Praise for *Bre*

'An impressive start in
The Sun

'A page tuner that will appeal to fans of *Broadchurch*.'
Adele Parks, bestselling author of *Platinum*

'Packed with authenticity.'
Mail Online

'Fresh, vivid and totally engrossing: this is gold-standard crime
writing bearing the unmistakable hallmark of authenticity.'
Erin Kinsley, *Sunday Times* bestselling author of *The Found*

'This could turn into a gem of a series.'
Sunday Post

'Fiendishly clever plotting. I was hooked from start to finish.'
Sarah Stovell, author of *Other Parents*

'A tightly-plotted, well-paced story with a disturbingly
manipulative, evil villain at its core.'
Country and Townhouse

'I genuinely found it hard to put down. The writing is beautifully
paced and the double viewpoint creates great tension.'
Alex Gray, *Sunday Times* bestselling author
of the DCI Lorimer Series

'It's difficult to accept that *Breakneck Point* is a debut novel as
T. Orr Munro's writing is exciting, genuine and convincing.'
My Weekly

'Fascinating and very compelling. Ally is complex
and engaging, and her character makes for a gusty,
unpredictable and emotionally taut plot.'
John Barlow, author of *Right to Kill*

'Fast-paced, suspenseful, with characters I want to
see again . . . Kept me guessing until the end.'
Alison Weatherby, author of *The Secrets Act*

T. Orr Munro was born in Aldershot in Hampshire to an English mother and a Greek-Armenian father who moved to deepest Devon after recognising it would be a great place to raise their children. She has a degree in Economic and Social History from Liverpool University and a PGCE in History and English. After university she trained as a CSI, then later became a secondary school teacher. She changed career at thirty-three to become a police and crime journalist and is currently freelance. She has since returned with her family to live in North Devon, the setting for *Breakneck Point*, but heads to Greece as often as she can. Her time as a CSI provided much of the inspiration for her novel, shining a light on what happens behind the crime scene tape.

BREAKNECK POINT

T. Orr Munro

ONE PLACE. MANY STORIES

HQ
An imprint of HarperCollins*Publishers* Ltd
1 London Bridge Street
London SE1 9GF

www.harpercollins.co.uk

HarperCollins Publishers
Macken House, 39/40 Mayor Street Upper,
Dublin 1, D01 C9W8, Ireland

This edition 2022

3

First published in Great Britain by
HQ, an imprint of HarperCollins*Publishers* Ltd 2022

ISBN: 9780008479817

MIX
Paper | Supporting
responsible forestry
FSC™ C007454

To my mum and dad and for my sisters,
Nicky and Dianne. Thank you.

1

I know what the perfect murder looks like and the slaying of Sian Jones isn't it. Far from it. Her killer, a no-mark called Danny Mainwaring, left a trail of clues bright enough to land a 747. The trial's just a formality. He's looking at life and I'm looking at spending my first rest day in two weeks with Megan. Or I was, until half an hour ago.

The corridors in Exeter Crown Court are the usual tense dance of lawyers, witnesses, accused, press and police. In among them, everybody's favourite Detective Inspector Jon Stride is sitting on a wooden bench outside Courtroom 1. Arms folded, long legs stretched out in front of him, he looks like he's been there days, which he probably has. He frowns when he sees me. He doesn't know what I'm doing here either.

'I didn't expect to see you.'

'Me neither,' I say, parking myself next to him. 'I'm meant to be having mother and daughter time over a chococino on Morte Sands.' I check my watch. 'I should still make it if they get on with it.' CSI appearances at court are surprisingly undramatic. If I'm called at all, I'm usually in and out in minutes.

I'm determined to make my date with Megan. I've already got a lot of making up to do with my daughter. I don't need more. The chococino is my sorry for ducking out of her school art exhibition the previous week. A papier-mâché mask Megan had worked on for months had won the school prize and pride of place in the exhibition, but I'd been called to photograph a 'fatal' on the Link Road in the north of the county. As I put the phone down on the court clerk this morning, Megan's stare challenged me to choose between her and my job, but it isn't that simple. It never is. I promised her I'd be back in time to take her to Morte Sands, but she just shrugged and said she was going back to bed. Something inside me shrank and I left determined to prove her wrong.

'How is Megan?'

Typical of Stride to remember her name. He knows the names of everyone's kids in Major Investigations, even the grandkids in some cases.

'Still fifteen.'

Stride laughs, but he can afford to. His kids have left home. Gone are the days his teenagers sought compensation for all the broken promises and missed milestones.

I nod at the door to Courtroom 1.

'How's it going in there?'

'Good. The CCTV evidence is enough to send him down.'

That's my memory of it too. There was ample footage showing Sian giving Mainwaring the brush-off in a club. He then follows her to her halls of residence. They argue outside. He grabs her, but she shakes him off and storms off inside. There are countless witnesses. Mainwaring leaves only to return ten minutes later. His hood up to cover his face, he enters the building when another student leaves the door open. A few minutes later, he re-emerges. Sian is already dead. There's so much CCTV, he practically has his own TV show.

Unusually for a murder scene like this, the rest of the forensics weren't great. Mainwaring may not look like a master criminal, but he knew enough not to leave behind any DNA or fingerprints. All I'm going to do today is confirm that.

'So why am I here?' Stride shrugs.

'Defence barrister's a new guy. Thinks he's Judge Judy. He'll learn, though.' He nudges my arm. 'Once he's seen you in action, I doubt he'll bother you again.'

His knack for quietly bigging you up is another reason everyone wants to be on his team, that and his legendary clear-up rate. We have a running joke in Crime Scene Investigation that if any of us are planning murder, we'll check Major Investigations' duty roster first and make sure Stride is on rest day or, better still, annual leave and preferably on the other side of the world with no Wi-Fi connection.

A woman with a clipboard appears in the corridor.

'Ally Dymond.' My hand shoots up. I want this over and done with. She smiles gratefully. The number of people who don't turn up for court is shockingly high. 'This way, please.'

As I get up, Stride lightly touches my arm, a move so rare it startles me.

'Just go with it, Ally. You'll be fine. Remember he's as guilty as hell.'

While I appreciate a pep talk as much as the next person, forensic evidence isn't like other evidence, the science does the talking and does it well. There's little room for argument. It's why court holds no hand-wringing fear for me, not like other cops. Even the best defence lawyers can't argue with the facts. Like I say, I'm not sure what I'm even doing here.

I enter Courtroom 1 by a side door. It's unnaturally quiet given that it's standing room only. The judge clearly doesn't put up with any nonsense. I'm shown to the stand and sworn in and there's a brief lull while the prosecution and defence teams whisper and consult their notes.

I avoid looking at Mainwaring, sat with the defence team, he's not worth it, and cast my eye around the courtroom. Sian's mother, Maureen Jones, is sitting in the public gallery at the back of the court, a tissue pressed to her nose, huddled under her husband's arm. Sian's father, Roy, stares straight ahead, eyes fixed on the wall behind the judge as if a single side glance will invite such horror in that it will break him, and he needs to keep it together for Maureen and Sian, his girls.

The jury leans forward on hearing I'm a CSI. They've seen too many cop shows. It won't last. Not when they realize the questions the barrister will ask will be no more challenging than confirming it's my signature at the end of my statement.

My interrogation, such as it is, begins.

'My name is Ally Dymond. I'm a Crime Scene Manager for Devon County Police's Major Investigations Unit.'

My notebook, an A4 ledger thick with times, dates, diagrams, and boxes ticked in triplicate is resting on the witness box. I quickly flick to the relevant pages.

The clock on the wall tells me there's still time to get to Morte Sands. The defence barrister will stand up long enough to say, 'No questions, your honour,' and I'll be on my way.

He doesn't. To my intense but suppressed irritation, he takes me through my evidence piece by piece. Go cut your teeth on someone else.

'Can you confirm, Ms Dymond, that the fibres recovered from Sian Jones' jumper matched those taken from a jacket recovered from the defendant's house?'

'Yes. That's correct.'

'My client argued with Sian outside the club as shown on the CCTV footage. He doesn't deny that. Is it possible that when he grabbed Sian, fibres were transferred from her jumper to his jacket?'

Sometimes in this job we have to give answers we really don't want to because science is science, but it still hurts to do it.

'Yes, it's possible.'

'Thank you.'

He gives me no opportunity to explain that they could also have been transferred when Mainwaring bludgeoned Sian to death, but I'm not concerned. No one thought the fibre evidence was particularly strong anyway and if the boy barrister thinks this will get his client off the hook, he has a lot to learn.

'Was there any blood found on my client's jacket?'

Movement catches my eye. Stride enters the courtroom, joining Detective Sergeant Rob Short and Detective Constable Will Lockhart who've already given evidence. Come to offer moral support, I suppose.

'No. There was no blood on your client's jacket.'

'Given the violent nature of Sian Jones' death, would you not have expected to have found blood on my client's jacket if he had killed her?'

Too easy. I address the jury directly.

'Not necessarily. The defendant could have taken it off

5

before he attacked Sian. Or more likely, he washed it when he got home. Any detergent with active oxygen in it will get rid of blood completely.'

The female jurors are nodding, almost willing me on. They're on my side and with me all the way. The sorry excuse for a human being sat with his defence team shakes his head. Shake away, son. You're going down.

'Thank you, Ms Dymond. You've been most helpful. I'd like to move on to the fingerprint evidence. I understand some fingerprints were also found at the scene, is that correct?'

This throws me. Why would he be interested in the fingerprints? None of the ones we lifted were of any use – by which I mean belonging to Mainwaring. We lifted what there was, but if it hadn't been a murder scene, I wouldn't have bothered.

'We lifted twenty-five fingerprint impressions from the scene, but I wouldn't call them fingerprints, more like smudges.'

An elderly female juror smiles. It's in the bag. The boy barrister won't be making his name today.

'And were they sent by you for analysis at the fingerprint bureau?'

'Yes.'

He then begins to lead me through all the fingerprints, one by one. Several jurors yawn.

'Ms Dymond, could you look at the screen and tell the court if this – Ref: Radley/11/18/01 – is one of the – what did you call them – smudges lifted from the crime scene?'

A small television screen next to me flicks into life. It's a photo of a transparent acetate sheet, but instead of a silvery fingerprint with its sharply defined contours, there's just a grey smudge where the aluminium powder has tried and failed to search out a loop or an arch, or any pattern that might identify the perpetrator. I check the reference number against my notes.

'Yes, it is.'

A second fingerprint flashes up. Even more of a blur than the previous one.

'What about this one, Ms Dymond? Reference Radley/12/18/02.'

I catch an exasperated sigh before it escapes. Never disrespect the defence no matter how much contempt they deserve.

'Yes, and that one.'

He's doing Mainwaring no favours. Juries aren't known for their abundance of patience. Judges even less so.

'Mr Lansley-Morton, unless there's a point to this can we move on? We are due a recess.'

A few more seconds and I can go. Megan better be out of bed.

'Of course, your honour. Ms Dymond, before you go, can you confirm this final print was lifted from the crime scene? The reference is Radley/13/18/03.'

A thumbprint flashes on screen. This time, its ridges and whorls are sharply defined, like contours on a map. A textbook lift from a crime scene. Only, I've never seen it before. Not that I remember every print I've ever lifted, but I'd remember this one. Christ, we'd have popped the champagne for that one. This is the kind of fingerprint that makes every detective's day, the kind that gets talked about for weeks, the kind that puts murderers away, which is why I know this print didn't come from the crime scene.

The barrister seizes the silence.

'Members of the jury, this fingerprint was recovered from

a glass found at the scene of the crime and was identified as belonging to my client who, may I remind you, has denied entering Sian Jones' room.' Jury members sit up, intrigued the defence appears to have condemned his own client. 'Ms Dymond, did this fingerprint come from the crime scene?'

I look at the mark on the screen again. The handwriting inked in black felt-tip pen could pass as mine, that's for sure, but it isn't. I loop my 'y's. It's a small detail, but enough for me to know I didn't write this.

I look to Stride, searching for some kind of telepathic guidance, I guess. His expression is impassive, unreadable, and that's when his words come back to me. *You'll be fine, Ally. Just go with it.*

Oh fuck. It wasn't a pep talk. It was Stride telling me to perjure myself. He's stitched me up. But that's impossible. He couldn't have tampered with the evidence, not without help. DS Short and DC Lockhart are both staring at me in a way that suggests I hold their future in my hands. Oh God, they're all in on it. Short or Lockhart must have lifted a fingerprint from Mainwaring's house. A pot of aluminium powder, a brush and tape are all that's needed. Someone, maybe Stride, substituted Mainwaring's gleaming fingerprint for one of the original ones before it went off to the fingerprint bureau. Surely, a fingerprint officer would have queried it. Unless the fingerprint officer is in on it too.

'Ms Dymond, could you tell the court if this fingerprint was taken from the crime scene?'

Panic whips through me. How the hell am I going to get out of this? I could brazen it out. Pretend I got confused with the line of questioning. Take ill. Christ, I'm on the verge of vomiting as it is.

In the public gallery, Maureen Jones sits upright and stares directly at me, sensing something isn't going according to plan. She doesn't want to be here, listening to people argue every detail of her daughter's murder. She's here because she wants justice for Sian. Because even in the maelstrom of her grief, justice matters. But justice doesn't look like this. This version is twisted and wrong. No matter how guilty Mainwaring is.

The court grows restless and awkward at my muteness.

'Ms Dymond, I'm going to need an answer from you.'

I check my notebook as if trying to refresh my memory, but I'm looking for answers I know aren't there.

'Ms Dymond, is there a problem?'

'No, no problem,' I respond, frantically trying to come up with a game plan. Stride is staring impassively at me.

'Then, I repeat, was this fingerprint taken from the crime scene?'

The dryness in my throat has spread to my lips. I flick through my notebook again, but the lines are blurred, and my head is spinning.

'Ms Dymond, please answer the question.'

I take a deep breath to compose myself. There is no way out of this. I shoot Stride a defeated look. His face is unreadable.

'This fingerprint didn't come from the murder scene.'

A collective gasp, the kind trapeze artists are used to, the kind my court performances have never drawn before, is released into the atmosphere.

'What are you saying exactly, Ms Dymond?'

Gripping my notebook, I utter words I never thought I'd ever hear myself say in a voice I don't recognize as my own.

'I'm saying this fingerprint was planted among the finger impressions that I took from the crime scene and was sent to the bureau without my knowledge.'

There's a silence that I want to last forever, but it's quickly filled with a sound, almost metallic, like a ship's girders bending and yielding to the sea just before it capsizes. It's the sound of a mother who knows her daughter's killer will walk free.

It's joined by other sounds and I can't tell where the sobs end and the shouts begin. Then cheers. Loud cheers. And angry exchanges.

In among the chaos, Stride is staring at me. His shaking head will come to represent many things: his conviction for perverting the course of justice, mass sackings and my own removal from Major Investigations after those left refuse to work with me, but mostly it speaks of his sadness that I've allowed a murderer to walk free.

2

Six months later

Someone is going to get it in the neck. Big time. This is the third tree-lined track I've driven down so if this isn't the right one, I'm calling it a day. It's not as if it's the crime of the century, for Christ's sake.

The narrow lane splays into a small copse, and there it is. Apparently, it was once a blue Nissan Micra, the pride and joy of a Mrs Jasmine Brownley, until its life took a turn for the worse and it was nicked by some scrote off the local estate to use as a plaything. I say apparently because its interior has melted to black plastic hillocks and its exterior is rocking black sootiness flaked with grey ash and rust.

I take out my phone and punch the number of the police officer in charge of the case, if you can call it that, but it goes to voicemail.

'PC 5831? It's Ally Dymond. What do you think you're doing sending me to this heap of shit? It's burned out. Just like the last one you sent me to. How many times do I have to tell you? This isn't *CSI* bloody *Miami*. I can't take fingerprints from a car that's been baked and left out in the rain for three weeks.'

I ring off. This is the sixth wreck I've been sent to since I was sent back to division six months ago. If it isn't an incinerated car, it's a dilapidated shed where the chances of me recovering any forensic evidence are slim to none.

I know it's punishment for the Mainwaring case. Send her to the shit jobs and maybe she'll get the message and quit. That's their thinking. I get it. The fallout from the trial was nuclear. Dozens of detectives and administration staff were suspended or sacked. It led to what the top brass like to call a 'root and branch' review of Major Investigations that filled the local papers for weeks. I did nothing wrong, but I've still ended up at a rural outpost in the far north of the county because cops have a weird sense of justice. Sure, Stride fiddled the evidence, but, hey, he was just making sure Mainwaring got what was coming to him. Anyway, Mainwaring probably did leave fingerprints at the scene and the CSI missed them. For some, maybe most, Stride is a hero for sacrificing his career to catch a killer and I'm the enemy for letting Mainwaring walk free. There won't even be a retrial because Stride broke the rules. That's the way it is. Well, they can shove it up their corrupt arses, because I'm not going anywhere. I'm not the crook. I could have fought it, of course, but what's the point when your colleagues won't acknowledge your existence?

I get my camera out and take a couple of photos, so it doesn't feel completely like the wasted journey it is. Not that this will ever go to court. Sorry, Mrs Brownley.

Back in the van, and the next job on my crime list makes me swear out loud. An allegedly kidnapped Cockapoo has turned up at a bus shelter. The officer dealing with it has returned it to its owner but took its collar back to the police station where it's waiting for me to just 'pop by and dust for prints'. Six years of investigating and solving some of the worst crimes imaginable only to be reduced to dog-nappings.

The radio crackles into life.

'November Juliet Two, we've reports of criminal damage to the public toilets at Morte Sands. Over.'

I squeeze the handset.

'OK, show me attending. Heading there now. Over and out.'

Morte Sands is only five miles away from where I am now, and two miles further along the coast from the seaside town of Bidecombe where I live. While Bidecombe boasts a picturesque fishing harbour, it also shoulders the embarrassment of a neglected high street which everyone tries to pretend has its own charm. It doesn't. There's nothing charming about short-lease shops selling Christmas decorations in mid-July. Morte Sands, meanwhile, is the true jewel in North Devon's crown. It's a glorious three-mile stretch of nothing but the finest golden sand. On rare days when the sun is high and bright, it casts water in azure, and you'd think you were on the Med. The road leading there is hemmed by those famous Devon high hedges sprinkled with cow parsley and, at this time of year, tall nodding foxgloves.

Mr Stavely, who owns the car park and its toilets, is already waiting for me when I pull into the car park.

'Thank God, you're here. What took you so long?'

Ignoring him, I fetch my silver case from the back of the van and he leads me to the gents' toilets, a grey block on the edge of the slipway leading to the beach. It's still early and a sea fret lightly veils the breaking waves. Three metres and clean, I wish I was joining the trail of surfers trooping towards the white froth. Instead, I'm in a windowless toilet that reeks of piss, staring at a condom machine lying on the floor.

'Look what the little shits have done,' Mr Stavely groans.

'Let's see if they've left us anything.'

Flicking open my case, I remove my thin-stemmed Zephyr brush from a plastic tube, unscrew the top off a pot of aluminium powder and load my brush with its contents.

Tapping the excess off, the soft squirrel hairs splay and I begin twirling it across the machine, working my way slowly across the shiny white surface. A hundred silvery fingerprints emerge, catching the light seeping through the door Mr Stavely has wedged open to relieve the odour.

Reloading my brush, I check the back of the machine and the pale patch of wall where it once hung. Both have been wiped clean as I suspected they might be. Mr Stavely isn't going to like what I have to say.

'There's nothing I can do here.'

'What do you mean?' he says, waving a hand over the fingerprints adorning the front of the machine. 'Aren't you going to take those?'

'There's no point. This is a public toilet, even if I get a hit on the fingerprint database, the offender will admit he came here to commune with nature. If they'd left prints on the back of the machine or had broken into it and left them on the inside, there might have been prints that would be very difficult to explain, but they haven't.'

'But their fingerprints will at least place them at the scene.'

Amateur sleuths. The bane of my life. Hollywood has much to answer for.

'I can also place you and I at the scene,' I explain, returning my brush to its home and snapping my case shut. 'It doesn't mean we ripped a condom machine off the wall.'

'So, you're not going to do anything?'

'No.'

It's not the answer he wants or is prepared to accept.

'I know the Police Commissioner personally.'

Judging by the number of times I've heard this line, the Commissioner has a very wide circle of friends.

'I'm sure you do. However, given police resources are so stretched, I'm also sure the Commissioner would want me to spend my time and expertise on those crimes where we have a realistic chance of a prosecution, but please feel free to call him.'

Actually, I'm not sure at all. The rare times I've found myself in the Commissioner's company he has always struck me as a self-serving, pompous prick.

My phone buzzes. It's Megan.

'Excuse me, I have to take this.'

Stepping outside, I check my watch. It's 8.15 a.m. No prizes for guessing what this is about.

'Before you ask. No, you're not taking a day off school.'

'But I'm really ill.'

'No, you're not. You've just got a maths test. So get dressed and go to school.'

Megan groans. 'Honestly, Mum, I'm really sick. Can't you come home and look after me?'

'No, I'm working and there's no one else.'

It isn't as if anyone matching the description of 'father' is going to swoop in and help. Julian fled the scene well before the end of my first trimester and I can't even bring myself to think of her stepdad, Sean, and no one I've met on Tinder would ever be a contender for Father of the Year. Penny, my friend and landlady, is out on her boat today and the further I keep Bernadette, my so-called mother, away from my life, the better my sanity. Besides, Megan isn't ill.

'You said you'd have more time for me when you got kicked off Major Investigations.'

'Thanks for reminding me.' But she's right. When I was sent back to division, the one upside was I wouldn't be trekking to police headquarters every day and I'd be around more for Megan, but the previous CSI retired and now it's just me covering seventy square miles of the moorlands and shorelands on my own. 'I still have to work.'

'So, what you're saying is your job's more important than your sick daughter?'

'No, it isn't because, fortunately, my daughter isn't sick.'

'Yes, I am. Anyway, I'm old enough to stay at home on my own.'

I can practically see her tossing her long cinnamon hair over her shoulder, wafting disdain in my direction.

'I don't have time for this. Go to school.'

'You never have time for me. You don't care about me, you only care about your stupid job.'

'If it weren't for my stupid job, you wouldn't be going on the school ski trip. I'm doing this for you.'

'Are you?'

For Christ's sake, she's relentless. It's true that crime doesn't keep office hours, and I've enough guilt to last a lifetime with all the parents' nights and musical debuts I've missed, but that's still not enough to let Megan skive off school whenever she feels like it.

'Megan, just get your arse to school.'

'God, Mum, you're such a bitch. You can't make—'

My phone beeps, interrupting her.

'I've got to go. It's work.'

'Of course it is.'

Megan rings off, leaving me wondering if she genuinely is ill and I should go home. I took a day off last week because she felt sick, but by lunchtime she was tucking into a tub of Ben & Jerry's Cookie Dough ice cream and shading her eyebrows. I take the other call.

'What is it?'

'Major Investigations are trying to get hold of you.'

My stomach flips like a teenager who's just spotted her crush in the street. I loathe myself for it.

'Major Investigations. Why?'

'They've got a body down on Bidecombe Quay. They want you there right now.'

I should tell them to stick it.

'I'm on my way.'

3

Trisha plonks herself down next to him; her vast backside hangs over the edge of the low harbour wall. She's so close to him her thigh brushes his and it takes all his will not to flinch in disgust. The woman has no concept of personal space. Without making it too obvious, he shuffles along the low quay wall.

They've been there since seven. He doesn't mind. He's used to it. Besides, it could be worse. The sun is shining. The seagulls are swooping overhead. The boats are bobbing in the harbour. It's going to be a beautiful day, the best in a long time, and, anyway, you can't hurry these things. A few more hours won't make any difference.

Trisha wanted them to go get breakfast and come back later, typical of her to be so unprofessional, but he told her they should stay close as they could be called any minute. They won't be, but he doesn't want to miss the show.

He's never seen so many police officers, marching up and down the quay, with their clipboards, looking very serious, knocking on doors, questioning people like they know what they're doing, when they haven't got a clue. It's very amusing.

Trisha hands him a coffee he hasn't asked for.

'Reckon we're going to be here for hours. Did you hear about my date with Bill from HR?'

'No.'

But he knows he's about to. He's had a ringside seat to Trisha's love life – or rather, loveless life – ever since they partnered up three years ago and if he's learned one thing it's that she goes through men even faster than a box of chocolate eclairs.

'We went to that new pub in Westlands Point, overlooking the sea. Dead romantic. I had the prawn cocktail and it came in a bowl as big as a fish bowl. Could barely finish it.'

'But you did.'

He looks at her. Everything about her screams round. Round body, round eyes, right down to the round dyed-red curls framing her round face, like a kid's drawing. And loud. She's so loud she hurts his ears. There's a name for people like her. Larger than life, that's it, but what it actually means is that the person is a fat, unbearable attention-seeker.

As if to prove his point, she glugs her coffee and projects a gasp across the road in front of them, attracting a frown from a woman pushing a pram on the other side. She really is repulsive.

'Yeah, but barely, Si. Then I had the steak which came with mushrooms, tomatoes and those giant onion rings. Bill chose exactly the same. His favourite, too, how weird is that? Reckon it means we must be compatible. Perhaps I've found my prince. God knows I've kissed enough frogs to fill a pond. Actually, a lake.' Her throaty laugh is louder than her joke deserves, but then she becomes unusually thoughtful. 'Never thought someone like Bill would go for someone like me. I know you think I'm a bit of a party animal, life and soul, always up for a laugh, but a lot of it is front, Si. I just want to meet someone I can grow old with. I think Bill could be the one. He said I was really pretty. No one's ever said that to me before.'

Well, he can certainly believe that. He blows the froth on his coffee and watches it migrate to the other side of the cup.

'Trisha, I think there's something you should know.'

'What?'

Shaking his head, he pretends to change his mind.

'Forget it. It doesn't matter.'

'You can't do that to me, Si. What is it?' Her smile deserts her, but he's in no hurry to reply.

A second crime scene investigator van pulls up opposite them on the quay. He watches the driver's door fly open and a leg already enclosed in a white forensic suit plant itself on the road.

Its owner gets out. The petite frame, the coal-black hair that skims her shoulders, the pointed chin and generous lips – it's her. It's Danielle. No, it can't be. That's impossible and he knows it, but he can't help but scrutinize the woman for further proof. He finds reassurance in her olive skin which speaks of the Mediterranean whereas Danielle's was pale and she wore her hair stair-rod straight, not frizzy and uncontrolled like this woman. But the resemblance is uncanny, and much as he'd like to, he can't take his eyes off her.

The CSI opens the back of the van and retrieves a large silver case before slamming it shut again. He watches her march towards the end of the quay where a small crowd is huddled around the police tape.

'Si, please tell me.'

'What?' Trisha's nasal whining pierces his thoughts, dragging him back to their conversation. He turns to her, pressing his features into what he hopes passes for concern. 'Look, I wasn't sure if I should say anything. We're friends, though, and, if it were me, I'd want to know.'

'Know what?'

'OK, but don't shoot the messenger. I was in the lunch queue yesterday, behind Bill, and he was with a friend. They were talking about a bet they'd made.'

'A bet?'

'Yes. Bill's friend had bet him twenty pounds he wouldn't take you out.'

Trisha's shoulders drop.

'A bet. He asked me out for a bet?'

Her lower lip quivers and her big round eyes shine with tears.

'Look at how upset you are. I shouldn't have said anything. I'm sorry.'

She runs the back of her hand under her nose.

'No, you were right to tell me. You're a good friend. What a total shit that Bill is.'

Turning away to hide his smile, his attention is caught by raised voices coming from the police cordon.

It's early, but already there's an eager crowd drawn by the half dozen police cars and the ambulance like it's some kind of fairground attraction. Even the seagulls are excited, wheeling and whining overhead.

But just as I'm about to lift the crime scene tape over my head, PCSO Christian Cobb steps in front of me.

'I'll need to see some ID.'

Of all people posted to guard the scene, it has to be him. I've pulled Cobb up several times for touching stuff at crime scenes and I know he's mates with DC Will Lockhart or just plain Will Lockhart, as he is now since he was sacked. I don't want to make a scene, but a burned-out car and a wrecked condom machine have already used up my admittedly low reserves of patience and it's not even 9 a.m.

'You know who I am, Cobb, now get out of my way.'

'Not till I've seen some ID.'

'I mean it, Cobb. Get out of my fucking way or I'll have you on school gate duty for the rest of your days.'

The audience, a mix of tourists and locals, falls silent with anticipation. A dead body and a fight between the CSI and the PSCO on the quay all in one day, this'll be talked about for years to come.

'Let her through, Cobb.' A weary voice cuts through our standoff. It belongs to a man in a badly fitting grey suit, his lower half obscured by a white forensic suit rolled down to his hips. He strides towards us, his jacket flapping at his sides like it's trying to keep up while the constant breeze tries to make off with the thin strips of hair covering a bald pate. People who want great hair don't live near the sea.

'What's going on here?'

The senior investigating officer, I assume.

Cobb's face flushes red.

'Just doing my job, sir.'

The SIO smooths his sandy-coloured hair back into place.

'What, by stopping other people doing theirs?'

'I thought she was off Major Investigations.'

'Well, she's not, otherwise she wouldn't be here, would she? I'm DI Bob Holt. Come through, Ally.'

I don't know Holt but guess he's Stride's replacement. After I was 'redeployed' I haven't paid much attention to what's been happening at the MI unit. I wonder how he knows me. Then again, the force's ranks aren't heaving with CSIs who've blown the whistle on police corruption halfway through a murder trial.

Ducking under the tape, I surface on the other side to see Holt marching back towards the end of the quay and Cherish, a twenty-metre bronze statue of a serpent coiled around a woman's naked torso, balanced on a tall plinth. Loaned by a local artist, it's loved and loathed in equal measure. I'm in the loathe camp. There's nothing positive about a dismembered body. I catch Holt up.

'Thanks,' I say, resisting the temptation to add that I can fight my own battles.

'Look, I'm not going to beat around the bush. If I had my way, I wouldn't have you anywhere near my investigation, but I've got one on long-term sick and the new lad, Jake Harris, would be out of his depth in a puddle and I need this wrapping up quickly so let's just get on with it.'

I'm guessing he's also a mate of Stride's, but this isn't the time or the place to launch into a rant about police corruption and, besides, I'm not looking for a new best friend.

'So, what have we got?'

'Young girl. Druggie. Probably strangled. Woman out walking her dog this morning found her.' He machine-guns his words like a man for whom time is a luxury only others can afford.

'Who else has entered the scene besides the dog walker?'

'A special got here first. Did a good job of securing it, by all accounts. That just leaves me, Alex, the pathologist, and Jake, of course.'

'No one else?'

'No.'

'Good.'

The forensic tent is perched awkwardly on the steps beneath

the statue. Any more than this light breeze and it'll be in the sea. Jake's clearly no architect.

PC Bryant, the police officer posted at the entrance, nods at Holt before eyeing me with what? Contempt? Loathing? Disgust? Hell. It's probably all three. I snatch his clipboard, scribble my name and thrust it back at him. I'm not the one who tried to fix a murder trial.

Holt zips himself back up into his forensic suit and we both slip on a fresh pair of blue shoe covers. I tuck my hair into the hood of mine, ensuring it fits snugly around my face and there are no loose strands.

Inside the crime scene tent a lanky young man also in a white forensic suit is leaning against the railings. Jake, I assume. God knows what Holt has said to him but his cheeks blaze with enough embarrassment to have raised the temperature in the tent by several degrees. Holt clearly gave him the hairdryer treatment. He introduces us and Jakes snaps to attention.

'This is Ally Dymond. She'll be managing the scene. Do as she says.'

'The DI told me to wait for you.'

'That's fine. You've laid the plates.' I nod at the metal rectangular plates placed at regular intervals round the plinth, protecting the scene from curious coppers and their size tens. 'Good job. Right, let's get on, shall we?'

The girl's body isn't immediately obvious which still surprises me, even after all these years. Violent death: such an abrupt, unprepared-for ending that I always expect the corpse to retain a residual aura, drawing me towards it. It doesn't.

Then, there she is, a scrap of a thing lying on her side across the steps, her white-blonde hair swept over her face, her mayonnaise arms flopped at her side and freckled with needle pricks – just another casualty of the town's buoyant drug business. Like I said, the real Bidecombe is never more than a few streets away from the tourist areas. She looks young, not much older than Megan, although I quickly archive that thought. It never takes me to a good place.

I kneel beside the girl's body for a closer look. Holt's right. There's only one obvious injury: a thick red mark rings her ballerina neck. It's the most likely cause of death and it wouldn't have taken much. It never does. I've met many horrified at how easy it is to snuff out a life. One hard squeeze would have tipped her into oblivion in less time than it takes to make a cup of tea.

'You said Alex has already seen her?'

Alex Blandford is the Home Office pathologist, but my question draws no response, forcing me to glance up at Holt who's engrossed in his phone. Sensing my eyes are on him, he slips it into his pocket and makes a show of hitching his trousers to squat beside me.

'Yeah, been and gone. Most likely asphyxiation caused by manual strangulation. Obviously, we'll know more after the PM.'

'What about time of death?'

'Only a rough approximation at the moment, but somewhere between midnight and three.'

'Do we know who she is?'

'Janie Warren, nineteen, local girl.'

The name triggers a memory. Her face obscured by her hair, I hadn't recognized her at first, but, of course, the white-blonde bob, the diminutive figure – we've met before.

'I photographed a Janie Warren five months back. A domestic.

Her boyfriend, Chris somebody, high on crack, beat the hell out of her.'

'Yeah, that's her. The local CID filled us in. It was a nasty assault.'

I remember Janie, hellbent on taking her 'bastard boyfriend' to court. He was a total deadbeat; the kind of guy Megan will bring home in a few years just to wind me up. Then, out of nowhere, she drops the charges. He's been under a lot of stress, she's been nagging him, it isn't his fault he snapped, etc., etc. She told me they were even trying for a baby. Everything's going to be fine. One big happy family. Things will be different, but they never are. I should know.

'So, what are you thinking? The boyfriend finished what he'd already started?'

Holt checks his watch.

'I don't think it. I know it.' He stands up, straightening his back then wincing with regret. He must be close to having his thirty years in, probably already booked tickets on a luxury liner somewhere in the Med. That seems to be what cops do when they retire – go on cruises. 'Doubt we'll even need to rely on forensics for this one so don't overdo it.'

I stand up too.

'How come?'

Holt's phone buzzes in his jacket. He fishes it out and carries on talking as he punches his reply. His multi tasking would be impressive if it wasn't so damned disrespectful.

'We've got CCTV showing the two of them on the corner of Argyll Street at around eleven. They turn left onto Quayside and head towards the end of the quay where they drop out of sight. Then at twelve-thirty, you see him, Chris Banstead, legging it back from the quay. There were only two of them on the quay and there's only one way in and one way out.'

'What about the live cam footage?'

'We checked. They don't record it because it costs extra, but we won't need it. The guy's as guilty as they come. We've already brought him in.'

'Has he admitted it?'

'No, but he will. At the moment, he won't even believe she's dead. Says they came here, smoked weed, had sex and he left her to clean herself up while he went off to a mate's to play *Call of Duty*.'

'Classy guy.' I run an eye over the steps. 'OK, we'll get the visuals done first. Then we'll bag up the spliffs and the cans. Do you have her phone?'

'No. We've searched. We're thinking he might have thrown it in the harbour.'

That isn't good. Phones are evidential gold, revealing every detail of our lives including the ones that help convict murderers, although it'll take more than a strangled drug addict to get the police divers out.

But something else is troubling me.

'That's odd.'

'What?'

'There's a lot of sand around.'

'Well, we are by the sea.'

I meet Holt's smirk with stone. Lame gags and murdered girls aren't a great combo for me. I glance at the harbour, now full and bobbing with boats.

'You're right, the tide was out last night.' I know full well that isn't what he means. 'But you said the CCTV picked them up on the corner of Argyll Street and Quayside, which means they walked around the harbour rather than crossing the sands to reach the quay.'

'Maybe they went for a romantic stroll earlier.'

Holt glances at his watch, tipping my irritation into annoyance and just a couple of phone beeps away from full blown anger. What little attention he's given this girl is rapidly waning. He's already ticked the boxes on this one and filed it under 'D' for domestic, but I haven't finished.

'You might also want to check the boyfriend's footwear.'

'Why?'

I point to a shoeprint on the top step, its delicate grooves perfectly sculpted in sand. There's even some lettering, a 'V', maybe. Probably part of the manufacturer's mark.

'It's too big to belong to a female so that rules out your dog walker. It's not a police boot either. I'd say it's most likely a brogue of some kind, though I reckon the boyfriend's more of a trainer kind of a guy, don't you?'

Holt fixes on the mark like he's trying to magic it away.

'Could have been left earlier by a tourist,' he says finally.

'Unlikely. It rained until around eleven-thirty last night. It would have been washed away. This was made after it stopped raining.'

It isn't the first time I've screwed with a detective's cosy theory and, in Holt's case, I can't deny a blast of pleasure because, as much as he wants to, he can't ignore this.

'OK, we'll check his shoes, but even if the shoeprint isn't his, I'm confident there was no one else involved in Janie's murder.' His phone stirs again. He leaves it where it is. 'Look, I've got to get back to the nick. We're massively short-staffed at the moment.' He looks at me like it's my fault, which it is. No one wants to join a unit that has the stench of corruption about it. 'I'm briefing on a child abuse inquiry going on in the south of the county.'

'What about the PM?'

'It's at two-thirty. I'll try to make it, but if I don't, carry on without me.' He turns to leave. 'And Ally?'

'Yes.'

'There's no need to sweat this one. We've got the guy. It's just a case of going through the motions. When you're done, send me a copy of your report.' In other words: don't think for one minute you're back on Major Investigations. 'One more thing . . .' He hesitates long enough for me to know I'm not going to like this. 'I want Jake's name on all the exhibits in case he's called to court.'

'What? Why?'

'You know why.'

Jake's frowning. He's no idea what Holt's talking about, but Holt's not getting away with this.

'I'm perfectly capable of giving evidence in court. I can't help it if your bent colleagues think it's a good idea to fix a trial. Besides, I'm leading the scene and Jake is too inexperienced for the dock.'

Jake's expression agrees with me.

'And I'm the SIO.'

Holt says this like it trumps everything and although I'm a civilian CSI and he can't technically order me to do anything, not like he can a lower-ranking police officer, he's right. It's his show, so much so he doesn't wait for my response, and then it's just me and Jake.

This time it's my phone that rings in my pocket. It's Megan again.

'Do you mind, Jake? It's my daughter.'

'Sure.'

Megan hurls a list of ailments down the line, evidence as to why I must collect her from school immediately. My temples begin to throb. I don't need this. Not now.

'I can't come. I'm at work. Go to the nurse and get some Nurofen.'

'They won't give me any. You never signed the consent form. Please come and get me, Mum.'

'I can't, Megan. I'll text the school nurse.'

'I could be dying for all you care.'

She hangs up on me for the second time today, leaving me staring at my home screen, my favourite photo of a pre-teen Megan flashing a smile I'd forgotten she had. Something's up. I'm not sure what, but it's not like her to phone me from school. I try to get hold of Penny, but she's not picking up and I can't bring myself to call Bernadette.

'Do you need to get your daughter? I can crack on here.'

Jake's words aren't dripping with confidence. I look down at Janie's pale, thin corpse that looks like it's been tossed aside like chip paper. I can't leave her. This needs to be done right if we're to nail her killer and Jake isn't up to it. Not yet.

'No. She'll be fine. Thanks, though. Let's get on with it. Remember, if in doubt, bag it. The first and most important rule of crime scene investigation, Jake, is assume nothing.'

But as we place the numbered markers next to the items we plan to remove, I can't help thinking about Megan. She didn't sound ill. She sounded upset.

4

The CSI appears at the entrance to the tent. She tugs back the hood of her white protective suit and wisps of dark hair dislodge themselves from her hair clip. Just like Danielle's would on a windy walk, before everything changed.

Scanning the quay, she spots him and gives him the thumbs-up. He waves back. 'They're ready for us.' He calls over to Trisha who is leaning against the wall of a takeaway, forking chips into her mouth, trying to chomp away the memory of Bill, no doubt.

She rolls her eyes. Interrupting mealtimes always makes her irritable and she hesitates, trying to decide whether or not she can save the chips for later, before reluctantly dumping them in the bin.

The crowd murmurs at their arrival, parting to make way for them, sensing they're finally going to get to see something interesting. He can't blame them. There's something beguiling about the dead. Some of them. He swings the police tape over their heads. The PCSO nods his approval. No one questions the paramedics.

Climbing into the back of the ambulance parked behind the police cordon, he unclips the trolley and guides it off the vehicle and towards Trisha. Between them they lower it onto the ground and wheel it towards the white tent and the waiting CSI.

'Hi, I don't think we've met before, have we? I was on Major

Investigations until recently. Most of our jobs were in the south of the county. I'm back on division so I guess we'll be seeing a bit more each other. I'm Ally Dymond, by the way, the CSI.' She looks down at her gloved hands, streaked with dirt. 'Probably best if we don't shake hands.'

'Hi, Ally, I'm Trisha Wilkins and this is Simon Pascoe.'

'Nice to meet you both. I just wanted to apologize for keeping you waiting so long,' the CSI says, but she doesn't mean it. She couldn't care less that she's kept them hanging around for hours.

'No problem,' says Trisha.

'Great, well, we're ready for you now,' the CSI says.

Hoisting the trolley over the railings which surround the statue, they park it just inside the tent's entrance, away from prying eyes, and follow the CSI inside.

'She's just round here.'

The CSI guides them around the base of the statue. In his peripheral vision, he's aware of a pale, ribbon-like form on the ground, but he doesn't dare look down for fear of how the sight might affect him.

The only other person present is the other CSI who is hovering on the steps below the statue like he doesn't know what to do with himself. He looks about fourteen, wet behind the ears and totally out of his depth.

The CSI turns to them. 'There's not much room in here so Jake and I will get out of your way while you move the body. If you can keep to the metal plates that would make our lives a lot easier.'

Trisha smiles.

'Of course. No problem.'

The CSIs leave and it's just the two of them.

'Poor kid,' mutters Trisha, heaving a sigh. 'Come on, Si, let's get this done.'

He nods and finally glances down.

There she is, draped across the stone steps, exactly where he left her.

Jake worries me. At first, he's quite chatty and our conversation flows, but after I task him to photograph Janie's body it trickles to nothing.

That's fine. He needs to concentrate. He gets one chance to photograph the body in situ and he can't afford to mess it up. He checks and rechecks the camera screen ensuring he's photographed her from every conceivable angle, but, by the time the paramedics remove Janie's corpse, he's slipped into one of those silences that long-in-the-tooth CSIs like me know to avoid.

We return to the CSI van with armfuls of brown exhibit bags and I search for something neutral to say, anything to drag him back from whatever dark hole he's fallen down.

'So, did you go to uni?'

'Yeah. I did Photography. What about you? Did you go?'

'For a while.' No need to mention an unexpected pregnancy and subsequent arrival of Megan cut short a Materials Science degree at Oxford. 'So why come here? It's not exactly a crime hotspot. It could be years before we have another murder.'

'I couldn't be anywhere else. I love surfing. If I'm not at work, I'm down at Morte Sands.'

'My favourite beach. Terrible signal, too, so there's no chance you'll be interrupted riding the waves.' Jake forces

33

a smile. 'Seriously, it's good to have interests outside your job. It'll keep you sane.'

'So, what are your interests?'

The question throws me. When Megan was young, I used to take her up to Exmoor where we'd photograph whatever wildlife crossed our path. The ponies mostly. Now, unless there's a purchase at the end of it, she won't walk further than a few hundred yards.

'My teenage daughter, I guess.'

'Sounds like a full-time job. My sister, Beth, is nineteen. She still runs rings around Mum and Dad.'

He smiles at the thought of his younger sister, but it's a smile tainted with something else – fear. Crime scenes resonate most when we identify with the victim in some way. I'm guessing Beth is small and blonde. Like Janie.

Jake glances back at the tent.

'Photographing that girl freaked me out a bit. When I first saw her, for a minute, I thought it was—'

'But it isn't Beth,' I cut him off for his own good. 'It'll never be Beth. If nothing else she's got her great big ugly brother to look out for her.'

My efforts to lighten Jake's mood fall flat, but at least it switches his focus.

'Who could do that to another human being?'

'The list is longer than you'd think, but I wouldn't dwell on it. You'll send yourself mad. Or worse, it'll affect how you do your job.'

He smiles at my lame joke.

'Yeah, you're right, but doesn't it make you angry?'

'Which part?'

'That the boyfriend'll get a cosy prison cell, Sky TV, drugs delivered by drone, and all paid for by us.'

'Assuming it's him.'

Jake loads his bags into the back of the van.

'We should do what the Americans do and give him a lethal injection.'

A popular sentiment in cop circles, but not one I share even though I've spent my life elbow deep in other people's depravity. Maybe I've just seen enough death to know that more death never fixes anything.

I'm about to steer the conversation towards the safe territory of last night's television when we're interrupted by voices loud enough to outdo the gulls in concert overhead. At the police cordon, a woman is gesticulating wildly in front of an unmoved Cobb.

'Why won't you let me through? I've a right to know what's going on.'

Her cheeks are stained with dark rivers of mascara applied that morning when she thought her daughter was still alive. This is Sue Warren, I realize, Janie's mother. I've seen her before at the hospital the first time Janie was beaten up by her boyfriend.

'Just tell me, is it her?' She pleads with Cobb, but her anguish makes no impression on him. He really is a prize prick.

'I'm not at liberty to discuss the details of the case.'

Jesus, the man is never at liberty to do anything.

'Someone told me it was my Janie. She's not answering her phone. I just want to know. Is it Janie?'

Her daughter's name is swallowed up by sobs that shake her body.

Cobb looks down at her, like she's just vomited on his shoes.

'You need to call the station and speak to Detective Inspector Bob Holt.'

Sue looks up, eyes flashing with fury.

'I just want to know if it's her.'

She tries to dodge Cobb, but he's too quick for her. His long arms wrap themselves around her torso.

'You're not going anywhere.'

'Get off me. You've no right to stop me. She's my daughter.'

But Cobb has her clamped in his arms. I know what's coming next. He has no power to arrest her so he'll call for back-up, tell the cavalry he's been assaulted and she'll be bundled into the back of a cop car and whisked into custody. He has form for it. Sure enough, holding Sue Warren with one arm, Cobb reaches for his radio.

'Shit, take these.' I thrust the brown exhibit bags at Jake and race over to the cordon.

Throwing the crime scene tape over my head, I grab Cobb's arm.

'For Christ's sake, let her go, Cobb.'

Had it just been the three of us, I've no doubt Cobb would have swotted me aside like a wasp, but even an idiot like Cobb knows a crowd of witnesses when he sees one. He releases Sue Warren, which both confuses and calms her.

'Come with me, Sue.'

Taking her by the elbow, I steer her behind the CSI van, out of sight from the crowd.

'My name's Ally. I'm not a police officer. I'm the crime scene investigator.'

Sue's sobs subside to chest-filling breaths.

'It's her, isn't it? It's my Janie.'

There's no way to sugar-coat this.

'Yes. I'm so sorry.'

'Where is she? I need to see her.' She pleads with Jake and interprets his helpless stare as refusal. 'You can't stop me. I'm her mother. I have a right.'

I slip my arm around her shoulder.

'Sue, she's gone. They've taken her to the mortuary.'

'But she needs me.'

'I know, and you'll be able to see her. I'll arrange for an officer to take you. We'll take good care of her, I promise.'

She looks at me and recognition seeps into her eyes.

'You photographed Janie when that bastard beat her up, didn't you?'

'Yes, I did.'

'You warned her about him. She told me when I picked her up from the hospital that you'd begged her to leave him, that he wouldn't stop, and now he's gone and killed her.'

Her words spark a fresh flow of tears.

'My baby gone, gone.'

She crumples into my arms. Her body heaves and shudders, her grief invading her like a virus, condemning her to terminally mourn the loss of her daughter. I hug her tightly.

'It's OK, Sue. I have you.'

Jake frowns at me as if to say, what the hell do you think you're doing, this isn't in the job description, but I ignore him. He's right, of course. Our domain is the dead, not the living. But, in that moment, I'm no longer a CSI, I'm a mother.

5

Just as he throws the last of the wet wipes into the disposal unit, the ambulance turns off the main road into the hospital grounds and pulls up in front of an anonymous door, tucked away around the back of the hospital: the mortuary. A few seconds later Trisha throws open the back doors. Even that's a performance.

'I knew I couldn't trust Bill, something about his eyes, too close together. I should've listened to my instincts. What a shitty thing to do. You know your Jackie's a lucky lady. Wish all guys could be as decent as you. You all right? You were very quiet in the back there. Thought you'd nodded off.'

He unclips the trolley and together they manoeuvre it off the back of the ambulance. Trisha presses the buzzer to the mortuary and a disembodied male voice invites them in.

They wheel the trolley into the building and park it in the corridor. Through a large window, the voice's owner, Gary, the assistant mortician, is sitting at his desk in the main office. He waves at them.

'Hi, guys. Come in.'

His face is half beard, and a scraggly ponytail hangs over his shoulder. He's heard that Gary's in a heavy metal band. He can just imagine this idiot screaming into a mic about drinking alcohol and having sex.

Trisha hands the paperwork over.

'There you go, Gaz. All yours.'

He smiles back at her.

'And how's my favourite paramedic?'

Trisha giggles like she's thirteen. So much for Bill being the only one for her. Faithless tart. His Jackie would never behave like that.

'Fine, how's my favourite assistant mortician?'

'Think you'll find I'm the only assistant mortician, but I'll take that.' Gary winks at Trisha and she giggles some more.

Their radios hiss into life and Trisha looks to him to respond, but he pretends he hasn't noticed, taking the paperwork from Gary to check something over. She taps her radio a few times before giving up. 'The reception down here is crap. I better find out what they want. Back in a bit.'

Trisha disappears and he passes the paperwork back to Gary who runs a surprisingly careful eye over it. He doesn't look the meticulous type.

'Thanks, mate. This is fine.'

Mate. He hates that word. He's not Gary's mate. He's not anyone's mate.

'Where shall I put her?'

'Just leave her where she is.'

'What, in the corridor?'

'Well, it's not like she's gonna get up and walk out, is it?' Gary's eyes mock him and it takes all his resolve not to punch this lout in the mouth.

'It just seems a little disrespectful, that's all, to leave her out in the hallway, like a piece of rubbish.'

'Nothing I can do about it, fella. We're full. Don't know what they're doing on the gerry wards, but these oldies are popping off all over the place.'

'But she's a murder victim.' He can't bear to think of her all alone.

'So? There's no pecking order down here, mate. It's first come first served. Don't worry. The undertakers are due. That'll clear the backlog and then we'll see if we can find her a cabinet. Anyways, she's in for a PM this afternoon. I might just take her straight into the examination room.'

He gives the idiot a side glance.

'You guys must be a bit worried at the moment.'

Gary continues ticking boxes on a form.

'Why's that?'

'I hear this place is next in line in the cuts.'

His pen stops mid-tick.

'What? You're kidding, right?'

'No. I know someone in the chief exec's office. They're thinking of cutting the number of staff and shifting some of the work to the Exeter Royal.'

He shakes his head.

'I can't go to Exeter. I live in Barnston, it's miles away. I'd have to give the band up and everything.'

Simon nods sympathetically.

'That's rough.'

'Too right it is. That band is my life.'

'Well, nothing's confirmed, but you might want to start looking for something else. Mate.'

'For fuck's sake. They won't be happy until they've got rid of us all. Thanks for the tip. Sign here for me.'

He holds his clipboard up and Simon signs his name with a flourish.

6

Holt catches up with me just as I buzz the mortuary to let me in. He takes a moment to catch his breath, adjusting his jacket and checking his hair is still in place. His phone is welded to his hand as if expecting a call any moment.

'I'm not staying. Just dropped by for the first few minutes to see what Alex has to say. Got a raid going down tonight. Need to brief the team.'

I get the message. Holt is a DI. He's constantly juggling more cases than is humanly possible, especially after all the cuts to policing, but he's got his priorities wrong on this one. Besides, I've a bone the size of my femur to pick with him.

'Sue Warren, Janie's mother, was on the quay and she was in a right state. She had no idea if it was Janie or not. No one had bothered to tell her.'

Holt can't ignore the accusation in my voice. Someone should have found Sue Warren long before she got wind it could be her daughter dead on the waterfront.

'We had the wrong address for her.'

'That's not good enough. The poor woman was out of her mind. I had to break it to her that it was her daughter

41

and I got one of the house-to-house team to bring her to the hospital.'

Holt prickles at the subtext – this is your job, not mine, only you'd already cleared off – and goes on the defensive.

'These things happen and, anyway, DC Trotter met her here and did the formal identification.'

I'm not happy, but I've made my point so I move on.

'So, how's the interview going with Janie's boyfriend?'

'Good.'

He isn't going to tell me any more. I'm not on the team. Unlike Stride who included CSIs at every stage of the investigation because no one understands a crime scene like a CSI, Holt's approach is strictly need-to-know and a CSI who hung her colleagues out to dry in court doesn't.

The door opens. It's Gary, the assistant mortician. Normally, he greets us with a grin, and a jokey 'not you lot again' followed by a quick plug for his latest thrash metal gig, but today all we get is a brief nod as he leads us into the white-tiled postmortem room.

Alex Blandford, the Home Office pathologist, is already there, scrubbed up and bent over Janie Warren's pale naked corpse, inspecting the red mark around her neck.

Lying on her back, her hair drawn aside, her face no longer lined by life and her body shrunken by drugs, she looks much younger than her nineteen years. A large, slightly wonky track, like a child's drawing, runs the length of her chest where she's already been opened up and sewed back together.

Alex greets me with a broad smile. It's been a while.

'Hi, Ally. Good to see you. It's been a long time.'

'Hello, Alex, how are you? How's Marjorie and the boys?'

Over the years and over corpses at various stages of decomposition, Alex and I have got to know each other well. Nothing drives you to cling to the normality of your life more than a sudden death. I've lived Alex's sons' GCSEs, A levels and degrees, his wife Marjorie's developing skill as a calligrapher and his irrational love for Harriet, his breakdown-prone Triumph Spitfire. In return, he's lived Megan's first day at secondary school, dental braces and my disasters on Tinder. It's kept us sane.

Alex grins.

'She's still nagging me to retire and then moaning that I get under her feet if I'm off for more than three days. How's Megan?'

'Still fifteen.'

He laughs.

'Don't worry. It doesn't last forever.'

Holt taps his phone against his palm, impatient to move on.

'So, what have we got, doc?'

'Yes. Right. We've narrowed the time of death to between twelve and two.'

Holt can barely believe his luck and throws me the smuggest of looks.

'Excellent. That fits with what we've got so far. CCTV shows Janie and her boyfriend, Chris Banstead, walking along the quay towards the statue at 11.17 p.m. and then, at 12.28 a.m., you can see the boyfriend running away back towards town.'

As Alex explains how ambient temperatures and body temperature mean it's entirely possible Janie's life was extinguished nearer to twelve-thirty than two, I set my camera case on the stainless-steel counter that skirts the room. Flipping the catches,

I remove my battered Nikon, click the close-up lens into place and slip the strap over my head.

'So, what about the cause of death?' says Holt.

Alex removes his pen from the breast pocket of his green tunic and circles the marks on the neck.

'It's as I thought, death by asphyxiation. He used his hands too. See, here – you can even make out the thumb marks on her front of her neck.'

Focusing the camera on her neck, I fire off some shots. Then I stand back and look at Janie's face. Something's different about her, but I can't work out what.

'Any other injuries?' I ask.

Alex scans Janie's corpse, like he might have missed something.

'No. She had recent sex, but it doesn't appear to be forced.'

Holt nods.

'The boyfriend has already admitted to having sex with her under the statue. Apparently Cherish is some kind of fertility symbol. Can't see it myself.'

For once, we agree. How a serpent coiled around a decapitated woman could possibly represent new life is beyond me.

'She didn't try to fight off her attacker, then?' I ask Alex.

'How could she if he had her by the neck?'

Alex raises an eyebrow at Holt's dismissiveness towards me. There's a rule in criminal investigations. We've all dealt with the bizarre and the unfathomable in our time which means no comment or question is too ridiculous to voice.

'It doesn't appear so,' he says. 'We couldn't find any defence injuries. Often a victim will claw at their own neck to try to get their attacker off them, but that doesn't seem to be the case here. We're still waiting for the toxicology report, but if she was drunk or on drugs that might explain why she didn't fight back.'

'I'll finish the photos and do the nail scrapes.'

'Sure, but I wouldn't hold out much hope. They were the cleanest nails I've seen in a while. No skin or blood. Not even any dirt.'

I kneel down, eye level with Janie's body, and fire off a few frames of her hands and enlarge them on my camera's display.

'You're right, her nails are spotless.' I turn to Holt. 'Doesn't that strike you as odd?'

Holt shrugs.

'Nothing strikes me as odd in this job.'

'She'd just had sex. The last thing on her mind would be the state of her nails.'

'Perhaps the sex was less than satisfying.'

I ignore Holt's facetiousness and my own urge to ask if he's speaking from personal experience.

'What if someone else cleaned her nails? After she was killed. Someone who's forensically aware.'

Holt rolls his eyes.

'The CCTV on the corner of Argyll Street and Quayside shows the only people on the quay were Janie and Banstead.'

Then I realize what's bothering me about Janie's face. It's been wiped clean of make-up. On the steps beneath Cherish, her eyes had a flick of eyeliner at each corner and her lashes were coated in mascara.

'Did you or Gary clean her face up when she came in? I'm sure she was wearing make-up on the quay.'

Alex shakes his head.

'No. Gary might have done although he'd normally wait until you've been in. Anyway, we've bagged up her clothing for you. Gary'll let you have it on your way out.'

Holt's phone buzzes.

'Thanks, Alex. I need to get going. If anything else crops up, let me know.'

Phone clamped to his ear, Holt steps out of the room. That's it for him. Job done. Case closed. Onto the next one. It doesn't matter what I think. He's the SIO. This is his show.

I unclip the lens from my camera and place it back into its foam compartment.

'How are things really, Ally?'

I'm about to brush him off with a 'fine' but he deserves better. He's asking because we've known each other for years and he cares.

'Pretty rough for a while now.'

I swallow back the urge to tell Alex how people I've worked with – some I thought of as friends – now blank me in the corridor or how when I enter a canteen, others get up and leave or how I've even been sent to jobs that don't exist.

He senses my discomfort and I'm grateful he doesn't pursue the cause.

'I saw the news. Seems like DI Stride was playing fast and loose with a few other cases too.'

'Yes. I heard it wasn't just Sian Jones' murder.'

That's often the way with corruption cases. Once uncovered, they tend to spawn. DI Stride cut his teeth on corruption long before Mainwaring entered the dock.

'You did the right thing, you know.'

'Did I? Then how come I've been exiled to the back of beyond?'

'That's the police service for you. Happy to catch criminals, but not so grateful when it's one of their own.' He pauses. 'I know you, Ally, you'll be fine.' I don't respond and Alex changes the subject. 'You're not convinced the boyfriend killed Janie, are you?'

'That obvious, huh?' I smile, relieved to be back on safer ground.

'Well, you never were one to keep your opinions to yourself. Good to see that hasn't changed.'

I look down at Janie's face, pale and serene, like the angels Bernadette used to tell me about when I was little, the ones bursting with love and jubilation. But there's no joy here, just despair.

'Something doesn't sit right with me.'

'What do you mean?'

'I photographed her when her boyfriend beat her up. He lost his rag, but he used his fists. Even when he was completely out of control, he didn't try to throttle her.'

'You know, two women a week are murdered by a current or former partner. The killer is most likely to be her boyfriend.'

'You're right. Maybe I'm looking for something that isn't there.'

'There's something else you should know. She had a miscarriage, fairly recently.'

'A miscarriage?'

Yes, of course. I remember now. The last time I saw Janie, all smiles, waving my concerns away. *It's fine now. We're good. Chris says he was just a bit stressed, we're even trying for a baby.'*

The classic response. A baby will make everything better. Only it doesn't and I seized my last chance to tell Janie to get out.

'They never change, Janie. You must leave him. He needs help.'

And then I did something I never do. Not in all the DA cases I've attended. I shared my story. It was the only way I was going to persuade this young girl she was in danger.

'A long time ago, I was with a guy who used to hit me. He always promised to stop, but he never did and the last time he almost killed me. Please don't go back to this guy.'

His name was Sean and it was my loneliness, that miserable state that tramples all reason, that brought him into our lives. He'd always had a reputation for being a bit handy in a fight, but saved his punches for the pint spillers down the pub. Then, one day, he turned on me and life became a cycle of slaps and sorrys until Megan and I escaped. I told Janie this, but she just gave me a look that said he never really loved you and wasn't really sorry for what he did, not like her Chris.

And now she's dead.

This time it's my phone that buzzes. It's an automated text from Megan's school.

'Oh shit.'

'What is it?' asks Alex.

'Megan didn't register for class this afternoon.'

Alex smiles and shakes his head at some distant memory, although I don't remember either of his kids bunking off school.

'Remember, it doesn't last forever.'

7

Jackie is where he left her. Her tiny frame clad in a shapeless grey shift, she looks lost in the large sturdy orthopaedic recliner that takes up most of the lounge. Not that she needs an orthopaedic recliner, but it suits him to let her think she does.

In front of her are three television screens stacked in a triangle and tuned into the live cams around North Devon. Jackie likes to watch the families on the various beaches.

Absorbed in other people's lives, she doesn't notice him at first, standing in the doorway. He doesn't want to interrupt her, not when she's attempting to extract one of the few remaining strands of hair clinging to her scalp, all that's left of what is meant to be a shoulder-length brown bob.

She scores a strand, lays it across her tongue, closes her mouth and swallows. There's nothing left of her eyelashes or brows, her face a beige blank canvas, waiting to be shaded and coloured in. She graduated to her head some time ago where now just a few tufts of hair reside. It's a symptom of her anxiety, and Jackie is anxious about everything. It's why she doesn't go out; that and she looks like someone has taken a Flymo to her head.

She's not alone. Dozens of miniature character teddy bears line every sill, shelf, ledge and even the sofa, fixing him with their glassy stares. Jackie says they keep her company when he's on long shifts which is most of the time. Balanced on her armrest watching the screens with her is her current favourite: a beige-brown bear in a white frilly shirt and black waistcoat called Darcy, apparently. Darcy has replaced Sherlock Holmes and before that Batman. One day, he'll burn the lot of them.

An unfamiliar woody smell hangs in the living room like she's just got in from a long stroll in the woods, only that's impossible. She's not left the house in two years although that doesn't stop her knowing what's going on in the world.

When he walks into the room, the movement startles her and she elbows Darcy to the floor. He lands at his feet, but he doesn't pick the bear up.

'You scared me.'

'Sorry.'

'Have you seen this? Isn't it awful? I don't know what the place is coming to.' Her upturned, hairless face is unusually flushed and it's then that he notices that all three screens are tuned to the live cam on Bidecombe Quay. She never watches the quay.

'Yes. Terrible business, we got called there this morning, but how did you find out about it?'

'Arjun told me they found a girl's body on the quay this morning. He gave me a foot massage today. Apparently, it was a local girl, a drug addict, so Arjun thinks it was an overdose.'

So that's what the smell is. Arjun is Jackie's carer and all-round busybody. He can't stand the man, putting ideas into her head, laughing and flirting with her as if he fancies her when he knows he's repulsed by her, everyone is. It's Barbara's fault. Jackie's health visitor. She said that with him at work for long periods of time, it would be good to have someone check up on her. What she really meant is that she couldn't be bothered to check in on Jackie, but before he knew what was happening, Arjun appeared on their doorstep.

He let him in knowing Jackie wouldn't allow herself to be handled by a foreigner, a brown one at that, and, sure enough, she was clutching her favourite teddies at the time, Edward and Mrs Simpson, for protection, when he strolled into the living room. Then he made some crack about how he 'only came to this country because he hates curry and couldn't get a decent roast back home' and it was like they were best friends. He even bought her a teddy dressed in a red-and-gold sari for her last birthday. It had one of those red bindi dots on its forehead. Now he comes every day.

'I wouldn't listen to anything Arjun tells you.'

'But he's very kind to me even though, you know, he's one of them. He used this juniper oil on my feet today. His mother swore by it. She had circulation problems too. She lived to ninety-two.'

'And he really shouldn't be using unprescribed medicine on you. Even homeopathic remedies can be very dangerous.'

Her smile fades.

'I didn't realize. I thought it was harmless.'

He pats her arm, the grey material crumples until his hand lands on a thin bony limb.

'It's not your fault. That's why I'm here, my love, to keep you safe.'

She nods and, like a child, her mind moves to something happier.

'Did you get them?' She knows full well he has, but she still likes it if he teases her a little.

'Mmm, let me see.' He slides his hand into his trouser pockets. 'No, not there. Wait. What's this?' He taps his jacket and produces a large bag of Haribo Gold Bears which Jackie eats by the cartload, but it doesn't matter how many she puts away, she never puts weight on.

Jackie reaches out for them, but her face clouds and she pauses.

'Arjun says that I should reduce the amount of sweets I eat as they might be the reason for my—' She points to her lower stomach. 'You know.'

They're not responsible for the pain in her lower abdomen and, anyway, they're better at covering up her noxious breath that no amount of Aquafresh or vigorous tooth-brushing can freshen – although as the day wears on it seeps through like a blocked drain on a hot day.

He withdraws his hand.

'Arjun this, Arjun that, anyone would think you fancy the man. Are you sure you're not having an affair with him or something?'

The idea that anyone would find her attractive is ludicrous, of course.

'No, Simon. I would never do anything like that. He just mentioned it, that's all.'

'Honestly, I go out of my way to buy you something special and you just throw it back in my face.' He stuffs the packet back into his pocket. 'Fine, I'll take it back to the shop.'

Her eyes, their largeness exaggerated by the lack of lashes, grow even larger and tear up with confusion and apology.

'No, please, don't do that. I'm sorry. I'm really grateful for the sweets. Thank you, Simon.' He lets her stew a few seconds more. 'Please. I'm sorry,' she whispers, and he relents and gives her the packet.

He picks Darcy up and puts him back on the armrest.

'You're beautiful just the way you are. Arjun's just a carer. What does he know about anything? I'm a medical professional and I say a few sweets won't do you any harm.'

'Yes, yes, you're right. Thank you.'

She digs around for a few seconds before finding what she's looking for. Pinching a Gold Bear between her thumb and forefinger, she holds it aloft her like a precious jewel before popping it in her mouth.

'What happened to the girl on the quay? How did she die?' she says, searching for a second Gold Bear.

'Strangled, I think.'

'My goodness, that's terrible. Do they know who did it?'

'No, but I heard she was there with her boyfriend, so I guess he's the prime suspect.'

'Who was she?'

He looks at her. She's not normally this curious.

'A local girl. I knew her. She had a miscarriage a few months ago and Trisha and I were called to attend.'

She was hysterical. There was so much blood she thought she was going to die, but he told her that wasn't going to happen. Then he went through the usual questions to calm her down and gauge her mental state. 'Can you tell me your full name?' 'What day of the week is it?' 'Well done. Let's try a harder one. What's your Instagram handle?' She was so grateful he'd saved her life she didn't think twice: Jamster2001. And his standard response, to pull a face and ask, 'What kind of a name is that?' made her laugh. A nurse at the hospital told him she'd been beaten by her boyfriend. It was then that he knew for certain she'd be perfect. Fragile and vulnerable, she wouldn't be able to resist anyone who showed her the slightest kindness. She wouldn't be able to resist him.

'She lost her baby too? That's sad.' A wistfulness passes over

Jackie, pausing the next Haribo between the bag and her mouth. She loves children. She spends hours cooing over the babies in their white frilly bonnets and the toddlers in their nappy swimmers that star on the live cams. She'd have loved her own children, but you have to have sex first.

'Yes, I guess it is,' he says, but he doesn't want to discuss her with Jackie. 'I met her boyfriend, too, and he was a complete thug. I've no idea what she saw in him.'

She rotates the sweet around her mouth.

'And now he's killed her.'

'Yes. It looks that way. Anyway, I better get on. I'm already late for my cycling club. The boys will be wondering where I am.'

He goes to kiss her cheeks, making sure his lips don't make contact. He executes the move swiftly, but not fast enough and he's caught in the stench of her breath.

She doesn't notice, of course, but picks up one of the remotes to change the live cam to Morte Sands, still dotted with families, enclosed in their striped windcheaters, even though the tide is out and the sun low and their skin has begun to pimple under the cooling breeze.

He never planned to marry again, not after the first time, but not long after he moved to Bidecombe, his little-old-lady neighbours started joking with him about why he hadn't been snapped up, a good-looking guy like him, own house, lovely smile, great job. Own teeth. Ha, ha, ha. Beryl, four doors down, would say things like, 'If only I was thirty years younger, I'd nab you for myself.' He sensed they weren't really joking and that they thought there was something abnormal about him. So, worried the lack of a wife was drawing attention to himself, he decided to remedy the situation.

If he knows one thing about churches it is that they are

a repository of the rejected: those souls that don't measure up to society's norms. Don't worry, God still loves you, but God isn't enough, misfits crave attention and affection, even the fake variety, just like everyone else so he began his search at St Joseph's, joining a committee called 'Friendly Faces' that went out into the community, checking up on God's flock.

At church one day, the vicar told him about a woman called Jackie. She had recently lost her mum who was also her carer. Bullied as a child for her small stature, Jackie suffered severe anxiety and agoraphobia. Her mum, when she was alive, was the only person she would leave the house with. Simon knew instantly he had found the answer to his problems. The vicar gave him her address and the next day, he turned up at her house with a bag of her favourite sweets, Haribo Gold Bears.

She still had eyebrows then, but her lashes were little more than a broken line of stubble. He couldn't believe his luck when he saw what she did with the hair she pulled out.

He was good at talking to people and it wasn't long before he became her new safe person and then her fiancé. They organized the wedding, a tiny affair for a church, and then, out of the blue, she broke it off. The vicar said the idea of marital relations terrified her as she'd never done it before. This just got better.

Over a family-sized bag of Haribo, Simon told her he wasn't like other men. His love for her was so great, he was prepared to forgo all that nonsense just to be with her. She cried with relief and gratitude while he tried not to laugh at the idea that she could possibly think he fancied her.

Anyway, he couldn't have done it with her even if he wanted to.

It's 8 p.m. I've called Megan's friends to ask if they've seen her. They've all said no, but they've reached the age where it's impossible to tell if they're lying, so having already trawled her usual haunts: the chip shop on the high street, a bus shelter near the quay and a bench in a particularly remote corner of Bidecombe rec with no success, I head to Morte Sands in the hope she might be there,

When the sun is high and unhindered by cloud, you wouldn't want to be anywhere else in the world and it's no wonder that the tourists flock to it, but the chances of Megan being here at the beach are slight. She wouldn't have walked, and she doesn't have the money for the bus, which is intermittent at best, but I have to try.

By the time I arrive, the sun is a great orange orb squatting low on the horizon. Its power is already waning, giving way to a fresh sea breeze that infuses the towels wrapped around the shoulders of the little kids until their stick-like legs begin to tremble, finally persuading their parents to pack up and head back to the car park. The knee-high, messy waves have already sent the surfers sloping to their camper vans which are now drenched in the cloying aroma of weed. It's been a while since Megan and I tugged on our wetsuits and took the bodyboards out and I'd do anything to return to those days where every one of my suggestions was grabbed with enthusiasm and joy, instead of sullen indifference.

On the edge of the beach is the Coffee Shack, a retro silver bullet-shaped van stationed at the entrance to the beach just below the main slipway leading from a car park carved out of the dunes. With his sun-dried hair and Hawaiian shirts, its owner Liam Greene does a convincing laid-back beach barista impression, but he was in the police once and nothing gets past him. If Megan has been here, he'll know about it.

I find Liam wiping down the counter. His surprise at seeing me quickly turns to a huge smile.

'You're brave,' he laughs. 'The water's a bit chilly this time of the day.'

'I'm not here for a swim. Have you seen Megan anywhere?'

'No, sorry. Why?'

'She's gone AWOL.'

'Ah. I see. Well, she's not been on the beach. I'd have seen her. Have you tried the rec?'

'I already checked it. She's not there either.'

'I doubt she's got far.'

'Yeah, you're right, but it's getting a bit late. Thanks, anyway.'

I turn to go back to my car.

'Ally,' Liam calls after me.

'Yes.'

'Let me help you look for her.'

His offer takes me by surprise.

'But you're not due to close for another hour or so.'

Liam looks over at the camper vans on the other side of the car park, their curtained windows opened just enough to release a pall of bluish smoke.

'I think finding Megan is more important that helping a few potheads stave off the munchies, don't you?'

I pretend to take a sharp breath.

'Well, I don't know, that sounds quite an important service that you're providing.'

He grins and unties his apron.

'Just give me a minute.'

'Thanks, Liam, that's really kind of you.'

'No trouble. We'll find her.'

He says this with such calm certainty that I believe him.

'While I'm finishing up here, why don't you ask those guys over there if they've seen her? They've just come from Bidecombe. They might have passed her on the coastal path.'

He nods towards the car park, now virtually empty except for a handful of camper vans in one corner and half a dozen men in jeans and windbreakers riding their battered mountain bikes in circles. Several are attempting a wheelie which is strangely unsettling given they are all over the age of thirty. I know most of them. They all live in Bidecombe, like me, and they all have learning difficulties. Some have been victimized and some even beaten up for their vulnerability which is where I come in, photographing the results of someone else's ignorance and cruelty.

Parked in the centre of them, like a circus ringmaster, is an older man. It's difficult to tell under the helmet, but I'd estimate he's late thirties. Clad shoulder-to-toe in black and red lycra that reveals a trim rather than muscular frame, he's perched on a matching sleek racer watching the others. Whether the spectacle is causing him pleasure or consternation is impossible to tell as his face is devoid of any expression.

When he sees me jogging towards him, he removes his helmet and gloves, like a racing driver. Sweat has dampened and darkened his baby-fine blond hair and it takes me a second or two to realize it's Simon Pascoe, the paramedic I met on the quay that morning.

I stand at the edge of the circle hoping one of the cyclists will see me and slow down to create a gap big enough for me to slide in between, but they're oblivious to me. I shrug at Simon, but he doesn't respond. Maybe he doesn't recognize me. Finally, I take my chances, narrowly missing one of the cyclists, not that he notices.

'Hi, Simon, I'm Ally Dymond, the CSI. We met earlier today.'

'Oh. Yes. Of course. What is it?' The softness of his voice throws me. I noticed it this morning, only because it was so at odds with his tight, chiselled jaw and impassive expression which give him a macho air.

'I'm sorry to interrupt your cycle ride, but I'm looking for my daughter, Megan. She's fifteen but much taller than me, about five-seven, with long auburn hair, pale complexion. Quite distinctive-looking. You haven't seen her, have you?'

I flick to my most recent photo of Megan on my phone, in which she's grimacing. It was the closest approximation to a smile she was prepared to muster, but it does the job of conveying the pallor of her skin and the unusual shade of her red-gold hair – the two things people notice most about her.

'I see what you mean,' says Simon.

'Sorry?'

'She is quite distinctive-looking, as you say.'

He slips his hand around mine to draw my phone towards him for closer inspection. Its damp clamminess feels oddly intimate but it's worth it if he recognizes her.

His intense blue eyes stare down at Megan and, for a moment, I take this as a sign that there is something familiar about her, but it comes to nothing.

'I'm sorry. No, I don't think I've seen her. I think I'd have remembered.'

'Oh. OK. Thank you anyway.'

I put my phone away.

'I hope you find her.' He glances up at the dusky sky. 'It'll be dark in an hour.'

Simon unclips a container from his handlebars and, holding it above his head, he squirts water into his mouth, swills and swallows. 'She won't have gone far.'

'Yes, I'm sure you're right.'

He tugs his gloves back over his hands and replaces his helmet, adjusting his strap.

'Well, I better be going, otherwise they'll get fidgety,' he says, glancing over at a man in a red anorak whose front wheel is lodged in the base of a dune on the far side of the car park. His name is Peter Benson. We were at school together. He has been warned for harassing women, which is unacceptable, but he also has learning needs, the phrase they use now, which classes him as a vulnerable adult and, to some, a legitimate target. He's lucky to have someone like Simon Pascoe to look out for him.

He turns back to me.

'Why don't you give me your number and then if I see her, I can call you straightaway.'

'Thank you. That's really kind of you.'

He takes a phone out of a breast pocket and I tap my number into it.

'It's the least I can do.'

Replacing his phone into the top pocket of his cycling suit, he swings his bike around, points it towards the path taking him back to Bidecombe and rides off. I wonder if he's forgotten about the others, but they notice immediately and fall in behind him, like the Lost Boys in *Peter Pan*. Only not a word is said. If only I had that control over Megan. Liam appears by my side.

'Any joy?' I shake my head, still watching Simon lead his silent troupe back down the trail. 'You all right?'

His question gets my attention.

'I think so.' I look up at the sky. Simon is right, the light is fading fast. 'What if something has happened to Megan?'

He looks at me like I'm mad.

'Why would you think that? Nothing's happened to her, Ally, other than she's bunked off with her mates.' Once again, I'm grateful for his unshakeable belief that Megan is fine.

'You're right. This is Devon, after all.'

'Where you do you want to try first?'

'The Tarka Estate. I've already called Megan's friends. They said they hadn't seen her, but I'm not sure they're telling the truth and they might not be so keen to lie to me face to face.'

I'm about to get in my car, when my phone rings and my day gets a whole lot worse. It's Bernadette. Haughty with a hint of Irish is the best way to describe my adoptive mother's tone.

'In case you're interested, I thought you might like to know Megan is currently at my house. Maybe you'd like to drive over. When you have the time, that is.'

'I'm on my way.'

I ring off. Liam looks hopefully at me.

'Well?'

'Well, the good news is I've found Megan. The bad news is, she's at my mother's.'

8

Bernadette Miller-Dymond's house is also in Bidecombe, but on the opposite side to Seven Hills Lodges where I live. Set high up on a wooded hillside, the building is very much like its owner: tall, thin and looks down on the rest of the town. It's also the last place I want to find my daughter.

Bernadette opens the front door, her face already dialled to disapproval.

'You took your time, Aloysia.'

She's the only person who uses my full name which I loathe. What woman goes through the hassle of adopting a baby only to christen them Aloysia?

'I was working, Bernadette. I couldn't just drop everything.'

She lost the right to call herself my mother the day she chucked me out of the house, seconds after hearing I was six months pregnant and had dropped out of Oxford. That and other things.

'Clearly.' Her overt dislike for my job is never far away. Bernadette had a number of career options lined up for me: CSI wasn't one of them.

In the living room, I find Patrick, Bernadette's current companion. Fifty years a fisherman, but now deep into retirement forced on him by crippling arthritis, he still can't bear to relinquish his navy sailor's hat and ribbed sweaters. From the look on his face, I'm guessing he'd rather be tackling thirty-foot waves in a Force 9 gale off Lundy Island than be in a room with three generations of the Dymond family. Talking of which, the third generation, Megan, is sitting on the edge of the sofa, curled into herself; the half of her face that isn't obscured by a curtain of pale red hair is channelling hurt and self-pity for all it's worth.

I stand over her.

'Right, what's going on, Megan?'

She doesn't look up, but her lower lip quivers impressively.

'I felt sick. I didn't want to phone you again because you told me you couldn't take time off work.'

Her Oscar-worthy performance doesn't work on me, but then it isn't meant for me and her words elicit a despairing sigh and shake of the head from Bernadette. She wallows in her concern for a moment before switching her attention to me, folding her arms in a way that suggests she's found herself in a terrible situation that only she is able to sort. I can't help but feel she's enjoying this.

'Well, it comes to something when you put your job before your sick child.'

I draw my breath in to stop myself saying something I doubt I'll ever regret, but accept will not help the current situation. Instead, I focus on Megan.

'Why didn't you tell your teachers you were ill? They'd have kept you until I got there.'

Megan hugs herself closer.

'I just wanted to go home.'

'But you can't just walk out of school. No one knew where you were.'

She gives me her best 'like I give a shit' shrug and I could slap her, but Bernadette has enough ammunition already.

'I think the real issue here is that Megan needed her mum, and you weren't there for her.'

Irony clearly hasn't reached this part of Bidecombe. I could say, 'Do you mean in the same way you weren't there for me when I was nineteen and six months gone?' But I don't. I'm meant to be an adult here.

'I *am* there for her.'

'Really, so what about six months ago when she hurt herself at school? Where were you then?'

Well, I walked straight into that one. Six months ago, Megan fell off the beam in gym class and hit her head. The school couldn't get hold of me because I was at a training day eighty-odd miles away, so they called the next person on my emergency contact list – Bernadette. It is the one and only time Bernadette has stepped in to help and, by all accounts, she took some persuading, but, boy, has she milked it for all it's worth. Still, she did it. That point goes to her.

I turn to Megan.

'So, what time did you get here?'

'About four.'

'So where were you in between times?'

Megan shifts in her seat.

'Around.'

'For Christ's sake, Megan, around where?'

'There's no need to blaspheme, Aloysia.'

She's right. There isn't. I started when I was Megan's age.

A petulant teenager railing against Bernadette's irrational attachment to religion and her insistence that I also adopt it unquestioningly, I did it to piss off the Irish Catholic in her and it kind of stuck. I refocus on Megan. 'You were hanging around the rec, weren't you? Was Jay Cox there?'

'No,' she says with the emphasis of a liar.

Jay Cox is a low-level drug dealer. He's sixteen, but he has the gangliness of a twelve-year-old who's had a sudden growth spurt. I caught Megan talking to him outside the kebab shop on Bidecombe high street a few weeks back when I was on lates and my heart folded in half. Jay Cox is the kind of boy mothers have nightmares their daughters will hook up with. He's a weaselly individual who doles out pills like M&Ms, drawing youngsters in before hitting them with his bill for his services. Mousy-hair and malnourishment must be in because the girls flock to him, including, it seems, Megan. Obviously, I challenged her about it, but she swore he was just asking to borrow money for his bus fare home and besides, 'he's not as bad as people make out'. Jesus wept.

'Jay is scum. He's mixed up in all sorts. I've told you before to stay away from him.'

'You're hardly perfect yourself.' In her apparent despair, Megan suddenly finds some fire. Bernadette nods in agreement.

'That's enough,' I snap. 'We're not talking about me.'

'I think we all need to calm down,' says Patrick, dividing a worried look between all three of us.

'Well, maybe we *should* talk about you.' A sly smile creeps across Megan's face. 'Helena saw you in the pub two nights ago, snogging the face off some guy.'

Oh God. I knew it was a mistake to meet someone in

Bidecombe, the town that doesn't know the meaning of discretion, especially when it was just another one of my nightmares on Tinder Street. As per usual, nerves and alcohol masked the awkwardness of our incompatibility to the point where it took physical contact to realize we really were wasting each other's time. The kiss wasn't me. It was a bottle and a half of Sauvignon Blanc.

Predictably, Bernadette throws her hands into the air. I might have known she'd make a big deal out of this which is, of course, why Megan has brought it up.

'For goodness' sake, Aloysia, what on earth's the matter with you?' Frustration brings out her Irish accent, reminding me with a shudder of the nuns at school. 'Have you no shame? You're a mother.' Here we go.

'Megan, get your things. We're going home.'

Megan picks up her school bag and traipses into the hallway.

'Bye, Nana.' She throws Bernadette her sweetest smile. 'Thanks for this afternoon.'

'Any time, my darling. You know I'm here for you.'

I'm biting the inside of my lower lip so hard it hurts.

'Go and wait in the car.'

Unbelievably, Megan does as she is told. Even she can sense this is about to escalate. I wait until the front door closes behind her before rounding on Bernadette, but she gets there first.

'What's wrong with you?' Bernadette hisses at me. 'Do you really think it's appropriate to be kissing men in public?'

'OK, one – this is the twenty-first century, not the Dark Ages, and two, I am allowed a social life, you know.'

'Is that what you call it?' I'm amazed Bernadette can unpurse those thin lips of hers long enough to get the words out.

'Now, Bernadette, this isn't helping.' Patrick's right, but I'm not going to back down. I'm sick of her lording it over me.

'I don't have a go at you about Patrick.'

'That's different. We're just friends and I'm not gallivanting across the countryside, dropping my knickers for all and sundry. It's no wonder Megan is going off the rails. You're just the same as you always were. Only thinking of yourself. No care for anyone else. You do what you want when you want. Well, you've got a daughter now and it's time you learned to take care of her properly.'

Ah, yes, here it is, Bernadette's tried and tested 'you've made your bed and now you've got to lie in it' approach to parenting. It never ceases to derail me. I know she had great ambitions for me. I had them for myself. Getting pregnant at nineteen wasn't part of my life plan either, but it happened. Bernadette was furious with me for, as she put it, throwing my life away and, for a time, she refused to have anything to do with us. Maybe if she had, I wouldn't have ended up with Sean. But you can't avoid anyone in Bidecombe and, besides, little kids have a way of winning you over and she couldn't resist Megan. She dotes on her now, but she's never forgiven me.

Before I can muster a response, Bernadette disappears into the kitchen, slamming the door behind her. I sigh at Patrick.

'I'm never going to please her, am I?'

Patrick shrugs and I feel guilty for pulling him into this family feud not of his making.

'Believe it or not, she loves you and she worries about you, and Megan.'

'Really? Well, she's got a funny way of showing it.'

I slam the front door hard behind me – two can play that

game – and get back into the car. Ramming the seatbelt into its catch, I switch on the engine before turning it off again. This can't wait.

'Jesus, Megan, what the hell are you playing at?'

But she just folds her arms and shrugs, her auburn hair draped forward hiding her face.

'Don't have a go at me, just because you don't get on with Nana.'

'This has nothing to do with me and Bernadette. This is about you skipping school. Do you have any idea how serious that is? What got into you?'

'Nothing, right. Nothing got into me. I'm sick of school. It's a waste of time and I'm sick of you going on at me all the time.'

'Fine, you're grounded for a week and if you bunk off again, it'll be a month.'

'Whatever.'

I turn on the car engine and pull away from the kerb sure of one thing. Megan isn't just having a Pink Floyd moment over education. She's keeping something from me.

9

Where would I be without Penny? Dead probably.

Boxing Day 2012. This time it was a broken oven, a raw turkey crown and six cans of Stella. Sean landed a few punches before the alcohol sloshing around inside him toppled him and that's when Megan and I made a run for it.

We found a bench in a corner of Bidecombe Rec, hidden from the main road and sheltered from the vicious wind blasting off the black wintry seas: me with a busted lip, Megan still in her My Little Pony PJs. I tried Bernadette first, but she had friends round for canasta and told me to make it up with Sean. 'Anyway, Aloysia, I'm sure it's not as bad as you say. Aren't you being a little dramatic about it all?' Years of bruised kidneys and expertly applied make-up said she didn't know what she was talking about, but there was no one else. Sean had made sure of that.

Next, I tried the women's refuges, but Christmas is their peak time and they were already full. The last refuge rang off and I knew we'd have to go back to Sean, but I couldn't move. Frozen with fear as much as the cold, one arm wrapped around Megan, I've no idea how much time passed, but a red woollen mitten closed over my hand and gently lowered my phone I'd been holding to my head like a loaded gun.

'You're coming home with me,' said a Scouse accent. It belonged to a woman in a purple-and-white, tie-dyed skirt and long grey hair punctuated with coloured beads. Home was the Seven Hills Lodges just outside Bidecombe. I knew little about the place because, like so many places in Bidecombe, it was for the tourists, not the locals. Nestled below the brow of a grassy hill that afforded the best views of Morte Sands, the Bristol Channel and beyond, it was home to thirty cabins sprinkled in among the pine trees that managed to survive the salty winds gusting off the sea. We were only meant to stay there a few days. Seven years later we're still in Cabin 27, but I've never forgotten that first Christmas. Penny took a photo of me and Megan clinking our glasses, filled with orange juice, over a huge turkey. Megan's smile is real – children have a way of living in the moment – but mine was purely for her and for the camera. You can still see the swelling around my left eye from one of Sean's more accurate punches.

Penny slides a cold bottle of locally made cider across the kitchen table and I take a grateful slug of the honey-coloured liquid. It's called Sam's Cider. I don't know Sam, but I do know that he knows how to make a good cider.

'Megan bunked off school again. I got a text from the school in the middle of a postmortem.'

Penny frowns.

'Why?'

'I don't know. She won't tell me, but I know it's got something to do with that piece of shit, Jay Cox. I saw the two of them outside Kebabs by the Coast on the high street a few weeks back.'

'Sharon Cox's son?' Penny knows everyone, although only I know her real name which is Sadie Macdonald. She hasn't used it in twenty years, not since she left Liverpool and her stalker ex. She shakes her head sadly. 'He's a soft lad, that one. Involved in all sorts. If Sharon was still alive, she'd be so sad to see what he's become.'

'Well, I've banned Megan from having anything to do with him, but she doesn't listen to me.'

'Megan's got too much sense to get mixed up with the Cox's.'

'I hope so, because I'm not sure how I can stop her. I've grounded her for a week, but I can't lock her up when I'm on nights and weekends.'

'I can keep an eye on her for you.'

'Thanks, Pen, but you already do so much. I mean, who else could have taught my daughter the Beatles' entire back catalogue?'

Pen is a huge fan. Her name, the first that came to mind when the previous Lodges' owner offered her a cleaning job, is a blend of Penny Lane and Strawberry Fields.

She laughs.

'Don't knock it. There's a lorra wisdom in those words.'

Twenty years in North Devon hasn't dulled her accent.

'Er . . . *she loves you, yeah, yeah, yeah*?'

She grins at me.

'OK, maybe not the early stuff.'

'Seriously, this isn't about someone else looking after Megan. This is about me being around more for her. You know, when she got fed up doing whatever she was doing this afternoon with Jay, she didn't come home. She went to Bernadette's.'

Penny's raised eyebrows signal her confusion and not a little hurt.

'Why? She knows I'm here for her. And you, for that matter.'

I smile gratefully. At times, Penny has been more of a mum to me than Bernadette ever was – although Bernadette would rather be horsewhipped naked down the high street by the Pope than wear a knitted rainbow poncho and neon feathers in her hair. It occurs to me that Penny's stalker ex, Ian, probably wouldn't recognize her now in all her bright finery, but she still moors an 'escape boat' in the harbour 'just in case'.

'Because she knew how much it would piss me off. She phoned to tell me she had Megan. I could hear the gloating in her voice. Then Megan pipes up that a friend of hers saw me kissing this guy in the pub the other night. Bernadette loved that, of course. More proof that I'm a fallen woman.'

Penny takes the top off another bottle of cider for herself.

'So you're not allowed boyfriends now?'

'I'd hardly call him a boyfriend. More an internet user error.'

'I don't know why you don't give that beach barista guy a go. It's so obvious he fancies you. He's always asking about you.'

'What, Liam? He's just being friendly. He's like that with everyone.'

Penny rolls her eyes in mock despair.

'No, he isn't and just because you've had a rough time in the past, it doesn't mean the future will be the same.'

'Save me the psychobabble, Pen. Adopted by an emotion-ally distant woman, impregnated by a man who scarpered five minutes after the first scan and beaten by my alcoholic husband, I think I'm entitled to have the commitment level of a rabbit in springtime. Anyway, you can't talk. When are you and Ringo ever going to meet?'

Ringo isn't his real name either. He's a guy Penny met in a Beatles forum a few months back. They've been exchanging messages ever since, mostly about their mutual love of the Fab Four. Recently, she found out he lives in South Devon. News of his close proximity unsettled her and she ignored him for a while. They're talking again, but so far she's knocked back his invitations to meet.

Penny shrugs.

'I don't know. Perhaps it's better that we don't.'

I place my hand on hers. I know what's on her mind because it's always there.

'It's been twenty years, Pen. You've changed your name. You're not on social media. Ian couldn't find you even if he wanted to. Ringo isn't Ian. You should give him a chance.'

She says nothing. I've already strayed too deep into her past and when she speaks it's to steer me away with a joke. 'Look at us. We're a right pair of commitment phobes, aren't we?'

She gets up and drops the empty cider bottles into the recycling bin by the back door. They smash against the others.

Maybe there are some things we can't escape.

10

When he walks into the house, Jackie's voice reaches him immediately, but her words are not for him. She's talking to one of her bears, probably Darcy, telling him what a pretty dress a little girl on the beach is wearing.

After two hours in the company of the imbeciles in the cycling club, he's in no mood to listen to Jackie drone on about the bloated lobster-skinned tourists she's watched on the live cams so he slips past the living-room door and heads upstairs. Jackie doesn't come upstairs, even to sleep. What would be the point? Upstairs is where the bedrooms are that contain beds where people have sex, so she stays downstairs which suits them both. It means he has the place to himself.

Exchanging the stifling atmosphere of Jackie's world of swirly carpets and a hundred hard stares for parquet flooring, white linen sheets and Venetian blinds feels like someone has slipped a mask over his mouth and blasted him with oxygen.

He lies down on his bed, hands behind his head, and takes a deep breath. Now he's alone he can think about more important things. Like last night.

It was touch and go for a while. He had waited hours, wedged under the V of the wooden struts holding the quay up, gagging on the stench of algae and dead fish. There, he listened to her and the thug having sex, him grunting like a pig at mealtime, her in total silence. When it was over, the thug took her lack of enthusiasm as a sign she must be 'getting it' somewhere else. She denied it, but he said that if he found out she was seeing someone behind his back, he'd kill her.

He stormed off, and Simon seized his chance. She was pleased to see him and knew who he was immediately. She practically fell into his arms. She thought he'd come to help her.

Even as his hands curled around her neck and squeezed, he could tell she thought it was all part of some master plan. Stupid girl. She didn't even struggle. They don't always. It's the shock. It was over in seconds although the best was yet to come.

He settles into the memory, like a warm blanket. His muscles relax and he drifts into a well-earned sleep, letting go of his mind, his thoughts taking on a life of their own.

He's back on the quay, sitting on the low wall. The white CSI van pulls up in front of him and the CSI gets out, already wearing a forensic suit. She scoops up her frizzy dark hair and pins it to the back of her head. He's staring at her, but she doesn't notice him as she walks to the back of the van and opens the door. She disappears inside to retrieve her case, but she's taking so long he gets up to see what's happening. He leans on the door just as she reappears. She looks straight at him and throws her head back in laughter. Shock rips through him and his eyes spring apart and fix on the bedroom ceiling to force the image from his mind. It isn't the CSI, it's Danielle.

11

I'm kerb-crawling Megan as she walks to school. It's not exactly the start to my day I'd planned. When I told my daughter over her Weetabix that I'd be escorting her to the school gates to make sure she didn't truant again, she either thought I was bluffing or was hoping to catch me unprepared as she threw her spoon down, grabbed her school bag and stormed out of the cabin.

She was wrong on both counts. Keys in hand, I followed her, jumping into my battered old red Volvo and I'm now crawling behind her at approximately three miles per hour.

As we reach the Park exit, I draw alongside her and wind the window down. The weather has finally broken and rain specks my hands and face.

'I'm going to follow you all the way to school, so I suggest you get in before one of your friends sees you.'

The public humiliation of your mother driving a metre behind you swings it and she gets into the car. Arms crossed and body twisted, she's practically facing the passenger door, reminding me I'm still public enemy numbers one, two and three after last night's clumsy attempts to understand why she skipped school.

I returned from Penny's to find Megan where I'd left her – sulking in her room. After a gentle interrogation along the lines of 'I won't be angry, if you tell me the truth', she finally admitted she was with Jay Cox because 'he's going through a tough time and just likes to talk to me'. It took considerable effort not to roll my eyes.

'Can't he do that outside of school hours?'

This was a genuine attempt on my part to be reasonable, but I get that it sounded like a cheap shot, earning me Megan's special 'you understand nothing' look.

'He's feeling really low at the moment.'

'It would help if he laid off the drugs – speaking of which, if he's offered you any, I'll kill him.'

'I knew I shouldn't have told you.'

'Look, I'm sorry for Jay. I know he's had it hard, but you're my concern, not him, and he's dangerous, Megan. He gets other kids hooked on drugs.'

'He wouldn't do that to me. He's not like that.'

It's at times like these that she reminds me of her dad, Julian. What I can remember of him. It's more than the auburn hair and freckles. It's the way she holds back on me, a sense of saying one thing, but meaning another, often the complete opposite. In Julian's case, he told me he loved me and would stand by me, both of which were total bollocks.

'Oh, Meggy, don't be so naive. He's a smackhead. That's what smackheads do.'

'No, he isn't. God, you moan about Nana being judgemental, but you're just as bad.'

'No, I'm not and, in Jay's case, I'm right.'

'I hate you.'

Well done, Ally. How to lose daughters and isolate them. So, this morning when I woke up, I decided it was out with bad cop and in with conciliatory cop.

'Look, I don't want to give you a hard time about Jay.'

Megan stares out the passenger window.

'Then trust me. Jay and I just talk. That's all. He's a friend and he's never offered me anything. Not even a can of cider. He wouldn't.' She throws me a side glance. 'I told him about Sean.'

Sean? Where did he come from? He's not been in our lives for years.

'What's Sean got to do with anything?'

My question is met with silence, but it doesn't matter because I've worked it out for myself. There's only one reason why Megan would speak his name now.

'You've seen him, haven't you?' She looks straight ahead and nods, which both horrifies and confuses me as I'd heard he'd moved away. 'Where?' She's fighting herself about what to say, what to censor. 'Just tell me, Megan.'

'He's working on the roof at school.'

'Why didn't you tell me?'

'I didn't want to upset you. I saw him a couple of days ago, but yesterday he said hello and I freaked out. I knew Jay would be around, so I called him and met him at the rec.'

She expels this like a breath she's held on to for too long. What else is she holding on to?

'Did – did Sean scare you?'

She nods and it crushes me, triggering a well-worn self-imposed trial by questions. How could I have ever let him into our lives? That's an easy one. Meggy and I were living in a shithole of a council flat on the Tarka Estate and Sean, a handsome roofer, built like a prop forward, offered us a way out. We were married six months later.

How could I have let him hit me? I don't know. It wasn't a nought to sixty thing, but small, barely noticeable, steps until finally I accepted everything was my fault, including his violence. The irony is he divorced me on the grounds of *my* unreasonable behaviour. Penny told me it was the quickest way to get him out of our lives. It felt like he'd beaten me up all over again, but that was then and this is now. This time, I'm not going to stand by and do nothing.

'I'll speak to the school. Get him removed. Meg, I'm sorry.' My apology joins a thousand others, but all the sorrys in the world can't erase the memory of her mum being pinned against a wall by her throat.

'Thank you. Sorry I bunked off. Seeing Sean freaked me out. I didn't know what else to do.'

'That's OK. It doesn't matter now.' We've nearly reached the school gates, but there's something else bothering me. 'I understand you were upset about Sean, but why did you go to Bernadette's after you met Jay?'

She doesn't miss a beat.

'Nana understands me. She knows how hard it is for me. She's got time for me.'

'Well, there's a first time for everything.' I can't help myself. A quip for every occasion, it's my public defence system, cauterizing any conversation that threatens emotional discomfort, but the message comes over loud and clear from Megan. Bernadette's there for me. You're not.

I pull up near the school gates. She opens the car door, but I grab her arm.

'Promise me you won't bunk off again.' But she just shrugs. 'I love you, you know.'

She stares at me and I brace myself for the usual 'whatever'. Then something seems to give. Anger and resentment, her constant companions these days, look away for a moment and the corners of her mouth turn upwards, even if they don't quite make it to a smile.

'I know.'

'And I promise you I will make this right.'

She reclaims her arm and slams the car door behind her, but it's enough. For now.

Rain streaks on the windscreen, producing a blurred and distorted version of Megan walking away. I flick my wipers on, bringing her back into pin-sharp clarity. She merges with her classmates and her face bursts into smiles. One of them says something to her and she throws her head back with laughter.

She disappears through the school gates, but I linger, scanning the entrance for signs of my ex. My head bobs from side to side trying to spot him in among the slither of black blazers. I know he must be here somewhere, but I can't see him.

I unclip my seatbelt just as my phone rings. It's Jake, asking if I'm nearly at the office in a way that suggests I need to be there now. He's going back to Exeter and there's been some kind of incident at the Commissioner's house and they're clamouring for me to attend. I tell him I'm on my way and ring off. I glance back at the school and then at my phone on the seat beside me. Maybe Sean isn't in today. Maybe Megan will be able to stay out of his way. I fasten my seatbelt and turn on the ignition. I wait for a gap in the traffic and am about to pull into it when I notice I am gripping the steering wheel so tightly the blood has leached from my knuckles.

12

Jake practically jumps out of his skin when I walk into the office. He's gathering paperwork at a speed that suggests he was hoping to vacate the place before I turned up. I suspect that, at some point between yesterday and this morning, someone, probably Holt, filled him in about me as his demeanour has shifted from wanting to please me to wanting to get the hell out of here.

He offers a weak smile as he slides his paperwork into a brown satchel.

'DI Holt has asked if you can send the forensic results to me and I can pass them on to him and the team.'

His tone has apology all over it and I'm angry Holt's got him doing his dirty work.

'He did what?'

But he can't look me in the eye.

'Just passing on the message.' He does the clasps up on his bag, hoping the distraction will soothe his burning cheeks. 'But there's no urgency, obviously.'

But it's not obvious to me. Most SIOs want everything yesterday.

'Really? Why's that?'

'Haven't you heard?'

'Clearly not.'

He seems surprised by my answer. I'm not. I'm on the outside of this investigation. Holt made that very clear.

'Chris Banstead has been charged with Janie Warren's murder.'

'Janie's boyfriend? Are you serious?'

Jake instantly regrets sharing the news. He wants to leave, but I'm standing between him and the doorway.

'Maybe I got that wrong.'

'And maybe you didn't. How can they have charged him so quickly?' A bit of CCTV isn't enough. Christ, the Mainwaring case should have taught Holt that much. 'Has Banstead confessed? If he has, he should sack his brief. And what about the shoeprint?' I wait for a response but Jake frowns, unsure of which question to answer first, so I make things easy for him. 'What the hell is going on here?'

'DI Holt told me to get rid of the photos.'

'What?' This comes out louder than I intended, startling the young man. 'Why?'

'He said there was no need to make life any easier for the defence team than it already is, so I deleted them.'

'You did what? Jesus, Jake, evidence is evidence. You don't just get rid of it because it doesn't suit the SIO's cosy theory.' His colour deepens. I feel sorry for the guy. I know how hard it is to stand up to a detective of Holt's reputation, but that's our job. And Holt should know better. 'Well, I'm not bloody standing for this.'

Taking the back stairs two at a time to DCI Lowe's office, I knock and enter without waiting to be asked.

'Steve, did you know Chris Banstead has been charged with Janie Warren's murder?'

DCI Steven Lowe, a small man, unusually lacking in presence and charisma for a senior police officer, stares at me and then at the person standing to my right: DI Holt. His unexpected appearance throws me, but only for a second.

'And what the hell do you think you're doing telling my CSI to delete photos?'

'Ally, calm down,' says DCI Lowe, getting to his feet.

'No, I won't calm down. I've just stood by and watched a shitfest of an investigation because DI Holt decided it was a domestic killing before I'd even got there.'

Holt steps forward.

'That's because it is a domestic killing. Banstead is as guilty as sin.'

'What about the shoe mark I found on the steps which you told Jake to get rid of? I told you it didn't belong to Banstead or the woman who found Janie and it certainly isn't a copper's boot. It rained until midnight that night so it had to have been made after that time, the time when Janie was killed. Christ, this is basic stuff. Someone else was there on the quay. I'm sure of it.'

I'm not, of course, but I am exceptionally pissed off that Holt won't even consider the possibility.

'I told Jake to delete the photos because they're not relevant and Banstead's defence will use the shoeprint against us. Anyway, it could have been made after Banstead killed her.'

I glare at Holt.

'What are you talking about?'

'Probably someone else found Janie but didn't report it to the police.' The straws aren't even clutched on this one. They've long been let go. Besides, people don't ignore bodies. 'Perhaps they didn't want to get involved. It happens, Ally, whether we like it or not.'

I've had enough. Holt isn't the only one who can rubbish a theory.

'This is Bidecombe, for Christ's sake, not Soho. People love to be involved. They get off on it. Janie's got more friends now than she ever had when she was alive.'

Lowe cuts in.

'But it is possible.'

His quiet voice of reason winds me up even more, but I can't ignore his point.

'Yes, it is possible, but it's not probable.'

'It doesn't matter, anyway.' Holt's smugness wafts over me. 'We've got a witness.'

'Someone saw Banstead kill Janie?'

'Not quite, but as good as. A lad living above the pub on the corner of the quay sleeps with his window open, heard them arguing. Banstead was accusing her of having an affair with someone else, called her all sorts of names. The witness says he overheard Banstead saying, and I quote, "I'm going to kill you, you little bitch."'

My anger drains away. If Holt had told me this before, I wouldn't have burst into the office like a jealous ex. But he's a cop. He understands the power of information and the power of withholding it. Just like in the court that day when DI Jon Stride and his cronies doctored my notebook and forged my statement. I've been had.

Situation diffused, Lowe sits down while I seethe in silence.

'Ally, are you sure there's not something else going on here?' he asks.

Oh, sweet Jesus. I know where this is going.

'Like what?' I snap back at him.

'DI Holt says there was an issue yesterday, a bit of an edge between you. That your comments weren't helpful and were actually quite obstructive.'

Holt meets my glare, ready to bat away any counterattack. You don't become a senior investigating officer without your Professional Investigator Practice Level Three Certificate in arse covering.

'Funny, you didn't say anything at the time. If I remember correctly, you told me I was the last person you wanted on the investigation. I'd say that's pretty obstructive, wouldn't you?'

'You kept obsessing about this fucking shoeprint.'

'And you kept checking your watch like your parking ticket was about to run out.'

Lowe holds a hand up.

'That's enough. Bob, it's probably best if you leave this to me.' The message is clear. Lowe believes Holt over me. As a detective chief inspector, Lowe outranks Holt and is his immediate superior, but – for all I know – they're training-school buddies and I never stood a chance.

Lowe waits until Holt closes the door behind him. He sits down and invites me to do the same. I stay standing.

'Look, Ally. Believe it or not, I'm on your side. I was never a member of the DI Jon Stride fan club as it happens, and you did the right thing in court. The guy was a bad apple.'

'But?'

'But you're not on Major Investigations any more and you have to put it all behind you.'

'Meaning?'

'Meaning leaving shitty voicemails after every job you're sent to just because it's not the crime of the century has to stop.'

'That's got nothing to do with it. I keep being sent to crappy scenes where there's no chance of any forensics. It's a waste of my time and police resources.'

'Still, it's pissing people off and, at the end of the day, I want the same result as you do.'

'And what about Holt? He made it very clear we weren't on the same side.'

'You're reading too much into this, Ally.'

'He's ignoring something that could be highly significant to the investigation.'

'He's a very experienced detective. If he says it's a domestic and Banstead did it, that's good enough for me.'

I ponder my options, but it takes less than five seconds to realize I don't have any. Lowe isn't going to take any notice of me.

'Is that it?'

'Yes, that's it.' I turn to leave, but he's not done. 'And I've had a call from the Commissioner. Someone's trashed his car again, you need to get over there right away and sort it out. He's got a meeting at ten.'

'But—'

He raises his hand to head off my protests.

'Ally, get over it or get out. The choice is yours.'

I close Lowe's office door behind me, wanting to scream. Fuck him, and fuck those that moan about me rather than admit they can't tell one end of a crime scene from another.

And, as for Holt, he only complained about my attitude to

deflect attention from his half-arsed investigation. I'm glad he made Jake put his name on all the exhibits we took from the scene. I don't want to be anywhere near this mess when it gets ripped to shreds in court.

13

'You'll live,' announces Trisha as she unplugs the stethoscope from her ears and peels the Velcro band from Cheryl Black's mottled pink arm. She's wearing a two-sizes-too-small dark pink flannel dressing gown, streaked with brown food stains. She couldn't roll her sleeves up to have her blood pressure taken so she slipped her arm out instead, exposing her right breast, creased and sagging like a punctured party balloon. She's watching him, a sly smile on her face, to see if he's noticed, but he doesn't give her the satisfaction and his eyes stay trained on Trisha. He's a professional after all.

This is the third time they've been called to Cheryl's house on the Tarka Estate in Bidecombe. Trisha can't stand the woman. She's spent the drive from Barnston to Bidecombe moaning about her.

'She's a time waster, Si.'

'Dispatch said she was having a heart attack.'

'No, she's not. There's nothing wrong with that woman other than she's lonely. No medicine can fix that.'

That doesn't stop Cheryl from trying. She's taking pills for everything: her circulation, her anxiety, her depression, her diabetes. Everything. All washed down daily with a litre bottle of vodka.

Trisha's announcement disappoints Cheryl. She was hoping for something more serious. She's enjoying the drama of it all. A lot of them do. Sirens, blue lights, paramedics running into her house. It makes her day.

'So why did I collapse?'

'You fainted. There's any number of reasons. Dehydration, low blood pressure, too much alcohol. Diabetes. You need to make an appointment with the GP and get yourself checked out,' says Trisha.

'I thought I was a goner,' she says, pulling her dressing gown together and finally covering up her right breast.

'You're not going anywhere, but alcohol, pills and fags don't mix, Cheryl. You've got to take better care of yourself.'

But then no one would take any notice of her, would they? If it weren't for the paramedics, the police and social services, no one would know she existed. In her head, they're her friends and family.

Cheryl is getting tired of being lectured by Trisha and he can't blame her. Trisha is fat and smokes twenty a day. Hardly a role model.

'Actually, I've given up the fags. I use them things now.' She nods at a vape on the mantelpiece. 'And I have to take pills for my nerves. Those little bastards next door make my life a misery.'

Trisha isn't interested. She's already packing their equipment away. He kneels in front of Cheryl. She parts her knees by just a fraction, but it's enough to tug her dressing gown apart at the waist. She isn't wearing any underwear, but he pretends not to notice.

'What have they done now, Cheryl?'

'Kicking a ball against my front door all hours of the day and night.'

'That must be terrible.'

He tries to sound like he cares; it seems to work.

'It is, Simon. Does my head in. I swear I've had enough.'

Trisha tuts and looks at her watch, but he ignores her.

'Have you rung the police?'

'Yeah, but they're not interested. I don't know how much more I can take.'

'You must be very frightened.'

She nods, her bloodshot eyes glistening with tears. Trisha rolls her eyes and bends down to whisper in his ear.

'Si, come on, we need to get going.'

Cheryl chokes back a sob.

'I'm scared witless.'

'Is there somewhere else you can go? Or someone that can come and look after you?'

'No, me and my sister don't talk any more. There's no one.'

'OK, I'll speak to the neighbourhood police officer. Ask him to drop in. Maybe have a word with your neighbours.'

She takes his hand. It's dry and scaly and he tries not to flinch.

'Will you? You're a good man, Mr Pascoe. If only the world had more people like you.'

He smiles.

'All part of the service.'

Trisha laughs.

'Believe me, one Simon Pascoe in this world is quite enough.'

It turns out the Commissioner's car hasn't been trashed at all, but someone has scrawled 'twat' in the dust on the bonnet. By the time I finish examining it, I have some sympathy with this observation.

The Commissioner greets me with a rant about my perceived lateness and how I've compounded his humiliation as his neighbours have now all seen the obscenity writ large on the bonnet of his classic E-type Jag. This then tips into apoplexy when I tell him the 'perp' wore gloves and forensically there is nothing I can do. He's still spitting about the breakdown of society and how national service would 'sort the lot of them out' when I drive away.

I continue to work through my 'list' for the day – mostly break-ins that have come in overnight, but I'm still seething about my run-in with Holt and Lowe and their decision to charge Chris Banstead with Janie's murder. Maybe they're right. Banstead had form for hitting Janie. Maybe this time, he just took it too far. It's the most likely explanation, but the existence of that shoeprint bothers me. Someone else was there that night. Maybe they're not involved in Janie's murder, but what if they are? It's irrelevant now, of course, because Holt has got rid of it and hunches don't cut it in modern policing. The only thing I can do is make sure I'm as far away as possible when the shit hits the fan at warp speed. Besides, I've got my own problem to deal with: Sean.

My shift over, I'm parked outside Megan's school. The thought that he is working just metres away from Megan makes me nauseous and nervous. That I could still fear him sickens me, but I can't ignore him, hoping he'll just go away. Sean is not the type to just go away.

It's late afternoon and most of the children have left apart from a few stragglers. I quickly find Sean, standing by some scaffolding clinging to the side of the gym hall. It's hard to miss him. He's built like the proverbial shithouse, but it's more than that. He always had the power to demand my full attention, throwing backgrounds into a blur, reducing sounds to low murmurs, like I couldn't allow myself to be distracted, not for a second, from the main event: him. I know now that this is what fear looks like.

He's shorter than I remember. And older, of course, but the years of working outdoors haven't been kind to him, introducing deep leathery lines to his once smooth laddish looks. I imagine that niggles. Looks were always important to Sean, who topped up muscles cultivated on a building site with long hours in the gym.

He sees me and speaks first, which annoys me. Already he's vying for the upper hand.

'Hi, Ally, good to see you. What's it been? Eight years? You haven't changed a bit.'

Charm oozes from every pore. He's a million miles away from the man who grabbed my throat because I hadn't made him a packed lunch and squeezed it so hard that I passed out. So much so that I could almost be persuaded it never happened. Almost.

'You can't be here. This is Megan's school.'

His wistful smile turns my stomach. 'I know. I saw her yesterday. God, she's grown. A proper young lady now, but it was really good to see her. I said hello, but she blanked me.' He laughs and raises his eyebrows. 'Typical teenager, eh?'

'She blanked you because she's terrified of you.'

His frown is genuine. Jesus, he doesn't think he's done anything wrong.

'That's crap. I loved her as my own. If she's got a problem with me, it's down to you and all the lies you've told her.'

'Or maybe, just maybe, it's because she watched you smash her mother's head against the kitchen table.'

Sean rolls his eyes like it's a trivial detail.

'Christ, Ally. Have you come all this way just to rake over stuff that happened between us years ago? I'm a different bloke now. I've married again. Got three kids of my own. I've moved on. Maybe you should too.'

He's twisting my words, like he always did, but he's right about one thing. I'm not here to talk about the past.

'Megan doesn't want you here. I'm asking you to leave for her sake, not mine.'

He looks me up and down. I shrink under his gaze, suddenly exposed and self-conscious. The smile returns, but this time it's different; it's mocking, designed to undermine me.

'You always were at your sexiest when you were serious. Maybe we could discuss this over a drink. I'm about to knock off.'

Christ.

'Please, Sean. Leave us in peace . . .' I pause because I don't want to say what I'm about to say but I have to. 'Please, I'm begging you.'

He folds his thick arms and casts an eye around as if he's seriously thinking about it, but he isn't because I've been here before, pleading with him not to shout at me, not to shove me and not to hit me.

'No. I'm not going anywhere.'

'In that case, I'm going to see the headteacher right now and get you removed from the school.'

He laughs.

'And tell them what?'

'That you're my abusive ex-husband and that Megan witnessed you assaulting me and that your presence here is upsetting her.'

'And what proof do you have of all this?'

'What do you mean?'

'Well, for a start, there's no police report. Nothing to say

I ever hit you.' He mockingly places his forefinger to the corner of his mouth and looks upwards as if he's trying to recall some fact. His face lights up. 'Ah yes, I remember now, I divorced you on the grounds of *your* unreasonable behaviour. From where I'm standing, this looks like a bitter ex-wife trying to cause trouble so I'm staying until the job is finished and there's not a thing you can do about it.'

He's won and he knows it.

'Fuck you, Sean.'

It's pathetic, but it's all I have left. He steps towards me, but I don't flinch. Is he going to hit me? Public scenes were never his schtick. Maybe he's changed, but so have I and I'm not moving.

The amusement in his eyes hardens into hatred.

'No, Ally, fuck you.'

A glob of warm spit lands on my cheek and slides down towards my chin. Still, I stand my ground, sealing my revulsion behind a defiant stare, but it's a pointless victory because I've lost the war.

He turns away. The only thing left in my arsenal is to close my eyes and not give him the satisfaction of me watching him swagger back into the school hall.

Opening my eyes, Sean has gone, allowing my surroundings to come back into focus; someone is watching me. I turn round and Megan is standing a few metres away. She's seen the whole thing – just like she did all those years ago, but it's not fear in her eyes, it's disappointment and anger.

'I tried.' A meaningless phrase that's more a gasp than anything.

'You promised. You always let me down.'

14

It's early evening and the sun has set low enough at Seven Hills Lodges for the midges to meet and merge in a frenzy of dull brown clouds in the shade of the pine trees.

It's a short stroll down the tarmacked path from Cabin 27 to Penny's white bungalow situated at the entrance to the site. A few of the lodges are occupied and in among the pine trees I glimpse the odd checked shirt or white floppy hat – mostly retired couples making the most of the out-of-season deals. It's still early July. High season doesn't kick in until the schoolchildren break for summer at the end of the month.

I've given up trying to talk to Megan. She refused a lift home from school and when she walked in, she went straight to her room. After a couple of one-sided conversations with her locked bedroom door, I conceded defeat and decided to decamp to Penny's.

Through the kitchen window, I can see Penny sitting at her kitchen table, already chugging her way through a bottle of cider. Smiling, she beckons me in, but on catching my expression, her own switches to concern.

'You look like you could do with a drink.'

'I'm OK, thanks.' There's no point holding back. I couldn't if I tried so I just blurt it out. 'Sean's working at Megan's school.'

Her bottle bangs the tabletop. She knows all about Sean, but he's not the only one on her mind. If Sean – my ex from years ago – can come back into my life after all this time, maybe Ian could come back into hers. Monsters from our past.

'Oh shit, no.'

'Actually, I will have that drink.' Penny grabs me a bottle from the fridge, takes the top off with the bottle opener and hands it to me. I take a quick swig. 'That's why she bunked off school. She's still terrified of him.'

'Oh my God. What are you going to do?'

'I already did it. I went to see him. Told him to leave. Begged him, in fact, but he refused. He's still the same manipulative bully he always was.'

'Can't you speak to someone at work? Get him arrested for harassment. Or get a restraining order on him?'

They're just words chucked out at random to try to make things right, but they don't mean anything because we both know the truth.

'There's nothing I can do. He's not been convicted of anything. I never went to the police, remember?'

I wasn't a CSI then. After I left Sean, I got a cleaning job at the local police station. It was Arthur, the station sergeant, who suggested I go for a job on the front desk. He urged me to put in an application to become a CSI too. 'If you examine scenes as thoroughly as you cleaned this place, no criminal will be safe,' he once told me.

Is there blame in my voice? Penny looks at me as if there

is. Part of me hopes there is. If I'd reported Sean, none of this would be happening. It was Penny who stopped me.

She knocks back the last of her cider.

'So, what are you going to do now?'

'Nothing. Just like I did all those years ago.'

'What about Megan?'

'She won't talk to me. Says I've let her down and she's right. I couldn't protect her then and I can't protect her now. What kind of a parent does that make me?' Silence fills the kitchen. Penny lost in her own nightmare scenario involving Ian, me searching for a solution. 'There's only one thing I can do.'

'What's that?'

'I'll keep her off school.'

'Are you sure?'

'None of this is Megan's fault. Why should she suffer? I'll call the school and tell them she's gone into hospital for a minor op and needs to convalesce. It's only three weeks to the summer break. By the time she goes back to school in September, Sean will have gone.'

Penny nods.

'I can keep an eye on her while you're at work. There's plenty of little jobs she can do around the site to keep her busy.'

'Thanks, Penny.' It's not ideal, but at least it's a solution and I feel a lot better at the thought Megan will be nowhere near Sean. My mood lifts. 'So any news from Ringo?'

Penny twists a row of coloured beads threaded through her long grey hair around her finger, a nervous habit of hers, especially when talking about men.

'Oh, I don't know. He's asked again if we can go on a date.'

'And what did you say?'

'I said I'd think about it.'

'If you keep him hanging on, he's going to get fed up sooner or later.'

She throws her hair over her shoulder.

'I just don't know if I'm ready for all that.'

'It's a date, not marriage.'

'I'm still not sure. He could be anyone. He could be a mad axeman.'

'And he could be the man of your dreams.'

'Or nightmares.'

'All I'm saying is you've got nothing to lose and plenty to gain. Message him, tell him you'll meet him.'

'I'll think about it.'

'Promise?'

'Promise.'

But I know she won't. I finish my drink and get up to leave.

'I better get back.'

'Ally.'

'Yes.'

'I'm sorry.'

Megan is in the kitchen that's more of a kitchenette as it's tiny and separated from the living room by a narrow breakfast bar. She's making her favourite meal: baked beans on toast, covered with melted cheese. It's what she makes herself when I'm not around. It smells good and I realize I haven't eaten since breakfast.

'Any leftovers for me?'

Megan glances at me.

'Maybe.'

This is teen language for 'I haven't completely forgiven you, but I'm not as mad as I was'. It's a start.

'Thanks.'

There's not enough room in the cabin for a dining table so we sit on the sofa in the living room, balancing our plates on our knees. I don't want to say anything for fear of saying the wrong thing. Just having Megan in the same room as me is progress so we eat in silence, scraping our plates clean. I'm beginning to wonder if this is the best I can hope for when Megan speaks.

'Why didn't you go to the police and tell them Sean was hitting you?'

This is the last conversation I want to have, mainly because of the utter shame that fills me every time I try to answer that question myself, but I owe it to Megan.

'After we left, I wanted him out of our lives. If I'd gone to the police, it would have meant court. They probably would have interviewed you too. I couldn't face it and I couldn't put you through that.' It's as rehearsed as it sounds and Megan knows it, which is why when I stop talking she says nothing. She's waiting for the truth. 'And I wasn't brave enough.' There. I said it. That's what it comes down to. I didn't have the guts. I ran away. Your mother is a coward. Penny isn't to blame for my inaction. I am.

Megan nods.

'That's OK. Seeing him again brought everything back.'

'I know and, if I could go back in time and change things I would. I'd give anything not to have met Sean Parker.'

'He's not a nice man, is he?'

'No, and I made a terrible mistake, but that doesn't mean I have to keep on making them.'

'What do you mean?'

'I'm taking you out of school until the end of term. By the time you go back in September, Sean will have gone and our lives can go back to normal.'

Megan tears up and throws her arms around me, sending her plate tumbling to the floor. The circumstances are terrible, but the feeling of her hugging me is glorious.

'Thank you, Mum. I've been so scared.'

'I'll call the school first thing Monday morning. Now, I've got two days off so how about you and I grab our bodyboards and hit Morte Sands in the morning? The surf's fantastic at the moment.'

She considers my proposition and I wonder if I've over-stepped the mark, but she smiles a smile that lifts me above Sean, above my job and all the crap that comes with it.

'Yeah, OK.'

Megan clears the plates away, declares she's exhausted in typically dramatic teenage fashion and turns in for the night, leaving me sitting alone in the front room. I rest my feet on the glass coffee table and lean back. I can't remember the last time I felt this relaxed.

Bernadette hates the cabin which she says is only fit for hillbillies, but it's been our home for eight years and we're happy here. The living-room wall is papered floor-to-ceiling in a mural of a beach somewhere in the Bahamas because we don't do white sand and palm trees in North Devon. I came in from work one day, about six years ago, to find Megan had taken her new Sharpies to it and added two people, playing in the surf, one with long straight hair, the other sporting a dark frizz, both with the biggest grins across their faces.

'That's you and me, Mummy.'

I couldn't be mad at her. In fact, I loved it. Just Megan and me. Having fun. And we did have fun. It's just that I've forgotten, in among the demands of the job which I could have done something about and her hormones which she couldn't. Over the years, other images were added – sailing boats, sharks, dolphins, submarines – but Megan's drawing of us is still there, a little faded with time, but it's still there.

15

The call comes in at 5.45 a.m., Monday morning. I'm not due on shift until 2 p.m. and my body responds accordingly by ensuring I'm in the deepest of sleeps when my phone starts buzzing.

Stumbling into my jeans and a sweatshirt, I scribble a note to Megan, thanking her for the best weekend ever, adding I don't know when I'll be back, but there's plenty of baked beans in the cupboard and cheddar cheese in the fridge.

Minutes later, I'm heading out of the site onto the road towards Bidecombe town centre. My destination isn't far. Jake's already texted me to say he's collecting the CSI van and it's stocked for all eventualities. He'll meet me there.

I take the road along the seafront and the stretch of gaudy amusement arcades which are brought to a merciful and abrupt end by Steep Hill, a great big implacable wedge of a cliff that defeated Victorian engineers and still juts stubbornly out into the sea. Dad and I used to climb the grassy hill when I was young. From the top, you could see Wales across the Bristol Channel and behind us the town, its buildings sitting awkwardly in the folds of the hills, trying to shelter from the winter gales gusting up the Channel from the Atlantic. By the time I reached my teens I'd grown to hate the town and I couldn't wait to leave. The whole place just seemed an embarrassingly tacky intrusion into nature, a lumpy rash slowly spreading inland over fields and woods, but now it's hard not to be impressed by its sheer resilience.

Beyond Steep Hill lies Bidecombe Quay, where Janie Warren was murdered, but I take the right fork and the road rises, rejoining the end of the high street where the shops peter out. Straight on, past the rec on the left, the road dips sharply. In the hollow, a right turn leads to the Tarka Estate, a cluster of grey pebble-dashed houses that have all the charm of a public toilet. No thatched cottages or honeysuckle hedges here: this is the Devon the tourists don't see, the Devon where I spend much of my time. It's home to some seasonal workers, but mostly generations of families who have never worked and dealers feeding off their benefits and boredom. It used to be my home too.

The blue lights of the emergency services vehicles guide me in and I add my car to the huddle. The fire crews are sitting on their rigs, yellow suits peeled back to their waists, helmets off, tucking into bacon sandwiches. God knows where they got those at this time of day. Firefighters have a knack of finding decent food no matter when or wherever they're called, perhaps it's in their training, but it means the fire is already out. There's no point calling us when it's still raging.

Leaning against the CSI van, Jake is knocking back a coffee. I get out of my car and a woman in a black trouser suit, standard uniform for a female detective, strides towards me, hand outstretched.

'Hi, Ally, I'm acting Detective Sergeant Shirwell.'

She's based at Barnston CID. I've never worked a scene with her, never been to one serious enough to coax a DS from out behind her desk. I'd like to think she knows me because I'm good at what I do and not because I got the force's favourite DI two years inside. I suspect it's the latter, but she seems pleasant enough.

'What do we know so far?' Jake hands me a forensic suit, mask and shoe covers which I put on while Shirwell brings me up to speed.

'Fire services were called just after 3 a.m. A neighbour – a bouncer, coming back from his shift at Climax Bar – saw the smoke. They put it out quickly, but not enough to save the female occupant, it seems. She's burned to a crisp.'

'Cheryl Black?'

'Yes, but how—?'

'I've been here before – a few times.'

Cheryl Black is one of those poor souls whom life has it in for. Her solution to her three failed marriages was alcohol and pills. She kept herself to herself until, recently, she made the mistake of complaining to the police about her neighbour's noisy kids. Since then, her life has been hell. Hammering on her door at all hours, throwing bricks through her front window and, when I last saw her three weeks ago, posting dog shit through the letterbox. It isn't anything you'd be sent down for, which her tormentors know, of course, but it's enough to tip anyone over the edge. And Cheryl was on the edge. That's how I know her.

There was nothing I could do, forensically, but I cleaned it up for her, made her a cup of tea and left a message with social services saying she needed help urgently, but mostly she needed CCTV installed so we could catch the scum destroying her life. No one called back and Cheryl didn't get her CCTV.

A tall, grey-haired figure emerges from the house that shows no outward signs there's been a fire. I've known Jeff, the fire investigator, for years. He's the best there is.

He shakes my hand.

'Good to see you, Ally.'

A car pulls up and out steps Alex Blandford, suited but dishevelled. I haven't seen him since Janie Warren's postmortem four days ago. He grins at me.

'Fancy seeing you here.'

We spend a few minutes getting suited and masked up and then Alex, Shirwell and myself follow Jeff into Cheryl's house. The dawn light is too watery for us to see properly so he swings his torch from side to side, guiding us from the hallway to the back living room.

'If you touch the walls, do it with the backs of your hands. We're still trying to make the electrics safe. One body is quite enough, thanks.'

The air in the hall is acrid, permeating my mask, stinging my eyes and the back of my throat. This discomfort intensifies when we enter the living room. The combination of smoke-blackened walls and poor light means we can barely see. Jeff points his torch into the corner.

A circle of light picks out a dark brown form. It looks like a piece of macabre modern art someone has welded together. It's not. It's the charred corpse of Cheryl Black kneeling in front of a mantelpiece – not that she is recognizable in any way. Her head is scorched of her burgundy bob and her hands have melted to stumps. Shirwell gasps. I'm guessing she hasn't seen many burned bodies.

'Why is she kneeling?' I ask.

The pool of light flicks to the corner behind Cheryl. There's nothing there but a pile of ash and melted metal. The wall behind it is tar-black.

'We think she was sitting in an armchair that was quickly reduced to nothing by the fire and so her body fell forward.'

'She didn't try to escape the fire, then?'

'She was probably overcome by smoke in her sleep. It doesn't take long.'

I squint into the gloom. The fire is localized. The firefighters got to it quickly, but not quickly enough to save poor Cheryl. It's summer so she wouldn't have had the two-bar fire on. There's really only one explanation.

'Cigarette?'

Jeff nods.

'You're learning. There's no obvious accelerant like petrol which might point it towards arson. The electrics are good. The fire was switched off. It's the only explanation.'

'Accidental, then?' asks Shirwell hopefully.

'Would seem so unless Alex has something to add.'

I admire Alex Blandford. It doesn't matter how awful the sight is, he's right in there. This time, he's five centimetres from Cheryl, scanning her body with his own mini torch for anything suspicious.

'She either died from smoke inhalation or possibly her burns, depending on how quickly the fire took hold, but I won't be able to say any more than that without a PM.'

Shirwell chips in.

'The paramedics said they were here on Friday. She had a bit of a turn. Nothing serious. Apparently, she was a very heavy drinker and on a lot of medication. She'd already accidentally overdosed last year. Maybe she passed out with a cigarette in her hand.'

Alex nods.

'That's very possible.'

Shirwell turns to me.

'In that case, it looks like we're just after the usual – visuals and any samples you and Jeff think are worth taking, Ally.'

I don't respond. A memory has planted itself in my mind and Shirwell isn't going to like it.

'Ally?'

'Cheryl didn't smoke. She gave up some time ago. She used vapes. Her favourite flavours were Gummi Bear and Blue Raz Cotton Candy.'

They look at me. They want to ask how I know this; when you're going through people's personal possessions in pursuit of the perpetrator, they often end up telling you things that are unrelated to the crime they've fallen prey to, but I have the kind of mind that remembers them.

When someone finally speaks, it's Jeff.

'I'm as certain as I can be this fire was caused by a cigarette. Obviously, I don't know who that cigarette belongs to. That's your job, but if you wanted to set fire to someone deliberately, you'd also want to make sure you'd done it properly. There's no way anyone could have stayed and watched this lady burn without being overcome by the smoke. You've not been here five minutes and you're all struggling to breathe and you're wearing masks.'

'Plus, she was an alcoholic, not the most reliable of people. Maybe she lapsed. Went back to the fags. We've all done it,' says Shirwell.

Jeff steps back in. It's a double act.

'And we've been through the house. You're welcome to check again, but there's no sign of any vapes.'

'I think you're overthinking this, Ally.'

I don't.

'She had a three-month supply. She told me. She bought it in bulk from a guy on the high street because he did her a special deal.' Like I said, people tell you the strangest things while you're crouched by their postbox, dusting it for prints. 'So where is it? The fact you didn't find anything, Jeff, makes this more suspicious not less.' I turn to Shirwell. 'I'm not happy with this scene. You need to get Major Investigations down here now. DI Holt needs to see this.'

Shirwell laughs. It's a brave and potentially foolish detective that rings an SIO early in the morning.

'No way. I'm not calling Holt. Not for this. There's not enough evidence to say this is a suspicious death.'

'And there's not enough evidence to say that it isn't. That's why we need to do this properly. If you don't call Holt, I will.'

Trisha is making a fool of herself with one of the firemen, fawning over him while he's trying to clear the hoses away. He's clearly not interested in a fat lump like her, but she's too stupid to get the hint.

They've been here for hours. The police and fire investigator disappeared into the house ages ago and haven't returned. Not that he's concerned. They won't find anything. He's made sure of that.

Cheryl wasn't his first choice, not by a long way. He hoped one of the others would come in first, but sometimes you just have to work with what you've got. He only gets a narrow window of opportunity to do what needs to be done and then be on shift so he's the one that's sent to attend when the call comes in. In a rural area like North Devon, where ambulance services are stretched, it's not difficult, but it's still a fine balancing act that takes some skill.

She opened the door to him in a swirling mist of sickly sweet vape smoke that mingled with the stale stench of booze. Leaning on the door to steady herself, she was already drunk, and still wearing that vile pink flannel dressing down.

'I was just passing. Thought I'd check up on you.'

But it was 3 a.m. and she knew this wasn't a normal call. She plumped her straggly purple hair and smiled at him. She was aiming for seductive, but her thin lips pulled back over her teeth, the colour of a rotting banana, made his stomach heave and he almost walked away, but how long would he have to wait for another opportunity? Cheryl was better than nothing.

Her living room reeked of cheap booze and rotting food. He wasn't normally sensitive to smells, but this was almost overpowering. Empty litre bottles of vodka and mould-crusted takeaway trays littered the sofa and the coffee table. He worried the squalor would put him off. It didn't.

She turned to him, letting her dressing gown fall from her shoulders, exposing her deflated breasts. That she thought this was sexy was pathetic and he wanted to laugh, but he didn't. Instead, he suggested a drink. She was so out of it she didn't see him spike hers with her sleeping tablets. He was relieved that they took effect quickly. Normally, he likes to take his time, but he didn't want this to last any longer than it had to.

Afterwards, the urge to get away from her was overwhelming, but he had to do this properly. He positioned her in the armchair, lit a cigarette and dropped it into her lap, firing it up with a slosh of vodka. The flames took hold of her gown almost immediately – she was practically pickled in alcohol – and her hair recoiled from the heat into tiny ringlets before melting into nothing.

The armchair went up in seconds giving off a black toxic smoke that clung to his throat, making him hack, but he needed to make sure nothing was left so he slipped on the oxygen mask from his kit and stood watching from the doorway into the kitchen, making sure the fire destroyed any evidence he'd ever been there.

There's a raised voice coming from the house. The CSI appears at the front door. She's on the phone. He tries not to stare, but he can't help it: that hair, those eyes, those lips. So like Danielle. She glances in his direction and he looks away, horrified she's noticed him looking at her, but when he looks back, he can tell the person on the other end of the phone has her full attention.

'I'm telling you, Bob, there's something not right. You need to see this.'

There's a short pause before she responds.

'Alex says at the moment it looks like she died of either smoke inhalation or of her burns, but he won't know for sure until he's done the PM. Jeff is as certain as he can be it's a cigarette, but she was a non-smoker. It wasn't her cigarette.'

Another pause.

'Yes, I know she was an alcoholic and, yes, I accept I may be wrong. All I'm saying is that you need to come down here and take a closer look – just to be sure.'

Her face hardens. The longer the other person speaks, the angrier she grows.

'So, that's a no then. Just to be clear. Your crime scene manager is telling you this is a suspicious death, maybe even murder, and you're refusing to come out.'

Another brief pause.

'I'm not overreacting. I'm doing my job and that sounds like a refusal to me and don't give me that resources-are-stretched shit.' She's about to say more, but the other person has rung off. She glares at the phone. 'For fuck's sake.'

She paces the front garden for a few minutes, too angry to do anything. The female detective emerges from the house.

'DI Holt has just told me this one stays at Barnston nick. I'm wrapping this up. It's accidental.'

She doesn't wait for an answer, but gets into her car and drives off, leaving the CSI furious. The boy CSI ambles over to her.

'You all right?'

'No.'

She's really angry.

'So, what now?'

But she's still staring at the empty road.

'We treat this for what it is – a suspicious death.'

'But—'

'Cordon off the house. I want every nook and cranny of the place videoed and then photographed. I want all doors and windows unaffected by smoke damage to be dusted for fingerprints and taped for fibres. And bring plenty of exhibit bags, we're going to be bagging everything. It's going to be a long day.'

He nods and goes back to the van. The CSI looks across at him. It's the first time she's noticed him.

'Hello again. It's not your lucky week, is it?'

He frowns. He doesn't know what she's talking about.

'First Janie Warren and now this poor lady.'

'Oh yes. You're right. I've been very unlucky, haven't I? Lots of people off sick at the moment. It's pretty much Trisha and I covering the whole county.'

'Hopefully, you'll get some time off soon. I'm really sorry about this, but we won't be moving the body for some time yet. It'll be at least a couple of hours.'

'The firefighters said it was accidental. Is there a problem?'

She checks back at the house.

'Honestly, I'm not sure. There's something not quite right.'

'I'm guessing the fire has probably destroyed a lot of evidence.'

She smiles politely at him. 'We'll see. Anyway, I won't keep you any longer.'

He goes to speak again, but she's already walking over to the other CSI like he doesn't matter. She was all over him when she was looking for her daughter the other day and now she doesn't want to know. Just like the rest of them, they're not interested unless there's something in it for them. Just like Danielle.

He searches around for Trisha and finds her performing her giggly girl routine for another fireman. The idiot falls for it and takes a pen from his top pocket and hands it to Trisha who scribbles something – her number, he guesses – on the back of his hand.

Simon calls over to her and she rolls her eyes like a child called in early from play. He climbs back into the ambulance cab and a few seconds later Trisha joins him with a stupid grin on her face.

'Oh my God, I think I've died and gone to heaven. That fireman just asked me for my number.'

'He's probably married.'

'No, I checked. He's definitely single. There's something really sexy about firemen. He's got big feet, too. And you know what they say: big feet, big dick.' Her laugh is deep and throaty and filthy. 'Right. I'm ready when you are.'

'Hang on a minute, I think I left my phone in the house.'

He gets out of the ambulance and finds the object of Trisha's lust around the back of the fire engine, out of her sight.

'Look, don't say I said anything, but the lady you were talking to, the paramedic, has herpes. It's not the end of the world, of course. Don't let it put you off. She's a lovely girl and she always insists guys wear condoms and she uses a dental dam, but I thought you should know.'

'Dental dam?'

'Those plastic things dentists put over your mouth to protect themselves. Anyway, I just thought you ought to know.'

'Er, right, thanks.'

He returns to the ambulance.

'Got your phone?' says Trisha, still smiling.

He taps his pocket and smiles.

'Good.' She glances across at the fire engine. 'He said he'd phone me tonight.'

'Then I'm sure he will.'

He's about to switch the ignition on when his phone buzzes. It can't be Jackie. He's told her never to call or message him at work or she won't be getting any more Gold Bears.

He takes his phone out and stares down at the screen. He really was not expecting this.

16

There's a narrow path that leads from behind Seven Hills Lodges up a steep hill. From a distance it appears to end in brambles, a natural perimeter to the site, but if you look closely it continues on up to the brow of the hill, where the pine trees wither and fade to nothing under the corrosive sea air and where only gorse and heather are able to thrive. There it joins the coastal path.

To my right, the path goes down into Bidecombe, but the left turn takes me out along the cliff top towards Morte Sands.

Halfway along is Breakneck Point, a small rectangle of land that pushes out into the sea. It's named after Mary Sewell, a young farm girl who, pregnant and jilted by her lover, leaped to her death. She was found at the bottom of the cliffs, her neck broken. Breakneck Point, Steep Hill: our ancestors cut to the chase when it came to place names.

The cliff path splits into two. The lower path is little more than a gap in the gorse, carved out by grazing sheep. Unless you're a local, you would assume it's a dead end, but it winds down towards the cliff edge before looping back up to join the main path.

Whatever time of the year, there's a constant wind that blows up the Channel, flowing over me and around me, like a playful sprite. Its welcome currents ruffle my hair and rustle my clothes, cleansing me of the smell of the dead and the despairing. By the time I reach the bottom of the path, the debris of the day has all but gone and I am restored. That's why I come here. This place always draws me in after a difficult shift. It removes me from humanity and the ugliness that can accompany it and subsumes me in all that is natural, reminding me there is still beauty in the world.

It's quiet at this time of day. Well, as quiet as it ever can be. Most of the seagulls have taken to their nests, but I still have the crash of the waves against the rocks below for company. Megan used to be my regular companion until her hormones intervened. Apparently exhausted by our bodyboarding antics over the weekend, she's spent the day playing games on her phone and sleeping. Her capacity to sleep never ceases to amaze me and yet she's always tired.

At the lowest point on the path is the only sign that the place has been touched by humans – a bench. It's dedicated to a Rex Gordon who enjoyed the wide expanse of the Bristol Channel enough to have a seat installed in his memory so others could appreciate it, too, but it's been long since requisitioned by Megan and I and renamed 'our bench'.

We've been coming here since she was tiny. Here, we would sit and make stories up about the people who lived on the other side of the sea. If we had the energy, we would take the path on to Morte Sands and reward ourselves with an ice cream.

But I haven't come here in search of nostalgia. The more I think about the fire at Cheryl's, the more I'm convinced there's been foul play. Maybe it was one of her neighbours. I wouldn't put it past them although pouring petrol through her letterbox is more their style. Besides, there was no evidence of a break-in. Jake and I both checked. Cheryl welcomed her killer into her home. Poor Cheryl. She didn't have much of a life and what she did have has been cruelly taken from her by someone she trusted. The worst betrayal of all. But who was it? Cheryl always gave me the impression that she had no friends or family. Was that true or just self-pity? If it was true, who did she open the door to? Surely, that deserves investigating, at the very least.

I'm still angry Holt refused to come out. First Janie and now Cheryl. Two separate murders in four days. Is that possible? This is North Devon, for God's sake. Murders in this part of the world are a once-a-decade event, if that. Maybe I'm reading too much into this, like Lowe said. And maybe I'm not.

I'm about to leave when I spot a figure heading down the path from the direction of Morte Sands. It's Liam, the beachside barista from the Coffee Shack, lost in his own thoughts. My presence startles him before he realizes it's me.

'Sorry, Ally. I didn't expect to find anyone here.'

It seems I'm not the only one who comes here seeking peace: what troubles bring Liam here?

'Me neither,' I smile.

He nods at the space next to me.

'Can I?'

'Of course.'

He sits next to me on the bench.

'You and Megan looked like you were really enjoying the surf this weekend.'

'Yeah, we had fun. Makes a nice change. Things haven't been great between us.'

'Is that why you're here? You guys had a row?'

'No, not this time. I had a tough job. There was a fire on the Tarka Estate. A woman died.'

'That's rough. Fires are the worst.'

Liam's palm-tree shirts and shoulder-skimming blond hair mean I often forget he was once a police officer who's seen his fair share of misery.

'It wasn't the fire so much. It was the DI in Major Investigations. I told him I didn't think it was accidental, but he refused to come out.'

'Who is it?'

'Bob Holt.'

Liam nods.

'I remember him, although he wasn't a DI when I was in the job.'

I look at Liam. Was he a mate of his? Under my careful scrutiny, he gives nothing away, but I don't care.

'I know he's busy and short-handed, and his desk is stacked with cases, but he cuts corners. God knows how he ever became a DI.'

'Like a lot of cops, he's got there because he's never screwed up enough, but that doesn't make him good at his job.' Not mates, then.

'That's not good enough. Cheryl, the woman who died, was an alcoholic who could barely dress herself. No one will miss her, but that doesn't mean we shouldn't try our best for her, you know? It shouldn't mean she gets a second-rate service. If she'd been the Commissioner's daughter, we'd be all over it.'

My words become a mutual thought that sits in silence between us until Liam turns to me with a seriousness I haven't seen before.

'Stick to your guns, Ally. Otherwise you become like them, not giving a shit about anything other than ticking boxes. You don't want to become that person. You wouldn't be able to live with yourself.'

We're not talking about Cheryl any more. This comes from a different place. I've never asked Liam about why he left the police service, sensing it wasn't a time in his life he wanted to dwell on. Until now.

'Is that what happened to you?'

Leaning forward, he clasps his hands in front of him, and stares out across the sea. How much shame has it witnessed because one person couldn't look another in the eye?

'Yeah. A stalking case. The DI thought she was being hysterical. The bloke was just a bit besotted. It did seem harmless stuff: flowers left by her front door, poems on her car windscreen, that kind of thing. The DI told her plenty of women would be flattered by the attention, but there was something about him I didn't trust. I told the gaffer, but he told me to drop it so I did. We had too much on as it was, and we couldn't arrest him for being in love. A few weeks later, she phoned me late one night because she thought she saw him in her garden. I told her it was probably her imagination and that she was overreacting.' He closes his eyes at the memory. 'Her mum found her the next day, strangled.'

'Christ. What happened to the guy?'

'Killed himself. I left the job shortly after that. I'd lost sight of why I'd joined and I couldn't forgive myself for doing nothing. Still can't.' Finally, he looks at me. 'So, do me a favour, don't let cops like Holt off the hook.'

Peter Benson is thirty-six. He still lives at home with his mum, and he's an idiot. He spends his days riding around the town and along the trails that loop around it on his yellow mountain bike staring at women long enough for them to complain to the police about harassment. You can't be arrested for looking, but you can be arrested for murder and Peter Benson is perfect. Almost too perfect.

He's known Peter for years and is a regular visitor to his home ever since his mum had a diabetic seizure.

Peter is at one of his usual haunts, sitting on a bench, midway up Steep Hill in Bidecombe which offers fine views of the Bristol Channel, but more importantly fine views of the female sunbathers below. He's not called Pervy Pete for nothing. His bike is propped up against the bench next to him. His hair is clipped at the sides, exaggerating a nest of dark brown curls on top. It looks ridiculously childish for a man of his age.

'Hello, Peter.'

More used to people avoiding him than talking to him, Peter looks instantly guilty. He doesn't ask why, but there's a woman in a low-cut top sitting on a bench directly below them.

He sits down next to him.

'How's your mum?'

The caution in his large brown eyes with their long, feminine lashes speaks of someone whose company is never sought.

'OK.'

Small talk only confuses Peter so he gets straight to the point. 'Peter, do you remember I told you a few weeks back about a very pretty lady that likes you a lot?' Peter's forehead moulds into several different positions like he's trying to physically squeeze the answer from his brain. It's quite funny, but he doesn't laugh. Peter's been teased all his life. 'You remember? She saw you riding your bike on the trail and thought you looked very handsome.'

Whether he remembers or not is irrelevant – the idea that a woman might be attracted to him unleashes a broad grin across the man-child's face.

'Yes. Yes. I remember. I like her too.'

'That's good because I have some news for you. She wants to meet you. Tomorrow.'

A rat-brown curl falls over Peter's left eye, irritating him more than it does Peter, who doesn't seem to notice.

'Me? Tomorrow?'

'Yes. Would you like to meet her?'

'Yes. Yes.'

'Good, I'll explain where in a moment, but first, there's something you need to understand. It's very, very important.'

'Yes. Yes.'

Peter's nods are vigorous enough to make him think he either really doesn't care or doesn't understand. Either way, it doesn't matter, but he has to take it slowly.

'You know I'm a paramedic. Well, the lady is a patient of mine. Like your mum.'

'My mum?'

Peter thinks he's comparing the woman to his mother.

'She's not like your mum. She's much younger, but she's a patient that I look after.'

'You look after my mum,' he replies.

'Yes, that's right. I'm not allowed to tell people who I visit about other people I visit because it's private.'

'Like a secret.'

He's catching on.

'Yes, like a secret.'

But the thought bothers him.

'It's bad to keep secrets. My mum says so.'

'Some secrets, yes, but not all because it's wrong to talk about people's private business.'

He shakes his head.

'Keeping secrets is wrong.'

This is all he needs right now, but he's not giving up. Not on this one. When she messaged him, his heart almost exploded. He hadn't heard from her in a long while and was sure she'd gone cold on him and then, bam, she contacts him out of the blue suggesting they meet tomorrow. He'd like more time, but he can't risk it. She might disappear for good and he can't allow that. He just needs to persuade this idiot to do as he's told.

'Listen to me, Peter. When this lady asked me to tell you that she wanted to be your girlfriend, I said no.' This confuses him. It doesn't take much. He's meant to be his friend. Why would he say this? Friends don't stand in the way of romance. 'I told her, I could lose my job, but she insisted, and I just know that you two would be so good together so I agreed.' Peter's eager smile returns. Good old Simon made it right in the end. 'But, Peter, you mustn't tell anyone that I told you about this lady. I mean it. You have to pretend you met her all by yourself.'

'Yes, yes, yes. I won't say anything.'

He presses his thumb and forefinger together and runs them along his lips to show he's zipped them up, but it's not enough. He needs to be absolutely sure he won't tell.

'I'm serious, Peter. You can't tell anyone. Ever. Because if you do, there will be no one to collect your mum's medicine for her.' He stops nodding. 'And then what would happen to her?'

His eyes flash with panic.

'She'll die.'

'Yes, Peter, she'll die. And it will be your fault. None of us want that, do we?'

'No, Simon.'

'So, promise me you'll never tell anyone. Not even your mum.'

There's a silence. He's very close to his mother. There's nothing she doesn't know about him or can't wheedle out of him. He looks down at the young woman below us and licks his lips.

'I promise.'

'Excellent. If anyone ever asks, just say you met her online. Now, I've bought a family pack of Minstrels for you to give her as a present as I know they're her favourites.' Peter takes the packet and turns it in his hand, like a piece of high-end jewellery. 'Remember, they're for her, not you. Now, listen very carefully. I've arranged for you to meet her tomorrow at 3 p.m. at Three Brethren Woods.'

17

DCI Lowe is not best pleased to see me in his office at nine the following morning. There are only two reasons for someone like me to request an audience with a senior officer. The first is to discuss career progression, but we both know I blew mine six months ago at Exeter Crown Court. The other is to make a complaint against a colleague.

I thought about what Liam had said about not letting Holt off the hook, changed my mind a dozen times and then decided I had to say something, even if I was wrong. There is no explanation for the cigarette and while I accept Cheryl wasn't the most reliable of people, there is enough doubt for us to consider the worst: someone murdered Cheryl Black. If Holt isn't going to listen to me then maybe his superior officer will.

To his credit, Lowe hears me out as I relay the events of yesterday morning.

'As far as I'm concerned as the crime scene manager, there was enough for this to be considered a suspicious death and yet Holt still refused to come out.'

'Acting DS Shirwell was there.'

'Acting DS Shirwell admitted to me that she'd never attended a fire death before. In fact, this is only the second death she's ever been to. She wasn't in a position to call this.'

'I understand you still examined the scene as if it were a suspicious death.'

This isn't going to plan. He's questioning my professional conduct here, not Holt's.

'Yes, in my view, that was the correct course to take.'

'Even though acting DS Shirwell told you she was writing it up as accidental.'

Strictly speaking, police officers can't order civilian CSIs around like they can each other but going against their decision is dangerous territory and a fast track to making enemies.

'Yes. There were inconsistencies that led me to suspect possible foul play.'

'And what were these inconsistencies?'

'The fire that killed Cheryl was started by a cigarette, but it couldn't have been hers. She gave up smoking months ago. It was a big deal to her. She said she was going to use the money she saved for a holiday. She even showed me how much she'd already saved and joked she'd become addicted to vaping.' Like I said, people tell you all sorts in this job. 'She was also being terrorized by her neighbours, putting dog shit through her letterbox, that kind of thing. I believed that was enough for us to do a more thorough examination.'

'But there's no evidence of anyone else being involved in her death apart from this vague nonsense about her smoking habits.'

'It isn't nonsense. The cigarette didn't belong to Cheryl. It belonged to someone else who she appears to have known because she let them in.'

'You're putting too much store in this Cheryl woman. The

sad truth is she was a paranoid alcoholic, given to calling the paramedics out on any pretext including having a heart attack.

'Yes, but—'

'She was on medication for just about everything, including self-medicating with a bottle of vodka every day, from what the paramedics told Shirwell.'

'Yes. I know.'

'And in among all of this she decides to give up the fags for the sake of her health. Have you any idea how ridiculous that sounds?'

'Yes, I do, but that doesn't mean it isn't true. In my professional judgement . . .'

'This isn't about your professional judgement, though, is it? This is about you having it in for Holt.'

'No, it isn't.'

'You're here to make an official complaint against Holt, though, aren't you?'

'Yes, but it isn't personal. I've nothing against Holt other than I believe he was wrong about Janie Warren and he's wrong about Cheryl Black.'

Lowe shakes his head.

'Drop it, Ally. You're way off the mark on this. I get it. Really I do and I sympathize.'

'What are you talking about?'

'You were on Major Investigations for six years. Your work was exemplary and then suddenly you're kicked off and you find yourself in a backwater like Bidecombe doing crappy little shed break-ins. No one would blame you for being bitter. I wouldn't even blame you for wanting to get your own back but going after Bob Holt is not the way to do it.'

'You think this is about revenge? Jesus, Steve, I don't give a shit about Major Investigations. I'm trying to get justice for Janie and Cheryl. I'm just doing my job. All I'm asking is for others to do theirs.'

'I'm not putting this on record and if you go higher I warn you there's every chance Bob will bring a counter claim against you and – let's be honest – you have a reputation for being difficult and there's plenty round here would like to see the back of you.'

'But—'

'No buts. For your own sake, drop this.'

He returns to his computer screen, signalling our meeting is over. There's nothing more I can do for poor Cheryl, dismissed in life and now dismissed in death.

'Si, sit here. Guess what?'

Trisha beckons him over. He has no choice but to collect his coffee from the counter and join her. They're in the hospital canteen, grabbing breakfast before the start of their shift. Trisha is already tucking into a fried breakfast. The state of her arteries.

As it happens, he can probably guess the answer to her question. The smirk on her face tells him it's likely to do with men. She thinks of nothing else, apart from food, and she devours both with equal enthusiasm.

'I met someone.' He says nothing: he doesn't care. He has more important things to think about. Somehow, he needs to get rid of Trisha this afternoon – just for an hour. That should be enough. 'This guy is a real gentleman. No dick pics, no messing around, just a nice bloke. We're going to meet up.'

He's hardly listening to her, but that's the thing with Trisha, it doesn't matter if you're interested in what she has to say or not, she'll say it anyway. He gives in. Just to be polite.

'So, what's his name?'

'Snakebite1988.'

'Snakebite1988?'

'Yeah, we met on OkCupid a couple of months ago. I thought we were getting on really well, but he went quiet on me. Then I got back last night to find a message from him.'

'What about the fireman? I thought you were keen on him.'

'The bastard never called.'

'So, what's this chap's real name?'

'Dunno. I'll find out tonight.'

She's so desperate, she'll go out with someone she doesn't even know the name of. She deserves everything she gets.

'But he could be anybody.'

Trisha is mid-chomp, but that doesn't stop her talking and she flashes him a mouthful of bacon rind. It takes all his strength not to gag.

'I know. I'm not stupid. He's taking me to the Crown tonight for a meal. Right posh. There'll be plenty of people around.'

'The Crown is really nice. You'll want to wear something new, of course. You want to create the right impression.'

Trisha pauses as she sweeps a slice of bread around her plate.

'You know, you're right.' She frowns at her plate. 'But my shift doesn't finish till six. We only get a half-hour lunch. I've no time to get to the shops.'

He knows this, of course, but he uses a few seconds to think of a solution, even though he already has it.

'Why don't you take an extended lunch break?'

She folds the bread smeared with beans and ketchup in two and takes a chunk off the corner.

'I can't.' He knows this too. Trisha's already had too much time off. 'I've got no time owing. Colin would say no, if I asked.'

He leans over the table, trying not to blanch at the wafts of eggy breath coming from Trisha.

'Then don't ask. I can drop you off at the end of the high street and pick you up, say two hours later. That should be enough time. Take your radio. If dispatch calls, I can come and get you.'

She thinks it through for a few seconds.

'Would you do that for me?'

'Of course. You're a mate, aren't you?'

He hates the word mate. It's for copulating dogs, not people, but Trisha uses it all the time.

'Thanks, Simon. That's really sweet of you. I owe you.'

'No problem and go for yellow. Yellow really suits you.'

'Yellow doesn't suit anyone.'

'Well, you're the exception, then.'

'Really, I always think I look like a great big zit, one of those whiteheads.'

He gives her his best 'don't be ridiculous' expression.

'Not at all, it brings out your complexion.'

'Thanks.'

'I'll tell you what. You finish your breakfast. Take your time. I'll go and do the vehicle checks.'

'Blimey. What did I do to deserve you?'

'You'd do the same for me, I'm sure. And remember, this is just between us. If Colin finds out, he'll go bananas.'

''Course. I'm not that stupid.'

The thing is, she is.

18

My first job of the day is in Lesser Worthington, a village in a valley five miles inland from Bidecombe where the air stands still and so does the life of its two dozen or so inhabitants. No one knows what happened to Greater Worthington.

I'm still seething after my exchange with Lowe. I don't know why. Lowe's attitude should come as no surprise. Of course, he backed Holt and Shirwell. Cops stick together. I'm just a 'civvie'. I was never sworn in to the office of constable and with that comes a lingering suspicion I can't be trusted. No point going to the Superintendent either. I'd be wasting my breath. He and Lowe were probationers together back in the day – bonded by night shifts and an unbreakable understanding they'll always have each other's back. Screw them all.

Penny's text arrives just as I park outside a bungalow on the road leading into the village, bringing with it a welcome chance to think about something else.

I'm so nervous.

You'll be fine. Enjoy yourself.

I must admit I was surprised to return from my walk last night to find an excitable Penny on my doorstep. Our conversation the other night made an impression because she had finally texted Ringo and agreed to go on a date with him. Clearly not a man to let the grass grow under his feet or let Penny change her mind, he suggested they meet today at a pub on the edge of Three Brethren Woods, just outside Barnston. I asked her what changed her mind and she said that she couldn't live her life in fear and, besides, they were having a late lunch in a busy pub so what was the worst that could happen? I hugged her.

My phone buzzes with another text.

I wish I'd dyed my hair. Grey is so aging.

I picture Penny sighing at her hair in the mirror.

Grey is the new blonde.

Do you think the feathers will put him off?

If they do, he's clearly not the one for you. Be yourself.

How about tie-dye? Too casual for a first date? What about my Sgt Pepper T-shirt?

Wear what feels comfortable.

What if he's really ugly?

I tap the laughing emoji.

131

😄

He won't be.

What if he's a mad axeman?

This time Penny gets an eye-rolling emoji.

😵

He's isn't. Just enjoy it. I've got to go. Speak to you tonight.
You can tell me all about it. Have fun!

I envy her the thrill of the first date. At least she and Ringo
already have a lot in common, even if that is the entire back
catalogue of the Beatles. My Tinder dates are based on little
more than a wish and a prayer, and I'm an atheist.

I collect my case from the back of my van. By the
time I shut the door, I'm fully focused on the job ahead.
Distraction burglaries are insidious, and we have more than
our fair share. North Devon is retirementville, full of the
elderly who've escaped the city to enjoy a pace more in
step with their own, but, lulled by the open spaces and
the seemingly open faces, they drop their guard, making
them easy pickings for those that make a profession out of
preying on them.

A wary ninety-year-old called Mrs Ellis opens the door to
me, but her suspicions over who I am come too late. When
I show her my ID, she expresses delight that there is such a thing
as a female CSI and invites me in.

This is not good, not good at all. Trisha is having second thoughts. He checks his watch. Peter will be on his way by now and he needs to get going. They're standing in front of a shop window and he's almost blinded by the sparkly, sequined tops and satin skirts stretched over the hairless, dead-eyed dummies. It's the kind of clothing that should only be seen on the ballroom floor, worn by a ten-year-old, not a fifteen stone, thirty-something paramedic. Obviously, he doesn't say that to Trisha. He needs to be rid of her as quickly as possible, only she's discovered she's got a conscience after all.

'I'm not sure about this. We've been pretty busy. What if a call comes in when I'm in the changing rooms?'

'It won't and if it does, I'll come and get you.'

'You're always covering for me, Si. No, I've got plenty of clothes at home. I'll wear what I wore on my date with Bill.'

'OK, it's entirely your call, but you'd look good in that one.' He points at a gold Lycra top with black sequins in the shape of a heart.

She stares longingly at it. He doesn't know why she's pretending to care about her job.

'It is nice, but I'll leave it. Thanks, anyway.'

'Sure, no problem. Let's go then. I'm hungry.' They amble back towards the ambulance. It's obvious she wants to stay. He just needs to say the right thing. They reach the ambulance, and he lets out a chuckle.

'What is it?' she asks.

'Nothing.'

'You can't laugh and then not tell me.'

'I was just thinking it would be a bit weird if you end up marrying this guy, Snakebite, and you'll always look back on your first date and think, Oh yeah, I wore that top I wore on my date with that idiot Bill from HR.'

She's appalled by the idea.

'Yeah, I guess when you put it like that, it doesn't sound like I'm making much of an effort, does it? And I do really like him, you know.'

He unlocks the driver's door. He wants her to think they're leaving immediately, put her under pressure to make a decision.

'I know. I just want you to make a really good impression on this guy, that's all. If you're OK wearing a top you wore on another date, then that's fine. Let's hope you don't call him Bill by accident.'

As he opens the door, Trisha glances back at the sequined top in the shop window.

'Actually, are you absolutely sure you don't mind?'

'Yes, I'm sure. I'm just going to park up in our usual spot, eat my sandwiches and then come back for you. To be honest with you, I could do with a bit of peace and quiet,' he jokes.

She grins.

'I do your head in sometimes, don't I?'

'No, no, not at all.' He says this in a way that suggests the opposite.

She laughs.

'Soz, I can't help it. I'm one of seven kids. I'm not good with silence or being on my own. Are you sure you're OK with this?'

'Yes.'

'And you promise you won't tell Colin. He already thinks I'm a slacker.'

'I promise. I'll pick you up in two hours.'

'Thanks, Simon. I've got a good feeling about this one.'

'Me too.'

19

Mrs Ellis has been relieved of her deceased husband's retirement watch and that week's pension. She doesn't care about the money, but she's distraught about the watch; hours after the crime was committed the soft folds beneath her rheumy eyes are still damp with tears.

'He loved that watch. He never took it off. Do you think it'll turn up?'

Distraction burglaries always depress me. The effect the crime has on elderly people like Mrs Ellis is heartbreaking and I want more than anything to nail the bastards that devastate their gentle worlds, but I only seem to make it worse. The truth is an assailant usually slips in unnoticed via an unlocked back door and goes through the house while their mate keeps the owner talking on the doorstep and they're almost always wearing gloves.

'Maybe.' The reality is it's long gone, but I don't tell her that.

'My son is on his way down from London, I could ask him to check the junk shops in town.'

'It might be worth a try.' It isn't, but I can't bring myself to tell her that, either – that most of this stuff is sold online now. 'Can you remember if the man touched anything while he was here? His accomplice might have worn gloves, but I'm guessing the guy who knocked on your front door didn't. It's summer and he wouldn't have risked you noticing and getting suspicious.'

A chink of hope brightens her.

'No, that's correct. He wasn't wearing gloves. I'd have remembered.' Her face falls. 'But now I come to think of it, I don't think he touched anything either. He had a clipboard and asked me lots of questions about my water usage.'

She looks at me like it's her fault this vile lowlife didn't touch anything.

'OK. Not to worry. Maybe his accomplice left his gloves at home. Where did you keep your husband's watch?'

Mrs Ellis leads me upstairs to a back bedroom. The door of a huge, dark wooden wardrobe is wide open; old clothes stored in plastic bags spill out onto the floor. The mattress has also been lifted and shifted to one side. I'm not surprised. I remain incredulous at the number of people who still stash cash under their beds.

'The officer said to leave everything as it is,' she says as an apology for the mess. 'Harry's watch was in that.'

She points at a red velvet box gaping open on the bed. Next to it are various boxes decorated in rose-patterned material spewing cheap pearls and paste brooches. It's not a great start. Even in the unlikely event he wasn't wearing gloves, I already know there isn't a fingerprint to be had among this. I can't dust material and the jewellery doesn't have a large enough surface area to give me a decent fingerprint. It's hardly worth digging out the aluminium powder, but I have to try. I'm about to open my case, when Mrs Ellis leans heavily against the bedpost. The enormity of what's happened has hit her.

'Fifty years with Williams Printers, Harry was. Man and boy. He loved it there. He wore the watch every day till he died. It was special to him and when he died it became special to me. Sometimes, at night, I slip it onto my wrist and pretend it's him holding my hand. Silly, I know.'

My heart flips and I place my arm around her hoping I'm not being presumptuous, but she sinks gratefully into me. Her tissue-thin skin is too big for her and puckers loosely around her neck. She reminds me of a newborn chick that has tumbled too soon from its nest: frail and helpless, just waiting to be picked off by a couple of hawks. Even if she had realized what was happening, she couldn't have stopped them. What it must be to be on your own in this world. At least I have Megan even if she is invariably glued to the latest Netflix series – which is how I had left her that morning, despite my gentle reminders that she was meant to be doing schoolwork. Still, I'd rather have her sulks and door-slamming than be alone like Mrs Ellis.

I hold the old lady tight in my arms until I feel her strength return.

'It's not silly at all. Look, why don't we go back downstairs, and I'll make you a nice cup of tea. I'll come back up and see what I can find here and then I'll tidy up for you.'

Mrs Ellis nods and shuffles towards the door where she pauses to look back over her shoulder at the mess in her bedroom.

'I feel such an idiot, falling for his lies. He seemed like such a nice young man and I don't get to talk to many people these days. I was so pleased when he said he'd come in for a few minutes.'

'Don't be too hard on yourself. These people are very convincing. It's easy to be taken in by them.'

But suddenly she's angry with herself.

'Yes, but I, of all people, should have known better.'

'What do you mean?'

She takes my hands in hers.

'Dear, I was a police officer. One of the first WPCs in this area.'

'Really? That's amazing.'

'My father was dead against me joining, but I was adamant. Of course, in those days we weren't allowed to do much more than make the tea and do the filing.'

'I'm sure you still caught your fair share of criminals.'

A twinkle returns to her eye.

'I had my moments. I know it's all science these days, but nothing beats the copper's hunch and I had a pretty good one and' – she waggles her finger at me – 'once I had them in my sights, I never let go of them. I always saw it through to the end even when my colleagues said I was barking up the wrong tree.'

'It sounds like you enjoyed your time in the job.'

'I did. Very much. It was a long time ago, but still I should have realized what was happening. I should have seen those scoundrels for who they were, then I might still have Harry's watch.'

She turns away and I watch her take the stairs, one step at a time, holding the rail and I find myself thinking about how easy it is to be deceived. We're all susceptible to a smiling face, a confident manner and the offer of company. You don't have to be ninety. I was just twenty-one when Sean strolled into my life promising all those things and I didn't see through him. Not until it was too late.

People rarely are who they say they are.

The smell of fish paste is released into the cabin as he peels back the lid of his lunch box. The sandwich feels soft and mushy in his mouth, but he doubts he'll have time to eat the orange. She'll be here any minute.

The ambulance is parked in its usual lunchtime spot when they're not busy, a lay-by on the edge of a new housing estate, just down from the Crown pub which backs onto Three Brethren Woods, a dense, steep wooded area edged by the trail beyond which lies the flat salty marshes of the estuary. It's perfect in every way.

While he's waiting, he retrieves his phone and rereads her messages. It's all happened so fast he can barely take it in. And her, of all people. Never, in a million years, did he think *she* would ask to meet *him*, but it just goes to show you never can tell. Sometimes the ones you think are pushovers tell you to get lost and those you think you only have an outside chance with are surprisingly easy. That's the thing with women. What they show on the outside is rarely what's happening on the inside. He's learned that from Trisha. Her brashness is just a cover. The truth is she's terrified of being alone which is why she bites the hand off the first man that gives her a second glance. He shakes his head at the topsy-turviness of it all. Still, he really didn't expect to land this one. There's definitely something more thrilling about the ones that appear beyond reach. The ones who tell themselves they'd never fall for it.

He puts his phone away and finishes his sandwich, flicking the crumbs from his shirt. His watch reads 3.10 p.m. She's late, but he knows she'll be here.

He wonders if it'll be as good as Janie, the girl on the quay? That had worked like a dream. He wasn't sure at first. He never is. Each time there's always a moment when he thinks it won't work, that it's over, but when he hovered his hand just over her forehead, it was as if someone had injected adrenaline straight into his heart. He knew then everything was going to be fine. He could relax.

In the back of the ambulance, on the way to the mortuary, he bent down to kiss her forehead and was startled by its iciness that exploded across his lips converting into a white heat that rushed his insides, nourishing him, reinvigorating him, reigniting him all at once. The dead have a coldness unlike any other, unyielding to the touch and yet possessed of magical properties.

She released waves of electric currents as he stroked her pebble-smooth cheek. It meant one thing only.

Yes, Janie was good, he couldn't deny that, but this one would be better. He's sure of it.

And there she is! Strolling towards him, a smudge of a smile on her face and a lightness underfoot that means only one thing. She's excited to see him. He's excited too.

She passes the ambulance, not bothering to glance in. That's OK. No one ever does, but his own heart does a little jig at the sight of her.

Dusting stray crumbs from his uniform, he replaces the lid on his sandwich box and drops it on the seat next to him. He checks himself in the mirror and smooths his hair into place. He wants to look his best for her.

From underneath his seat, he pulls out a metal bar. There's a plastic bag tied to one end, the end with Peter Benson's fingerprints on it. It's from the shed in his garden. Unbuttoning his jacket, he slides it inside his uniform. It feels cold and hard against his chest.

One last check in the mirror and he's ready for action. People say he looks a bit like Daniel Craig, the chap who plays James Bond. Same eyes. Same colour hair. No wonder Jackie can't believe her luck. Pity Danielle didn't feel the same way.

There's no one around when he gets out of the ambulance – the drizzle has seen to that – but he doesn't linger, just in case, and swerves into a narrow path that runs down the back of the housing estate and towards Three Brethren Woods, towards her.

20

Holt is already here, wrapped in despair. Forget the TV cliché of the hard-nosed detective, the ones I know are seriously affected by sights like these.

I know what he's thinking because I'm thinking it too. Who could do this to another human being? But we've both been around long enough to know the answer to this question is: lots of people. I lived with one of them for years.

Through the thick glass partitioning me from the ward, at the far end of the room, I can only just make out a profile of a face distorted by bulging, purple-black bruises. Her head is bound in a thick turban of bandages spotted with blood. Wires and tubes criss-cross her body, attached to machines monitoring her and their ability to push life into her. My camera case is in my hand, but I doubt I'll be taking photographs anytime soon.

The call came in just as I was leaving Mrs Ellis's. It was the usual half message. 'You're needed at Barnston Hospital to photograph a female. Head injuries.' But the words don't do justice to the woman encased in the incubator, like a plastic tomb, in the far corner of ICU.

I don't mention Janie Warren or Cheryl Black. The horror of this attack has shoved that to one side. For now.

'So, what have we got?' I sound as depressed as Holt looks. He sighs himself back into investigator mode.

'Not sure yet. Just got here myself. Serious assault at the moment. A member of the public found her in Three Brethren Woods, just off the trail.'

'Three Brethren Woods?'

Penny is meeting Ringo in a pub nearby.

'Yeah, why?'

'Nothing.'

Penny said she was meeting Ringo for a late lunch. Did they decide to go for a walk after? After all that's happened to her, she wouldn't go into a wood with someone she barely knew.

'Do we know who she is?'

Holt ignores the phone buzzing in his pocket.

'We're working on it, but there was no ID on her. No driver's licence, nothing.'

Penny keeps her driver's licence in her purse.

'Are you OK?'

'Yeah, yeah, I'm fine.'

It's not Penny. It can't be. But I have to be sure. I take out my phone.

'Can you excuse me a moment? My friend was meeting someone near Three Brethren Woods. I just want to make certain she's OK.'

'Of course.'

Penny's number is on speed dial and already ringing. She doesn't pick up, so I leave a voicemail.

'Pen, it's Ally. Call me back as soon as you get this. There's been an attack in Three Brethren Woods, I need to know you're safe.'

'Is your friend OK?' asks Holt.

'She's not picking up, but I'm sure she's fine. I can't think why she'd go for a walk in the woods with someone she'd only just met.'

But that doesn't mean she didn't.

The doctor catches sight of us and is already shaking her head by the time she joins us.

Holt flashes his card.

'DI Holt and this is CSI Dymond.'

'You're wasting your time, Detective Inspector. There's no way you'll be able to photograph her injuries or interview her today. She's in a very bad way. Her skull is fractured in several places. She's heavily sedated. We're prepping her for surgery.'

Holts nods, but he isn't finished.

'Any thoughts on the weapon?'

The doctor studies her patient through the glass as if she can see through the bandages.

'Some kind of blunt-ended instrument. A bat or a metal bar, maybe. It's difficult to say. I've never seen anything like this. The ferocity needed to do that is off the scale.'

'Is she going to make it?'

The doctor gives my question some thought, her eyes still trained on her patient.

'Difficult to say. The next forty-eight hours will be crucial.' She turns to me. 'We'll let you know when she comes round and you can take your photographs then.'

There's a finality in her voice that suggests there's nothing more to say, but Holt has plenty.

'Any other injuries? Any signs of sexual assault?'

'No. Nothing. The injuries are all concentrated around the head. It's a miracle she's alive and we're doing everything we can to keep her that way. Now, if you'll excuse me.'

The doctor steps back inside ICU, leaving Holt and I standing in front of the glass trying to fathom what all this means. He's thrown by the news she hasn't been sexually assaulted.

'Maybe he was disturbed.'

'Maybe.'

'But if it isn't sex then we're looking at a different motive.'

'Perhaps he just hates women.'

'I think that's a given. I'll stay here until we get an ID on her.'

'OK. I'll get down to the scene.' Whatever bad blood there is between us has gone. We've both got a job to do.

'It's cordoned off. There's a couple of PCs guarding it at the moment and Jake is on his way.'

'Thanks. I'll radio you if we find anything of interest.'

'A signed confession by her attacker nailed to a nearby tree would be useful.'

A lame joke is Holt's attempt to repair our relationship, the way those that have won are wont to do, but I appreciate it and concede a smile.

'I'll see what I can do.'

'Ally?'

'Yes.'

'I know you think I jumped the gun on Janie Warren, but Banstead is our man and I went over acting DS Shirwell's notes on Cheryl Black. It was accidental.'

Maybe he's right. I don't know and I'm in no mood to argue.

'OK.'

145

'And look on the bright side,' adds Holt. 'At least we know Banstead couldn't have done this one too.'

I glance back through the glass at the beaten and broken woman fighting for every breath. There is no bright side.

I check my phone. Still nothing from Penny.

He can't understand it. This is wrong, all wrong, but it had all started so well.

They were called to attend to her. First on the scene. Like he knew they would be. When they got to her, he felt her neck and there it was – the faintest of pulses. He didn't tell Trisha, of course.

'There's nothing. She's gone.'

He figured if she wasn't dead yet, she didn't have more than a few minutes to live and anyway he could let her bleed out in the back of the ambulance, but Trisha had other ideas. She did something she's never done before. She insisted on checking herself.

He should have known something was up. She'd been acting weird since he picked her up outside the clothes shop, telling him to hurry up and effing and jeffing at the other drivers blocking their route.

She kneeled down on the ground, practically pushing him out of the way.

'She can't be.' Her fingers pressed and prodded her neck then stopped. 'Wait, she's still alive. Thank God, but we have to hurry.'

Still, it didn't bother him. He'd finish her in the back of the ambulance.

'OK. Let's get her stabilized as quickly as we can and get her to hospital.'

They worked on her to the point where they were happy to

146

stretcher her down to the trolley parked on the trail. He tried to drag his heels, even pretended to stumble, but Trisha kept telling him to 'get a march on'. The cheek of it. She's normally the one slowing them up.

They wheeled her to the ambulance at the entrance to the woods and slid her into the back just as the police car arrived. He showed the officer where they'd found her so he could cordon off the scene but, by the time he returned, Trisha had already jumped into the back. She hardly ever rides up back. At times like this he despised the woman more than ever. Always interfering, always making things difficult for him.

'I'll ride with her, Si.'

'But you're a much faster driver than me.'

She placed her hand on the girl's arm. 'No, Si. I've let her down once. I'm not doing it again.'

He dithered. This wasn't the plan. Trisha's patience ran out.

'Come on, we're wasting time.'

So they set off. Him driving, Trisha in the back. A couple of times she poked her face through the hatch.

'Hurry, I'm not sure how much longer she can hold on.'

Stupid cow. She's ruined everything. She denied them his special time. He could kill her. Maybe one day he will.

'What if she dies, Si?' Trisha's question snaps him back to the present.

They're in the canteen in the hospital. Colin sent them there after they got back from Three Brethren Woods to 'collect themselves' and get over the shock of what they'd just brought in. But he's not in shock. He's raging inside.

'Si, did you hear me? What if she dies?'

'If she dies, she dies.' He regrets his words the moment they

147

leave his mouth and the shock registers on Trisha's face. 'But she won't die,' he adds, hastily.

'But she's in a bad way, Si.' Trisha hangs her head. 'If she doesn't make it, I'll never forgive myself.'

'OK, you did a terrible thing.' Her eyes are glassy with tears. 'But what's done is done. Anyway, we don't know that if we'd have reached her any sooner it'd have made any difference.'

'I do. I worked it out. You were parked in our normal spot, right? I reckon that's five minutes max from the entrance to the woods. The call came in at 3.52 p.m.; I checked, you collected me at 4.05 p.m. We didn't get to her until 4.17 p.m. That's a difference of twenty minutes which . . .' She stops, unable to finish the sentence so he picks up where she left off.

'Which could be the difference between life and death.' Her lower teeth grab her upper lip. She closes her eyes and nods. 'Look, there's no point dwelling on it. It's out of our hands now.'

'It's gonna take a miracle to save her, Si.'

Well, hopefully, God is looking in the opposite direction because if she wakes up, he's finished, but he doesn't plan to trust this to God or anyone else. He needs to think, to come up with a way out, and he can't do that with Trisha whining in his ear.

On the table is a pink plastic shopping bag, the words BABE NATION in black written on the side. It contains Trisha's outfit for her date, some tarty top that's two sizes too small, no doubt.

'At least you have your evening with Mr Snakebite to look forward to.'

She pulls the bag out of sight, exhibit A in her guilt.

'I'm going to cancel. I don't feel in the mood any more and I want to make sure she's in the clear before I clock off. I thought I'd go up to ICU later.'

A thought pushes into his mind. Maybe there is a way to save the situation.

'That's a shame. You were so looking forward to it.'

'Honestly, I'm not feeling it, Si.'

'But what if he's the one? You said yourself, you had a good feeling about him.'

The thought she may miss out on the man of her dreams after a lifelong search stirs her. She reeks of desperation. It's pathetic.

'I did feel we connected.'

'There you go then. It was meant to be.'

Her mind wanders elsewhere: Three Brethren Woods, at a guess.

'It just doesn't seem right. Not after today.'

He reaches across the table and places his hands on her enormous man-hands.

'Trish, we have to go on living. TV dinners, *EastEnders*, dates with men called Snakebite, life goes on and we have to live it, otherwise we can't do the job that we do.'

She nods. Simon's the sensible one. If he says it, then it must be true.

'Maybe you're right.'

'Your Uncle Si is always right.' She calls him her Uncle Si all the time. He hates it, especially as he's only five years older than her, but he wants her to feel he's on her side. 'I'll stay on and finish the paperwork, you get off. Tell you what, I'll drop by ICU later and call you with any news. How does that sound?'

She doesn't mull his offer for long. He knew she wasn't that bothered about her. She was just scared of being found out.

'Thanks. You're a mate.'

'And promise me you won't let Mr Snakebite down.'

'I promise, Uncle Si.'

She grabs the plastic bag, holds it close to her chest like some precious keepsake, and disappears through the canteen's double doors, leaving him to think things through.

If he leaves it late enough to go to ICU, there'll be hardly anyone around. He can already picture the gratitude of the overworked nurse, probably a bank nurse doing nights for the extra cash, when he offers to sit with her while she takes a well-earned break. Then they can say their goodbyes properly. He's already looking forward to it. It will be much more dignified than the back of an ambulance. He's surprised it's never occurred to him before. Maybe this is the start of something new.

21

The drizzle has graduated to a steady downpour. Sliding my camera case into the back of the van, I shut the door and climb into the driver's seat, relieved to be out of the rain. I check my phone again. Still nothing from Penny. Penny who was meeting an unknown man at a pub near Three Brethren Woods. I glance back up at the hospital. It can't be Penny. She promised me she wouldn't take any chances and she'd stay in view of other people. She would never go into the woods with a guy she'd only just met.

I need to get down to the scene and secure it straightaway. Maybe we'll be able to start examining it today, but the dark clouds will pull nightfall forward by a few hours which means that we'll get the tent erected and examine the area immediately around where she was found, but wider searches will have to wait until tomorrow. But, apart from the diminishing light, the weather has sided with us. The rain will have softened the hard ground, making it perfect for foot impressions. I just hope no one trashes the scene before I can get there.

I radio my intention to drive to Three Brethren Woods. Almost immediately, Jake responds with an 'Echo Tango Twelve also on route'. My relief at hearing his voice doesn't surprise me. After the usual initial flurry of activity, crime scenes can be solitary, even eerie environments, especially somewhere like Three Brethren Woods, named after three brothers who drowned cockle picking in the estuary. I've always thought it a strange name. Like a warning. A place where no good happens.

Buckling myself in, I switch the van engine on, push it into reverse and ease out of the parking space just as my peripheral vision registers a marked police car turning towards me. I ignore it, but it speeds towards me like it's playing chicken, screeching to a halt inches from my bonnet.

I hit the brakes and glare at the driver. It's Cobb. What the bloody hell does he think he's doing? I'm in no mood for his games so I throw my seatbelt off and swing the car door open. It groans under the force.

'Get out of my way!' I shout through the gap.

Cobb ignores me and speaks into the radio clipped to his lapel. Arrogant shit. I get out and lean over the van door.

'This is the second time you've stopped me doing my job. I'm putting in a formal complaint. Now fucking move.'

But he doesn't move. Instead, he gets out of his car so I slam my door shut, ready for another showdown, startling an elderly couple sheltering under an umbrella.

'We've just ID'd the woman who was attacked.'

Normally, I'd ask who, but this is Cobb and I've had enough of him.

'Good, now get out of my way. I'm meant to be at the scene.'

I go to get back into the van, but his next line stops me.

'She's registered at the same address as you.'

'What?'

'Seven Hills Lodges. That's where you live, right?'

My mind does the maths. Two plus two equals Penny. Oh God. It's Penny.

'Yes. Penny Fields runs it.' My voice is tight and thin. I need Cobb to tell me this is a mistake as my mind won't accept anything less. He frowns hard at me and I realize this is the first time he's heard that name.

'No, that's not her name.'

Thank God. He's got this wrong. God knows, it's not the first time, and for once, I'm pleased he's an idiot. But Cobb doesn't move, his face swaying between puzzlement and concern.

'Do you have a sister?'

'No. What's going on?'

'Does the name Megan Parker mean anything to you?'

Parker is Sean's surname, but Megan doesn't use it, hasn't done since the day we left him. Whatever database the police are using it's way out of date.

'My daughter is called Megan, but her surname isn't Parker. It's Dymond.'

But what's Megan got to do with anything? Surely, she hasn't bunked off again and been picked up by the truancy patrol? I'll kill her when I get a hold of her.

'Your daughter?'

He doesn't know I'm a mum. Not many at the nick do.

Cobb removes his hat.

'Ally, I'm sorry.'

'What for?'

He glances up at the hospital and then at me. He can't speak. He doesn't have to. Oh God. No.

'No,' I say aloud. It doesn't make any sense.

'I'm sorry.'

'No.'

I need to call Megan. She'll be home, probably texting her mates right now, complaining about what a bitch her mother is. I take my phone out from my pocket. I dial Megan's number. Her phone is turned off. It's never turned off.

I look at Cobb. Tell me it isn't true, but his face is ashen, his eyes fixed on the bonnet of my van, refusing to bear witness to the terrible situation he's found himself in. No one signs up for this.

I shove past him, past the disapproving old couple and race back towards the hospital entrance, barging through the doors, almost taking out a man propped up by a Zimmer frame.

Mistake. It's a mistake. It can't be Megan, she's at home.

I slalom the people in the reception area, standing still like ninepins in my way, paralysed by the sight of a small dark woman hurtling towards them.

It can't be Megan. She wouldn't be on the trail. It's sixteen miles from Bidecombe.

Through the blur of fluorescent lights and doors banging shut, I hear calls to slow down, but I need to go faster. No time to wait for the lift. I take the back stairs two at a time to the third floor and burst through the doors into ICU.

It can't be Megan. I'd have known if it was her. I'm her mother.

Holt stands in the middle of the corridor, his face rinsed of colour. He knows. That's who Cobb spoke to on his radio. And then I know. For certain. It's Megan.

Holt steps towards me, arms outstretched, not to embrace me, but to bar my way. I try to dodge him, but he wraps himself around me and holds me fast.

'You can't go in there.'

'Let go of me.' I have to be with Megan. She needs me. I'm her mum. Not the best mum, I accept that, but still her mum. I can't wrench myself free of him, years of policing have perfected his grip. The bastard won't let me go.

'No, Ally.'

I kick his shin hard. He gasps in pain but tightens his hold.

'She needs me.'

'Not yet.'

Not yet. What does he mean, not yet?

I twist around in Holt's arms and stare through the window. I can't see Megan. There's people, so many people fussing around her bed. Calm, methodical, practised. The crash team. The sight sucks the fight from me and I can do nothing but watch as strangers try to bring my daughter back to life.

Holt feels the fight leave me and lets me go. I press my hands against the cold glass. The team pause. Megan's body arches silently – possessed of five hundred volts – and I tense as if I too have experienced the surge. Her body levels, limp and lifeless. Come on, Megan, respond. Respond. You can have the six-inch heels from New Look. Just respond.

Nothing.

Machines scrutinized. Heads shaken. Instructions reissued. Paddles repositioned. People ordered to stand back. Another shock. Megan's body jumps, higher, stronger. Forcing life into her. This is it. The time it will work. Respond, Megan. Come on, Megan. You can have your nose pierced for your sixteenth. Respond. Just come back to me.

They wait. Machines checked and rechecked. More heads shake. Shoulders sag in defeat. It's over. She's gone.

Then something happens. I can't hear anything, but someone

says something and they all stare at one of the machines. No one moves. It comes again. This time it's enough for people to exchange nods of relief. Someone mouths 'Well done, Megan' at my daughter. She's back. She's alive. My legs buckle. Holt catches me.

A nurse emerges from the room.

'Please. Can I see her?'

'Don't get too close. We're still trying to stabilize her.'

I stand in the doorway, watching the doctors and nurses administer to Megan. All I want to do is push them out of the way and hold my child, convinced that my life force will work better than their medicine and machines can. I just have to hold her long enough, that's all, and she will return to me as she was, I know it, but I can't. Instead, all I can do is stand watch over her from a distance – one thought stapled to the front of my mind. *I wasn't there for her.*

I don't know how much time passes before I'm vaguely aware of a beeping noise, but it's not coming from the hospital's machines. It's my phone. Instinctively, I get it out. There's a text from Penny responding to my voicemail.

Oh my God, that's awful, but I'm fine.

But she's talking of a different time, a time when I thought the worst thing that could happen was that my best friend had been attacked, but it wasn't the worst.

The phone trembles in my hand. I can barely keep it still long enough to tap the letters in, but Penny needs to know.

It's Megan.

22

His key card lets him into ICU. It's late enough for the lights to be dimmed, throwing the corridors into shadow. A single light illuminates the reception desk where the nurse in charge is tapping her mobile phone, like her life depended on it, engrossed in some silly game when she should be caring for her patients.

She looks up and smiles at his uniform.

'Hi.'

'Evening. I brought the young girl in today. The one found in the woods. I just thought I'd drop by and see how she is, sit with her while you go and have your break. I know the family.'

The nurse puts her phone down, but the tinny music from her game still blares out. He wants to tell her to switch it off. This is ICU, not an amusement arcade, for goodness' sake.

'Are you a relative?'

For someone who thinks it's acceptable to play games at work, her sudden decision to take her job seriously surprises him.

'No, as I said, I'm the paramedic that brought her in. I saved her life. I just wanted to pop my head round the door to make sure she's OK.' He glances down the darkened corridor, trying to gauge which room she is in.

'She's still in the operating theatre.'

'Oh?'

She nods in agreement, interpreting his response as a bad sign.

'I know. It's been five hours. Not good.'

Five hours. They're fighting to keep her alive. Hopefully, it's a battle they'll lose, not that he can share that with this excuse for a nurse.

'So what time are you expecting her?'

'No idea.' The nurse shrugs.

He hesitates, trying to decide what to do. He can't wait. That would look odd.

'I'll pop back later.'

'I'm not sure they'll let you in. She's in a pretty bad way. The mother's around here somewhere. She just went to get a coffee. If you wait, she'll be back any minute. Maybe you could speak to her.'

He'd forgotten her mother would be around. He definitely can't risk being seen by her. Not that she would suspect him. He's a paramedic.

'It's fine. I don't want to bother her unnecessarily.'

'Yeah. I'd leave it if I were you.' She checks both ways and leans across the desk. 'Between you and me, I don't think she's going to make it. Sorry, I know you guys did the best you could.'

'Thanks.' He makes for the exit, pauses and turns back to the nurse. 'By the way, I heard one of the ward sisters moaning about the night staff spending too much time on their phones. They've been checking the CCTV and anyone they catch is looking at a disciplinary.'

She squints at the camera as her phone disappears under the desk.

'Shit. Really?'

But he's already buzzed himself out.

*

The toilet cistern digs into his back, but he doesn't care, he's spent. He's been through hell, these last hours. First, Trisha changes her mind about going shopping and then she insists on riding up back with the girl. Then, just when he's managed to bring it back from the brink of disaster, she's not even on the ward.

He was so looking forward to it too. It all seemed so perfect. Just the two of them, surrounded by the dark and the quiet. But it's all been for nothing and now all he's left with is the memory of their meeting on the trail. What use is that?

Maybe, just this once, if he concentrates hard enough, it will be enough. Closing his eyes, he makes himself as comfortable as he can on the toilet seat.

People always see the uniform first and she was no different. She was wondering what a paramedic was doing there, but then as he drew closer, she recognized him and smiled. It made his heart swell. Not everyone remembers him.

He remembered her even though it had been six months since they had met in the school hall and even then they had been surrounded by flapping teachers muttering about health and safety and a grandmother who was seriously put out at being there.

When he met her, he assumed she would be too difficult a nut to crack. Teenagers usually are. Their natural contempt and in-built defensiveness towards anyone more than five years older than them can make them more trouble than they're worth, but she was different. She was happy to answer his questions in the back of the ambulance, but then she's probably been taught to trust men in uniform. By the time they reached the hospital she had told him everything he needed to know. Even then, he wasn't sure about her. You might win a teenager's confidence, but can you trust them to keep their mouths shut? They're so unpredictable alongside a predisposition to share their every waking thought with the world and his dog. Still, he gave it a go, but when she batted away attempts to meet, he began to admit defeat. Besides, he had other options. At that point, the girl Janie was a much better bet anyway. It wasn't until he saw her photo in the car park at Morte Sands and realized she was the CSI's daughter that his interest was reignited. The CSI was so like Danielle that he struggled not to stare at her. He seriously considered switching his attentions to her. It would almost be reliving history, every glorious moment of it. But these things take time, and she'd be wary. All police people are suspicious. She'd take a lot of planning. No, right now, he'd make do with her daughter, but the CSI was definitely one for the future.

He didn't immediately react, he didn't want to spook her, so he kept it casual and walked by before pausing and turning back.

'We've met before, haven't we?'

She nodded, still smiling, pleased to see a friendly face out on the trail.

'Yes, I fell off the beam at school and knocked myself out. You took me to the hospital, to make sure I didn't have a concussion.'

'That's right. I remember. You were with your gran.'

'Yes. My mum was working so the school called my nana.'

'Let me think . . . TwilightSparkle – right?'

'Er, yes.'

She squirmed at the mention of her Instagram username. Like her friends, she didn't use her real name. Maybe she was embarrassed by its childishness, maybe it was because she'd shared it with him as he tended to her. He didn't care.

'So, how's the head?'

'All better.'

160

'What are you doing here?'

'Waiting for a friend.'

'Who's the lucky boy? I'm guessing it's a boy. With all the effort you've made.'

She smoothed her long auburn hair, but it was a self-conscious act, like she was embarrassed he'd noticed.

'Yes.'

'Guess he must be special, though, if you're meeting him out here?'

He was being childish, but he wanted to hear her tell him how amazing he was. She didn't disappoint.

'Yeah, he is. Really funny and sweet.'

'And good-looking, I'll bet.'

Her cheeks flushed red.

'This is the first time we've met.'

'Like a blind date.'

'S'pose.'

But she wasn't interested in him. She was turning her phone in her lap desperate to read its screen and find out where her Prince Charming had got to. He wanted to grab her there and then and tell her: Ruggerboy666 is me.

'Look, he sounds perfect. You have fun and be careful, right. There's a lot of weirdos out there.'

She laughed and he strolled away, distracted by the curlews out in the estuary, spearing the mudflats with their knitting-needle-thin beaks, until he rounded a bend and ducked back into the woods.

Keeping low, he climbed the steep bank and tracked over to where she was sitting. Leaning against a tree, looking down, he had a direct view of her back.

She glanced at her phone and scanned the trail. Ruggerboy666, or rather Peter, was late. She wasn't going to wait much longer. He couldn't blame her. It was rude to keep her waiting, but he couldn't make his move. Not yet.

He spotted a yellow bike frame through the trees. He'd come, Peter, wearing the red puffer jacket like he'd told him to. He skidded to a halt in front of her, his back tyre swinging out. It was meant to impress her, but she was surprised and annoyed by the act, shifting in her seat, turning her head sideways, hoping her body language would be enough to repel him. But Peter isn't the type to pick up on signals.

He said something to her and she shook her head. He spoke again. He couldn't hear what Peter was saying, but he didn't have to. The words that came out of Peter's mouth were his.

Then he heard him.

'You're very beautiful. I want to stroke your hair and kiss your lips.'

'Go away.' She said this loudly enough for him to hear, her eyes sweeping the trail for her knight to rescue her. Don't worry, you won't have to endure him for much longer.

Peter dug around in his pocket and produced the bag of Minstrels he'd given him. It had already been opened. He offered the bag to her, but she ignored him. Never take sweets from a stranger. Everyone knows that.

Peter helped himself to a handful of Minstrels and shoved the packet back into his pocket. He crunched happily on them for a few minutes, still sitting on his bike, while she pretended he wasn't there.

'I want to make love to you.'

He almost burst out laughing at the suddenness of this although he knew it was coming, but she didn't find it funny. She leaped to her feet, her phone clattering to the ground, and shouted at him.

'Look, just fuck off or I'll call the police.'

Such language for one so young. So coarse, but he had to take some of the blame. Her anger sent Peter into retreat. A face full of confused hurt, he swung his bike round and cycled back towards the town, but he'd been there long enough to condemn himself.

He made his way down the bank and emerged from the woods, feigning breathlessness.

'Was that boy bothering you?'

Still flushed from her outburst, she didn't question what he was doing in the woods.

'A bit.'

He felt her relief. It had been bravado: Peter had scared her.

'Do you want me to call the police?'

'No, it's OK. Thank you.'

She smiled at him. She was in safe hands now. He was no threat to her. She could relax now. Silly girl.

'I better be going.'

He took her arm. She tensed but was too polite to brush him off.

'There's no hurry.'

'My mum's waiting for me.'

Ah, that old chestnut. The thing is, he knew she was lying. She didn't tell her mum she was there because she hated her mum and, anyway, she didn't care about her. No one cared about her. That's what she told him.

'It's OK. You're safe with me.'

And then she understood. That delicious moment when they realized they'd got it wrong, but before she could resist, he had slapped his palm over her mouth. But he must move on.

He calls up the memory of her body lying on the ground. Like

163

studying a great painting in a gallery, he examines every inch of her form until he reaches her face. Still. Serene. At peace. His.

His breath shortens and his heart begins to beat so hard it hurts, forcing the blood through his veins, like it's willing him on. It's working. *You can do it, Simon.* He squeezes his eyes tight to make sure her face, her stillness remains anchored in his mind. He wants this so badly, surely that counts for something. Yes, yes, it's happening, this is it. He knows it.

He looks down and the sight drives the air from him.

Nothing.

He nudges it, but it just lies there: flaccid, limp, lifeless, impotent. Useless. Tilting his head back, he stares up at the grubby grey ceiling and he just wants to scream. He touches his cheeks. They're damp and he realizes he is crying big, fat, silent tears.

Danielle would have found this hilarious, of course.

23

Megan is out of surgery and back on the ICU ward. A tangle of leads and tubes connected to banks of machines either side of her bed do the job of keeping her alive: one breathes for her; another feeds her; another empties her; and another tells me her heart is still beating. She's in the deepest of sleeps, and unresponsive to my touch, but she's in there somewhere. She's still here.

The consultant smiles down at my daughter.

'She did really well. The surgery went according to plan. Obviously, the next few days and weeks will be crucial, but she's a fighter.'

'Yes, she's a fighter,' I echo his words.

'Is there anything you'd like to ask me?'

Warm relief has eased my numbness enough to release a dozen questions that then jam my mind so I'm unable to articulate any of them. All I can do is stare at Megan – bruised, bandaged and still, her body slack, even the muscles around her mouth unable to muster a grip on the ventilator tube – and wonder how the girl I left smiling and full of life yesterday morning ended up in a hospital bed, kept alive by machines. That's something the consultant can't answer, but he's used to voices silenced by the fear and horror of seeing a loved one hooked up to monitors and answers as if I asked my questions.

'Megan has what we call a Traumatic Brain Injury caused by several very severe blows to the head. She's heavily anaesthetized at the moment, what we call an induced coma. It's nothing to be concerned about. We do this to protect the brain and allow it to heal. It's entirely normal in cases like this.'

Only it's not normal to me. None of it is. This is all wrong. Megan shouldn't be here. Neither should I. I'm the CSI. I'm the one that comforts victims, catches their attackers, tells them we will get justice for them. I'm not the one who sits by bedsides, bewildered and distraught. This isn't meant to happen, and it isn't normal.

'In the meantime, be with her, talk to her as much as you can. It may not seem like it and she probably won't remember, but she can hear you.'

'When will she wake up?'

For once, I'm grateful for Bernadette's directness. Patrick dropped her off a few hours ago just before Megan came out of surgery. As she marched towards me down the corridor, I'm ashamed to admit I stood up and braced myself for a slew of recriminations. Instead, she took me in her arms and hugged me tightly, tighter than she has ever hugged me before.

'It'll be all right,' she said with a gentleness I didn't know she was capable of. How many times have I wished Bernadette had said that to me over the years, but she was saying it now and for that I was grateful. She let go of me and sat down. I took my seat next to her.

'I want to say a prayer for Megan.'

Religion and I parted company many years ago, Bernadette

knows that, so what was this? Some twisted attempt to lead me back into God's fold? I wouldn't put it past her. But scrutiny for confirmation of an ulterior motive only revealed a woman of faith seeking comfort from her God.

'OK.'

'Thank you.' Bernadette took my hand, and she began to utter numerous self-crafted sentences that all amounted to one plea: don't let Megan die. At the end, we both said: 'Amen.'

'We're hoping to start to bring her out of the induced coma later today,' said the consultant. 'The drugs will wear off slowly and then it's a waiting game, I'm afraid, but she's young and she's resilient.'

'Will she have brain damage?' Bernadette's bluntness takes him aback.

'It's too soon to say, much too soon, but the brain is a remarkable organ. I've seen worse cases make a full recovery, but we must be careful not to raise expectations until we know more.'

'What sort of things should we talk to her about?'

Penny is also here. She flew into the hospital, her eyes sore and her cheeks already puffed from crying. She held me like she never wanted to let go while Bernadette looked on, her expression a mix of confusion and distaste.

'Anything and everything. Memories, stories of childhood, favourite places. If you get stuck, the Highway Code will do. She just needs to hear her loved ones.'

I find my voice. I have a question.

'Will she remember who did this to her?'

Bernadette delivers a disapproving 'tut'. I ignore her. The

consultant appears not to notice Bernadette's disapproval, but he pauses, and pauses are never good. Pauses mean I'm not going to like what's coming next.

'I would say that even if she makes a full recovery which, of course, we're hopeful that she will, I very much doubt she'll remember any of the events leading up to her attack, but let's not get ahead of ourselves. It's going to be a long road to recovery. For now, the most important thing you can do is be here for her. I'll leave you to it for now, but I'll come back later and we can talk further.'

The consultant leaves.

'Is that all you can think of?' Bernadette hisses in a low voice in case the consultant is still within earshot. 'Whether or not she'll be able to give a police statement about who attacked her?'

What passed between us last night is beginning to feel like a temporary truce.

'Not now, Bernadette. Please.' My voice is also barely above a whisper. I don't want Megan to hear this.

'Well, you asked the question so it's obviously on your mind.'

'Because the person who did this needs to be caught and Megan is our best hope. I don't understand why you think that's unreasonable.'

'Because you're treating it like it's just another one of your cases to be solved. This is your own daughter. Can't you put her first, just for once?'

'Megan has always come first.'

'If that were true, she wouldn't be here in the first place. What was she doing out on the trail, miles and miles from home, for goodness' sake? I told you she was going off the rails, that you needed to be around more.'

There it is – that old anger festering under the surface of our relationship just waiting for the opportunity to burst forth and remind me how I always mess everything up, but I give her the benefit of the doubt: it's the shock talking.

'This has nothing to do with my job or how I parent Megan.' I don't sound as convinced as I'd like, but I put that down to the weariness of battling Bernadette when all I want to do is sit with Megan.

'So why wasn't she at school?'

She doesn't know about Sean and I don't have the energy to tell her.

'She wasn't feeling well so I kept her off for the day. She's fifteen. She's capable of looking after herself and if she needs anything Penny is nearby.'

Bernadette looks at Megan.

'Well, clearly she's not capable of looking after herself, is she?'

I can't believe what I'm hearing.

'Christ. You think it's my fault Megan was attacked?'

Penny sighs.

'For God's sake, will the two of you just shut up? This isn't helping Megan, is it?'

Bernadette presses her lips together. The conversation is over, but it doesn't matter. She's had her say. I'm to blame for the fact that Megan is lying in a hospital bed, clinging to life, her skull caved in.

'There's a text from Helena. It says, *Get well soon, smelly. I need you by my side. Who else is going to defend me against that cow, Leah?* I'm not sure that last bit is appropriate, but it was nice of her to think of you, wasn't it? You've known Helena for years now, of course. Since nursery school.'

My voice is both tight and breezy, a distortion of itself. It's barely recognizable to me so I'm not sure how it helps Megan. If she could speak, she'd laugh at me, 'You sound so fake, Mum,' and she'd be right. I'm fighting to keep the fear and anguish out, but the result is fooling no one.

Bernadette has left, having delivered her verdict on how Megan ended up in hospital and Penny has gone to get us some coffee. It's just me and Megan and the machines, blinking and beeping.

The nurses have said to keep talking, but there are only so many times I can tell her she's doing really well, that everything is going to be OK and that she's to keep fighting, so now I'm reading out text messages like a second-rate disc jockey on the radio.

I tap the next text.

'This one is from Liam. He says, *Get well soon, Megan. There'll be a chococino waiting for you when you next come bodyboarding. Maybe you could give me a lesson or two. It's about time I learned.* You know Liam. He runs the coffee bar at Morte Sands. You always . . .' My voice fractures as my mind catapults back to just a few days ago on the beach and our laughter at the waves that got the better of us. I pause to let it heal then press my lips into a smile, hoping it's enough to inject something approaching sunniness into my words. 'You always say Liam makes the best chococino in the whole of the county.'

Returning to my phone, there's a text from a number I don't

recognize so I check to see who the message is from. Him! How the hell did he get my number? And why in God's name does he think it's OK to send me a text? Especially as I already passed his name to Holt as a person of interest. He's a suspect, for Christ's sake. I'm about to delete it when I stop myself. Much as I loathe the thought, what if this is the one that reaches Megan?

I sigh.

'OK. This one's from Jay. He's a – a friend of yours,' I fail miserably to mask my disapproval. It says, *WTF, tell Meg she's got to get better from me. Ta, Jay.'*

My eye lingers on his words. Jay Cox, Bidecombe's friendly neighbourhood drug dealer. Does he have a hand in this? If he has, would he send Megan a text afterwards? It's what the guilty would consider a clever move to cover their tracks, but Jay's not that clever, and while there's a raft of crimes he could be locked up for, he's never been done for assault. He isn't the violent type. A lifetime of neglect has left him with the shape and strength of a stick insect. And he never leaves Bidecombe.

Jay has filled my mind and, to my horror, I realize I've stopped talking. I take Megan's hand in mine, taking care not to dislodge the thin tube running from the back of her hand.

Her fingers lay limp in mine and I frantically search for something to say, convinced her life force, hastened by my silence, is fading fast, bleeding out, and I need to stem it.

But there's only one thing that comes to mind.

'Who did this to you, Megan?'

24

He had had a terrible night, barely getting any sleep, his mind churning the possibilities. What if she survived the operation? What if she remembered? Just recalling his green paramedic's uniform would be enough for the police to track him down. Perhaps she had told the police and they were on their way to arrest him right then. No. No. That couldn't be possible. But how could he find out? He couldn't go near the ward and he couldn't keep asking people.

In the end, he couldn't stand it. At least if he was at the hospital, he might hear something, so he left early for work the next morning before Jackie had even stirred in her recliner. His head pounding with the lack of sleep, he had tucked himself away in a far corner of the canteen in the basement to wait for his shift to start, but Trisha had still managed to find him.

She slaps him on his back and plonks herself down in the chair in front of him.

'How you doing, my old mucker?'

She's ridiculously upbeat which can mean only one thing.

'The date went well then.'

Trisha winks at him. He hates it when she winks at him like he's meant to know or care what's going on in her head.

'You could say that.'

And he notices, for the first time, the purple ragged-edged bruises on the side of her neck. Lovebites, they're called, but they're nothing but a filthy brag that she'd had sex the previous night. Danielle never gave him lovebites.

'And you'll never guess who it turned out to be?' There's a pause. He's bored of her games. 'It was Gary! You know, the guy from the mortuary.'

'Gary.'

'Yeah. I know. He's better looking out of his uniform, but who'd have thought it, eh?'

'Who'd have thought it?'

'He's in a band and, between you and me, he put on a pretty good performance in the sack too.'

She cackles at her own joke. He wonders if his disgust is visible through his forced smile, but he's past caring.

'Guess we'd better get on.'

She's disappointed not to have the opportunity to expand on their bedroom antics. No doubt that'll come later.

'Yeah, you're right. You OK to start the vehicle checks while I pop down to the mortuary? He had to start early this morning. Surprised he had the energy to get out of bed. Poor lamb.'

'Take your time.'

'Aw, thanks, Si.'

She saunters towards the canteen exit. She really is a vile-mouthed, loathsome individual. Perhaps he'll put in a request to move.

When she reaches the corner, she stops and turns back. He looks away, not wanting her to know he was watching her.

'By the way, did you hear?'

'Sorry? No. Hear what?'

'That girl. The one who was attacked in Three Brethren Woods yesterday?'

'Yes.'

'She survived the night. She's in ICU. Critical, but stable. They're hoping she's going to wake up soon. Si, we got to her in time. Isn't that the best news?'

He stares at Trisha.

'The best.'

A voice startles me. For a moment, I think it's Megan, but her lips are stone still, the ventilator tube awkwardly hooked to the corner of her mouth. I turn my head towards the nurse standing in the doorway.

'There's a detective here to see you.'

Over her shoulder, Holt's face appears, pale and drawn. He hasn't had much sleep. His appearance triggers thoughts of Janie and Cheryl and traces of my anger at his refusal to listen to me. In his mind, their cases are both closed. In mine, they most definitely are not, and I almost ask him about them before realizing I don't have the energy to fight their corners, not right now.

'How is she?'

I rise to meet him. He doesn't want to come into the room, and I don't want him to, either. Megan can't hear this, so we move into the corridor.

'OK. The surgery went well.'

He nods and says no more. He's waiting for my permission to move the conversation beyond Megan's condition. It would be crass of him to do so, but there's only one reason he's here.

'How's the investigation going?'

'Early days, but we're hopeful of a quick result.'

'What have you got from the scene?'

It slips out without me thinking and takes us both by surprise, but now it's out there I want to know.

'We – er, think we may have the weapon. Jake recovered a steel pole nearby with what looks like blood on it.'

'The weapon? Really? Megan's attacker didn't make any attempt to get rid of it?'

My questions are a reflex. Suddenly, we're not talking about Megan, we're talking about a crime like it's any other crime on the crime sheet.

'Doesn't look like it.'

I'm not expecting this. Even criminals have watched enough cop shows to know to dispose of the weapon and Three Brethren Woods with its dense woodland is the proverbial haystack – not to mention the estuary on the other side of the trail, its black silt the keeper of many secrets. It's a basic error that raises my hopes that the scene is right out of a training manual.

'What else did Jake find?'

Holt shifts uncomfortably.

'Nothing else.'

'But it was wet. There must have been shoeprints.'

'Yeah, plenty of those, but all accounted for.'

'Really? What about Megan's phone?'

'No sign of it. It's probably in the estuary.'

'So, the assailant remembers to get rid of Meg's phone, but not the weapon?'

'I know, but maybe he got spooked and dropped it.'

'Maybe.'

'We'll keep looking, and we've got Megan's laptop. I wanted to ask you, what social media is she on?'

'Facebook and Snapchat, but she mostly uses Instagram. Her username is SubmarineGirl227. It's the same username for all of them. Do you think she met someone she was talking to online?'

'It's one avenue we're exploring. Most teens communicate through their social media.'

'So you think it's someone she knows?'

'That's the mostly likely explanation, but it could be someone she has only met online . . .' He pauses because he knows no parent wants to hear what he's about to say. 'Someone who groomed her. We're not ruling anything out.'

I want to tell him not to bother. Meg wouldn't be so stupid as to arrange to meet someone she'd only encountered online, but now I'm not so sure any more. I would have sworn on Bernadette's Bibles there is no way she would have taken herself off to the woods sixteen miles away without telling someone, but she did. Unless she was taken there by force.

'I know we've already spoken about this, but does she have a boyfriend?'

'Have we?' Then I remember Megan being taken down to theatre and Holt standing next to me. 'Ally, I know this is hard for you, but I don't need to tell you time is of the essence.' He didn't. It's called the golden hour of investigation, those first sixty minutes where the race is on to secure as much evidence as possible when scenes are at their freshest and memories have yet to fade and become corrupted. But it normally applies to murders. 'Not that I know of. I told you about Jay Cox, but I think they were just friends – although I'd banned her from having anything to do with him. He deals drugs.'

'We checked him out. He had the best alibi there is. He was being stopped and searched in Bidecombe High Street by the local uniform yesterday afternoon.'

'That's about right.'

'So how did Megan seem yesterday?'

'In good spirits, the best for a while. I kept her off school. She'd seen her ex-stepdad working on the school roof. He's a building contractor. There's a lot of history there so I kept her off.'

'Sean Parker, right? Yeah, we spoke to him too. He was working on site all day. His boss confirmed it. Actually, he was very upset to hear what had happened to Megan and then got all angry because he thought we were accusing him. Unpredictable type.'

'Sounds like Sean, but he's been off the scene for years.'

'OK, well if you can think of anything else, anything at all, call me. Anytime.'

'There is one thing. It's been bothering me ever since Megan came out of surgery.'

25

It's late and there's no moon. The night is on his side, but he isn't taking any chances. He parks his car in a lane behind the hospital grounds which is nothing unusual; lots of hospital workers do it to avoid paying the astronomical parking permit fee.

He gets out of his car and pulls up the hoodie that he bought after work. He hates them. It's the type of thing sex-mad yobs like Gary wear to try to look younger, but it's perfect for hiding his face.

There's a gap in the hedge that the staff use as a cut through to the back of the hospital. It's an unofficial entrance and they regularly receive letters requesting them not to use it. More importantly, it's not covered by CCTV.

Keeping to the deep shadows thrown by the tall broad chestnut trees lining the perimeter fence, he slips into the main hospital building through an open fire exit door. The doors are always left open. It's against hospital policy, but people are always forgetting their passes and wedge them open so they can get back in after their fag break.

He takes the back stairs two at a time to ICU on the third floor. There's no CCTV there either. The lights in the corridor have been dimmed. It's quiet. Hospitals run 24/7 but the truth is there's barely anyone around after midnight. The corridors are empty, the wards are mostly staffed by one person – two, if you're lucky.

Through the glass window in the door, he can see into the ward, a wide corridor with rooms leading off it. Halfway along, a nurse, a different one to the one last night, sits at her desk, doing paperwork.

He doesn't know which room she's in, but it won't take long to find her. He's already decided he's not going to make it complicated. She'll be on a ventilator. All he needs to do is flick a switch, but first he has to get past the CSI.

She's bound to be still around, but his luck is in. A door opens and the CSI emerges, rubbing her eyes. Her dark hair is frizzy like she's not brushed it for days. She rolls her shoulders back, easing the stiffness, and approaches the reception desk where she trades a weak smile for some pity.

She's asking something. The nurse suddenly points in his direction and he darts out of sight. She's giving the CSI directions which means the CSI is heading his way and, any second now, she'll come through that door and see him.

He dips down a small corridor to the left of the main corridor, his back flat to the wall. Behind him, the ICU door opens and closes and footsteps lead away in the opposite direction. He risks a glance and is rewarded with the sight of the CSI stepping into the lift.

She's gone, probably to the canteen. That's two floors away and on the other side of the hospital. He's got a good fifteen minutes, even if she buys something and comes straight back.

He returns to the door leading to ICU and observes the nurse for a few moments more before making the call.

'Hi, it's the Path Lab here. I've got the test results you requested. I'd send them electronically, but our systems are down. I'll print them out for you, but any chance someone can pop up and collect them?'

'I've not requested any results.' Her voice is curt, no nonsense.

'Well, someone did, and we've got it flagged as urgent. I've just come on shift so I'm picking up someone else's job.'

'Can't you bring them down? I'm on my own.'

'Sorry, no can do, I've got another rush job on here.'

There's a pause. She rolls her eyes and shakes her head.

'OK, I'll be there in a moment.'

Reluctantly, she gets up and walks towards the exit. Once again, he ducks around the corner and waits for the door to open. He's banking on the nurse not wanting to be away from her station and hurrying to the Path Lab which means he's got around five seconds to get to the door. He's right. She's already out of sight by the time he checks the corridor.

He lunges towards the closing door, sliding his fingers into the gap just in time. He's in. And alone. He could have used his hospital pass, but that would show up on the system. This way, the most they'll have on the ward CCTV is a figure in a black hoodie. He can live with that.

Through the window to her room, he spots her. Her bed is raised at a thirty-degree angle, the metal side bars are up, the machines fussing and flickering. She looks so peaceful, so still, it's hard to believe she's even alive. Something stirs within him which takes him by surprise. If only he had more time, but he doesn't.

He pushes the door handle down. It opens a fraction and the sound of the machines grows louder, as if calling out to his own heart thudding against his rib cage. He steps into the room. He must be quick, but oh, how he would give anything to stay longer. Anything. He sighs with regret.

He's about to take another step when a hand grips his shoulder hard. A man's hand.

'Excuse me, sir.'

He twists round to find himself eye to eye with a police officer.

26

The last thing I remember is returning from the canteen with a coffee. It must have been about three in the morning. The nurse was nowhere to be seen, neither was the police officer that I insisted Holt provide. He said no, of course: police resources are already too stretched, Megan's attacker wouldn't dare try anything so risky and no one can get into the ward without a pass, but I'd seen people coming and going all day, politely holding doors open for each other. No questions asked and not a hospital pass in sight. Besides, public spaces don't seem to bother this guy. He's not the shy type. I told Holt this and that he'd never forgive himself if something happened to Megan and, reluctantly, he agreed to put a Special on guard.

So, when I found the corridor empty, my heart pumped hard with the possibilities, none of them good. I rushed into Megan's room, but she was as I'd left her, sleeping peacefully to the rhythm of the machines.

Revived more by the exceptional bitterness of the coffee than its caffeine content, I sat down next to Megan and began reading some trashy crime novel that Penny had bought in the hospital bookshop. It was that or *Fifty Shades of Grey*, apparently.

The next thing I know, natural light is flooding the room, my head is resting on Megan's bed, the book is on the floor and Penny is here.

Her grey hair, still threaded with beads, is tied back in a loose ponytail, which she has decided is more appropriate for the hospital environment, and the redness around her eyes has gone, only to be replaced by dark smudges of sleep deprivation.

'Morning. The nurses said Megan's had a good night.'

'I was reading to her, but I must have dropped off.'

'Has there been any response?'

'No. Not yet.'

She brushes off the bad news.

'Well, the doctors said it would take time. She'll come round.'

Penny sits in the armchair in the corner of the room. I lean over the metal side bar and I take Megan's hand.

'Megan. Guess what? Penny's here.'

'Hi, Megan,' Penny calls and waves. 'How's it going, love?'

'Penny runs Seven Hills Lodges where we live. You know Penny. The lady who wears the brightly coloured skirts and feathers in her hair.' I exchange smiles with Pen. 'She put feathers in your hair once for your tenth birthday party, bright pink ones, but they made you sneeze. She's looked after you a lot, especially when I've had to go to work. She taught you all the Beatles songs, although I've just about forgiven her for doing that.'

'Unfortunately, your mother has no musical appreciation. Lucky you and I do, eh, Megan?' Penny chips in, her Scouse accent broadening in defence of anything remotely connected to her home city. I laugh and look to Megan to join in. Nothing.

I lift her hand to my lips and kiss her cool skin warm. 'Megan, please, come back to me.'

Nothing.

I don't know what to say any more. I've run out of words. My brain has stalled. Even the inane is beyond me. Staring down at my hand clasped around Megan's, I search for inspiration. But there is only one thought suspended, midway in my mind like a neon light on the darkest of streets. *Who did this to you, Megan?*

I throw Penny a pleading look. She stares at me and then opens her mouth, but not to speak. Instead, she starts to sing. Quietly, at first, just under her breath, almost as an act of self-comfort, but my smile wills her to sing louder and she responds. Each note is clear and confident. She's singing 'Yellow Submarine'.

The song is so familiar to me. Penny taught it to Megan when she was about nine. She loved it, singing it in supermarkets, the back of the car, the beach, our bench, everywhere until it drove me mad.

Penny gets up from the chair and joins me by Megan's bedside, placing her hand on my shoulder, connecting herself to Megan, through me. Then as suddenly as she started, she stops singing.

'What is it?'

'Her eyelids flickered.'

'Are you sure?'

'Yes.'

I stare down at Megan, but I'm sure she hasn't moved.

'Keep singing.'

Penny starts from the beginning again. She gets as far as the third line when Megan's eyelids twitch. Just for a second.

'Oh my God. Megan. You're back.'

27

The consultant tells us it's too soon to hang out the bunting, but everything is moving in the right direction and, for that, we must be grateful.

'She's doing really well. Well done, Megan.' He turns to me. 'And well done to you too.'

'It was Penny's singing that did it.'

'It all helps. Look, now might be a good time to give yourself a bit of a break. Can I suggest that you go home, get changed, get some fresh air even? Your friend Penny is here and we'll take good care of Megan while you're gone.'

Penny is beaming, and almost giddy after the effect her singing has had on Megan.

'He's right, Ally. Go and get some proper rest. I'll read to Megan. Or if she's really unlucky, I'll sing to her again.'

'I'm not sure.'

'Honestly, Megan and I will be just fine, won't we, Megan?'

She smiles at my daughter and I feel the mildest of pangs that I'm ashamed to admit is envy. Why did Megan respond to Penny? I dismiss it before it morphs into something uglier. The important thing is Megan reacted and, anyway, didn't the consultant say it was our combined efforts that had made the difference?

I don't want to leave for fear of missing the next step of Megan's recovery, but, put simply, I feel gross. I haven't left the hospital since Megan was brought in two days ago. I risked a glance in the toilet mirror and instantly regretted it. Lack of sleep has darkened and sagged the skin around my eyes. My hair has taken on a greasy gloss and my teeth are tacky to my tongue's touch. I suspect my breath stinks and there's every likelihood that I smell. I am the epitome of someone letting themselves go, but I need me back for when Megan returns. I don't want her to see the toll her attack has had on me.

I smile back at Penny.

'Thanks, Pen.'

The high green hedges and outlying villages that line the route of the Barnston to Bidecombe road flash by until I reach Heale Cross, a desolate peak where the road splits, left to Morte Sands, right towards the moor or straight on to Bidecombe.

The road curves down towards the town, passing the cast-iron railings that surround the old rec. I'm half expecting to see Megan monopolizing one of the benches with her friends, tiredness and my need for normality still scorching all reason. It's empty, of course. At this time, the kids are still in school and Megan is lying in a hospital bed. The new normality.

Just as I'm about to take a left turning towards Seven Hills Lodges, movement catches my eye and I spy a figure in jeans and a hoodie shuffling across the wide expanse of grass on his way to cause misery.

Before I've thought it through, I've pulled over, jumped out of the car and am running towards him.

'Jay! Stop!'

He turns at the sound of his name and, when he sees it's me, considers doing a runner but even he knows his skunk-nourished limbs and lungs are unlikely to get him far so he just stands and waits for me to reach him.

'I had nothing to do with it.' Denial is his default setting although, in this case, he's telling the truth. 'And thanks for grassing me up to the pigs.'

I'm not apologizing for that. He might not be guilty of hurting Megan, but he's guilty of plenty of other things.

'I know you had nothing to do with it. I just want to talk to you, that's all.'

'I told you. I already spoke to your lot. Not that I had any choice. The detective with the stupid hair was a total dick.'

Holt obviously leaned on him a little too hard. For once, I'm with Holt.

'I'm not asking you as a CSI, I'm asking you as Megan's mother.'

He shrugs, but he doesn't tell me to fuck off. That's progress for Jay.

'You hung out together a few days before she was attacked? How was she?'

He takes a deep drag on a roll-up so thin he's in no danger of a nicotine rush, using the time to decide if he'll answer me or not. To my amazement, he does.

'She was upset. She'd seen her stepdad at school. She told me he'd been a right bastard to you and her when she was little. She was scared of him.'

My heart pinches on hearing this.

'Are you and her in a relationship?'

A laugh turns into a hacking cough.

'No,' he says through watery eyes. 'I asked her out. Of course I did. She's a stunner, but I got the impression she was interested in someone else, know what I mean?'

I don't. This is the first I've heard of this.

'Have you told the police this?'

''Course not.'

'But it might help them find her attacker.'

Jay gives me a 'so what' look. I picture his interview with the police. Monosyllabic, evasive, aggressive, he's never going to be a leading light in his local Neighbourhood Watch. I hope Holt gave him both barrels.

'It's nothing to do with me, is it?'

'So, who was this someone else she was interested in?'

'Dunno. Didn't ask.'

'Was it someone she met online?'

He shrugs and I ignore the urge to slap him.

'Jay, Megan was brutally assaulted. If you cared for her, you'd want to help catch the person who did it.'

'I don't know, right? We didn't talk about stuff like that, know what I mean?'

'So, what did you talk about?'

'Stuff.'

'Like?'

'Just stuff.'

It's pointless. This is all I'm going to get. This kid is genetically programmed to hate the police.

'OK. Thanks.'

I'm about to leave when Jay starts talking again.

'How is she? I sent you a text.'

'I know. I read it out to her.'

'Really? Thought you hated me. That's what Megan said.'

'Hate? No. Disapprove? Yes. Can you blame me?'

'Fairs. Has she woken up?

'Not yet. But she will.'

He nods and takes another drag before flicking the butt to one side.

'She was nice to me, you know, but I never gave her nothing. She wasn't into it. She was just really nice to talk to. She was really proud of you, of the job you did. Talked about you all the time. Said she wanted to join the police when she was older. Be like you.'

I didn't know this. Why don't I know this? How come he knows more about my daughter's hopes and dreams than I do? Christ, where the hell have I been?

Bernadette's condemnation, Megan responding to Penny's voice and now a fucking drug dealer knowing more about my daughter than I do suddenly meet and merge into a dark swell of emotion that forces its way into my throat, and threatens to burst out of me. I press my lips together in a way that would make Bernadette proud. I have to hold on; I can't let it out, not here.

Jay places a hand gently on my arm. The suspicion, the defiance, the easy hatred of authority has gone, and his eyes simply reflect my pain back to me. His father got locked up when he was eight and his mum died of a heroin overdose when he was twelve. This boy has known heartache. A tear breaks in the corner of my eye and I quickly wipe it away with my knuckle before it goes fully public.

'She's a great girl,' he says.

'I know.' Christ, of all the people in all the world, I find comfort with Jay Cox. Another tear threatens to replace the first and I plug my nostrils with the back of my hand hoping it'll do the job of stemming my emotions. It doesn't and I just give into it.

'I just want her back,' I say through the blur.

'Sorry,' he says, and he means it.

'Me too.'

I walk slowly back towards my car.

'Ally!'

I turn back to Jay.

'What? Have you remembered something?'

'Just make sure your lot catch the fucker.'

28

He knocks on the door of cabin 27. This is a much better idea, after last night's setback.

The cop insisted on escorting him back down to the main reception on the ground floor. Jim was on the front desk. Luckily, he remembered they'd brought in a man who'd had a heart attack during the week so he told Jim he wanted to check in on a patient, but had been given the wrong ward name. When the police officer realized he was a paramedic – a member of the bluelight family – he couldn't do enough for him, falling over himself to apologize, he was. He accepted the idiot's apology, of course, told him he understood he was only doing his job.

The CSI opens the door, towel-drying her hair. She's so like Danielle, it takes all his resolve not to start at the sight of her.

'Simon, hello, er, is everything all right?'

Through his uniform, his heart is pounding.

'Yes, sorry, I didn't mean to scare you. I said to the other paramedics I'd drop by and ask how Megan is. We're all very worried about your daughter, but I didn't like to disturb you on the ward. One of the nurses said you'd gone home.'

She relaxes.

'Oh, I see. Yes, I just came back to shower and change. I'm heading back to the hospital now.'

'We heard she was still in a coma. We're all praying for her to recover.'

'That's very kind of you. Thank you and please pass my thanks on to your colleagues.'

'We bought this for you. It's not much, but we wanted you to know that we're thinking of you.' He holds out a card. She stares down at it. 'It's affected us all really badly, if I'm honest. I can't get the image of Megan out of my head.'

She smiles and steps to one side.

'Why don't you come in for a moment?'

They enter the living room with a small kitchenette to one side. There's a pile of unopened cards on the kitchen bar so he tucks his in among them. He's rather proud of it. It wasn't cheap either.

She directs him to a large, lumpy sofa facing a huge mural of a Caribbean beach that has been spoiled with childish drawings of boats and people swimming.

Those full lips of hers are still smiling.

'I never thanked you and Trisha properly for what you did. Megan wouldn't be alive if it weren't for your actions.'

'I'm just glad we got there in time. How is she?'

'Actually, she's beginning to respond.'

No. That can't be.

'That's fantastic news. Did she say anything?'

'No, it's much too soon for that. When I say respond, her eyelids flickered to the sound of my friend singing.'

'So she's not awake?'

'No. Not yet.'

'But you're still expecting her to wake up?'

She frowns at him.

'Yes, of course.'

He pulls back.

'We know so little about the brain, don't we? You hear of people waking up after months of being in a coma as if nothing has happened to them.'

'Yes, that's true.'

'Although I guess she won't remember anything of the attack.'

'No, the doctor says she's very unlikely to have any memory of that day, but maybe that's a good thing. I'm not sure I want her to remember any of this.'

'I can understand that.' Of course, she won't remember! He knows that. He's a paramedic.

The CSI stands up, signalling their conversation is over.

'Anyway, it was very thoughtful of you to drop by and thank you for the card, but I ought to get back to the hospital.'

She moves towards the door, but he hangs back. He doesn't want their conversation to end.

'Are you OK?' she asks.

'I'm fine. Just a bit upset about everything, that's all.'

'I know. I understand.'

'I can't imagine how you felt when you found out.'

'Yes, it was terrible.'

'You're à CSI. You've seen lots of terrible things, but it's different when it's your own flesh and blood. The paramedics with kids always say their worst nightmare would be to attend an incident and discover it's their own child.'

'Yes. I can understand that.'

'How do you even begin to come to terms with that?'

'We're just taking things day by day. Look, I'm sorry to rush you, but I really need to go.'

She walks towards the front door and holds it open for him, signalling for him to leave, but he isn't finished.

'Your daughter spoke before she lost consciousness.'

It isn't true, of course, but she closes the door. The hospital and her daughter can wait, after all. Satisfaction fires his insides.

'Megan spoke?'

'As I held her in my arms.'

Her body stiffens as if she's trying to absorb an electric shock that's passed through her.

'What did she say?' Her dark brown eyes trawl his for the answer. He couldn't look away even if he wanted. She's bewitched him. She moves so close to him he could almost reach out and touch her. 'Simon, what did she say?'

'I think she thought I was you. She just said, "Mum, I'm sorry."'

Her lips part to take a tiny breath and her face pinches like the oxygen in her lungs has been replaced with poisonous gas.

'I see.' She exhales the words.

'I thought it might help to know she was thinking of you before she lost consciousness.'

She smiles.

'It has. Thank you, Simon.'

29

Apologize? For what? Oh, Megan, you've nothing to apologize for. None of this is your fault.

The idea that her last thought before she slipped into unconsciousness was to say sorry to me is almost unbearable. A man beat her senseless and all she could think of was how she was to blame, how I would be angry with her for what this monster did to her. Part of me wishes Simon had kept this to himself. He thought he was doing the right thing but it has just dredged fresh agony to the surface. My daughter called out to me in the moment of her greatest need. Convinced herself I was there, cradling her. I wasn't.

As I turn into the hospital grounds, I try to ignore this hard mass of guilt wedged inside my chest, hoping it will fade if I focus on the good. Megan's eyelids twitched at the sound of Penny singing her favourite song. I don't dwell on it being Penny's voice that she reacted to. Why wouldn't it be? Penny is like a second mum to Megan. The important thing is she responded. She's on the road to recovery and when she's better things will be different. I will be around more. I'll be there for her.

Strolling across the hospital car park, someone calls my name. It's Gary, the mortician's assistant.

'Ally, hi, how are you? Alex and I heard about your daughter.'

I haven't seen him since he and Alex Blandford, the pathologist, did the postmortem on Janie Warren, but I'm touched that he has gone out of his way to talk to me when it would have been easier to avoid me.

'OK, thanks.' We both know it's a lie. I may have had a shower and brushed my hair, but I look exactly like someone who hasn't had more than a couple of hours sleep in the last forty-eight hours. Shit, in other words.

'How's she doing?'

'Better, thank you. Still a long way to go.'

'It's a terrible thing to happen to a young girl. Trisha is just so pleased that she's going to be OK.'

'Trisha?'

'My girlfriend. She's one of the paramedics that saved Megan. Trisha Wilkins.'

'Yes, of course. I've just seen Simon. He dropped a get well soon card off at my cabin. Please pass on my thanks.'

'I will. It'll mean a lot to her. It's been rough. She's still feeling a bit guilty.'

'She has nothing to feel guilty about.'

'That's what I said, but she reckons the delay in getting to Megan cost them a good few minutes.'

'What delay?'

Gary opens then closes his mouth. He glances around the car park.

'It's er – it's nothing, just that Simon had to go and pick her up before they could respond to the call. She'd stayed with a patient while he went for lunch.'

'I see. Look, tell Trisha from me those few extra minutes honestly wouldn't have made any difference. She and Simon couldn't have done more for Megan and I'm indebted to them both.'

'Thanks, Ally. She'll appreciate that. I'll see you around.'

He turns to leave when another thought occurs to me.

'Actually. There's one other thing.'

'What's that?'

'Did Megan say anything to Trisha before she lost consciousness?'

He frowns.

'I thought they found her unconscious. Why?'

'Oh, it's just that Simon mentioned that Megan spoke, and I wondered if she said something to Trisha too.'

He shrugs.

'Trisha didn't say anything to me about it, but she really doesn't like to talk about it. I think she just wants to put it behind her. Sorry.' He looks at me, guilty that his girlfriend has moved on.

I place my hand on his arm.

'It's OK and it's not important. Trisha saved Megan's life. I'll always be grateful to her for that.'

Poor Trisha. She has nothing to reproach herself over.

I walk into the hospital. Suddenly, I have an overwhelming urge to be with Megan. Too impatient to wait for the lift, I take the back stairs two at a time up to her room on the third floor of the hospital. A nurse buzzes me into ICU.

'Good news about Megan. We're all cheering her on.'

'Thank you.'

I quicken my pace, excited to be back with her and for the

next sign that she's coming back to me. Christ, I'll sing the Beatles' entire back catalogue myself if that's what it takes.

But as I open the door to her room, there's a man standing by Megan's bedside, leaning over her.

He turns the key in the front door and laughter rushes into the gap. It's coming from the living room. It's Jackie and her carer, Arjun. His chest sags. He doesn't need this. He has work to do.

Things have moved quickly – much more quickly than he could have anticipated – and he needs to come up with a plan.

He puts his head around the living-room door. Arjun is kneeling before Jackie massaging her feet. The earthy smell of juniper oil permeates the air. Jackie is just loving all the attention, giggling like a lovestruck teenager. She's even made some attempt to brush her few remaining strands of hair.

'Hello, my love. Arjun is giving me a foot massage.'

'Is he now? I've bought you some sweets.'

He produces the packet from his hoodie pocket, but, eyes fixed on Arjun, she waves it away.

'Just put it on the side. I'll have them later. We've had a wonderful morning, haven't we, Arjun?'

Arjun, in his grey carer's uniform, looks up at him. His face breaks into a broad grin and he flashes a perfect set of white teeth that he'd dearly like to put his foot through.

'Yes, we've had a great time.'

Jackie is red in the face, almost giddy with excitement. It's pathetic.

'We've been to Morte Sands.'

This throws him.

'You go to Morte Sands every day.'

Arjun frowns at her. Jackie laughs that slightly-too-loud fake laugh.

'He means I watch it on the live cam. No, we went there for real, didn't we, Arjun? Arjun bought me a chococino from the nice man that runs the Coffee Shack.'

What is it with this 'didn't we, Arjun?' nonsense? She's talking as if they're lifelong friends.

'What do you mean, you went there for real?'

Arjun replaces the top on his massage oil.

'The company I work for has bought a minibus and hired a driver, Stan, so he took a few of us out for the morning. I thought the fresh air would do Jackie some good. Put some colour in her cheeks.'

How dare he? Who does he think he is, taking his wife out without his permission?

'Oh, I see. Well, it's all right for some, I suppose.'

'Simon, it was so lovely to be outside, feeling the sun on my face, watching all the children running up and down the beach. We even had ice cream.'

'You did really well. I'm really proud of you. I didn't think you'd get out of the van, but you did. I think the live cams have made Morte Sands feel familiar and safe for you,' says Arjun.

'Is that so?' He sounds calm, but his insides are churning with anger, anger that will keep. 'Well, thank you, Arjun. It was a very kind thing to do for Jackie.'

'No problem. Maybe, in time, we might hire one of the dune buggies. They're specially adapted for the disabled.'

'That sounds fun, doesn't it, Simon?'

'If you like that sort of thing.'

Arjun fixes Jackie's slippers back onto her feet and stands up.

'Right, that's me done. See you tomorrow, Jackie. Simon, can I have a quick word?'

The two men step out in the hallway.

'Jackie complains a lot about stomach pains and she's definitely lost weight these last few months. I think she should see a doctor. It's probably nothing serious, but she should get it looked at.'

He doesn't need to take Jackie to the doctor. He already knows what she's got. It's called Rapunzel Syndrome and it's where people compulsively pull their hair out and eat it. Jackie has been doing it for years, before he met her, but hair isn't biodegradable which means it's just sitting in her stomach, a huge black tangled mass of a million hair strands slowly damming up her intestine. It's why she lives on sweets; it's the only thing she can consume that doesn't give her severe stomach ache. It's also why her breath stinks, but an ulcer can't be far away now and, untreated, that'll be enough to shut down her vital organs.

'You're absolutely right, Arjun. I've noticed it myself. I'll get her an appointment.'

Arjun leaves and he returns to Jackie, but the smiles have all gone. They were just for Arjun but *he's* the one that cares for her around the clock. *He's* the one that buys her Gold Bears and puts up with her ridiculous obsession with the miniature furry variety.

'You're annoyed with me for going out, aren't you?'

He takes her hand.

'No, I'm not annoyed, my love. It's just that I can't stand the thought of all those people staring and laughing at you. I can't bear it.'

Jackie looks down at her hands.

'No one was staring. Everyone was just having a good time. Arjun wouldn't let anyone say anything mean to me or about me.'

He crouches beside her chair and is rewarded with waves of her pungent breath escaping from the huge hairy knot in her stomach.

'I just worry about you, that's all. Remember the comments you used to get when I took you out. "There's goes Gollum."'

'Yes,' she nods.

'I couldn't stand it if that happened again.'

No one called Jackie Gollum or anything else for that matter, but he needed a reason to stop taking her out. It was tedious and embarrassing to be seen out with her, so he began to tell her all the terrible things people said behind her back. She was devastated, but he told her that she couldn't let these people get to her. He, for one, was proud to be seen in her company. It wasn't long before she told him she didn't want to go out any more, until now. Arjun was apparently her new safe person, and he couldn't have that.

'But I'm sure Arjun would protect me. He's my friend.'

'Oh, Jackie. Arjun is paid to be nice to you.'

She looks horrified. The thought has never occurred to her.

'What – what do you mean?'

'He doesn't really care about you. I bet you anything he's in the pub laughing with his mates about you right now.'

'I thought he really liked me.'

Unable to tolerate her breath any longer, he stands up.

'I'm sorry, I didn't want to upset you, but it's better you know the truth. Look, I don't mind if you want to go out. Go out every day, all day, if you want to, I'm only trying to protect you, that's all.'

Jackie nods.

'Why don't you see what's happening at Morte Sands?'

He presses the button on the remote and the screens light up with images from the live cams on Morte Sands.

'Look, the tide's coming in. There's lots of sandcastles on the beach today. And, look, someone's drawn a massive heart in the sand.'

She's not interested. Her mind is elsewhere, and she picks up Florence Nightingale and strokes her furry head, but he has no intention of letting her sulks ruin his day. He isn't going to make her a doctor's appointment either. He picks up the packet of Haribo and goes upstairs.

30

Sean is standing by Megan's bedside, holding a bunch of wilting petrol station flowers in one hand, the other on her forehead. It's a tableau from one of my more disturbing dreams where Sean is back in our lives as if nothing happened and I am mute and immobile, but this isn't a dream.

'Get away from her!'

This explodes from me with enough force to startle Sean into taking a step back from the bed, giving me time to plant myself between him and Megan, arms outstretched, guarding her against him.

'I'm still her dad.'

His entitled 'I'll do what I want' tone sickens me. *You're my wife. If I want to hit you, I will.*

'No, you're not. You never were. Now get out.'

He shakes his head at what he sees as my unreasonableness.

'For God's sake, Ally, calm down. I've only come to see how she is.'

'We don't want you here. Megan is terrified of you. Just go.'

His eyes invite me to make him leave and he stands his ground. No one pushes Sean around, especially not a woman. Then he moves closer to me. He has a foot on me and uses this to the full, leaning over me, reminding me of his strength and what he's capable of.

'She was pleased to see me at school the other day.'

I let out a dismissive laugh that I didn't know I was capable of, which again disorientates Sean because he's never heard it before, nor seen the sneer on my face, but it feels good. I'm not frightened of him, not any more.

'She was pretending, you prick. It's called fear – fear that unless she behaves the way you want her to, you'll hurt her. '

'What? I would never hurt her. It's you. You've turned her against me.'

He might be up for a row, but I'm not.

'Just leave us alone, Sean.'

'No, I've every right to see my stepdaughter.'

He's enjoying the drama of it all. Christ, he's probably been telling his mates down the pub that the girl that was attacked is his and that he'll be the one to bring her out of her coma because her mother is useless.

'I said, get out.' This time my voice is loud enough to bring two nurses running into the room. One look at the size of Sean brings them to an abrupt halt and they huddle in the doorway.

'This man isn't a relative. He shouldn't be here and I want him to leave.'

'She's lying. I'm Sean Parker. This is my stepdaughter, Megan Parker.'

'I want him out. Now.'

One of the braver nurses steps into the room and takes Sean's arm.

'Sir, you'll have to leave, otherwise we'll call security.'

He snatches his arm back. His eyes never leave mine.

'This is your fault. If I'd have been around, this would never have happened. This isn't the end of it.'

The nurses accompany him out. He glares at me through the window, his face hard with fury. He's not used to losing and certainly not to me.

I turn to Megan and pray none of this permeated her consciousness. I sit on her bed and lean over her, navigating the tubes and wires, to enclose her in my arms in an awkward one-sided embrace.

'I'm so sorry, Meggy. I didn't know he was going to be here.'

But it's too late. I've let her down again. That's what she said to me when she overheard my conversation with Sean at her school. *You always let me down*. And she's right.

I know what a monster Sean is. I should have known he would do something like this. I should have stopped him, but I didn't. I stood by and let it happen just like I did all those years ago. I didn't protect Megan from Sean and I didn't protect her from whoever did this to her.

I stroke Megan's hair releasing an almond aroma, her favourite shampoo.

'No more excuses, Megan. I promise.'

Holt appears in the doorway. I intercept him before he gets any further and we step into the corridor outside Megan's room.

'You OK? I heard there was a problem with your ex. He told the PC he was her dad, so he let him in. The idiot. He could have been anyone. Anyway, I've bollocked him for it. Your ex won't be allowed anywhere near her again.'

'Thanks.'

'How's Megan?'

My smile relaxes him slightly.

'Actually, she's starting to respond so the signs are positive. We've just got to wait.'

'Ally, that's great news.'

He's genuinely pleased. He's already lived this a hundred times in a hundred different cases, but when it's one of the police family it crosses some invisible threshold, and it's felt more keenly.

'What about you? How's the investigation going?'

Who did this to you, Megan?

'Good. So the blood on the steel pole found near the scene *is* Megan's. Jake also appears to have got a partial fingerprint from it.'

'That's good. Anything on the system?'

'No. Nothing. It's a good print, so whoever did this hasn't got a criminal record.'

I don't know why, but the news doesn't surprise me.

'OK.' My mind is still trying to wrap itself around the idea Megan's attacker dropped the weapon – complete with blood and fingerprints on it – but remembered to get rid of Megan's phone and not leave any other forensics at the scene. Did Jake miss something? He's very inexperienced. It's entirely possible. Holt told me he'd done the scene alone because they couldn't get hold of any CSIs from the south of the county to help and the weather was closing in. I don't blame Jake. I should have been there. 'Anything else? What about her laptop?'

'Digital forensics has turned her laptop inside out.'

'Did you get into her social media accounts?'

'We did.'

'And?'

His expression tells me it's not good news.

'*Nada*.'

'Nothing at all?'

'Nope. She didn't use social media that much. She's got a few pictures of Morte Sands on her Facebook and Instagram. A couple with her friends at the park. That's it.'

'What about her private messages?'

'The usual. Lots of conversations about the teachers she hates, the boys she fancies at school, how unreasonable you are etc., etc. Like I said, the usual.'

'Nothing else? No conversations about going to Barnston to see someone?' I ask.

'No. If she arranged to meet someone, she didn't do it through her social media.'

We both look at Megan like she's let us down.

'I don't understand it. I was sure you'd find something. Jay said he thought she was interested in someone.'

'You spoke to Jay Cox?'

'By accident. I happened to see him on my way back to Bidecombe this morning.'

Holt isn't happy about this but keeps it to himself.

'Well, if she was, she wasn't talking to him on Instagram. Everyone on her messaging system has been accounted for. Unless she has another account. Is that possible?'

'No, I don't think so. I don't know why she'd bother.'

'What about other devices? Although you can have more than one account on the same phone.'

'No, she only has one phone. If you let me have her social media passwords, I could take a look at those messages for you.'

'You know I can't do that.'

'Please, Bob. I'll have a far better chance than you guys of spotting something suspicious, something that doesn't sit right.'

'I'm not sure.'

'Look, we can just keep it between ourselves. If I see something, I'll tell you. If I don't, no harm done.'

He stares at me, weighing the options. Then he takes a pen and an old receipt from his pocket and jots down a jumble of letters and numbers and hands it to me.

'You didn't get this from me.'

'Thank you. I'll have a look later. So, what are your thoughts at the moment?'

'That she was in the wrong place at the wrong time.'

My insides cave. It's the theory detectives trot out when they don't have much of a clue. The victim was unlucky. It could have been anyone. The problem is it's rarely true. Most attackers know their victims, but I'm not going to argue. Holt doesn't have to tell me any of this. He's doing it because I'm in the job, but if I contradict him, he'll more than likely withdraw this privilege, so I go with it. For now.

'OK. Are there any witnesses?'

'None that have come forward.'

'Really? A young girl is attacked in broad daylight and no one saw anything?' Holt shrugs. It happens. 'So, what now?'

'We're running a reconstruction on tonight's news while it's still fresh in people's minds.' Kudos to Holt. He hasn't wasted any time.

'Great.'

'And we want you to go into the studio, make a direct appeal for people to come forward.'

He doesn't say any more. He doesn't have to. The mother

of a brutally attacked girl appearing live on TV? It's a ratings winner. We both know it.

'Of course.'

'Good. I'll pick you up at 5 p.m. and take you to the studio and bring you back to the hospital afterwards. Have you got someone who can sit with Megan?'

'My friend Penny will be here.'

'Good. We'll get him, Ally, I promise you.'

This is intended to lift my spirits and I oblige Holt with a smile so he leaves, content he's doing everything right and it's only a matter of time before Megan's attacker is caught, but I'm not so sure.

Something feels wrong, but I can't quite make it out. If only I'd attended the scene, I would know what it is, I'm sure of it. I would know why Megan's attacker dropped the weapon but managed to leave no other evidence behind.

31

When he wakes up, it's already early evening. Downstairs, there's a sound coming from the front room. For a moment, he thinks it's that dreadful Arjun as he's Jackie's only visitor, but that can't be right. Arjun was there this morning. He's not due again until tomorrow. He realizes the voices are coming from one of the televisions. Two of the screens are tuned to Morte Sands, all but empty at this time of day, but the third is tuned to the news.

'Why are you watching that rubbish?'

Jackie practically leaps out of her recliner.

'Oh. They're doing a reconstruction of that terrible attack on that girl. Didn't you attend that one?'

'You don't want to watch that nonsense. You'll only scare yourself.'

He goes to take the remote out of her hand.

'The mother's doing a special appeal.'

Her mother? He switches his attention to the screen. '. . . Still no concrete leads three days after it happened . . .' a lady with an immaculate blonde bob solemnly informs him.

'Maybe I'll watch a little longer. Just to keep you company.'

'That would be nice. Thank you.'

Lowering himself onto the flowery sofa, he knocks Laurel and Hardy to the floor.

'. . . We have in the studio, DI Holt who is leading the investigation, and Ally Dymond who is Megan's mum.'

The camera pans out. He catches his breath. It's Danielle, but it isn't. It's not just her hair and eyes, it's her air. She thinks she's better than everyone else. Just like Danielle.

'. . . But first we have a reconstruction of the events leading up to the attack . . .'

The film sequence begins to roll. They've found a good lookalike for her daughter. He'll give them that. Tall, red hair, it's hard to believe that mother and daughter are related. The lookalike goes into a newsagent and buys a chocolate bar. Yes, he remembers her chocolatey breath.

'I've been in that newsagent. Not for a while, but it makes you think, doesn't it?' Jackie tells the television.

The stand-in walks with purpose along the trail. That's all wrong. She was much more of a dawdler, reading her phone the whole time. Silly him, they won't know that, of course, will they?

Then a voice tells viewers to cast their minds back to the day of the attack. It had been a warm, but wet Tuesday. Wimbledon was on the television and that evening someone scooped £157 million on the EuroMillions.

'Lucky beggar,' mutters Jackie, popping a Haribo Gold Bear into her mouth.

The girl stands in the middle of the trail while the voiceover explains the route she took and how police believe she had arranged to meet someone there, but who? They even do that thing where the camera looks like someone is spying on her from a distance, but it's in the wrong place. He was at least another ten metres further along.

Then it ends. But they haven't shown her sitting on the bench. There's no mention of a man on a bike, either. Why not? Then he realizes why not. The police have nothing. They're so incompetent they've even missed the false trail he laid – the weapon with her blood on it and Benson's fingerprints – what more could they ask for? Peter has been pestering women for years, *surely* his prints are on file.

The lady with the blonde bob is talking again.

'DI Holt, this was a very brutal attack on a young girl. Local residents are frightened it may happen again. How close are you to finding the person that did this?'

The camera is on wide-angle, but he's not interested in the detective next to her and fixes on the CSI, but she may as well not be there for all the use she is. She's just staring down at her hands as if none of it is anything to do with her. You wouldn't know it was her child that had been attacked.

'Well, Suzy, I'd like to assure local residents that this is a very rare crime for this area and there's no reason to suspect it will happen again. Having said that, I can also assure you we're doing everything we can to apprehend Megan's attacker. We're working on a few theories which I can't talk about at the moment. That's why we've done the reconstruction. We have lots of information, but we need more. We need people to think about what they were doing that day. Were you in the area? Did you see Megan? Did you see anyone else in that area at that time? It was just after lunch, and it was drizzling quite hard, but there would have been people about.'

Still she keeps her head bowed. She's a waste of everybody's time. She just wants to be on TV, probably wants everyone to feel sorry for her.

'And you think someone close to Megan's attacker might suspect something. They might even be protecting them,' says the presenter.

'Poor love,' says Jackie, dropping another Haribo into her mouth.

'Yes, we think someone – a friend, a family member – must suspect something. He would have had blood on his clothing when he got home.'

A reaction. Barely perceptible, but he sees it. She tenses at the mention of blood, her jaw clenches. He smiles. She's trying to hold it all in.

'Please, an innocent girl was viciously attacked that day. We're appealing to anyone who may know something, have seen something, no matter how small, to contact us.'

'Thank you, DI Holt. Ally, would you like to say a few words? Perhaps you could tell us what kind of a girl Megan is? We understand she is still critical. How are you coping?'

He leans towards the television, ignoring a teddy in a soldier's uniform that tumbles off the sofa. She'll have to look up at the camera now. The presenter is addressing her directly. It'll be rude not to.

But she doesn't move. The presenter tries again.

'Ally, I know how hard this must be for you, but is there anything you'd like to say?'

What's she playing at? Even the detective looks embarrassed. The camera lingers on her and just as he's sure it's going to cut away, she looks up and there it is, right there, in her eyes. He knows that look; it's a look of defeat welded to acceptance of one's fate.

He sits back and lets her expression flow over him, as soothing as if he'd just injected himself with morphine.

'Megan is kind, loyal, funny, beautiful, infuriating – a normal teenager,' she says.

Not bad, but it has a rehearsed feel to it and is a little rushed. She needs to speak more slowly, with more emotion. Tears would be good. Even if she doesn't mean them. 'And she is very loved.'

Lies. The only person she loves is herself. She couldn't care less about her daughter, leaving her alone all the time. He wants to shout at the screen, 'TwilightSparkle hates you. She told me. She told me how you left her alone for hours on end, how you never had any time for her because you were always at work.'

'Poor lady. She's broken-hearted,' says Jackie.

'Yes, poor lady.'

The camera pans out. The detective throws a look at her and then the presenter as if to say, that's all you're going to get, but the newsreader ignores him.

'Take your time, Ally. Is there anything else you'd like to say to people watching this?'

The tips of her fingers dance around each other on her lap. The camera homes in on her once again, but it's obvious she isn't going to say any more.

He's been duped into watching a laughably inaccurate reconstruction and an emotionally stunted and media-obsessed mother. He stands up to leave, but then stops and lowers himself back down onto the sofa.

Something's changed. Her fingers are still. Slowly, deliberately, almost robotically, she raises her head. Her eyes. Her eyes are unblinking, defiant, no pain, no sorrow; her pupils are black with fury and she's staring right at him. Everything around him blurs.

'I know you're out there.' Good grief, she's talking directly to him. A heat rises from his neck to his face. 'But you will be caught—' She says this with absolute certainty, like it's inevitable.

She pauses a while, searching for the right words. No, he's wrong, she's already selected those. She's making sure she has his attention. The bitch has it all planned. She *knows* he's watching.

The camera closes in on her face, just as she expects it to. She stares down the lens at him. Now, it's just the two of them. Jackie has gone. The studio has gone. No one else exists. Her eyes anchor his.

'Because I'm coming for you.'

Penny is by Megan's bedside when I return from the TV studio. She immediately gets up and offers me her seat. I take it along with Megan's hand.

'How is she?'

'Good. I don't think she's moved again, but it's so difficult to tell.'

'She will.' I kiss Megan's forehead. 'Well done, love. Keep doing what you're doing.'

Penny sits in the armchair in the corner of the room.

'I watched the appeal on TV.' I nod. There's an unfamiliar terseness in her voice. 'So, what was all that "I'm coming for you" stuff at the end?'

'Honestly, I don't know.' That's the truth. I hadn't gone to the studio planning to do anything other than describe Megan, make her real to the viewers and convey my anguish in a way that would spur them to pause their lives and reach deep into their memories. But as I watched the reconstruction and I listened to Holt, it was obvious to me that the police have little to go on, and I became convinced Megan's attacker was watching

216

and would know that too. I couldn't bear the thought of him sitting on a sofa wearing the smuggest of smiles thinking he'd won. 'But Holt was furious with me. As soon as the cameras stopped rolling, he had a right go at me.' I couldn't blame him. Heartbreak gets results. Confrontation doesn't. 'He told me I'd jeopardized the investigation and if Megan's attacker was watching I might even have turned myself into a target which they could do without, seeing as they're already guarding Megan.'

'Maybe he's got a point.'

Her response takes me by surprise, so much so I think I've misheard.

'What do you mean?'

'Well, they've got enough on their plate without having to watch out for you too. Why don't you just let them get on with it?'

It irks me that Penny is siding with Holt. It's not as if the police did her any favours over her ex, Ian.

'Well, I would if—'

'If what?' she snaps.

I sense there's something else going on here that I'm not up to speed with, but I've no idea what.

'I don't think the investigation is going very well.' There, I've said it. It's not in the league of major cock-ups, but something isn't chiming. I wait for Penny's reaction to my revelation. There isn't one. It's like she hasn't heard me or hasn't understood the significance of what I'm saying so I fill her in. 'They haven't found Megan's phone. There's nothing on her laptop. They've no idea why she was there in the first place. Nobody seems to have seen anything. They don't have anyone in the frame. It's slipping away from them.'

'I thought the weapon had a fingerprint on it,' she offers, half-heartedly.

'It does, but—'

'But what?' There it is again, a shortness that wants to head off the conversation, but why? She must want to know who did this as much as me. I plough on.

'Something doesn't sit right. First rule of crime – get rid of the weapon. Second rule – wear gloves. This guy failed on both counts but managed not to leave a single shred of any other evidence at the scene.'

'Perhaps he panicked. Anything could have made him drop it.'

'Maybe. But I can't help thinking they've missed something.'

Penny is staring at me oddly.

'Leave it alone, Ally. Let them do their jobs.'

'Even if they're not doing them properly.'

'Even that,' she sighs. 'Megan needs you here, not swanning around the countryside playing Sherlock Holmes.'

Why is she saying this? This isn't like her. And I don't swan anywhere.

'It happens to be my job and there's nothing wrong with taking an interest in the investigation. This guy needs to be caught, Penny.'

'And that's exactly what the police will do and they don't need any help from you.'

'That's the point. They *do* need help.'

Penny shakes her head.

'I get it. You're a CSI, you want to do your bit to catch this guy.' She pauses. 'But you're a mother too. Maybe you need to remember that.'

32

So, the CSI thinks she's coming for him, does she? That's a joke. He'd like to see her try. What a stupid threat to make, and on television too. She made a complete fool of herself. She can come after him as much as she likes but she'll never catch him. She's not as smart as she thinks she is. None of them are. Didn't he just stand in her house, right in front of her, asking her about her daughter? She doesn't have a clue.

There's a tap on his window. It's Trisha. He rolls it down.

'Come on, Si, we've got work to do.'

He gets out of the car and the two of them stroll towards the hospital car park towards the ambulance station.

'Did you see that TV appeal last night on the young girl in the woods?'

'No,' he says.

'Poor kid. I hope they catch him, evil piece of shit. Who'd do that to an innocent young girl?'

But he isn't listening. Two people are standing outside the entrance to the ambulance station: a man in an ill-fitting grey suit, a long, thin layer of hair swept over a bald scalp, and a young woman in a blue jacket-and-skirt combo, her hair scraped back into a tight bun.

'That's the cop who was at the murder of that girl on Bidecombe Quay, isn't it?' says Trisha.

The detectives walk towards them. His insides flip, but he keeps his composure.

'Simon Pascoe? Trisha Wilkins?'

'Yes.'

'I'm Detective Inspector Bob Holt. This is acting DS Shirwell.' The young woman nods at them. 'Can I have a word with you?'

'Sure,' says Trisha.

'I don't know if you saw the TV appeal last night about the attempted murder of the schoolgirl, Megan Dymond.'

'Yes,' says Trisha.

'I'm afraid I didn't,' he says, 'I try to avoid them. My colleague and I were first on the scene.'

Don't hold information back. Give him more than he asks for. Make him think you can't do enough to help with his inquiries.

The detective gives him a sympathetic nod.

'That can't have been easy.'

'No. It wasn't.'

'Anyway, as a result of the appeal, we had a caller who said they saw an ambulance parked up in a lay-by near the back of Three Brethren Woods on the day of the attack.' He senses Trisha stiffen. 'Your boss, Colin, said it would mostly likely be you two. Apparently, it's a favourite place to stop for a bit of R&R.'

'That's correct, yes.'

'Can you tell me what time you got there?'

He turns to Trisha, but she's no help, staring at the detective, her face a pale round disc of fear.

'Let me think, Officer. We'd just come from a suspected heart attack at the old people's home just up the road in Fleetham, so it must have been around 3 p.m.'

'And how long were you parked there for?' asks Shirwell.

'Gosh, I'm not sure. An hour maybe. What do you think, Trisha?'

Without taking her eyes off Holt, Trisha agrees, 'No more than an hour.'

'And did you see anything?'

'No, nothing. Sorry,' says Trisha, but her hurry earns her a frown from the officer. He turns back to him.

'What about you, Mr Pascoe?'

He gives the question much thought: trying to appear as obliging as possible so the detective thinks he really wants to help.

'Actually, wait – yes, we did see something, or someone, now you come to mention it.'

'Really?'

The detectives swap side glances. He can practically smell their excitement and he pictures them, heading back to the office, self-satisfied and triumphant at their 'breakthrough'. This is too easy.

'Yes, a youngish-looking man. He stood out because he was cycling on the pavement and I remember thinking he was going a bit too fast.'

'Can you remember what he was wearing?'

'Yes. A bright red puffer jacket.' He nudges Trisha. 'You remember him, don't you?'

She looks at him.

'Er, yeah, now you come to mention it.'

'Which direction was he heading?'

'Towards the trail, I think. It was like he was late for something.'

'What did he look like?'

He sucks the air through his teeth.

'Difficult to say. It was raining. I didn't get a great look, but I'd say he's white, well-built, twenties, maybe older. Sorry, I can't be more specific, but he must have passed the Spar near the entrance to the trail so I'm guessing their CCTV will have picked him up.'

That last bit peps up the detectives even more.

'Thanks, you've both been really helpful.'

'No problem.'

He watches them walk across the hospital car park with a haste that suggests they think they're onto something. Idiots. So easily fooled. Call themselves detectives. They couldn't see through a spring-cleaned window.

Trisha lets out a long sigh.

'Fuck, that was close. Thank you, Simon, thank you, thank you. I owe you. Shit, if Colin finds out I went shopping on work time, I'll be out. He's already pissed off with me.'

'It's no problem. What are friends for? And he's not going to find out. No one is.'

'Thanks, Si. She nudges him playfully. 'And you might just have solved an attempted murder. The detective was really interested in this kid on the bike. From now on, I'll call you Simon, the super sleuth.'

Sometimes, he wishes Trisha would just shut up. For good.

33

Holt finds me in the hospital cafeteria, grabbing a coffee while the nurses tend to Megan. I haven't seen him since the TV studios and if he's still angry with me, he doesn't show it. In fact, he looks positively upbeat. He drags the chair from underneath the table and sits down in front of me.

'I hear Megan's making good progress.'

'Yes, she is. Her eyes twitched again this morning. Just for a moment.'

I was reading a book she loved as a child, *Guess How Much I Love You*. I haven't read it in years, but I found it in the hospital library and remembered Megan's joy at the idea of Little Nutbrown Hare measuring his love for Big Nutbrown Hare to the moon and back. Megan told me she loved me all the way to the other side of the Bristol Channel and back which she estimated was much further than the moon. As soon as I started it, her eyelashes quivered. The smallest movement that took my breath away. I stopped reading for a moment, but then continued and it happened again. Megan is on her way back to me.

'Is there any chance she'll remember any of it when she wakes up?'

'The consultant says it's very unlikely and, you know, I'm not sure I want her to.'

Holt looks at me. We both know that if Megan remembers the attack, it could be key to catching her attacker, but she's my daughter and I can't bear the thought that it might play on repeat in her head forever.

'Yeah, I can see that. Look, I'm sorry I flew off the handle after the TV appeal yesterday. You're under a lot of stress and it makes people say all sorts of things. I shouldn't have shouted at you. I was just worried that it could have a really negative effect on the case. You know the deal. People want to see victims' families hurting, not fighting back.'

'And did it?'

'Did it what?'

'Did my threat to go after Megan's attacker have a negative effect?'

'Actually, no, it didn't, not if the number of calls we've had is anything to go by, I guess.'

'Anything useful?'

'We're following everything up, but we did get one call in particular. A resident from the housing estate above Three Brethren Woods said they saw an ambulance parked at the end of the street. Apparently, they park there a lot as it's a quiet spot to have lunch and they're close to the main road out of Barnston, if they get called up.'

'Ah yes, a guy I know is going out with one of the paramedics that attended Megan. He mentioned it. I should have told you, I guess, but it didn't seem relevant.'

'You've got other things on your mind, Ally. Anyway, we've just spoken to the paramedics.'

I'm sure I can detect a slight excitement in his voice.

'And?'

'And they saw someone. A man on a bike riding towards the trail just a few minutes before Megan was attacked. They didn't get a good look at him, but he's showed up on the CCTV outside the Spar. We're trying to get an ID on him now. Might be nothing, but no one matching his description has come forward to be eliminated.'

'That's good news.'

'I thought you'd like to know. Obviously, I'll let you know as soon as we have more, but I've got a good feeling about this one.'

'Thanks. I'd appreciate that.'

'I'll be in touch.'

He gets up.

'What do you mean by "they"?' I ask.

'Sorry?'

'You said *they* saw a man on a bike.'

'The paramedics. They were parked up in that housing estate on the hill behind the woods having lunch when they saw this guy.'

'But there was only one of them.'

'What?'

'Trisha was with a patient. Her boyfriend told me. The other paramedic, Simon Pascoe, was alone when he got the call.'

Jackie is in her reclining chair, as usual. As he walks into the living room, she looks up and smiles hopefully. He knows what she's after.

'I haven't had time to get you any sweets,' he snaps. His conversation with the detectives had put him in a good mood, but a day of Trisha banging on about how good Gary is in the sack meant it hadn't lasted long. 'And don't start blubbering. You're a grown woman, for goodness' sake. It's pathetic.'

She sniffs hard and nods in agreement.

'Yes, I'm sorry.'

There's an aroma of juniper in the air.

'I take it that Arjun fella has been in again, giving you another foot massage.'

'Yes.'

He picks up one of her teddies. It's wearing an eye patch and a blue jacket with gold epaulettes and buttons: Nelson, he guesses.

'Are you sure there's nothing going on between you two?'

She looks at him in horror.

'No, no, Simon. Never.'

'You're always going on about him. I reckon you're seeing him behind my back.'

Jackie searches out several shafts of her hair, wraps them around her forefinger and gives them a sharp tug. They come away easily and she slides the prize into her mouth. She doesn't even know she's doing it. The hairball inside her must be enormous.

'No, no. I would never do anything like that. He's just nice to me, that's all.'

His eyes are fixed on Nelson.

'How nice, though? That's the question.'

'It's not like that. He's my friend. He keeps me company.'

'I told you, he's paid to do that. Do you think he'd come here for free?'

Her fingers re-explore the moonscape that is her scalp, searching out a strand.

'No,' she says quietly.

226

He's bored of their conversation, bored of her fawning over Arjun.

'I've got work to do. Oh, and I've been asked to do extra shifts, so I won't be around much for the next few weeks.'

'Can't someone else do it? They always ask you. Couldn't they ask Trisha?'

He hasn't been asked at all. He volunteered to increase his chances of meeting someone suitable. Colin snapped his hand off, of course, telling him how the NHS was lucky to have such a dedicated paramedic.

'No, I'm the only one who knows what they're doing.'

He turns to leave.

'Don't go, Simon.' Her eyes shine with tears. 'Stay with me a little longer. I get so lonely here on my own all day.'

'Well, maybe you should give your friend Arjun a call then,' he says, tossing Nelson to one side.

He leaves, but at the top of the stairs he pauses and takes his phone out. He should have done this weeks ago.

'Bidecombe Carers?'

'Yes.'

'I'd like to speak to the manager.'

34

The path down to Breakneck Point is so steep I have to tackle it sideways or the incline will convey me all the way down and over the cliff, if I'm not careful. Our bench is stationed at the lowest point of the path, but it is still high above the waves below.

Megan is making such good progress the consultant suggested I go home for a rest. I couldn't leave her alone – not even now when the news is so positive – but I found myself suddenly yearning to walk along the cliffs where I could give myself up to the cool breeze sweeping in from the Channel, rinsing my hair and clothes of the cloying smell of hospital disinfectant.

I thought about asking Bernadette to come in and watch over Megan. She has been in a few times to see her, but it's taking its toll on her. She doesn't stay long and I wonder if this is because she fears the sight of Megan will break her if she lingers, so I called Penny instead. If my friend was still annoyed with me about my television performance, she didn't show it. Instead, she agreed that the break would do me the power of good. Thirty minutes later she walked into Megan's room.

I sit down on the bench, its aged and faded wood is rough, but so familiar to my touch. Names, dates, hearts, even the odd penis have been penknifed into it over the years, a biography of lives.

I remember the first time we came here. I lifted Megan up onto it and her legs dangled over the edge. We shielded our eyes from the sun to look out to sea across the Bristol Channel to the Welsh coast, wondering if anyone was sitting on a bench on the other side, looking back at us.

Just in case, hands cupped around our mouths, we shouted hello into the sea breeze and waved like we needed rescuing. We didn't want the people who lived there to think we were unfriendly.

Then Megan asked me if I'd take her to the land on the other side of the water and I said I would. She swung her legs backwards and forwards with excitement. 'We could go in a yellow submarine.'

'Well, I'm not sure where to buy a yellow submarine, but Penny has a blue boat. Perhaps we could ask her to take us.'

Megan clapped.

'Yes! Let's.'

Since then, over the years, this old bench has silently charted Megan's life: who she's inviting to her ninth birthday party, how her real dad can't love her because if he did, he'd come and see her, what friends she'll make at secondary school, the period talk, the sex talk – there is nothing this bench doesn't know about our lives.

Jobs? Megan was always changing her mind. When she was little, she wanted to run a café and call it The Yellow Submarine, but she told Jay she wanted to be a CSI. She'd be good too. She's tenacious, like me. Marriage? Never, she said. I take responsibility for that one. Sean and I were enough to kill anyone's idea of a happy ever after. Babies? Disgusting, she told me not six months ago. I thought the same at her age, but when she was little she planned to have two children and call them Desmond and Molly, two characters from the Beatles song 'Ob-La-Di, Ob-Lah-Da'. Penny has a lot to answer for. One would have auburn hair like her, the other would be dark like me.

I smile at the memories, but they quickly fade.

Who did this to you, Megan?

There it is. That question. Always there, loitering in the foreground of my mind, seeking my attention.

Whoever he is, he knows Megan personally. I'm sure of it. That's the only explanation as to why she went to Three Brethren Woods. She went there to meet someone. So, does he go to her school? No, the registers have been checked and revealed nothing more sinister than the usual round of doctors' and dentists' appointments. So, is he a friend of mine? Surely, he's not one of my Tinder disasters. No, that's not possible. I don't even use my real name and I've always been very careful not to reveal details about myself. None of them knew I had a teenage daughter. So, how does Megan know him? If she didn't meet him online, where did she meet him?

A voice tramples over my questions. It's Liam. I haven't seen him since I came here after Cheryl Black's death.

'Sorry, didn't mean to startle you. I thought I was the only person who came here. How's Megan?'

'Getting there. She's moving her eyes.'

'That's great to hear.'

He sits down next to me on the bench.

'I saw the TV appeal.'

'Are you going to give me a lecture about compromising the investigation too?'

Liam frowns.

'No. I'd have done the same. In fact, I'd have gone further. I'd have told the bastard that when I find him, I'll kill him.'

I look at Liam. I never had him down as the violent type, but his anger over Megan is genuine and I believe him.

'Thanks. Not sure what Holt would have done if I'd said that. He already thinks I've blown the investigation.'

'And how is the investigation going?'

He's the first person to have asked me, but he's an ex-cop. He gets it and it's a relief to be able to talk freely about it without feeling guilty that I've shifted the conversation away from Megan's prognosis and progress.

'Honestly? Not great. First, they thought Megan was meeting someone she'd found online, but there's nothing on her laptop. Now they think she was in the wrong place at the wrong time.'

'It happens.'

'Yes, it does, but it doesn't explain why she randomly got on a bus and travelled sixteen miles to Barnston to walk along the trail.'

'Teenagers aren't the most rational of people.'

'True, but in my experience, they also don't exert themselves without reason either. Something's wrong.'

'What do you mean?'

'For a start, her attacker dropped the weapon with a fingerprint on it.'

'Sounds like a schoolboy error.'

'Exactly, but the rest of the scene was clean, apparently.'

'Apparently?'

'What criminal does something as basic as dropping their weapon, but remembers to get rid of any other forensic evidence? None of it adds up to me.'

'Bob Holt's the SIO. I can see why you're worried.'

'Yeah, he wants to solve it – of course he does – but I'm not sure that he's up to the job. I just hope I'm wrong.'

'Did the TV appeal lead to anything?'

'Yes, it did. Someone rang in saying they'd seen someone on a bike heading towards the trail which at least gives them something to go on, but that's it and the only thing I can do about it is make idle threats on TV. To be honest, you're the first person I've spoken to about this. Penny isn't interested and I try to avoid speaking to Bernadette about anything.'

He looks at me intently.

'You know I'm always here if you need someone to talk to.'

I sense that if I accept Liam's offer, he would play a much bigger part in my life which isn't an unpleasant thought but, for some reason, I can't bring myself to open up to him, not in the way I suspect he wants me to, so all I offer in return is a non-committal smile and a 'thanks'.

Besides, the mention of their names has resurrected my uncomfortable conversations with Bernadette and Penny.

'What is it?' he asks.

'Nothing, just Bernadette being Bernadette. She thinks it's my fault that Megan was attacked because I'm never around.'

'Jesus. That's a bit of a quantum leap.'

'I know and I wouldn't take much notice normally – you know what she's like – but Penny then said I needed to leave the investigation to the police and be a mum to Megan. It feels like she blames me too.' I shift around on the bench to face him. 'There's a part of me that can't help wondering if they may be right.'

He raises a hand to interrupt.

'Whoa. Hang on a second. That's rubbish. Teenagers are devious so-and-sos and – for what it's worth – I think you're a fantastic mother. I've watched you both on Morte Sands for years now. You have an amazing bond with Megan. God, I'd love to have that relationship with my two girls. Since I split with their mum and she took them back up north, I'm not much more than a FaceTime father. Their digital dad.'

I knew Liam had kids; I've seen the messy-haired, toothy-grinned photos in the van, but he never talks about them.

'I'm sorry. I didn't know.'

He shrugs it off.

'It's OK, we make it work, sort of. Summer's tough because the Coffee Shack is 24/7, but I try to make up for it in the winter. What I'm trying to say is, there's nothing wrong with your relationship with Megan. Bernadette and Penny are missing the point and so are you.'

'What do you mean?'

'The reason you want to find out who hurt Megan so badly isn't because you're a CSI. It's precisely because you are her mother.'

When I get back to the cabin, there's a letter waiting for me on my doormat – delivered by hand. From my doorway, I check the site to see if the person who delivered it is still around, but there's no one. It's too official-looking for it to be a get well soon card for Megan and I consider leaving it, but maybe it's a bill. Despite the catastrophes that happen in life, debts still need to be paid.

But it's not a bill. It's from a solicitor's firm in Barnston, writing on behalf of Sean Parker. The last time I saw his name on a document it was to inform me my divorce had come through, so what the hell does he want with me now?

Bad news is best delivered quickly, so I scan it. Words like 'court order' and 'parental care' leap out at me until I begin to understand that they form the basis of a demand. Oh God, Sean's applying for custody of Megan. This is a joke, right? He's not been in Megan's life for eight years and even then his idea of fatherhood was to beat her mother, putting the fear of God into her. But it's no joke. It's there in black and white. Ludicrous as it sounds, six years of parenting someone else's daughter means he has a claim. Sean is planning to take Megan away from me.

My hands tremble at the thought of Sean anywhere near Megan. Who the fuck does he think he is? Shortly after I left him, I heard he'd got a job upcountry somewhere and I thought I was rid of him for good. Now, after all these years, he's waltzed right back into our lives, making demands like he's entitled to have a say in the life of a girl who isn't even his blood relative. How dare he? But he has dared because he can. He thinks he has a chance. Just like Bernadette and Penny, Sean thinks I can't look after my daughter properly. He thinks it's my fault she was attacked. I can picture him with his mates down the pub. 'It would never have happened if I'd still been around.' Well, screw him.

I should call him up, tell him that hell would have to freeze over twice before I let him anywhere near Megan, but

I haven't the energy. The consultant's confidence in Megan's recovery allowed me to relax the tiniest amount and just enough to open the sluice gates that have so far contained my exhaustion. I just need a few minutes rest then I can deal with Sean. I can deal with them all.

I lie down on the brown sofa knowing that not even its lumpiness can keep me awake and Sean's letter slips from my hand.

35

Someone has buzzed the front door, but he's not expecting anybody. They don't have visitors. Not any more. Margaret, a friend of Jackie's mother, used to drop by when they were first married, until he told Jackie that Margaret said her efforts to make a cake for the church cake sale looked like vomit. She didn't really say that, of course, but it was enough for Jackie to refuse to open the door to her and, in the end, she stopped coming round. Perhaps it's the odious Arjun come to flirt some more with Jackie.

He calls out to Jackie that he's 'got it' and opens the door to find the detective on his doorstep, smoothing his ridiculous hair into place. Keep calm. He can't know anything. This is just a routine call. No one ever suspects a paramedic.

'Evening, Detective Inspector.'

'Mr Pascoe. I'm sorry to bother you at home.'

'That's no trouble at all. I wasn't busy. How can I help you?'

He doesn't want to let him in because when he leaves Jackie will be all over him, asking stupid questions.

'I wanted to clarify something you said earlier.'

'Oh?'

'Yes, you said that you and your colleague were having lunch together in the ambulance in the lay-by on the housing estate that joins Three Brethren Woods. Is that right?'

He holds the officer's gaze. Why would he ask him that? He's already told him what happened. Then he understands. The detective knows he was lying, but *how* does he know? Trisha shooting her mouth off, no doubt.

He needs to think fast. He shakes his head.

'Actually, no, Detective Inspector, that's not right. I was alone.'

'Can I ask why you lied to me?'

'Yes. I was protecting my co-worker, Trisha Wilkins.'

'And why would that be?'

'She went shopping on work time. She's already on a final warning. If our boss, Colin, found out she'd be sacked so I covered for her. I know I shouldn't have. I can see it was a serious lapse of judgement. I was just trying to help Trisha.'

'You do know it's an offence to lie to the police?'

'I'm sorry, but I didn't think it would make much difference. I saw the man on the bike. That's all true. What's going to happen to me?'

'Nothing. This time.'

It is, as he thought, an empty threat, just a cop wanting to make a point, but he lets out a loud sigh of relief.

'Thank you. Thank you so much. My wife is disabled. If anything happened to me, I dread to think how she would manage.'

'OK, but can I strongly advise you not to lie in the future. Another officer might not be so sympathetic. Anyway, I won't take up any more of your time.'

He turns to leave.

'Yes, Detective Inspector, you're quite right. It was a spur-of-the-moment thing and I'm proud of Trisha for speaking up.'

The detective pauses.

'It wasn't your co-worker that told us. Ms Wilkins' boyfriend mentioned it to the mother of the girl who was attacked, but it's all sorted now and, as you say, the information about the man on the bike has been very useful. Anyway, I'll leave you in peace.'

Simon closes the door behind him and leans against it.

'Who was it, my love?' Jackie calls from the front room.

'No one important, but I have to go out.'

'It's late,' she shouts back.

He doesn't reply but grabs the car keys and leaves. He's under-estimated her, but he won't make the same mistake twice.

Sliding out from behind the thick trunk of a pine tree, the clear night sky and full moon light his path to her bedroom window. The curtains aren't drawn. Why would they be? No one can see in. The nearest cabin is forty metres away and barely visible through the trees.

Her bedroom is empty. There's no one in.

He moves to the side of the small wooden structure and peers into the living-room window. There's the round dining table to one side and at the back of the room the kitchen counter jutting out from the wall. Behind it, in the shadows is the kitchenette that's nothing more than a nod to those tourists who prefer to cook than have takeaways. His eye falls on the sofa that's too large for the room. There's something piled up to one side. At first, he dismisses it as cushions and throws, but as he looks closer he can see it's a person, curled up, fast asleep. It's her. It's the CSI.

He moves to the front of the building. A solar light attached to a tree throws a watery white light around the veranda, so he has to be quick, although there's no need to break in. He still has TwilightSparkle's keys. She might have changed the locks, of course, but he doubts it. He guesses she has other things on her mind right now and he's right. The key slides silently into the lock and turns.

The cabin is made of wood, but that works in his favour. She'll be used to creaks and knocks at all hours of the day and night. A few extra aren't going to rouse her.

Once inside, the moonlight seeps through the window illuminating the hallway past the kitchen area. There are three doors leading off it. The CSI's room is the door to the left. The door opposite, he guesses, is her daughter's room. He knows he shouldn't, but he can't resist taking a peek.

On the wall above a bed framed in fairy lights is a notice board, pinned with photos of TwilightSparkle-hugging, similar-looking girls, sticking their chests out and pouting like wannabe porn stars. There's a poster that says GIRLS KICK ASS and several pictures of horses. On the dressing table there's a heart-shaped photo frame. The photo inside has been taken on a beach. It's her and the CSI. The two of them are clinging onto each other, laughing. There's a phrase written around the end of the frame. *Memories are made with the ones you love.*

He makes his way back into the living room. Each step slow and measured, it will take just one loose board to loudly betray him.

She's lying on the sofa on her side, her dark hair splayed on the cushion. She looks so like Danielle. It's the chin – pointed and determined, even in their sleep. They could be sisters.

He would watch Danielle sleeping too. He liked to study the smooth contours of her face: the gentle slope of her forehead, the curve of her brow bone, the straightness of her nose and the smooth rise of her lips. Sometimes she would open her eyes and freak out to find his face inches from hers and the moment would be ruined. Danielle was always better when she was asleep.

He kneels beside the sofa level with the CSI. Her breathing is so light, it's barely audible and there's no rise and fall in her chest. He leans in closer. He can't feel her breath on his cheeks. She's so still she looks dead.

Oh my. The rush is so sudden and surprising that he springs backwards onto his heels and almost loses his balance. The blood pumps into his groin and his breath shortens to a gasp. Through his trousers, he's already pushing and straining to be released. How can this be happening?

His hand reaches down to his fly. He's hard, harder than he can ever remember being. Even in the early days with Danielle, it was never like this. He stares at the CSI like she's cast some spell over him. How can this be?

Before he can comprehend what's happening, his hand dives under his belt and he reaches inside his pants. His other hand reaches for her.

36

A persistent knocking sound reverberates inside my head until I realize it isn't a dream and I open my eyes. The clock on the wall says 10 a.m. I've been asleep for twelve hours. My phone contains numerous missed calls from Penny and texts swerving between anger and terror:

> Where the hell are you? You said you'd only be a few hours.

> Are you OK? That's it. I'm calling the police.

The banging grows insistent and is accompanied by Holt's voice.

'Ally, it's Bob. Are you OK? Can you open the door?'

By the time I bring myself to a sitting position, Penny's master key is already in my lock and the door flies open. She rushes towards me. Behind her is Holt.

'Thank God, you're all right,' she says, throwing her arms around me. 'When you didn't answer my calls, I thought something must have happened to you.'

I rub the sleep from my eyes with the base of my palm. My heart is still pounding from being woken so abruptly.

'I'm fine. Who's with Megan?'

'Bernadette. Sorry. I had to call her. I was worried about you, so I called DI Holt.'

She's beside herself. I place my hand on her arm.

'No, I'm sorry. I didn't mean to frighten you. I must have fallen asleep on the sofa.' I pull my head from side to side to work a crick out. 'Bob, you've had a wasted journey, too, I'm afraid.'

'No need to apologize. I was on my way over anyway when Penny called.'

'Oh?'

He smiles.

'You might want to sit down.'

'I'm OK standing.'

'We've got him, Ally.'

The oxygen leaves my body.

'What?'

My head is light and I'm teetering. Penny plants a firm arm around my shoulders and steadies me.

'You OK?'

'Yeah, thanks, I just wasn't expecting it, that's all.'

'We're only questioning him at the moment, but we're quietly confident he's our man.'

'So, it's over,' says Penny.

'Who is it?' Holt must have anticipated that I would ask this, but he still hesitates. I don't blame him, but I need to know. 'It's OK. I'm not going to do anything stupid to undermine the investigation. I probably don't know him anyway.'

'His name is Peter Benson.'

But I do know him. Everyone knows him.

'Peter Benson?'

He's maybe not the last person I would consider capable of murder, but he's still fairly far down on the list. Even Penny frowned at the sound of his name.

'You do know him, then?'

'Yes. Everyone does. He has learning difficulties. He likes to ride his bike around town.'

'That's the one. Thirty-six years old. Lives with his mum, still.'

He says this as if it seals his guilt.

'And you ID'd him from the CCTV.'

'Yep, it's definitely him. He's denying everything, of course, but it doesn't matter. He's going down for this.'

'So, had he arranged to meet Megan on the trail?'

'Yes, he's admitted meeting her. He even bought her a packet of Minstrels.'

This is sounding more bizarre by the minute. There is no way Megan would knowingly meet Peter Benson on a trail just outside Barnston. Minstrels or no Minstrels.

'So, what happened?'

'He said she was very rude to him, so he just cycled off back to Bidecombe. He swears he didn't touch her.'

'OK.'

'There's something else.'

'What's that?'

Holt smiles.

'That fingerprint on the side of the steel pole. It's his.'

Penny lets out a breath.

'So, it is him.'

'Yes.'

'He wasn't already on file then?'

'No. He'd been warned a few times against harassing women,

but it never got as far as a caution. This isn't confirmed yet, but we're also fairly certain the pole came from his shed. It's part of an old trampoline. We've also seized his computer and his phone. The techies are already looking at them. His ISP records show his browsing history, and he was definitely on Instagram a lot in the run-up to Megan's attack.'

He pauses. There's more, but he's holding back.

'What is it?'

'He visited other sites, too, including a website about the best way to kill someone.'

'Oh my God,' says Penny.

'And you think he met Megan online, through Instagram, and then groomed her?'

'We think so, although he's adamant he's never been on Instagram. He's also saying he never accessed those other websites either, but it's definitely his IP address so it's either him or his mum.'

'So, have you got into his Instagram account?'

'Not yet. He won't give us his details. He didn't access it using either his computer or his phone, so we think he was using another device which we haven't found it yet, but we will.'

'But you already checked Megan's Instagram messages. There was nothing suspicious in them, either.'

'That's true. I know I asked this before, but is it possible Megan has another account?'

'Maybe, but I can't think of a reason why she would do this, though. Like I said, I didn't know her password so I couldn't have read her private messages anyway. I trusted her.'

He shrugs.

'To be honest, it doesn't matter. We've got his fingerprints on the weapon which came from his shed and an eyewitness putting him near the scene, that's more than enough. The CPS will think it's Christmas.' He's right. In murder investigation terms, this is top-drawer evidence. 'Don't worry, we'll get to the bottom of his Instagram account.' Holt is waiting for me to respond, but my head is still whirring which he interprets as doubt. 'It's him, Ally. I promise you. And, before you ask, I also spoke to Simon Pascoe and asked him why he lied to us.'

Simon Pascoe. I'd forgotten about him.

'And what did he say?'

'To be honest, he was bricking it. Couldn't apologize enough for his serious lapse in judgement, as he called it. He was covering for his co-worker who'd bunked off to go shopping. Apparently, she's on a last warning.'

'OK. That makes sense.'

'Look, I've got to get back to the station. You take care of yourself, OK? If you need a FLO to come out and be with you, let me know.'

I watch Holt leave. Peter Benson. Peter. Benson. Whatever I was expecting, it wasn't this, but Holt is certain he attacked Megan. He somehow groomed her online and arranged to meet her in Three Brethren Woods. He cycled there, having taken a metal pole from his shed, and he attacked her. Then he got rid of her phone.

Penny hugs me.

'Isn't that great news?' she breathes. 'Now, we can just focus on Megan getting better. That's all that matters, which reminds me, Bernadette wants you back at the hospital at ten. Apparently, she's got book club at eleven. Ally?'

'Sorry, my mind was elsewhere.'

'What is it? What's wrong?'

I look at Penny. She isn't going to like what's coming next, but I have to do this. Liam is right. I need to know who did this to Megan, not because I'm a CSI, but because I'm her mother. 'Can you go back to the hospital and I'll meet you there in a bit?'

'What? Why?'

'Please.'

Penny's shoulders sag.

'Ally, Megan needs you.'

'I promise. I'll be an hour. Tops. I wouldn't ask if it wasn't important.'

She's about to protest further, but stops herself, knowing it's a waste of breath and she's right. My mind was made up as soon as Holt said it was Peter Benson who attacked Megan.

37

He checks the tyres on the back of the ambulance and as he straightens himself he catches his reflection in the side mirror. He looks pale.

He's still feeling out of sorts. It was a strange night. Not what he was expecting at all and he still doesn't know what came over him. Why her? Was it her resemblance to Danielle? He didn't know, but thank God, he realized what was happening before it was too late. It certainly won't happen again.

Trisha's bright red face appears from round the back of the ambulance.

'I don't fucking believe it.'

'What's happened?'

'Some dickhead has only gone and complained to Colin about me and Gary behaving inappropriately during work time.'

'What?' He shakes his head in disbelief when he couldn't be more delighted. Colin had taken his complaint seriously when he spoke to him the previous day. 'That's terrible. Who would do such a thing?'

'I don't know, but when I get my hands on them, I'll bloody murder them.'

'So what did Colin say?'

'He was right out of line. Said we'd been seen snogging behind the station and that I was being unprofessional. Told me off like I was fourteen. He even told me Gary had a terrible reputation with women and I should tread carefully.'

'Is that true?'

'No. Anyway, I called Gary, he's on earlies too, and he's furious. He's all for coming over and giving Colin a piece of his mind, but I said to him, Babe, I appreciate it, but you'll just make things worse.'

'Poor Gary, but you're right. It wouldn't solve anything. So, did Colin suspend you?'

'No, thank God, but he said that if he gets any more complaints about my behaviour, that'll be it for me.'

'You're kidding.'

'No. I'm right upset about it. I've a good mind—'

A radio in the cab buzzes into life. He nips round to the front and picks up the handset. A girl has gone off the cliffs near Breakneck Point. She's alive, but they're not sure how badly injured she is. All he hears is: *a girl.* The news stokes his heart. A glimmer of hope. His decision to take on extra shifts looks like it could be about to pay out.

Twenty minutes later, the ambulance pulls up in the beach car park below the cliffs. He can't wait to get out, not just because of his excitement at what awaits but because Trisha's anger at being disciplined by Colin subsided by the time they left Barnston and she returned to her favourite topic of conversation: how good Gary is at oral sex. 'Most men are all fingers and thumbs, working a fanny like Play-Doh, but Gary just seems to know what I like.' Her crudity is repulsive. Nothing is off limits. He can't believe Colin didn't suspend her. What a spineless man he is.

Directed by the car park attendant, they lug their equipment up a narrow lane towards Breakneck Point, a chunk of the cliff that juts out into the sea. The coastguard rescue team in their red uniforms and white helmets are clustered around the top of the cliff guiding them to the right spot.

When the team leader spots them, he peels away from the group and approaches them, rope slung over his shoulder.

'She's about fifteen metres down on a narrow ledge. One of our guys has reached her. She's conscious, but we don't want to move her until one of you have had a look. The plan is to lower one of you on a rope. If not, we'll have to get the chopper out.'

He steps forward immediately, not that Trisha would volunteer. Far too much effort.

'There's no need. I'll go.'

Trisha grabs his arm.

'Si, you sure about this?'

'You'll be secured at all times, but your partner's right, you don't have to do this.'

'Look, we don't know what her injuries are, which means we can't afford to waste any more time.'

The man slaps him on the back.

'Thanks, mate.'

They spend a few minutes kitting him out and testing the clasps and ropes before finishing with a crash course in abseiling.

When they're ready, he leans back into the void. One of the coastguards feeds the rope through his hands and he begins to descend, his feet walking himself down the cliff face.

He draws level with the girl. She's curled up on a narrow ledge, but when she sees him, she lifts her head; her eyes are wide with fear. She's perfect.

'It's OK. Everything's going to be fine now.'

His toe catches the ledge and he uses the grip to inch himself in until he's standing securely on it. The girl instinctively moves towards him.

'No. Stay where you are. I'll come to you. You're safe now.'

Still attached to the harness, he kneels down beside her.

'What's your name?'

'Gemma.'

'OK, Gemma, we're going to get you out of here.' The girl manages a weak smile. 'Does it hurt anywhere?'

'My head.'

He removes the rucksack from his back, fishes out a pair of gloves and slips them on. Parting her fair hair, he tries to concentrate on a deep gash along her hairline, but inside he's giddy with excitement.

'That's a nasty cut. OK, Gemma, can you tell me what day it is?'

'Saturday,' she says immediately.

'Excellent. And the month?'

'July.'

She's eager to please.

'Good. Can you tell me your address?'

'Fifty-six Doone Way, Bidecombe.'

He takes a small torch from his pocket and, gently holding her upper eyelid, shines it into her left eye.

'Just off Williamson Drive? That's near me.'

The torch switches to her right eye.

'OK, we've done the easy ones. Let's try something a bit harder. Let me think . . .' He pretends to think. 'Ah yes, I bet you can't tell me your Instagram handle?'

'TruffleDelite,' she announces without a second thought.

'Good.' He puts his torch away. 'Although I'll have to take your word for it. Bet you can't spell it, though.'

'T-r-u-f-f-l-e-D-e-l-i-t-e.'

'That's an odd one, but very good. OK, let's get you out of here.' He presses the button on his radio. 'Patient conscious, but she has a head injury. There's no obvious signs of concussion. It's hard to say what other injuries she's got. I'll need a neck brace and a backboard just in case she's damaged her spine.'

'On its way.'

'The stretcher's on its way right now, Gemma. So, what happened?'

'I was out walking. I took a selfie and must have got too close to the edge.'

He senses that's not the whole story.

'Did you black out?'

'I'm not sure. Maybe.'

The stretcher is just a few metres above them.

'OK, TruffleDelite, just a few more minutes and we'll have you out of here. I need you to stay awake for me. So, what's your boyfriend called? Snizzlewhizzle909?'

The girl smiles coyly.

'No.'

She's holding something back.

'Something you want to tell me? It won't go any further. I promise.'

She drops her eyes and blushes.

'I wasn't taking a selfie. I was running away.'

'Why were you running away?'

'Because my parents have banned me from seeing my boyfriend and I'm sick of them telling me what to do.'

'Well, I'm sure they only want what's best for you.'

Her eyes are damp with tears.

'They're horrible about him, having a go about him all the time. I couldn't stand it. I came up here to get away from them.'

'Well, don't worry, everything's going to be fine now. I'm here to save you.'

He grabs the stretcher and pulls it towards them.

38

Three Brethren Woods occupies a stretch of steep slope on the edge of Barnston between a housing estate and the old railway line that's been converted into a trail, fringing the estuary the town stands on.

A thin strip of plastic police tape still knotted to a branch acts as a helpful marker, guiding the ghouls to gawp at the site of Megan's attack. I rip it off and stuff it into my jacket pocket. My daughter is not entertainment.

I'm about to step across the unseen threshold into the crime scene, when I stop myself. I know I shouldn't be here. Not just because I'm Megan's mum, although that is reason enough, but because this isn't my crime scene. It's Jake's and I should respect that. I have no business being here. If I thought he'd missed something I should have asked him to check again. That said, I'm not doing anything illegal. That's what I tell myself as I take the next step.

Crime scenes are examined mostly before the perpetrator has been identified, but Peter Benson has all but been charged with Megan's assault. I start with Peter Benson.

According to Holt, he cycled along the trail to meet Megan. He propositioned her and she told him where to go. In a fit of anger, he dragged her the ten or so metres up a steep slope to a very conveniently placed clearing.

The clearing is ringed by beech trees, their foliage meshed into a deep rich green wall that hides it from the trail. A dense canopy overhead stifles the sunlight. Accessible, but completely secluded. It's a good choice.

But I have a question. What did Peter do with his bike? He wouldn't have been able to drag both Megan and his bike into the woods so he must have left it on the trail, risking it being seen. Another schoolboy error, as Liam would say.

It had rained that day, softening the ground which means it would have been near impossible to pass through here without leaving a foot impression, but Holt said the shoeprints had been photographed and all been accounted for. None belonged to Peter Benson. So, did Jake miss one? Did he check beyond the clearing? It's what I would have done. Or was Peter smart enough to get rid of them? If he was, it means he abandoned his bike in full view, dropped the weapon, but had the presence of mind to obliterate his shoeprints. I'm not buying it.

My hand runs over the bark of one of the trees. Jake would have taped them for fibres, all of them, I've no doubt about that. Despite Holt's misgivings, what I saw on Bidecombe Quay that day when we examined Janie's murder scene was a CSI as diligent and determined as any I've ever known, including myself. Knowing the victim was my daughter would have energized and extended his efforts. No, Jake didn't miss anything. So where does that leave me? Did Peter come here with the intention of hurting Megan? Or did something go horribly wrong and he lost his temper? Or what if Peter is telling the truth that after Megan rejected him, he left her unharmed?

No shoeprints, no phone, but the weapon left in plain sight. The longer I'm here, the greater the sense that this scene is straight out of the local theatre. Every single aspect of it has been stage-managed. But that would mean this was not a spontaneous act. It was premeditated and planned to the last detail. Peter Benson doesn't strike me as a planner.

For the moment, I take Benson out of the equation and do what I always do at crime scenes: put myself into the perpetrator's shoes and ask myself what would I have done, factoring in how even the most calculated mind can be disorientated by the adrenaline surging through them.

Through the foliage below me, I can only just make out a patch of grey gravel that is the trail. High above me a swatch of red brick from the high garden walls that rim the back of the housing estate pushes through the trees. This is a risky place to commit an attack to the point of idiocy. It's a favourite among dog walkers and it wouldn't have been unreasonable for one of them to be exercising their pet in these woods even on a wet weekday afternoon.

Why here?

The county is pocked with empty caves and deserted coves, none of which have been visited by humans for years, so what's special about this spot? Does he live nearby? Or is there another reason why it had to be here?

And how did he get here? Did he walk along the trail or come down through the woods from the housing estate? Either route is enormously risky. The trail borders flat marshlands that edge the estuary, filling and draining with the tide. There's another trail on the other side of the water. You can spot people on both trails for miles and there's always twitchers out stalking the wading birds with binoculars. The woods have multiple entry points. It's easy to slip in unseen and once you're in, the bracken is dense enough to hide you. No contest. I'd have chosen the woods.

I stand in the middle of the copse, my back to the trail, and scan the tangle of bramble and weeds covering the ground. Just to the right, the bushes appear slightly depressed. A patch of drooping stinging nettles catches my eye; their stalks bent and bowed. Elsewhere, bracken has been crushed underfoot. Someone has been through here. Could it be Jake or other police officers? Possibly, when they were doing a wider search.

I follow the route upwards. There's no obvious path, but it's possible to zigzag through the trees to the top. Every few steps, I pause to check low-hanging branches and that's when it catches my eye: a sharp ragged end, its pale-yellow innards exposed against a grey-brown branch no wider than a finger. Further up, there's another. And another. A slow and systematic search wouldn't have caused this. The search team would have inched forward, like I'm doing, gently pushing the branches to one side. This was caused by someone running fast. Towards the estate.

At the top of the steep slope a high wall skirts the back of the housing estate. Below it runs a narrow path. Which way would I go? Left brings me out alongside the Spar and the main road which takes you to the official entrance of the trail. Too public. Right takes me to the end of the estate, where the houses peter out. I go right. The path here is wide – there are no overhanging branches – and I keep going and finally it ends in an iron kissing gate. I pass through it and the narrow, high-hedged path, no more than twenty metres long, deposits me onto the pavement.

To my right is a lay-by. It's empty, but it wasn't empty the day Megan was attacked. That day, an ambulance was parked there and in it was Simon Pascoe who lied to Holt that he was there with his colleague when he was alone.

A shiver runs through me. Could Simon Pascoe, the paramedic who saved Megan, be in on this?

My phone goes off, startling me. It's Penny.

Get back to the hospital now. It's Megan.

He's the hero of the day. Colin is even talking of nominating him for an award for going above and beyond the call of duty. He can't deny he's quite enjoying all the attention and gratitude. It's about time.

Colin takes his hand and shakes it vigorously.

'Top effort, Simon. You're definitely in line for a commendation for this. The *Herald* has also got wind of it. They're sending someone over to do a story on you. They want a photo with you and the girl.'

'I don't really want any fuss and, anyway, I did what anyone would do in my position.'

'Rubbish. You're a hero. Get yourself smartened up. They'll be here in a minute and besides, it's good PR.'

Before he knows it, there's a journalist in front of him asking him all sorts of questions and a photographer snapping away. Then Colin herds them all up to the hospital ward to see the girl. She's with her parents, but she's not badly hurt. He really doesn't want to be photographed with her, but, when he thinks about it, it doesn't change anything. He's too clever for that.

He has to admit that it feels good to be appreciated, even by Trisha, who threw her arms around him on the cliff top.

'You're a bloody legend, Si. Wish everyone was like you instead of the sneaky little shit that spied on me and Gary.'

But as he drives home, there's another reason for his high spirits: TruffleDelite. She's expected to be discharged later that day and when she is, he'll be ready for her.

His good humour doesn't last long, though. As he walks through the front door, he's greeted by loud sobbing coming from the living room. It's at times like these that he wonders if he needs Jackie any more. She was useful to him once when he first moved to Bidecombe. Single men, especially good-looking ones in their thirties, still attract questions, like it's somehow unnatural not to have settled down with a wife or now even a husband. But, of late, Jackie has become so needy, so clingy, that widowhood is beginning to have its appeal.

Her sobs are too loud to ignore. Like a child's, their volume is designed to snare his attention rather than signal real distress.

As he walks into the room, Jackie looks up at him, all red-eyed and wobbly lipped. She's clutching a teddy in a white loincloth and pebble-glasses. He hasn't seen it before.

'What is it, my love? Why are you so upset?'

She dabs the corner of her eye with a tissue twisted into a peak. She's been crying a while.

'Something terrible has happened.' Another sob chokes her once again and he's annoyed he has to wait for her to get a grip of herself. He really doesn't have time for this.

'Oh my goodness. What? And where's Arjun?'

She presses the teddy up against her mouth to stem her emotions until she's able to compose herself and then she replaces it, its fur damp with her tears and snot, on her lap.

'It's about Arjun.'

'What about him?'

'He just came by. He said he's been sacked. Someone told the care home that he'd been stealing money from an old lady with dementia.'

He puts his hand on her shoulder.

'That's a terrible thing to do. He always seemed like such a nice chap, but why come here?'

'He came to tell me that he'd miss looking after me. He said he'd come to see me as a friend. He brought me this teddy. It's Gandhi. A man of honour. He told me that he was a man of honour too and that he wanted me to know the truth. He didn't do it and I believe him. The old lady probably forgot where she put her money.'

'Oh, my love, so innocent, you always believe the best in people, but the care company wouldn't accuse him if they weren't sure.'

'I know, but he was really nice to me. He was going to take me to Morte Sands again. We had such a lovely day.'

'I've told you before. People aren't always what they seem. That's why I'm here to look after you.' He takes one of the remotes and turns on one of the televisions. 'It's still light. Why don't you check out the Live Cam on Morte Sands? I bet there's still plenty of families enjoying the beach. Perhaps I'll call the care company in a day or two, see if they can send someone else.'

He's lying. Arjun was a mistake. He should have got rid of him sooner. He doesn't want people in his house, snooping around and filling Jackie's head with silly ideas.

He leaves her sniffling into her hanky, telling Gandhi that Arjun had been a bad man after all, and that someone new is going to come and look after her.

The care company was surprisingly quick to embrace the news

that Arjun was a thief. He thought they'd ask him for evidence, but they just sighed as if it happened all the time, which meant, coupled with a dose of racism as the woman on the other end of the line muttered that 'you could never trust them', Arjun was out the door almost before he put the phone down.

39

Megan. Hang in there. I'm coming.

Flying into her room, three faces twist towards me: Penny, Bernadette and the consultant. Megan is lying peacefully in her bed, just as she has done for the past five days. I can't read their expression, so I look to the machines for answers. The heart monitor registers a steady beat. The ventilator is still pushing air into her lungs. She's alive.

Penny, tearful and angry, speaks first.

'Where the fuck have you been?'

I ignore her and address the consultant.

'Wh-what happened?' The dash from the car park has stolen my breath and I can barely get the words out.

'She's had a mild seizure.'

I look at Penny and Bernadette and sense I'm playing catch-up here.

'What does that mean?'

'Megan had a sudden onset of what we can only describe as erratic electrical activity in the brain.'

I don't understand and his answer leaves me frustrated.

'Why has she had one now when she was doing so well?'

'It can happen with traumatic brain injuries. In the first week we call them early post-traumatic seizures.'

'Has it caused any permanent damage?'

'We don't know. As I said, it was a mild seizure. We also won't know for some time if this is a one-off or if Megan will be permanently affected. About a quarter of people who have a seizure will have another later on in life, but there are anti-epileptic drugs that can be taken to control them.'

'Is she going to be all right?'

'She's comfortable now. We'll keep an eye on her. Like I said, it was a mild seizure and we're hopeful there's no lasting damage.'

He leaves and I take Megan's hand.

'It's OK, Megan, I'm here now.'

'What good is that now?' Bernadette says and I throw Penny an accusing 'what's she doing here' glare. She shrugs defensively.

'I had to call her. I didn't know where you were. And she is Megan's gran.'

'I told you I wouldn't be long.'

'Don't blame Penny. You should have been here and you weren't,' Bernadette says, latching onto her favourite subject: Ally, the terrible mother. 'So typical of you. When will you learn?'

I have no intention of answering this. It only encourages her and she's consumed enough by her self-righteousness. I turn to Penny.

'What happened exactly?'

'I was reading to her and suddenly the machines went haywire and she started making these weird jerking movements so I called the nurses. They were here in seconds.'

'Thank you, Penny.'

I move to hug her, but she steps away. Her face is hard, unyielding and judgemental.

'Don't thank me. Bernadette is right. You should have been here.'

'I know, I know. I'm sorry.'

'Where were you?'

I can't lie to her.

'I went to look at the crime scene.'

'You're kidding?'

'No.'

She shakes her head.

'You've got to stop this, Ally. You've got to let the police get on with their jobs. For Megan's sake.'

Billy Strudwick opens the door with more cheerfulness than is normal considering he's spent the last four years caring for a cripple. His dad, Ken, was paralyzed from the waist down in an industrial accident. Just after it happened, Billy's mum left them to it. He'd have done the same. Who wants to spend their life wiping a grown man's backside twice a day?

'Hi, Mr Pascoe. How's it going?'

'Hello, Billy. I was just passing and I thought I'd drop by. How's your dad?'

'He's OK, thanks.'

He holds up a white plastic bag.

'I bought him a DVD. I remember him saying how much he liked old war movies and this one's a classic.'

'Thanks. Do you want to come in and say hello? I know he'd like to see you.'

'Sure.'

He follows Billy into the front room. Ken is in his wheelchair and he's as cheerful as his son. He can't for the life of him work out why. It isn't natural. If he ended up in a wheelchair, he'd kill himself.

The living room is small and he struggles to manoeuvre his chair to face him, knocking into the coffee table so often it makes him want to laugh out loud, but Ken perseveres and shakes his hand like an old friend.

'Simon, good to see you. Have a seat.'

'I bought you this.' He takes the DVD out of the plastic bag and passes it to Ken who studies the blurb on the back.

'*Where Eagles Dare.* I don't think I've seen this one.'

'I think you'll like it. It's got Clint Eastwood in it.'

'I'll look forward to watching it.' He smiles up at him. 'I'm really touched that you should think of me. Thank you.'

It's not that big a deal. It was £2.99 from the bargain bin, but he's come to understand that people like Ken don't get shown much attention so the smallest things overwhelm them. So much so, they'll do anything for you – which brings him to the real reason he's there.

'How's things generally, Ken?'

'Great. Did Billy tell you he's passed his driving test?'

That's not what he meant.

'No, that's great news. Congratulations, Billy.'

Billy grins at him.

'Yeah, I've already taken Dad out. We went down to the quay and had an ice cream, didn't we, Dad?'

'We did, son. I bought Billy a car with some of the money left over from my payout. Been saving it.'

He's not interested, but he has to pretend he is. Sometimes, it feels like he spends his whole life pretending.

'Great.'

'It's just a little runaround, but it'll do for now.'

'Absolutely. So, everything else OK with you? You look a bit pale.'

The news takes Ken by surprise.

'Can't complain, but the wheelchair's a bit knackered. It's getting harder to move around.'

Bingo.

'Oh? Can I help? Who is it you're dealing with at the hospital?'

'The wheelchair service department.'

'I know the chap who runs it. He never answers his phone, but I'll drop him an email now for you, if you like.'

'No, it's OK. It just needs a service. There's no rush.'

'It's no bother. It'll take two minutes. He's off on holiday in a few days' time so if you don't do something now, it'll be weeks.'

'Oh, OK, then.'

He gets out his special phone and holds it up in the air. 'I'm not getting much signal here, though.'

'That's odd,' says Billy. 'We usually get 4G here.'

'It's my phone. It's a bit dodgy. You don't happen to know your Wi-Fi code, do you?'

'Sure.'

Ken laughs.

'Kids these days. They don't know what day of the week it is, but they all know their Wi-Fi codes.'

He smiles and taps the code in. Then he writes an email and pretends to send it.

'There, all done. Let me know if you don't hear anything from him and I'll get on to it for you.'

'Thank you, Simon. I really appreciate it. I know you're busy.'

'Think nothing of it. And enjoy the film.'

They say their goodbyes and he strolls back to the paramedics' car parked around the back of the Strudwicks' house on a small industrial estate. He pulls his phone out and immediately he drops into the Strudwicks' Wi-Fi. Perfect.

Now it begins.

40

Bernadette left hours ago, but Penny has stayed although her lingering anger stilted my attempts at conversation. I tried to explain where I'd been and why it was important, but she batted me away. She couldn't have been less interested and now she's now asleep in the armchair.

I've been awake most of the night, talking to Megan, trying to make up for not being here. Seems like I've been doing that her whole life.

'I wasn't that far away. The doctors say your seizure was just a minor setback. You're still doing really well.'

But she's as still as the night, a deserving punishment for my neglect. Eventually, as the dawn breaks and a new day establishes itself, my throat runs dry and there's not enough water in the world that can coax any more words out of it, so I climb onto the bed and cuddle her like I did when she was a little girl and she couldn't get to sleep. Only now I want her to wake up.

The silence feels like I've failed all over again. I begin to hum tunelessly so she knows I'm still here, but it requires so little thought that my mind drifts back to Three Brethren Woods and Simon Pascoe.

Does he have something to do with this? Or is it just

a terrible coincidence that he happened to be parked nearby? CSIs don't like coincidences. The 'I just happened to be in the vicinity' line doesn't wear with us. Yes, it's possible, just not probable. And there was evidence that someone had run from the crime scene back to the housing estate. It could be anybody; it's public woods. It could also be somebody: Simon Pascoe. Are he and Peter Benson accomplices? It's an unlikely pairing.

But I can't get my head around the idea that Peter groomed Megan. Peter has learning needs. Firstly, how did he find Megan online? Did he just stumble across her account by accident? Even if he did, how was he then able to entice Megan to meet him when he is barely literate? Unless he had help. Did someone else tell Peter what to write? Was that someone else Simon Pascoe? A person he knows and trusts. Did Simon Pascoe set Peter up in some way? But that doesn't explain how Pascoe knows Megan?

There is a way I can find out. It's a long shot. She may not even speak to me, but I can get around that. What I can't get round is that it means leaving Megan again. I shoot her the guiltiest of glances like she knows what I'm thinking. I can't go. Not after what happened. What if she has another seizure?

But I have to know the truth. I *have* to know: did Peter Benson really attack her? Holt's evidence says he did. And where does Simon Pascoe figure in all of this? Because he is involved, I'm certain of that.

Drawing Megan closer to me, I breathe in her soapy disinfected skin and almond-scented hair, and whisper in her ear.

'I won't be long. I promise. And Penny is here.'

I wait a beat as if giving her the option to protest and – taking her silence as tacit approval – I kiss her on her cheek and get off the bed. My trainers silent on the shiny tiled floor, I slip past Penny, but she's fast asleep, her arms draped over the sides of the armchair, her head lolling to the side. Still I mouth a silent 'sorry'.

Easing the door open, I pause once more to look at Megan. I don't want to leave her, but I don't have a choice. I have to do this. For her sake.

He's parked as close to the back of Billy's house as he dares in an industrial estate that's little more than a small cluster of units. Apart from the odd lorry, there's no one about, but even if there was, it doesn't matter. A paramedic who's found a quiet spot for a bite to eat mid-shift is unlikely to attract much attention.

It's morning. TruffleDelite will be in school, but lessons won't have started yet. His phone hooks up to Billy's Wi-Fi in seconds and he searches for TruffleDelite on the social media channels. A distinctive username like that means it's not long before he finds her.

There's nothing on her profile to give away her identity, just a photo with 'life's a beach' written in sand, but she isn't as clever as she thinks she is. Her account isn't private and there are plenty of photos of her and her friends, pouting at the camera.

His thumbs hesitate over the keypad. It's crucial he gets it right. One wrong word and she'll block him.

Ruggerboy666: You OK? Heard about your accident.

He stares at it for a while, changes the 'your' to a 'ur' and then presses send. He's not expecting an immediate response and is about to put the phone away when a message flashes up on the screen.

TruffleDelite: Do I know you?

Satisfaction oozes through him. He's in.

Ruggerboy666: Yes but can't say here. Just wanted to make sure you're OK. I heard you had a big fight with the 'rents.

TruffleDelite: Who told you about that?

Ruggerboy666: Word gets around.

TruffleDelite: It's no one's business but mine.

She's feisty, but they all are to begin with. It doesn't last. Who can resist a secret admirer? It's what young girls dream about.

Ruggerboy666: Sure, but I want it to be my business too. Ur cool.

TruffleDelite: Who are you? U at my school?

Ruggerboy666: Wish I could say. It's complicated.

TruffleDelite: Yeah, right.

Ruggerboy666: OK, I'll tell you, but keep it to yourself. I'm seeing someone else. She's in your class and I'm trying to finish it. Told you it was complicated.

TruffleDelite: Lol. Yeah, I see now. You at Riverside then?

Ruggerboy666: Yeah. Year above you. Thing is. I've always liked you and when I heard you'd gone over a cliff, I knew I had to say something. Hope you don't mind.

TruffleDelite: I don't mind. So, what else do you know about me?

Ruggerboy666: I know ur parents hate this guy you fancy and they're right. I know him, he's an idiot. You should watch him. He says stuff behind your back.

The cursor winks at him for a long while. He's gone too far. Got carried away. It's been a while and he couldn't help himself. In his excitement, he rushed things and he's blown it.

But wait. She's typing.

TruffleDelite: He wouldn't do that.

Darn it. Wrong move. He's got to get off the subject.

Ruggerboy666: I also know you've got the most beautiful green eyes I've ever seen.

A blushing emoji comes up on screen: 😊

Ruggerboy666: Thanks for talking to me and not being freaked out.

TruffleDelite: Why would I be freaked out?

Ruggerboy666: Because I could be a paedo or a mad axeman.

TruffleDelite: That's true. 😄 😄 😄

Ruggerboy666: Can we talk again?

TruffleDelite: If you want.

Ruggerboy666: Probably better if you don't tell anyone about this. If my girlfriend finds out, she'll go mad.

TruffleDelite: I don't know who you are – lol!

Ruggerboy666: Oh yeah. Let me sort stuff out and then I can tell you.

She's his.

41

Mrs Benson's son is on an attempted murder charge and someone has sprayed 'Paedo' across her front door. She's a broken woman; her world has been shattered beyond repair, but I need to speak to her about her son.

I flash my CSI card at the wary eye that's appeared in the narrowest of gaps between her front door and its frame.

'Hello, Mrs Benson. My name is Ally Dymond. I'm a crime scene investigator.'

She relaxes, but only slightly.

'You people have already been,' she says in a broad Devonian accent.

'I know, but I just need to do a follow-up search of Peter's bedroom. It's standard procedure.'

Standard procedure. Two words people never seem to question.

Defeated, she unhooks the chain and opens the door. Her first name is Lily. Wrapped in a threadbare green cardie, her unevenly cut hair with its blonde home-kit highlights can't distract from the deep trenches running the length of her cheeks. She's only fifty-five, but she looks seventy.

'His room's up the stairs, first on the left. He didn't do it. He'd never harm anyone.'

Poor woman. Still fighting his corner. She's been on her own with Peter for as long as I can remember, and I've known Peter since we were eleven. We were at the same school. He was in a different year, but I still knew of him. We all did.

His mum attended almost as often as he did, a constant presence at the front desk or on the red chair outside the head's office, always there defending her son to the end.

Simple, guileless and desperate to belong, Peter would do the older boys' bidding without question. No matter how often Lily Benson told him to stay away from them, the promise of attention lured him back in. Then he spied on the girls' changing room and got expelled. Seems he's been spying on girls ever since. But that doesn't make him Megan's attacker.

I open the door with a Harry Potter movie poster on it. Inside is a shrine to the boy wizard who stares sternly from a duvet, pillowcase, calendar and even the lampshade.

'He loves Harry Potter. He'd really like Dumbledore's wand.'

I slip on a pair of latex gloves and make a play of checking bedside drawers and flicking through the pages of the unread books on the shelves.

Lily hovers by my shoulder, close enough for me to catch a whiff of body odour. She can't cope with herself, let alone her son. They needed help a long time ago.

'I know he had a bit of trouble with girls saying he hassles them, but he just wants to make friends with them. He doesn't mean any harm.'

Complaints to the police suggest he's much more interested in making friends with a girl's breasts, but I keep that to myself.

Scanning the room, my eye falls on the empty rectangular space on a desk by the window where Peter's computer stood before the police seized it. Lily follows my gaze.

'They say he was speaking to this girl on 'is computer, but I don't see how. He's never been good at writing. He just plays games on it, but the police won't listen.' Her cold clammy hand closes over mine. 'He didn't hurt that maid. He didn't even know her.'

Her final sentence catches my attention.

'How do you know he never knew her?'

'He told me. I read it about it in the papers and I know he likes to cycle the trail to Barnston so I asked him. He said to me, "Mum, I saw her, I thought she liked me, she didn't. I didn't touch her, I promise."'

'If Peter had never met her before, why did he think she liked him?'

Lily shrugs.

'Dunno, but I believe him. The thing is, whenever he's been in trouble before he's always admitted it to me.'

There's a pride in her voice and I believe her. Peter wasn't talking to Megan online and he didn't attack her, but he was there that day. My mind flashes back to our school days and the 'naughty boys' who led Peter on. Did someone persuade Peter to go to Three Brethren Woods and approach Megan, like some kind of decoy? Was that someone Simon Pascoe?

'Did Peter ever let anyone else use his computer?'

'No, no one else ever went into his room.'

'What about Peter's friends? Did they ever come round and visit? Were any of them ever here alone?'

Lily lets out a cackle.

'Friends. Peter doesn't have any friends. It's just him and me. That's the way we like it.'

'What about your friends? Do they come and visit you?'

'Like I said, it's just me and Peter.'

This doesn't make sense. No one has accessed Peter's computer, other than Peter, but I know as well as Lily does that he wasn't messaging Megan.

'Are you sure no one comes to the house, Mrs Benson?'

But I've lost her.

'And that's the problem. I got diabetes, see, and my blood pressure is sky high, not that my GP cares. 'E won't even return my calls. Peter normally gets my medication for me. Without it, I'm done.'

'So who gets it for you now?'

She shrugs.

'I go without.'

'Isn't there anyone who can help look after you?'

'No. Mr Bates used to check on me, but he's in hospital.' She taps her temple. 'Gone doolally.'

'What about the health visitor?'

'No, silly cow says I'm fit enough to get myself to the surgery, but I'm not.'

'So, there's no one to check up on you?'

'Only that nice ambulance man. He pops in from time to time, on 'is way to work.'

The ambulance man.

'He's sounds a lovely chap. I probably know him. What's his name?'

'I'm not sure. Sean maybe, no Simon. It's Simon.'

'Simon Pascoe?'

'That's the one. Such a quiet voice, can hardly make out what he says sometimes, but he's a lovely man. He's a hero too. He rescued a girl who'd fallen down the cliffs. It was on the lunchtime news.'

Simon Pascoe, the man who told me Megan's final words were an apology to me to help soothe my guilt.

'Yes, he is, isn't he? He runs the cycle club that Peter goes to, doesn't he?'

'Yes, but I know him from way back.'

'Oh, how's that?'

'Silly me, I forgot my medicine once and had a funny turn. Bless Peter, when he couldn't wake me, he ran over to Mr Bates over the road who called the ambulance. He was all there then. It was Simon who came out. I didn't know that, of course, because I was in a coma, but he came to see me in hospital, brought me flowers.'

Simon Pascoe who, having dropped his partner in town, was parked just yards away from Three Brethren Woods. Alone.

'He even tried to email my GP for me to sort out a repeat prescription, but his phone wouldn't work.'

'What do you mean?'

'He said this street was a bit of a blackspot for mobile reception.'

There are plenty of mobile blackspots in a place like North Devon, but I know where they all are. Everyone in the emergency services does. It's so we can avoid them when we need to talk to call handlers, which is why I know Mrs Benson's street isn't one of them. There's no reason for Simon's phone not to work here.

'So, what did he do?'

'It's OK. He sorted it out in the end. Peter told him some numbers and letters and that seemed to do the trick.'

'You mean Peter gave Simon your Wi-Fi code?'

'Don't ask me, maid. Is that what it's called?'

'Thank you for your time Mrs Benson. I think I have everything I need.'

'Oh, you leaving so soon, love?'

'Yes. You've been very helpful. Thank you, and, for what it's worth, I don't think your son hurt anyone.'

She smiles for the first time.

'He's a good boy.'

I get back into my car and get my phone out. There's someone I need to call.

'Liam, it's Ally. You free to talk?'

'Sure.'

'How far does a Wi-Fi signal reach beyond a house?'

Of all the questions he might have been expecting, that most definitely was not on his list, but he once told me he'd done a spell in the hi-tech unit so I'm guessing this is his area.

'Er, right. OK. Well, you need to factor in a few things, like walls and weather, but I'd say the signal from a Wi-Fi router, like the one you have in your cabin, could reach up to ninety or so metres outside.'

'That far?'

'Sure, if the conditions are right.'

'So I could sit outside my house or nearby and access my Wi-Fi?'

'Absolutely.'

'And I could surf the internet and set up social media accounts using that Wi-Fi?'

'Of course.'

'And those web addresses would show up on my ISP records?'

'Yes, they would.'

'But you wouldn't know which device had been used?'

'No, you only see the web address and time and date stamp. What's this all about, Ally?'

'I can't tell you, but you've been a great help. Thank you. I owe you.'

'Er. OK. Anytime.'

I ring off. There's one more thing I need to do. I switch on the car engine, ram it into gear and head over to Bernadette's.

Unsurprisingly, Bernadette isn't pleased to see me. Her last words to me were a lecture on not being with Megan and now here I am on her doorstep, ringing her doorbell.

'Who's with Megan?'

'Penny.'

'She's too good to you.'

'I'm about to go back. I just need to speak to you. It won't take long. It's important.'

'It's always important.'

I'm already beginning to think this is a mistake, but I can't leave until I have what I need.

'Please.'

That I haven't bitten back surprises her. She frowns at me.

'What is it, Aloysia?'

'It's about the time when Megan hurt herself at school, about six months ago. Do you remember?'

'Yes, I remember.'

Of course, she does. She only raises it every time I see her.

It was a Tuesday afternoon when Megan's school rang me to say Megan had fallen off the high beam in gym class and knocked herself out. She'd come round, but an ambulance had been called, as a precaution. I was eighty miles away on a training day and couldn't leave so I called Bernadette. The ambulance was already there when she arrived.

'The paramedic who treated Megan. Were they male or female?'

'Male, why?'

'What did he look like?'

Silence, but there's no reward at the end.

'I've no idea. I was too busy worrying about Megan.'

She stares hard at me, eyebrows raised, in case I missed her little dig. I haven't, but I'm not here for a row.

'Was he fair or dark?'

She sighs, irritated at being asked what she regards as pointless questions.

'Oh, Aloysia. I don't know. This is so difficult. It was so long ago. Fairish, I think.'

'Tall or short?'

'I've no idea. He was kneeling next to Megan most of the time.'

This is hopeless.

'OK. Thanks for trying. I best get back to Megan.'

I turn to leave.

'I remember his voice, though.'

'His voice?'

'Yes. He was very softly spoken. I had to get him to repeat himself a few times. He also said there wasn't enough room in the back of the ambulance, and I'd have to follow in my car. He was very insistent. I remember not being happy about that; I am Megan's grandmother, after all, and you know how I hate driving the Bidecombe to Barnston road. It's a death trap. All those bends. Aloysia, are you all right?'

'Yes.'

'Are you sure?'

'Yes. I'm sure. Thanks.'

'Wait. What's this all about? Is this to do with what happened to Megan?'

'It's OK. It's nothing for you to worry about.'

But Bernadette is following me down the steps to the car.

'What's going on?'

'Nothing. I just wanted to check something, that's all.'

I get back into the car and go to pull the door shut, but she grabs it with surprising strength.

'Aloysia?'

I'm about to brush her off, but there's something in her eyes I don't recognize: fear.

'Yes.'

'I know we don't always see eye to eye, but promise me, you'll be careful. For Megan's sake.'

'I promise.'

She lets me close the car door and takes the steep steps back up to her house. She's not as sprightly as she used to be. The door closes behind her and I'm alone in the car with just one thought. Simon Pascoe – I've got you.

42

Holt is reticent, but I insist we meet in person because I can't do this over the phone. He might put it down on me.

The drive back to Barnston is filled with Simon Pascoe. It all makes perfect sense. He met Megan at her school. God knows how, but he managed to get hold of her social media details. Then he accessed Peter Benson's Wi-Fi and used it to make contact with her so he could groom her and set Peter up to take the fall.

Holt is waiting for me in the corridor outside Megan's room.

'What is it? What's wrong?'

Doubt. I have to introduce doubt Peter could have acted alone and raise the possibility that someone else was involved.

'OK, hear me out. Quite a few things have been bothering me about Megan's attack.' He tenses. We have history, but I can't help that. 'First, the crime scene with the weapon, complete with fingerprint, but nothing else left behind just felt all wrong. So, I went back and examined the scene myself.' He rolls his eyes and opens his mouth to speak, but I cut across him. 'There's definitely evidence of someone running from the copse up to the housing estate. There's too much bracken and leaves on the ground for shoeprints, but branches have been snapped.'

I pause.

'And?'

Good. He's interested.

'And we both know Simon Pascoe was parked up alone in the lay-by on the housing estate on top of the hill.'

He computes what I'm saying and, as anticipated, arrives at a different answer.

'Yes, because the paramedics always have lunch there, only that day his colleague had gone shopping.'

'But did you know Peter Benson and Simon Pascoe know each other? Peter is in Pascoe's cycling club.'

'So what? Everyone in Bidecombe knows each other.'

I ignore this truism.

'Not only that, Simon regularly goes to their house because Peter's mum, Lily, isn't well and he likes to pop in and make sure she's OK.'

He looks at me passively.

'Again, so what?'

'You said yourself Peter's IP address showed he had accessed various incriminating websites including Instagram, but there was nothing actually on his computer or his phone and you thought there might be a third device.'

'Yes, and we will find it.'

'OK, but you won't find it in Peter's house.'

'What are you talking about?'

'The thing with Peter is that he isn't very bright. You've interviewed him, you've probably already worked that out

283

for yourself. Now, obviously, we don't know what he said to Megan because you haven't found his Instagram account yet, but whatever he said would have to be clever enough to fool my daughter who is by no means stupid.'

'Ally, come on. You and I both know these people can be pretty clever at persuading young girls to do all sorts of things.'

'Exactly, but Peter isn't clever. He has learning difficulties.'

'So, what are you saying?'

'Bob, Peter doesn't have an Instagram account and he didn't go on to those websites.'

'And you're going to tell me it was Simon Pascoe?'

'Yes, because it's true and I can prove it.'

'Can you now?'

'I went to the Bensons' house.'

'You did what?' He's appalled at the flagrant abuse of my position. 'And his mother let you in, just like that, did she?'

'No, I told her I was working, and we had to do another search.'

'What? Have you any idea how stupid that was? You do know I could have you on a charge of gross misconduct.'

'Yes, I know, but the fact is Peter gave Pascoe his Wi-Fi code. He could easily have set up an Instagram account and sent those messages just by sitting outside Peter's house and tapping into his Wi-Fi. In the same way that he could have accessed all those suspicious websites. The reason Peter denied ever having been on Instagram or the other sites is because he's telling the truth.' Big breath. Here it comes. 'Simon Pascoe attacked Megan and then pinned it on Peter.'

Holt actually laughs.

'You call that proof. That's the biggest load of crap I've ever heard. You're ignoring all the evidence. Peter Benson took a steel pole from his own shed and he cycled to Three Brethren Woods where he brutally assaulted Megan. Something disturbed him and he dropped the weapon and legged it. That's what happened. End of. This Instagram stuff is nonsense. You'll see once we get Benson's account details out of him.'

'No, that's what Simon Pascoe wants you to think happened.'

'You're not serious.'

'Of course I'm serious.'

'So, let me get this straight. A paramedic assaults your daughter and then saves her life so that when she wakes up, she can ID him.'

'His luck ran out. He thought he'd killed her. He came to my house with a get well soon card, asking questions about what she'd remember when she woke up.'

'Because he cares. Christ, Ally, you know what it's like; we're not robots. We turn up to scenes. We deal with the injured, the dead. It affects us. Do you think I'm ever going to forget seeing your Megan lying in that hospital bed? I've interviewed Simon Pascoe. If he was in on this, I'd know.'

He's challenging me to contradict him, to accuse him of not doing his job properly. Janie Warren and Cheryl Black drop into my mind. They're on his mind too. He knows I don't rate him, but I need him onside.

'Please, Bob, this isn't about you or me. Simon Pascoe did this.'

But it's too late. I've lost him. He throws his arms in the air.

'I had enough of this. You don't have a shred of evidence to tie Pascoe to the attack on Megan. It's pie in the sky. You're a CSI. You know evidence is everything and you don't have any and, quite honestly, I'm sick of you undermining me at every opportunity. Christ, I don't know what more I can do. I nail the guy who almost killed your daughter and you come to me with all this conspiracy crap. What's the matter, can't stand the thought that I might actually be good at my job? Or are you still pissed off at being kicked off Major Investigations for shopping Stride?'

'No, no, that's not it at all. I just know Peter didn't do this.'

Holt lets out a long sigh.

'I give up – but let me tell you something.' He leans into me. 'It's only because of what you're going through with Megan that I'm not going to take this further, otherwise you'd be facing a suspension for gross misconduct. But I'm warning you, stay away from Lily Benson and stay away from Simon Pascoe.'

He stalks off down the corridor. The door to Megan's room opens and Penny's furious face appears. She must have heard Holt and I talking.

'What the fuck do you think you're playing at, leaving Megan without telling me?'

Tossing his special phone onto the passenger's seat next to him, he slams his palm against the steering wheel. Why isn't she responding? This is unbearable. First thing this morning, he was certain he had her, but now nothing.

The drizzle gathers and trickles down the windscreen, the inside of which has begun to steam up, obscuring his view. He's been parked up behind Billy and Ken Strudwick's house for nearly an hour now, but he can't stay much longer, not without some nosy parker calling the ambulance station and complaining he's sitting around doing nothing, wasting taxpayers' money.

He can't understand it. He was certain she was interested in him. What could have happened?

He stares down at the screen and the long list of comments and questions left hanging by themselves on one side. The other side is empty.

Hi. Not heard from u. U OK?

Saw u at school. Looking good.

Wanna chat?

He starts typing.

Can't stop thinking about u.

Darn it, that's far too needy. Any more and he'll sound really desperate, or worse, like a stalker.

His eyes are stinging with the strain of watching and waiting for those magic italics: *TruffleDelite is typing*. But there's nothing. Just a blank screen.

The little bitch. How dare she ignore him? Who does she think she is? *I saved your life*. He should have pushed her off the cliff. It wouldn't have taken much and it would have served her right for pretending she needed saving. She doesn't deserve to live. She's just like all the rest, all innocent and grateful when it suits them and then it's all forgotten. But he won't forget.

A knock on the window startles him.

'Yes.'

It's a white-haired old man, out walking his white-haired old terrier. His face is veiny and pink. Much as he doesn't want to, he winds the window down.

'Thank God,' the old man says, leaning on his window to catch his breath. 'There's an old lady. She's fallen over in the street. I don't think it's serious, but can you take a look? She's in a bit of pain.'

'I can't. I've just had a call for a suspected heart attack. Call 999. They'll send someone else.'

The window whirs back up, dislodging the man's arm. Before he can protest, he drives away. He has more important things to attend to.

43

'I can't believe you walked out of here without telling me.'

Penny is seething. I've never seen her like this before. I can't blame her.

'I'm sorry. I needed to do something, and I knew you'd try to stop me.'

But she's not going to be placated.

'Damn right, I would have. What's got into you, Ally? I don't recognize you any more. You always need to do something, but when are you going to need to be with Megan?'

'That's not fair, Pen. I'm doing this for Megan. You know Peter Benson couldn't have done this. Megan was attacked by Simon Pascoe, the paramedic. He was parked nearby the whole time.'

Penny is shaking her head.

'You don't get it, do you? I don't care. I doubt Megan cares either. She just wants you by her side. Now more than ever.'

'I know that and I'm here now.'

'But for how long? She responded to my voice, Ally, not yours. Doesn't that tell you something?'

I hold her gaze.

'It tells me you happened to be singing to her when she came round for a moment.'

Penny shakes her head.

'You're unbelievable.'

'Penny, they've got the wrong guy.'

'So what?' she snaps. 'Wrong guy, right guy. None of it gets Megan better, does it?'

'You can't send an innocent man to jail. And it *does* matter. What's to say he isn't going to do this again to another young girl? Or even have another go at Megan?'

'Leave it, Ally.'

But I know why she's so reluctant to talk about it.

'What? Like you left it with Ian? Only you didn't, did you? Ian has been with you these last twenty years. He's stopped you having children, having relationships, having a life. You still think he's going to turn up any day now. You're still living in fear of him. That's why I can't leave it. I don't want that for Megan.'

She's horrified I've raised the spectre of Ian.

'That's not true,' she says quietly.

I feel bad and I know I should leave it, but I can't. Penny needs to understand why I have to do this.

'It is true. In the same way that it's true about Sean. I left that, didn't I? And look where that's got me? I don't want that for Megan. I want her to be free from all of this, free to live her life without fear.'

'She has to be alive to be free and you need to be here to help her get better.'

'And I will, but first I have to do this, and I need your help. Holt doesn't believe me. I need evidence to prove Pascoe is guilty and I can't do that by being in the hospital.'

It doesn't take her long to work out what I'm saying. She grabs my arm.

'You're leaving again, aren't you?'

'Just for an hour or two.'

'I don't believe this.' She points at the door to Megan's room. 'Megan is in there and she needs you right now.'

I keep my back to the door. If I turn around, I'll cave in.

'I won't be long. If I don't do this, it will never end. We both know that.'

Penny folds her arms, her lips tightly pursed; she reminds me of Bernadette.

Simon Pascoe lives at number 19 Lavender Gardens, a beige brick house on an estate on the edge of Bidecombe that's as nondescript and unmemorable as its owner.

An estate car bearing ambulance insignia is parked on his driveway. He's borrowed the works car overnight. That's not unusual in rural areas like this. It means we can get to jobs quicker. I do it, but I don't use it to steal someone's Wi-Fi and groom young girls.

I park some distance away, but with clear sight of his front door. Pascoe's on a day shift, the ambulance station told me, when I called pretending to be HR wanting to check his holiday entitlement with them. He's in at nine, call back then.

The door opens and there he is, in his green paramedic uniform, talking into a mobile. The sight of him momentarily throws my theory into doubt. His slight figure and barely-above-a-whisper voice make it almost impossible to believe he could hurt anyone. He's devoted his life to saving people. How in the hell could a person who does that do what they did to Megan? But he did.

Pascoe's car passes by me and I launch myself across the passenger seat in case he sees me. A good ten minutes elapse, enough to ensure he's not returning any time soon, before I get out of my car and walk towards the house. I'm about to press the intercom when the voice in my head reminds me that what I am about to do is illegal. I just about got away with visiting the crime scene and Lily Benson, but this is a different level. It's not too late; I can walk away, take Penny's advice and leave it up to the cops. For some strange reason, the image of Mrs Ellis, the old lady who was robbed of her husband's watch, slides into my consciousness. Follow your hunch, she said, and never give up, not even when those around you doubt you.

I press the buzzer.

'Who's there?'

'My name's Linda Smith. I'm a colleague of Simon Pascoe's.'

'He's not here. Come back tomorrow.'

The voice belongs to a woman. I don't why, but this shocks me.

'It's not Simon I'm after. I was hoping to speak to someone who knows him. We want to nominate him for an OBE, and we're collecting information. Confidentially. Could I come in?'

'I'm not sure. I'm on my own. Normally Arjun's here, but he's gone.'

There's a sadness in her voice.

'I'm sorry to hear that, but this won't take long. Sorry, are you related to Simon?'

'Yes, I'm his wife, Jackie Pascoe.'

Pascoe has a wife. I was not expecting that.

'Jackie, your husband is a wonderful paramedic, as you know' – the words almost choke me – 'and we, at the hospital, strongly believe he should be recognized for all that he's done.'

Silence. She's not buying it. 'And, of course, he, and you, will get to meet the Queen.'

The door opens for me, but the hallway is empty. Its shiny laminate flooring and white walls give the impression of a dentist's waiting room, but for the sickly synthetic lavender aroma drifting from one of those plug-in air fresheners.

'In here,' a voice calls. I trace it to an open door on the right that leads to a different world of flowery rose wallpaper, matching curtains with frilly edges and dozens of miniature teddy bears, perched on every available surface – the mantelpiece, the windowsill, the sofa – watching me with fixed hard stares. There are three television screens, all paused on the image of a beach. When it suddenly refreshes, I realize it's the live cams on Morte Sands.

'You work with Simon?'

In the centre of the room, in a recliner that dwarfs her, I find Simon Pascoe's wife. Little more than a waif in a grey dress that reminds me of a hospital ward gown, her legs are no wider than my arms and she has severe alopecia. The table next to her is piled with empty Haribo packets.

'Yes, at the hospital. I'm in HR. Linda's the name.'

She takes my hand limply like she's not sure what to do with it. Hers feels lighter than air.

'I'm Jackie.' She presses her hairless brow bone down into what I discern must be a frown. 'You look familiar. Have we met before?'

Shit. My TV performance.

'No, I don't think so. So, as I said, we'd like to nominate Simon for an OBE and we're just gathering lots of evidence to support his nomination.'

Her large eyes widen with interest.

'An OBE? I wish Arjun was here. He'd be so excited for him.'

'Is he a friend? Perhaps I should speak to him too.'

'No. He used to be my carer, but Simon says he's not what he seems.' She lowers her voice and puts the back of her right hand next to her mouth like we're in a crowded room. 'He got fired for stealing.'

'I see. Well, as I was saying, we believe Simon should be recognized publicly for his heroic work.'

She nods.

'Yes, yes. Is this about what happened the other day?'

I've no idea what she's talking about, but I can't let on.

'Er, yes, that and all the other wonderful things he's done.'

'He was so brave, going down the cliff face like he did. That young girl is lucky to be alive. If it hadn't been for my Simon, God only knows what would have happened to her.'

'Yes, it was a very brave thing to do. We're all very proud of him.'

'It's in the papers and on the internet, you know, and his boss said that he'll probably get a medal, too, but you'll know that already.'

'Yes, absolutely. Simon's bravery is just one of the reasons we think he should be put forward for an OBE. Obviously, we know all about the fantastic work he does as a paramedic, but could you tell me about any charity work he's involved in?'

'Yes, he belongs to the church. That's how we met.' She looks down at herself, her tiny body outlined in her voluminous grey dress. Why is she so thin? Is Pascoe starving her? If he is, what's with the sweets? 'I could get out a bit more in those days before my thyroid problems started.'

I make a play of jotting down some notes.

'He's clearly very special. What sort of work does he do at the church?'

'He runs the cycling club for men. They're not all there.' She taps the side of her head. 'They're not easy to deal with, but they adore Simon. He drives some of the elderly parishioners to the day-care centre, too, and he's on the fundraising committee. They've raised around £400 for the new church roof.'

A regular fucking saint.

'Crikey. You must never see him,' I joke, but it has the opposite effect and her mood darkens. I've touched a nerve.

'What do you mean?'

'Nothing. Just that he's a busy man.'

She selects a beige teddy in a pair of white pants and horn-rimmed glasses. Surely, that's not meant to be Gandhi?

'He is out a lot, but I'm so lucky to have him. Everyone says so.'

'Yes, he's a lovely man. Well, I think I have enough information. Thank you. Just to remind you, this has to be absolutely confidential. If Simon finds out, it will jeopardize his nomination. He can't know a thing about it.'

'Yes, yes, I won't say anything.'

'Do you have a toilet I could use?'

'Yes. Use the one upstairs. It's the first door on the left.'

'Thanks.'

The bathroom smells differently to the hall. The stench of disinfectant clings to its stark white walls and shiny white tiles, reminding me of the mortuary. I shut the door loudly for Jackie's benefit.

There's another door that leads into a large room – a bedroom with no more furniture in it than a prison cell. One corner is occupied by a single bed, its white covers crisp and crease-free, like it's been iced. At the end, there's a desk with nothing on it. Even though it's daylight, the Venetian blinds are down, and the room is barely illuminated by the light seeping through the slats.

I try the desk drawers. They're locked. I could easily open them without leaving a mark, but I won't be able to relock them and Pascoe will know someone has been in his room. I abandon the idea and try a fitted wardrobe.

The door opens with a sigh, displaying a rail of three white shirts, brown jackets, slacks and jeans all crisply ironed. I quickly check the pockets. Nothing. Next to Pascoe's civvy clothes are two paramedic uniforms.

Just as I'm about to pull the wardrobe door to, something catches my eye on the floor beneath the clothes – a row of identical brown brogues, polished to perfection.

I pull the first pair out by the laces so as not to leave any trace of myself on the shiny leather and lift them high enough for me to see the underside. Imprinted on the sole is a crest and above it the name of the manufacturer: Windsor Shoewear.

I have seen this before. Only I thought it was a V, not a W. It was cast in sand on a stone step beneath a statue of a serpent coiled around a woman's torso on the night Janie Warren was murdered. Oh God. No. I knew someone else was on the quay that night. I had no idea it was Simon Pascoe. Pascoe killed Janie Warren. Pascoe is a killer. It repeats over and over in my mind and my heart spikes with fresh fear that I'm dealing with something greater and far more evil than I could have imagined.

My instinct is to get out of the house, to run and to keep

running. I stand up to leave when something else in the bottom of the wardrobe catches my eye and, once again, my breath stalls in my throat.

At first glance it looks like a child's whistle. I don't want to touch it so I gather my hair behind my head and bend forward to inspect it at close quarters. An aroma hits my nostrils – it has that sickly sweet artificiality that makes it impossible to work out what fruit it's mimicking, but I've smelled it before. It's Cheryl Black's vape and there's no other reason for Pascoe to have this other than he killed her too.

Simon Pascoe murdered Cheryl Black and Janie Warren. And he almost killed Megan. But why these women? They're all different to each other. What, if anything, connects them? Another thought comes to mind. Are there any others?

44

A full hour passes before TruffleDelite finally leaves the house. Mobile phone clamped to her ear, chewing gum furiously, she ambles down the street.

How dare she mess him around like this, ignoring his messages, treating him like a piece of dirt?

Waiting for her on the corner is a tall skinny youth in ripped jeans and a faded black T-shirt. A mop of black hair flops two inches over a face of fierce acne. He's guessing this creature is the object of her desire: the boy who apparently wouldn't say anything horrible about her behind her back. He's the reason she's stopped speaking to him online, he's sure of it.

She removes the gum from her mouth and throws her arms around his neck, her open mouth clamping onto his. He shudders at the thought of the fluids passing between them. They break off. He slides his hand into hers and they wander towards the end of the street, laughing and giggling, thinking their so-called love is forever when he knows it won't last the week. And anyway, a goofy teenager with bad hair is no match for him.

When they're out of sight, he gets out of the car and approaches her house. He rings the bell and eventually an unshaven man in a grey tracksuit opens the door. He doesn't bother to hide his irritation at being interrupted, although judging by the sight of him he doesn't look like he has much going on that day or any day.

'Yes,' he snaps.

He has the same green eyes as his daughter.

'I'm very sorry to disturb you. You probably don't remember me. My name is Simon. I'm one of the emergency personnel that attended your daughter when she fell off the cliff.'

Recognition flickers across his face, but he's still confused as to why I'm there.

'Oh yeah. I remember. You're the one who kept her company. Is there a problem?'

He needs to take this slowly, draw him in.

'No, not at all. But this is a bit awkward.'

He screws his bristly face up.

'What is? What are you going on about?'

'OK. I was driving home from work yesterday and I saw your daughter. Now, I shouldn't be doing this and I'd appreciate it if you didn't say anything to anyone, but I know the boy your daughter is going out with.'

The news confuses him, just as he thought. The dad has no idea what his daughter gets up to.

'My daughter isn't going out with anyone.'

'Judging by their behaviour, I'd say she is. Look, he's probably a nice lad, but you should know his dad spent time inside, for molesting young girls.'

'What? The dirty bastard.'

'It was a long time ago and his son probably knows nothing about it.'

He runs a hand over his greasy greying hair that's too long for a man of his age.

'Still, I don't want him anywhere near my Gemma.'

'Like I said, I'm sure his son is a nice lad, but I just thought you might like to know. I know I would, if she was my daughter.'

'Yes, sure. Thanks.'

'I'd really appreciate it if you don't mention what I told you. Stuff like that can get out of hand in a place like this and the guy has served his time in prison.'

'You're a lot more understanding than me, but I won't say anything.'

'I'll leave you to it then.'

'Thanks . . .' he holds his hand out, 'for taking the time to drop by. Sorry I was a bit short with you earlier. We get a lot of cold callers. Thank you for all you did for Gemma too. She's lucky to be alive and she's lucky to have you looking out for her.'

'It was nothing. Just doing my job.'

'Still, you guys don't get enough recognition for what you do.'

He strolls back to the car. Job done. It's just a matter of time now, he tells himself on the drive home to collect his special phone. He wants to be ready to pick up TruffleDelite's messages as soon as she sends them.

Simon Pascoe: paramedic, husband, carer, killer. I sit back on my haunches as the words career and collide in my mind, unable to comprehend how a person devoted to saving lives can show equal devotion to extinguishing them. I've read of cases like this, but if I hadn't seen it for myself, I'd never have believed it.

Janie, Cheryl, Megan – their names, too, churn in my mind. I picture Janie in the mortuary, the fierce red bruise around her neck stark against her pallid skin, and Cheryl, little more than a charred silhouette crouched on her living-room carpet, and

Megan. My Megan, battered and bandaged, lying in a hospital bed hooked up to machines forcing life into her. Are there others? There must be others.

Who else has been lulled by Pascoe's soft voice and green uniform? Men like Pascoe don't go from zero to murder in sixty seconds. It happens in stages. Each time testing how far they can go, each time thrilled by their success. There's more. I know it.

But I can't think about that now. I have to concentrate. I have to get this right. If I don't, any barrister worth their hourly rate will get this thrown out of court on some shitty little technicality and the fact that I lied my way into the house is more than enough for Pascoe to walk free.

Think, Ally. The shoes don't prove anything, but Cheryl's vape does. Pascoe would have a hard time explaining why he has it in his possession. It would be enough for Holt to rethink the investigation, but I can't take it with me. I'm here under false pretences and Pascoe would simply say I have no proof it was ever in his house. I could have planted it. It wouldn't even get to court. Holt has to find it for himself.

I close the wardrobe door and return to the living room. Jackie and her all-seeing teddies glare accusingly at me. She smiles.

'I was beginning to wonder where you'd got to. Are you all right? You look a little flushed.'

'Yes, thank you. It's just I haven't been well recently. Anyway, thank you very much for your time.'

'Are you leaving?' She's crestfallen. 'I was hoping we could chat a bit more. I wanted to tell you how Simon's always visiting his patients even when they're better. My Simon always goes the extra mile.'

'He sounds wonderful, but work will be wondering where I am.'

'Maybe another time, then. I don't get many visitors, not now Arjun's gone.'

There's a sadness in her voice that is heart breaking. She's lonely. I suspect Pascoe spends little time with her – does that mean she has no idea what her husband is?

'Maybe. It's been lovely to talk to you. Take care of yourself.' I say the last line with meaning, but she just picks up the remote and switches to a different live cam.

Outside in my car, I dial Holt's number. I'd rather do this face to face, but I don't have time to waste.

'Bob, it's Ally.'

'What is it now?'

'I've got him.'

'What?'

'I've just been to Pascoe's house.'

'You did what? What the hell are you playing at?'

I've asked myself the same question. I revisited the crime scene, blagged my way into Mrs Benson's and now the Pascoes' home. Behaviour I wouldn't tolerate in others and yet here I am treating the rules with the same contempt as DI Stride did six months ago.

'I had to, Bob.'

'I told you to stay away from Pascoe.'

'This isn't just about Megan any more.'

'What?'

'Pascoe has got Cheryl Black's vape and that shoeprint from Janie Warren's crime scene, it matches the tread on a pair of shoes in his cupboard. He killed them, Bob.'

'I'm not listening to this. Cheryl Black's death was an accident.'

He doesn't refer to the foot impression because we both know he told Jake to get rid of it.

'So why has he got Cheryl Black's vape then?'

'How do you know it's hers?'

'Because I've seen it in Cheryl's house and now it's in the bottom of his wardrobe.'

'Doesn't prove it hers – and what were you doing in Pascoe's house?'

'Bob, we don't have time for this now. If you seize the vape, I'm certain it will have Cheryl's DNA on it.'

'Are you asking me to get a search warrant? No chance.'

'You said yourself, I didn't have any evidence on Pascoe. Well, this is evidence. He has Cheryl's vape. What's it doing there? When did he take it from her house? Come on, that's enough for you to suspect his involvement in Cheryl's death and get a search warrant.' Silence. I restore my voice to a more measured tone. 'Bob, Pascoe killed Janie Warren, Cheryl Black and he tried to kill Megan. I don't care what's gone on between us before, you can't ignore that. You need to stop him before he does it again because he will.'

The silence at the end of the phone lasts so long, I think the reception has cut out.

'OK. I'll organize a search warrant.

'I won't say anything.'

He rings off.

I need to make sure I'm nowhere near Lavender Gardens when Holt turns up with the heavy mob so I drive away, taking a final look at the house with one thought in mind. This is the end for Simon Pascoe.

45

The detective is standing in his living room, holding a piece of paper – a search warrant – while uniformed police officers go from room to room, rifling through the cupboards.

They've already searched the front room, scattering Jackie's teddies over the floor. She's managed to save four of them that are clutched to her chest.

He knew something was wrong as soon as he walked into the house. Jackie's face and scalp were unusually flushed, like she'd caught the sun, but she couldn't have gone out unless that awful Arjun had turned up on their doorstep, trying to worm his way back into Jackie's affections. No, something had happened.

He hates secrets more than uncertainty and, eventually, he managed to coax it out of her. He knew instantly it was the CSI and that she's on to him. He doesn't know how, but she is. She also doesn't have enough evidence to do anything about it and that's why she came to the house.

The thought of her rummaging around in his belongings made him boil up inside, but he needed to keep calm. He wanted to shout at Jackie for being so stupid to let her in, but he couldn't bear the thought of all that blubbing and, anyway, something was niggling at him.

He was sure she'd found what she was looking for, but if she had why hadn't she taken it straight to the police station? Then he understood. She had lied her way into the house. Anything she found would be inadmissible in court so she went bleating to the detective instead, but it was too late. When the idiot detective turned up with a search team, he was ready for them.

A police officer enters the living room and whispers something in the detective's ear.

'Are you sure?' the detective says out loud.

'Absolutely. We've turned the place inside out.'

The detective nods, but his face is hard with fury.

'We've finished our search, Mr Pascoe, thank you to you and your wife for your cooperation. I'm sorry to have disturbed you.'

He throws the detective a look of innocence.

'Is this to do with the lady who came here earlier today?'

'I'm sorry?'

'Yes, it was the mother of the girl who was attacked in Three Brethren Woods. She's a CSI, I think. She came here pretending to be someone from my work who is nominating me for an award.'

The colour drains from the detective's face.

'When was this?'

'About three this afternoon. I wouldn't have thought too much of it until you turned up with a search warrant. I'm guessing she called you saying she'd found something that connected me to her daughter's attack.'

Mention it before he does. The detective says nothing.

'I'm sorry, Mr Pascoe, I had no idea she'd been here.'

The detective is lying.

'It's fine. It's not that unusual for a relative to fixate on the person who saved their loved one's life.'

The detective frowns at him.

'What do you mean?'

'Well, I've seen her watching me at the hospital a couple of times and I think, although I can't be completely sure, she's driven past my house several times too.'

'Is that so? Do you want to file a complaint for harassment?'

'No, not at all. I feel sorry for her. It's a terrible ordeal to go through.'

'That's still no excuse.'

'She's got it into her head I've got something to do with what's happened to her daughter.'

'Which is completely unacceptable.'

'Like I said, you'd be surprised how often it happens. We get accused of all sorts, Detective.'

The detective can barely contain his fury.

'Well, I can assure you she won't be bothering you again.'

There are messages on my phone from an irate Penny demanding to know where I am and when I'll be back, but I can't face her empty-handed. I need to know Pascoe has been arrested before I face her so when I reach Heale Cross I don't take the road to Barnston but turn towards Morte Sands.

I take my place among the tourists in their Hawaiian swimming shorts and bikinis that just look like strategically placed bandages and queue for one of Liam's coffees. Once at the front, he smiles warmly and tells me how good it is to see me, but with people waiting behind me I don't linger. But it's good to see him too.

I sit down at one of the small round tables Liam provides for those who want a brief break from beach antics and back-ache-inducing deck chairs.

I close my eyes, drawing a lungful of salty air that carries notes of coffee, but as I let go of my breath, hoping it will take with it a modicum of the stress of the previous hours and days, my eyes spring open and lock onto the live cam mounted on a tall post on the slipway to the sands and I think of Jackie, the silent voyeur. I shudder at the thought she has watched me on this beach with Megan. Is she watching me now? Is Simon watching with her?

I check my watch. No. Holt should be there by now with a search team. They'll struggle to keep a straight face at the sight of all those teddy bears – that'll do the rounds of the station for weeks, but the triangle of television screens tuned into the live cams dotted around North Devon's beaches will unnerve even the long-timers.

'How's Megan?'

Liam joins me with a coffee.

'She's doing OK. She's no longer in an induced coma so we're just waiting for her to wake up. The doctors are hopeful she'll come around soon. I fancied a bit of a break and some sea air, but I'll be heading back in a bit. Thank you for the text by the way.'

'When she's awake, I'd love to drop in and say hello if she's feeling up to it.'

'She'd like that.'

I want to tell him that I'd like it, too, but I don't. Some warped defence mechanism, I guess, that says admitting feelings just leads to a trail of regret.

'I heard they got the guy.'

'Shame it isn't the right one,' I say without thinking.

'What?'

I shake my head, not wanting to take Liam into my confidence. He might take it to mean I have other confidences I'm willing to share.

'Long story.'

He shrugs.

'Well, I'm not going anywhere.'

'It's OK. It's all sorted now.'

'Sorry. Now you've lost me.'

'Let's just say DI Holt needed a little nudge in the right direction.'

'Well, I'm still none the wiser, but the main thing is they get the right guy.'

'Yes, but I do have a question for you, though.'

He brightens at the prospect of being useful.

'Another one?' He smiles. 'Fire away.'

'I was trying to find a bit of background on someone, but I could only find information on them going back three or so years and then nothing. A complete dead end. They seemed to vanish into thin air. Any thoughts as to why? I wondered if they'd been abroad.'

As soon as Pascoe's name had sidled into my mind at Three Brethren Woods, I had wanted to know more about him, but a deep trawl of the internet yielded nothing before he took up his job as paramedic, nothing at all.

'Maybe. Or the name they're using now isn't their real name. It's not that difficult to change your name by deed poll.'

'But what about applying for jobs and that?'

'You would just apply under your new name.'

'What about your national insurance number?'

'That doesn't change, but when you change your name,

you just tell the tax office and they update their records with your new name.'

'So how would I go about finding the person's original name?'

'That depends. If they registered it, then there would be a public record of it at the Royal Courts of Justice. You'd have to contact the court and ask for it.'

'What if they haven't enrolled it?'

'Then you've got no easy way of finding out.'

A customer trudges up the slipway, loose sand fanning from his steps, eyeing the coffee shack. Liam drains his coffee and lobs the cup into a bin. 'I better get back to it. Good to see you, Ally. And if you have any more questions, let me know.'

'Thanks.'

The tourist is leaning over the counter searching for someone to serve him. He strolls back towards the van but pauses at the steps up to the side door and turns back to me.

'And I'm here if you need me for anything else.'

'I know. Thank you.'

He appears back behind the counter, delivers the tourist a hundred-watt smile and asks what he can get him. I return to my coffee. So Simon Pascoe isn't his real name. No surprises there. I think I can guess why he might have changed it, so who was he before? But it isn't down to me any more. Pascoe is likely already cuffed and in the back of a police car. When Holt calls, I'll let him know. He can take over. I've done my bit. I need to get back to Megan.

As if on cue, my phone goes off. It's Holt. At last. Pascoe is going down and this ends now. Relief rushes through me before Holt even has a chance to speak, so much so, that when he does, it takes me a few moments to make sense of what he is saying.

'You've really fucked up this time. I'm sorry, Ally, but I'm done protecting you. You're on your own.'

It's late evening when he pulls up in the deserted industrial estate behind the Strudwicks' house. He parks at the end of a cul-de-sac of dull green units, built in the hope businesses would appear and snap them up. They didn't.

His special phone beeps and vibrates a dozen times as soon as he turns it on. Someone's keen to reach him: TruffleDelite. The thought of her impatiently firing off messages at him and then becoming increasingly anxious waiting for a response leaves him glowing with satisfaction.

He's glad he hasn't been able to check them until now. She's got herself into a right state which makes it a whole lot easier.

Swiping his screen, most of her messages are complaints about her parents who are 'total bastards' because they've banned her from seeing that boy, but they won't tell her why. Life's so unfair and now she wishes her parents were dead because she's so sick of how they keep trying to control her life.

He says a silent thank you to her father. He's guessing he didn't hold back and he doesn't blame him. What dad would want their daughter hanging around with the son of a paedo?

Ruggerboy666: They'll come round.

TruffleDelite: No, they won't. I'm not allowed ANY contact with Luke.
😭😭😭😭😭

Ruggerboy666: That's rank. Got the impression you guys are really into each other too.

TruffleDelite: Yeah, we are, but I'm not giving up that easily.

Ruggerboy666: U still seeing each other then?

TruffleDelite: Nah. Can't risk it. Don't want to even message him. Parents threatened to send me to my aunt's up north, if I have anything to do with him.

Ruggerboy666: Seriously. They're mad. What you gonna do?

TruffleDelite: Dunno. If I can't see Luke, I'll die.

Ruggerboy666: I get it. What if I said I know Luke. He's the really tall lad with long black hair, right?

TruffleDelite: Yeah, that's him. How come you know him? Are you his mate, Tim?

Ruggerboy666: No, bit insulted you should think I'm that spanner!!!

TruffleDelite: Soz. I know. He's a right idiot. Btw, thanks for listening to me. Can't talk to anyone else. Luke was going out with my best mate, Shana, before we got together. He cheated on her to get with me. She'd kill me if she found out.

Ruggerboy666: Don't worry. Ur secret's safe with me. I got my own troubles.

TruffleDelite: Oh yeah. How's that going?

Ruggerboy666: Good, been a bit tough, but we had a long chat last night. We've decided to stay together.

TruffleDelite: So you don't have a secret crush on me any more?

Ruggerboy666: Lol. No. Soz. Think it was because of all the stuff we were going through. We're still mates though?

TruffleDelite: 'Course.

Ruggerboy666: You serious about this guy?

TruffleDelite: Yeah.

Ruggerboy666: OK. I'll talk to him for you. See if we can get you lovebirds together without the parents knowing.

TruffleDelite: You'd do that for me? I'm desperate to see him.

Ruggerboy666: Sure. That's what mates are for. Will message you.

TruffleDelite: Thx. You're the best.

Ruggerboy666: I know.

46

Lowe is sitting behind his desk. Next to him stands Holt. He's already bawled me out for not finding anything during the search. After Holt called me, I returned to the hospital where I tried to explain to Penny what had happened, but she left without saying a word beyond a perfunctory discussion that there was no change with Megan.

I apologized to Megan for my absence and determined my penance would be to stay awake all night reading to her, trying to make up for the hours I'd been away.

Penny made it clear that she would only return to sit with Megan this morning so I could attend this meeting, but I had to get back immediately after it finished.

'Take a seat, Ally.'

'I'm OK standing.'

'So be it.' Lowe takes a huge breath. 'Do you know why you're here?'

I glance at Holt. How much has he told Lowe? Lowe appears to read my mind and duly answers my question. 'I know you tipped DI Holt off about evidence in Simon Pascoe's house that related to Janie Warren and Cheryl Black. I also know you visited Pascoe's house yesterday morning.'

So, Holt has told him everything. This is what it feels like to be hung out to dry, but while my methods are questionable, the facts are unalterable. Pascoe attacked Megan and killed Janie and Cheryl.

'That's right. I suspected Pascoe was involved in Megan's attack. I told Bob of my suspicions, but he said there wasn't enough evidence to act so I went to the house to find that evidence. What I found was Cheryl Black's vape. I contacted Bob immediately. Clearly, by the time the police arrived, Jackie Pascoe had already told her husband of my visit and he had disposed of the vape.'

'Did DI Holt have prior knowledge that you intended to go to Simon Pascoe's house?'

'No. I acted alone.'

'You made me look like a right idiot, that's what you did.'

'That wasn't my intention and I know what I saw. Like I said, Pascoe got there first.'

'You do realize how serious this is, don't you?'

'Yes, but I had to do something. Simon Pascoe set up Peter Benson and attacked Megan. I went to Pascoe's house to look for proof and I got it, and much more. Pascoe killed Janie Warren and Cheryl Black. Maybe there are more. Maybe we even have a serial killer on our hands.'

Holt sighs.

'Warren was the victim of a domestic and Black died in an accidental fire.'

'That is what Pascoe wants us to believe. Like he wants us to believe Peter Benson attacked Megan.'

'That's bullshit,' says Holt.

'No, it's not. Why would I make it up?'

'Because you're still pissed off at me over the Warren and Black case and now, unbelievably, you're trying to screw up the investigation into your own daughter's attempted murder.'

'I'm not screwing up anything. I'm trying to get to the truth.'

'What – by threatening the guy on TV? By going around to the suspect's house and bothering his mother? By intimidating innocent members of the public?'

'What?' interjects Lowe.

'Oh yeah, you'll love this one. She went to Benson's house, pretending she needed to do another search. Five minutes there and she decides Simon Pascoe somehow broke into his Wi-Fi and used it to groom her daughter. You're in the wrong game, Ally, you should be writing crime fiction.'

Lowe is rubbing his face.

'OK, thank you for your input, DI Holt, I'd like to speak to Ms Dymond in private.'

Holt leaves. Lowe lets out a long, disappointed sigh. The kind of sigh a senior officer releases when one of their own has fallen short.

'What the hell is going on with you? I've read your file, Ally. You've never even had a parking ticket. You alienated your colleagues on Major Investigations because you weren't prepared to protect a bent copper and see a kid go down on false evidence. That is the Ally Dymond I know.'

'Steve, hear me out. I admit I've done a couple of things that are inappropriate.' We both know that's stretching it, but I ignore his raised eyebrow. 'But I wouldn't put my career on the line if I didn't think I was right.'

He nods. He can relate to this. No one jeopardizes their career without good cause.

'Go on.'

'I've been a CSI for a long time. I've examined more crime scenes than I can count and – from the very beginning – this one didn't add up so I went and checked it out for myself. I'm absolutely certain someone walked down through the woods from the housing estate and attacked my daughter before running back to the estate. That someone was Simon Pascoe, who was parked alone in an ambulance at the back entrance to the woods the whole time. He'd already met Megan when she had an accident at school, and he was called to attend her. God knows why but I think Megan has another Instagram account and somehow Pascoe got those details out of her and began grooming her online. He set Benson up. Benson is telling the truth. He's never been on Instagram. I bet he doesn't even know what it is. Simon used Benson's Wi-Fi to communicate with Megan. And I saw those items at Pascoe's house. I'm telling you, Pascoe is a killer. You have to stop him. He will kill again. Megan just got lucky.'

Lowe is shaking his head.

'I've looked at the files, Ally. They're watertight. Chris Banstead strangled Janie Warren, a stray cigarette killed Cheryl Black and Peter Benson attacked your daughter. I know you're upset and angry that the paramedics didn't get there more quickly.'

'Wait, no, that's not true. I'm not upset about that. Did Pascoe say that?'

He ignores my protests.

'I also know you're under huge stress with your daughter still ill in hospital, but I can't ignore this. You don't need me to tell you your behaviour constitutes gross misconduct in a public office.'

'Steve, no, wait. I know I shouldn't have blagged my way into Peter's house or Pascoe's, but please listen to me. I did it for good reasons. Suspend me, sack me, do what you want, but please investigate Simon Pascoe. He's a killer. In fact, I'm pretty sure that isn't even his real name. And there's only one reason to change your name and that's because you have something to hide. Christ, he could be a serial killer.'

'That's enough. I have listened to you and I've listened to the others. Your behaviour isn't rational and neither can I ignore it. I'm suspending you immediately, pending an inquiry and, Ally, I strongly advise you to get a decent brief.'

Penny and I are sitting either side of Megan's bedside. Her gaze trained on Megan, she listens, stony-faced, as I relay my meeting with Lowe. When I finish, she looks over at me.

'So what happens now?'

'I'll be referred to Professional Standards. They'll investigate and decide if I'm guilty of gross misconduct.'

Me. On a gross misconduct charge. I don't even park the CSI van on double yellows and now I'm facing the prospect of losing my job. I left Lowe's office numb at the thought. Nothing I could say would change his mind and now I'm facing the sack while Pascoe roams the streets.

'And if you are?'

'I'll be kicked off the force.'

Surely, they'll see sense. My phone will ring any second now and it'll be Lowe telling me he's gone over the files again and he believes me. Pascoe is a killer and because of my part in bringing him to justice, I'm exonerated. 'Just don't do it again, Ally.' That's what would happen if this were a film, but this is real life governed by process and rules and I've broken them. Forget Pascoe, this is now about bringing me to justice. Is this how Stride felt? OK, he bent the rules, but for the right reasons and what better reason than seeing a murderer get sent down. But it's Stride that's seeing out a prison sentence and Sian Jones' killer is still out there.

Penny nods.

'Maybe it would be for the better.'

Her words come at me like a sucker punch and it takes me a few seconds to recover.

'What? Are you serious?'

She shrugs.

'Yes, I am serious. You should be here with Megan.'

So there it is. Penny doesn't have my back at all, but this isn't just about me, her or even Megan any more.

'Yes, you're right. I should be here, but what if Pascoe attacks someone else?' I spread my arms and cast around the room. 'I wouldn't wish this on anyone.'

She shakes her head.

'But that's not why you're doing it, is it?'

'Of course it is, and to get justice. Not just for Megan now, either, but for Janie and for Cheryl.'

Penny rolls her eyes.

'That's assuming you're right and Pascoe is guilty.'

I can't believe I'm hearing this, Penny of all people doubting my honesty.

'Pascoe had Cheryl's vape.'

'How do you know it was Cheryl's? Lots of people have vapes.'

'I recognized the flavour.' Penny raises an eyebrow. I know

how weak this sounds. 'I'm certain if Pascoe hadn't got rid of it we'd have found Cheryl's DNA on it.'

Penny shakes her head.

'But you didn't, did you? And now you're probably going to lose your job over him. Maybe this would be a good time to leave it be, concentrate on what's important.' She looks at Megan. 'Concentrate on Megan. Put her first.'

'That's just the point. I *am* putting her first. I'm making sure she'll be safe from the man who attacked her. Don't you think he's wondering when she's going to wake up and what she'll remember when she does? Megan isn't safe. And neither is anyone else.'

She nods, finally seeming to relent. Maybe she's remembering what it's like to feel unsafe, to live in fear of someone.

'OK,' she concedes, 'but if the police don't believe you what else can you do? You've tried everything.'

I hold her gaze.

'Not quite everything.'

It's something that I've been mulling over since I left Lowe's office. It's what's known in the trade as a long shot, but there may be a way to end this.

'What do you mean?'

I stand up to leave.

'Look, I can't go into it now, but can you stay with Megan just for a little bit longer? Then, I promise, this will all be over.'

Penny gets up too.

'No. Not this time. You're Megan's mother, not me.'

'What's that supposed to mean?'

'It means I'm tired of being picked up and dropped whenever it suits you. Good old Penny, she'll take care of Megan. She doesn't have her own kids. She's probably grateful for the opportunity.'

'That's not true.'

'Yes, it is. You've always got somewhere else to be, but never here by your daughter's bedside because you've always got me to fall back on. Well, guess what? I don't want to be a surrogate mother for Megan.'

'Penny, you've been brilliant. I know that I'm lucky to have you and so is Megan. Please. Let me do this one last thing and then I promise I'll never ask anything of you again.'

I move towards the door expecting her to give me a defeated wave and tell me it's OK to go, but don't be long. She doesn't.

'I mean it, Ally, if you walk out of that door, our friendship is over for good. When Megan is better, you can start looking for somewhere else to live. I want you out of Seven Hills.'

I don't know where this has come from; I've never seen her so determined before. She means it, but so do I.

The door closes behind me.

47

A wiggle of a paperclip and the lock on the back door of Pascoe's house gives way.

Breaking and entering. In other words, burglary. Not that I plan to take anything, but I have forced my way into a house without the owner's consent. That makes me a burglar. Me. Ally Dymond. Straight down the line, always by the book, upholder of the law. Only, I am none of those things any more. I have hammered many nails into my career coffin over the last few days; this is the final one.

My hands sheathed in latex gloves, I ease the door open in case it has a repertoire of noises ready to alert its owners. It doesn't and I slide between the narrow gap I've created and into the kitchen. Its shiny white units and white-tiled floor smelling of bleach have all the welcome of a hospital examination room. This is Pascoe's territory, not Jackie's, and its coldness causes me to hesitate, but only for a moment.

The house is silent. Pascoe's car is gone from the driveway and maybe he's taken Jackie with him, although they don't look the day-trip type. It's been a wasted journey if he has.

Slipping off my trainers, I move into the hallway, my socks gliding silently across the parquet flooring. I need to go quietly.

The door to the living room is open. A low whine drifts out from within. At first I think Pascoe has got a dog, but the noise comes again and it's less of a growl, more a groan and this time it has a human quality. It's not a dog. It's Jackie Pascoe and she sounds in pain.

I take a step nearer to the living room and peer in. Dozens of glassy eyes seem to turn in my direction, but they're powerless to warn their owner. The TVs are on, tuned to the live cam on Morte Sands.

Jackie is in her reclining chair, her legs poking out from under her dress like straws. On the side table is a bundle of screwed-up sweet wrappers. Her shoulders shudder and her face is buried in a teddy, the one with the white loin cloth and glasses that I think must be Gandhi. She's crying, not in physical pain, but in despair.

My heart heaves. I know she told Simon about my visit, but I feel nothing but pity for her. She's a victim too. I don't know what he's done to her, but I do know she's wasting away and needs to get out of here.

Another, louder groan slips out of her and something aches inside me like a bruise has been pressed that I thought had long faded. I am Jackie and she is me. She thinks she's free. She thinks every thought is her own, but it isn't. It belongs to Pascoe in the same way that mine belonged to Sean. That's how it works. You're subsumed into them and you can't even see it yourself. You are a satellite moon to their planet, believing you determine your own existence when you're entirely dependent on them, body and mind, never free from their orbit.

But it's not too late. She can leave with me today. She can stay at the cabin for as long as it remains my home. I can get her help. I can save her.

I step silently into the room just as Jackie takes a sudden deep breath like her inner voice has just given her a talking to, telling her to stop with the tears. She lowers the teddy onto her lap and strokes his head.

'All I want to do is go to the beach with him. It'd be such fun. I know it would. He works so hard and it makes him grumpy, but I know a trip to the beach would cheer him up.' She heaves a huge sigh like a teenager with a crush on an unattainable pop star. 'If only he knew how much I love him.'

This is going to be harder than I thought. She's besotted with Pascoe, but she's my only hope of bringing him to justice and preventing him from hurting Megan again or anyone else.

First, I need to make sure she can't call for help. Taking a deep breath, I rush into the room. Immediately, her head twists round. Shock registers across her face and she goes to grab the mobile phone from the table beside her, but I already have it in my hand. She grips the arms of her chair in fear.

I raise my hands to show I mean no harm.

'It's all right, Jackie. I'm not going to hurt you.'

'What do you want, then?'

'I just want to talk.'

Her lips wobble.

'I trusted you and you tricked me. You said Simon was going to get an OBE.'

'I know. That was very wrong of me. I'm very sorry. Please, I just want to talk.'

She's terrified, but not just of me, though. Her mind is full of what will happen if Pascoe were to walk through the door. Not to me, but to her. How much will she be blamed for my presence? How much will she be punished? I know what that feels like, to take the rap for the delivery man not showing up on time or the live football stream not working. I'm on your side, Jackie. I just want you to be on mine.

'I see you're watching Morte Sands. It's a lovely beach.' She glances at the screen and then back at me, but my eye remains on the screen. 'My daughter Megan and I have been going there for years. Do you ever get the chance to visit?'

Her head turns towards the screen and we both watch a family playing beach cricket. I sense her relaxing a little.

'Arjun took me once. Before he got the sack. Until then I hadn't been for years. Not since before I was married.'

'Arjun? Yes. You told me about him. He was your friend, wasn't he?'

She smiles.

'Yes, I miss him.'

'Would you like to see him again?'

'Oh yes, but Simon says he's a crook, a bad man.'

'Do you think he's a bad man?'

She thinks for a moment and gives a little shrug.

'He was never bad to me, just nice.'

'Sometimes, it's difficult to know if someone is good or bad. Sometimes good people do bad things and bad people do good things.' I let that sit for a moment, but I've no idea if she understands what I'm getting at. She appears to mull it over like a thought that's never occurred to her before, but she says nothing. I decide to take a risk. 'Jackie, I think you know why I'm here.'

She shakes her head.

'No, I don't.'

'I need your help.'

This catches her interest. It's been a long time since anyone asked her for anything.

'What do you mean, my help?'

I pause. Christ, how do I put this? Jackie, your husband has murdered two women and tried to kill a third. Will you testify against him for me?

'Well, someone hurt my daughter Megan and has hurt other women too. I want to find that person before they hurt anyone else.'

'I don't know what you're talking about.'

I nod.

'I know how hard this is for you, but these women have done nothing wrong.'

'I don't see what this has to do with me.'

'I think you do. I think you know I'm talking about your husband, Simon.'

Jackie bites her lower lip, like she's trying to stop her words spilling out of her. A part of her wants to tell me, but that doesn't mean she will.

She shakes her head.

'That's ridiculous. He's a paramedic.'

'I know and I know that he's saved lots of people too. Like I said, good people can do bad things. Life isn't black and white.'

'Not Simon. I know him. He wouldn't hurt anyone.'

She looks down at her fingers interlaced on her lap. She can't look me in the eye because we both know she's lying.

'Jackie, I wish it wasn't him, really I do, but Simon attacked my daughter, Megan, and he has hurt other women.'

For some reason, I can't bring myself to say the word kill,

as if I need to protect Jackie from the horror of what her husband has done.

'No, not Simon.'

But it's whispered. She doesn't believe her own words.

'Yes. Simon. It's true, isn't it?'

She bites her bottom lip again, but the emotion within her finds another outlet. A tear rolls down her bony cheek.

'Jackie, it's true, isn't it?'

She nods. I want to ask a hundred questions: How much does she know? When did she find out? Has he ever hurt her? I don't need to ask why she didn't call the police. I already know the answer to that one.

'I can help you. I know what it's like living with someone who wants to control you, who persuades you that everything they do is for the best, even though it makes you feel sad.'

'Simon loves me.'

I have to go so very carefully.

'Yes, I think he does, in his own way, but you deserve better. Much better. And he's hurt other women, Jackie, really badly.'

'He wouldn't hurt me.' There's defiance in her voice and I believe her. He's never touched her and that makes things much harder. It makes her special. She's the only one that really understands him. The other women deserved what they got because they didn't know how to behave, and he didn't love them like he loved her.

'That's what I used to say about my ex. Yeah, he's got a temper on him, but he'd never lay a finger on me. Until the day he did.' She's looking at me hard, trying to work out if I'm feeding her a lie. 'It's true.' I lift up my shirt to reveal three pale white streaks across my stomach. 'I got these when he pushed me and I fell onto a glass coffee table. I have others too.'

'I love him.'

I roll my shirt back down over my stomach. No. No, you don't. You think you do because he gives you attention, tells you he'll keep you safe from the world, maybe he even brings you gifts, but it's all a lie.

'I know you do, and that's OK. But how many times have you worried about saying the wrong thing in case it sets him off? How many times have you dreaded him coming home in a bad mood? How many times have you told yourself it will get better, you just have to learn not to upset him?' Another tear joins the first. I lay my hand on hers. She doesn't flinch. Instead, her fragile hand turns and closes around mine. 'The trouble is, Jackie, it doesn't get better.'

I stop talking, allowing her time to take it all in.

'What will happen to me?'

There it is – the first call for help. I let out a silent sigh of relief.

'I'll make sure you'll be well looked after. You'll be safe. I promise. I can talk to Arjun and arrange for him to come and visit you.'

It's too much. The reality of what happens next hits her and she removes her hand from mine.

'I don't know.'

'I know it's hard for you, but things can't go on like this. You have a right to be happy and you can be, but not here.'

She looks around the room.

'It's not so bad.'

Oh Christ. She's talking herself out of this.

'Jackie, things could be so much better for you. You could visit Morte Sands as often as you wish.'

She shrugs. I'm running out of time.

'The thing is, Simon is a very, very dangerous man. If we don't stop him, he could hurt someone else's daughter.' I glance at the live cams. A group of young girls are sunbathing in the foreground. 'You see those people on Morte Sands. One of them could be next. Imagine watching the screen, only it isn't full of people enjoying the beach, it's full of police and ambulances and imagine you know the reason why.' Guilt seeps into the corner of Jackie's eyes. She looks away from the screens. Then it hits me. 'Oh my God. It's already happened, hasn't it?' Jackie can't meet my eye, but I don't need her to. I know the truth. 'There's a live cam on Bidecombe Quay. Janie Warren, the young girl that was murdered there. You saw it, didn't you?'

She hesitates.

'I fell asleep in the afternoon and when I woke up, I couldn't find the TV remote. I wouldn't normally go upstairs, but it was a lovely day and I wanted to see the children on the beach so I went into Simon's bedroom and found it there. I don't sleep very well at night and I like to watch the moonlight on the water in Bidecombe harbour. It's so pretty. I noticed someone under the quay, I didn't know what they could be doing there at that time of night so I watched them. It was dark, but I knew straightaway it was him. I put the remote back in his room before he got home.'

'Does Simon suspect anything?'

'I don't think so.' She pauses. 'I don't see that much of him. He has a very stressful job, you see. When he gets home, he's usually too tired to spend any time with me. He often just goes straight to his room, leaving me downstairs.'

'Oh my God, Jackie. You poor woman.'

I curl my arm around her; she doesn't pull away.

'Maybe it was an accident,' she says quietly.

'Maybe, and if it was that will all come out. All you have to do is tell the police what you saw.'

She picks up Gandhi and strokes his fur.

48

Something has shifted. He senses it as soon as he walks through the door. It was the same with Danielle. She didn't have to tell him she was seeing someone else. He already knew. There was something different in her, not in how she looked or acted, but in the air around her. It's the same now with Jackie. Something has happened.

In the living room. Jackie's chair is more upright than usual. She has a teddy in each hand. Judging by the laurel wreath and the snake crown, it's Caesar and Cleopatra. Gandhi has finally been relegated to the mantelpiece. The three of them are studying the television screens intently. They're all tuned into Morte Sands which is all but empty except for a couple of teenage girls flaunting themselves.

Jackie starts at his appearance.

'I didn't hear you come in. I was watching the youngsters on the beach.'

'Did anyone visit today?'

'No.'

'Are you sure?'

'Yes. You told me not to let anyone in and I didn't.'

She looks at him levelly. Something's wrong.

'Has that CSI been here?'

Jackie colours instantly and gathers her teddies closer to her.

'I promise I didn't let her in. I don't know how she got in, but she just appeared in the living room.'

'Shush, there, there, don't get upset. I'm here now. She can't hurt you.'

'I'm sorry. I didn't know how to get rid of her.'

'Why should you? She's very sly. What did you talk about?' Jackie looks away. 'Actually, let me guess. She told you what a terrible man I am.'

She nods. The tears flow effortlessly.

'I didn't believe her.'

She's lying. My smile confuses her.

'That's OK. I understand. You were scared. You said what you had to say to get rid of her.'

She nods like a wind-up toy.

'Yes, that's it. I didn't know what else to do. She had my mobile.'

'So what did she say?'

'Horrible things about how you've hurt people and that you would hurt me. She said she could help me leave you.'

He laughs.

'It's a trick, you do know that, don't you?'

'What do you mean?'

'The woman is obsessed with me. She's just trying to get you away from me because she wants me to herself. When I dropped a sympathy card off for her daughter, she practically threw herself at me. She's forever sending me filthy messages. I should have told you. I'm sorry. I didn't want to upset you. Can you forgive me?'

He crouches beside her and takes her hand; her skin is crinkled and loose, like an old lady's.

'Yes.'

He wipes away a tear and gazes into her eyes.

'You do know that I love you, don't you? I'd never leave you. There isn't a woman on this earth that can compare to you, my dear sweet Jackie.'

She smiles.

'Perhaps you should tell that detective. He could arrest her for harassment. Then she'd leave us in peace.'

He pretends to think about it.

'Yes, that's a good idea. The thing is, people like her don't know when to stop and I can't bear the thought of you being here on your own, terrified she might break in at any moment and hurt you. I could never forgive myself.'

Jackie tenses at the thought.

'So, what are we going to do? I'm scared.'

He blows out his cheeks and releases a long sigh as if they've been left with little choice.

'We need to think of a way to stop her for good.'

Instead, he idly traces the lines on the palm of her hand, like he once saw Gary do to Trisha behind the ambulance station. She seemed to love it, but she's easily pleased. Smiling up at her, he kisses her palm and presses it against his cheek. Its clamminess repulses him and he has to unpeel it sooner than he'd like, but it's already had the effect he wanted. Her thin lips work themselves into a smile and her pupils have expanded into big black pools of submission.

'You know I love you, don't you?'

She nods.

'I love you too.' Her words are croaky with emotion.

'You trust me, don't you?'

'With all my heart.' She lifts her hand towards him, but he moves out of range and it falls by her side.

'There is a way out of this. A way where she'll never ever bother us again, but you need to do exactly as I say.'

She nods.

'I will.'

'Good, because I'm going to need you to be extra brave.'

49

It's quicker to take the new road to Exeter unless you know the old one like I do and can navigate its sharp corners and hidden dips with the requisite easing of the foot off the accelerator, saving vital minutes, but still, today it feels interminable.

Jackie has agreed to leave Simon and I promised her that I would speak to Holt first and then some police officers would accompany social services to collect her within an hour, two at the most. Once she's away from him, she'll open up.

My preference would be to waltz into the Major Incidents suite so Holt has no choice but to listen to me, but Lowe demanded that I surrender my security pass so I pace reception, hoping Holt will deign to put in an appearance.

I'm about to ask the receptionist to call him up again when he finally appears, but he's not alone. With him are two uniformed officers. Before I have time to speak, he nods in my direction.

'That's her.'

The officers move towards me.

'What's this? What's going on?' But I know what's going on. I've seen it enough times. I just can't work out why it's happening to me. I look to Holt for an explanation.

'Ally Dymond, I'm arresting you on suspicion of assaulting Jackie Pascoe.'

But his words make no sense.

'Assault? What are you talking about? I would never lay a finger on Jackie Pascoe.'

Then it hits me square on. Oh God. Pascoe. He got to her first. What have I done?

Holt's face remains impassive. Despite our differences, I sense this is giving him no pleasure. We never like to nick one of our own. 'You do not have to say anything, but anything you do say . . .'

I have to stop this. For both our sakes.

'Bob. Wait. Don't do this. You know me. You know I couldn't have done anything like this. I never touched Jackie.'

Holt gives a weary sigh; he's had his fill of people protesting their innocence.

'We've got proof that says otherwise.'

'What proof? You can't have because I didn't touch her.'

Holt stares at me for a moment before picking up where he left off, reciting my rights in the same way he's done since his police training days thirty years ago. When he's finished, one of the uniformed officers grabs my arm like I'm planning to do a runner, but I shake it off.

'Don't fucking touch me.'

I regret it immediately. It's enough to make him go for his cuffs. His mate steps in, grabs my right arm and twists it behind my back smacking my face onto the front reception desk. Pain shoots up my arm which feels like it'll snap any second.

'Ow. Get off me.'

But I'm wasting my breath. While his mate holds me still,

the first cop slips the plastic loop over my wrists and tightens the plastic cuffs, cutting into my skin.

'Right, let's get her down in custody,' says the first cop.

They jostle me towards the door to the inner sanctum of the station.

'Christ, there's no need to be so rough. Bob, please get them to take the cuffs off. I'll go quietly.'

Jesus, I'm a walking criminal cliché, but he ignores my request and nods at his goons. One officer opens the door, while the other shoves me roughly through the doorway, the plastic slicing my skin like a wire through cheese.

'Bob, you're making a massive mistake,' I call over my shoulder, but the door closes on me.

Jackie's eyelids flicker open to the narrowest of slits under the pressure of the bruises that have ballooned her brows. Her bloodied eyeballs swivel before settling on him. 'How are you, my love?'

He says it loud enough for the nurse tending the patient in the next bed to hear. She looks on as if she wishes her husband spoke to her that way.

'Water,' whispers Jackie.

Her arms aren't broken, Jackie's perfectly capable of reaching for it herself. She's not been conscious five seconds and she's already making demands.

'Of course, my love.'

He holds the straw a little way away and watches her swollen dry lips protrude and pucker as she searches it out. She lifts her head and gasps from the effort before her lips clamp around the straw.

As she sips, he nudges the straw out of her mouth. Water

dribbles down her chin and onto her chest. Where's your precious Arjun now?

He puts the plastic cup on the side.

'Did we do it?' she whispers.

The nurse has left the ward, but he leans in close to Jackie.

'Yes, we did it. The CSI has been arrested. She won't bother us again. I promise. Things can get back to normal now.'

A wince accompanies her nod.

'That's good. Thank you.'

At last, some gratitude.

The effort of those few words appears to take its toll; Jackie closes her eyes and relaxes back onto the bed. A few minutes later, she's asleep again.

By the time he'd finished explaining to her what a threat Ally Dymond was, she was practically begging him to hit her as hard as he could.

He told her that the CSI was obsessed with him and if she couldn't have him she would hurt him instead. Jackie would end up in a home. No more sweets, no more live cams, no more miniature teddies. But it was worse than that. He's regularly called to care homes. He's seen the physical and psychological abuse that happens there first hand.

She dissolved into a quivering, watery mess and begged him to do what needed to be done then and there, but these things needed to be done properly.

Jackie chose which bear she wanted to be with her, opting for Florence Nightingale. He patted her hand, told her she was doing the right thing and left.

An hour later, he crept downstairs and into the living room where he found her absorbed in the live cam and the sight of a little boy and his father trying to shore up their sandcastle against the incoming tide. He was suddenly irritated that these strangers had her attention and not him, so he coughed to announce his arrival.

She looked up, terror in her eyes, but she didn't try to defend herself. It might have been better if she had, more authentic, but it was too late now and he swung the CSI's spanner down hard onto her crown. Florence Nightingale tumbled to the floor.

She slumped to one side of her chair, blood oozing over her scalp from the gaping wound. Head injuries always look bad and it was difficult to tell if it had been enough so, pulling her back into an upright position, he struck her a few more times just to be sure. He dropped the spanner by her side. It landed next to Florence Nightingale.

He checks his watch. It's nearly midday. He wants to leave. He's been there since 4 p.m. yesterday. Surely, that's long enough. The nurses keep remarking on his determination to be by his wife's side and how lucky she is to have him to look after her. Trisha even put in an appearance. She was really shocked and angry at what had happened to his 'lovely Jackie' and Colin told him to take as much time as he needed. Work can wait.

A nurse ambles in just as he's getting up. She checks the machines Jackie is hooked up to.

'She's doing well. She'll be out of here in no time.'

The thought doesn't cheer him.

'That's good to hear.'

'Although your wife has complained of stomach pains when she eats. Would you like me to ask the doctor to take a closer look?'

'Thank you, but there's no need. We've already seen the doctor about it. They're caused by her General Anxiety Disorder. Same as her alopecia. She was severely bullied as a child. She's never really got over it. They used to spit on her food so eating makes her particularly anxious.'

'That's terrible. I could speak to our mental health team instead.'

'Honestly, we've tried everything, it's hopeless. Being in hospital will make it worse too. The sooner she's home, where I can take care of her, the better.'

The nurse nods.

'It must be hard being a paramedic and caring for your wife.'

'Yes, it can be,' he says, rubbing his eyes.

'You look tired. Why don't you go home and get some rest? We'll call you, if we need to.'

'Yes, OK.'

Outside of the hospital, he pauses to inhale the cool unrecycled air, but he's not going home. TruffleDelite is about to finish her morning lessons.

50

Holt announces the time, date and names of everyone present, for the purposes of the tape.

He's sitting opposite me, avoiding my eye, as if I've yet to enter the room. He lays the beige file on the desk and smooths his hair in preparation. He's ready to do battle. Next to him is acting DS Shirwell, the detective I met at Cheryl Black's house. Her hair is dragged into a ballerina bun and she studies me with a mix of curiosity and contempt. I'm guessing she's there to learn the ropes. Lesson ten: what happens when one of us goes bad.

I've refused a brief. It slows everything down and I need to get out of here.

Clasping his hands in front of him, Holt finally looks me in the eye.

'Ally, can you tell us where you were at precisely 3 p.m. this afternoon?'

'We don't have time for this. You need to get over to Pascoe's house now.'

'I repeat . . .'

I'll take a burglary charge if it gets me out of here quicker.

'OK. I was breaking into 19 Lavender Gardens, the home of Simon and Jackie Pascoe.'

Shirwell glances at Holt, her superior, for guidance on this unexpected start to the interview. Holt remains unmoved by my confession. He's got something up his sleeve, I can sense it. He wouldn't have nicked me on Jackie's say-so no matter how convincing her story. He's got proof of some kind that I was there, most likely CCTV, putting me close to Pascoe's house, but that's not enough.

'Why were you breaking into Mr Pascoe's house?'

'I wanted to talk to Jackie.'

Shirwell frowns; she's more used to the 'no comment' kind of response. Holt continues to draw me down some planned-out path. I just can't fathom what it is and I have no choice but to go along with it.

'Why would you want to do that?'

'Because I wanted to persuade her to leave Pascoe before he hurt her. I also wanted to find out if she knew her husband had attacked Megan and killed Janie Warren and Cheryl Black.'

Holt ignores my references to Janie and Cheryl.

'We have the person who attacked Megan. You know that.'

'You've got the wrong man.'

He turns to Shirwell and rolls his eyes.

'We're getting nowhere here. Let's move on.'

But I'm not ready to move on.

'Bob, listen to me, Pascoe knew Megan. He met her months ago when she hit her head in a PE class. Somehow, he got her username.'

Holt interrupts.

'We already checked her social media.'

'Then she must have another Instagram account and she

341

gave that username to Pascoe who began grooming her online and then lured her to Three Brethren Woods, but not before he'd set Peter Benson up to take the rap.'

Shirwell rolls her eyes.

'You do know that Mr Pascoe is a hero. He not only saved your daughter's life, but he was in the papers just last week for rescuing a girl from the cliffs at Morte Sands.'

Holt is irritated at Shirwell's interruption.

'I'm not listening to this. Simon Pascoe has been ruled out of our inquiries.'

Holt opens the beige file in front of him and spreads out a series of photos on the table which make me gasp. Assault is such an emotionless word which, in law, can cover anything from a scratch to a beating. I don't know what I expected, but it isn't this.

Jackie Pascoe's lower lip is purple and swollen and cartoonish against her pale hollowed-out cheeks. Down the centre of her scalp is a long dark track of stitches: Jackie Pascoe is lucky to be alive.

'Jesus Christ. That's horrific. You don't seriously think I did this, do you? This is Pascoe's doing.'

'Are you saying Simon Pascoe beat his own wife?' asks Holt.

'Well, it wouldn't be the first time a man has taken his fists to his wife so yes, that's exactly what I'm saying. I told you he's a killer. There's nothing he isn't capable of.'

Holt lets out a heavy sigh.

'Cut the bullshit, Ally. You were warned to stay away from the house. So what happened? You just snapped?'

I stare at Holt and, for the first time, I think he actually believes I did this. Panic surges through me at the thought that I could go down for something I didn't do. Worse, Pascoe would still be free to strike again.

'It would be totally understandable, Ally.' Shirwell is speaking. I deeply resent her using my first name like we're friends, but this isn't the time for a discussion about boundaries. 'Your daughter has been brutally attacked. You've been through hell. We understand that. You're angry and that can make you irrational, even dangerous.'

Patronizing cow.

'I'm angry because no one will listen to me and there's every chance Pascoe will attack some other innocent woman. Bob, you don't honestly believe I could do something like this.' He doesn't respond, of course. This isn't about what he thinks, this is about the evidence so I take a look at it again, lining the photos up in front of me allowing me to switch from one to another. Something's wrong. 'Are these all the photos of her injuries?'

Holt nods. Shirwell frowns again, even harder this time. She's unhappy with the way this is going. Suspects don't ask questions in her world. They say nothing or spill everything.

'Look here,' I tap the photo. 'There's one hard blow to the top of her head, but the rest are superficial, like the attacker pulled back. This isn't a frenzied attack. If it were, the blows would become more forceful. And if these are the only photos then that means there are no defence wounds. Jackie didn't attempt to stop the person doing this to her.' It's a shock to realize that Jackie may have allowed Pascoe to beat her up. The things we do for love. I tap the photo again. 'That's a controlled assault. Your theory that I snapped and lost it doesn't hold up.'

Holt sits back, arms folded.

343

'That doesn't mean anything. You could have crept up behind her. The first blow almost certainly knocked her out. Maybe you panicked. You just wanted to hurt her rather than kill her.'

I shake my head.

'Why would I do that? It's Pascoe I'm after, not his wife.'

'You went looking for Pascoe and when you couldn't find him, you got angry with Jackie because she wouldn't believe your nonsense either.'

'What? No. That's not true. She's as much a victim as the others. She just doesn't know it. Jackie told him I had been there, trying to persuade her to leave him. She knows what he is. He realized I was never going to give up and this was a surefire way of getting rid of me.'

Holt leans forward again.

'So, you're denying you attacked Jackie Pascoe?'

'Of course, I'm denying it because I didn't do it. Simon Pascoe did this to his wife and then framed me.'

'We've already spoken to him. He says he came home and found his wife like this.'

Holt nods down at the photos.

'Well, he's lying.'

'The man's completely distraught.'

'He's faking it.'

God, I sound ridiculous and we all know it. Shirwell doesn't even bother to hide her contempt, rolling her eyes at me. Holt just lets out another long sigh.

'OK. I've given you every opportunity to come clean. Let's get on with it. If you didn't attack Jackie Pascoe, as you say, can you tell us how your fingerprints came to be on the weapon which was found at the scene?'

'What?'

He takes another photo from the file and slides it towards me. It's a spanner, one end of which is smeared in blood.

'You don't deny this is your spanner?'

I shrug.

'It could be. I have one like it. It's under the kitchen sink.' Or was. 'Oh shit. Pascoe must have broken into my house and stolen it.'

The thought of him in the cabin sends shudders through me.

Acting DS Shirwell laughs.

'Oh, so now Mr Pascoe is a burglar as well as a killer.'

I want to tell this Shirwell that sneering at your suspect is not the way to get them to talk, but Holt steps in.

'What proof have you that Simon Pascoe broke into your house?'

'None, but it's the only explanation for why the spanner ended up in his house. He took it from me.'

There's a long pause until Holt speaks again.

'It's not the only explanation, though, is it?'

'No.'

Bob tidies the photos away.

'You do realize you're likely to go to jail for this, don't you?'

'How many times do I have to tell you, I didn't do it?'

But it's like he hasn't heard me.

'Ally, you know how this goes. Tell us what happened and things will be easier for you. It might, at least, keep you out of jail.' He pauses to let me speak, but I decline the opportunity. 'You know what happens to people like us inside.' Another pause. He tries again. 'And what about Megan? What good are you to her if you're banged up?'

He doesn't get it. I'm doing this *for* Megan.

'I've told you what happened. I'm not confessing to something I didn't do.'

Bob exchanges looks with Shirwell who returns a smug smile.

'Then you leave me no choice.' I know what's coming next and there's nothing I can do about it, but I have to try.

'Please, Bob, don't do this. You're making a huge mistake. Simon Pascoe killed Janie Warren, Cheryl Black and he almost killed my Meg.' But justice – fickle at the best of times – is slipping away from me, I can see it in their eyes. They don't believe me. Their minds are made up. It doesn't matter what I do or say, it won't make any difference. Is this how Maureen Jones felt in court that day? Justice for the murder of her daughter, Sian, was within her grasp only to be snatched away by me, by my actions. I remember the pain in her voice as she cried out in court. Now it is me that is being denied justice and now I know what that pain feels like. It is deep and intense and primeval, and I want it to kill me because I have failed in the most basic of maternal duties – to keep my daughter safe. I keep going, but it's all for show. I've already lost. 'He'll kill again. I'm sure of it. Do whatever you have to do with me but bring him in before it's too late.' Impassive, Holt at least waits for me to finish.

'The interview has now concluded. Ally Dymond, I have to tell you that I now intend to make an application to the CPS to formally charge you.'

51

Up ahead, a tractor trundles along the road oblivious to the queue of traffic forming behind it. If he was in the ambulance, he'd just put the lights on and speed past him, but he's not and, with no passing places along the route, he's forced to crawl back to Bidecombe with everyone else.

He could have killed Jackie. Maybe he should have. He never expected to be married to her this long – the hairball in her stomach should have killed her by now – but he had held back. Her death would only invite the cops to go snooping through his life and then they'd eventually find out that he hadn't always been Simon Pascoe. He used to be Michael Flowers and that would lead them to Danielle.

They met in college. What with her dark sultry looks and his razor-sharp cheekbones, they were the best-looking kids in the year; it was inevitable they would get together. People said they'd have beautiful babies.

Looking back, he'd never given sex much thought, not like other boys his age who were obsessed with 'how far they'd got' with a girl – not as far as they bragged, he suspected. He assumed his Christian upbringing had taught him to value sex as something sacred and not to be contemplated until the wedding night, so he didn't.

Danielle found his request that they wait cute, even sexy; other guys had only ever wanted one thing from her, he was different, she liked that. By the time their wedding night arrived, Danielle had giggled, they'd be desperate for each other's bodies, but, he discovered, he wasn't desperate for hers at all and the whole thing was a disaster. Danielle said not to worry, the pressure of the day had got to him and, anyway, everyone's first time was always horrible. But what about the second or third or fourth time? Because it didn't get any better. He kept trying, what else could he do? But then the sharp tuts and bored sighs began to replace the fake gasps and encouraging whispers killing off any hope of arousal.

Oh, Danielle was sympathetic, at first. Given her desirability, the problem would only be temporary, and she liked a challenge. He'd come in from work to find her in black lacy underwear. She'd massage him with lavender oil and book weekends away at 'couples retreat' hotels, but nothing worked, and her frustration turned to scorn. When he told her he'd made an appointment to see the doctor, she laughed and said doctors were there to heal people, 'not raise the dead' so he cancelled it. She found his stash of Viagra ordered off the internet and wafted the all-but-empty packet in front of his face: 'You need reinforced scaffolding to hold it up, not pills.' Then one day she told him she'd met a real man called Johnny, like some kind of country and western singer, who had a 'cock you could hang a coat on' and she was leaving him.

Not long after, he bumped into her on the high street. She was wearing a long lemon-yellow summer dress, her dark hair loose and flowing, and she didn't so much as walk but bounce along the pavement. She was holding hands with a man in washed denim and dark stubble. This was the famous Johnny and, by the look on Danielle's face, he had no trouble getting it up. They exchanged brief nods, but, as they walked away, they started laughing and he knew she was telling Johnny all about his lifeless dick. So, he watched and waited and one night he followed her home, intercepting her as she took a shortcut through the park. She wasn't laughing then.

He had planned it, of course, but he hadn't planned what happened next. He knew the longer he stayed, the greater the risk of getting caught, but he was transfixed by the sight of her lying on the ground. She was the most beautiful creature he had ever seen. It was as if she had gone for a walk, grown tired and fallen asleep under a tree. He was so lost in her that he barely noticed himself stirring and, when he did, the shock knocked him for six. After all this time, it was happening. He had tried everything: girls, boys, both, porn, creams, pills, whores: it didn't matter, nothing aroused him. The answer had been right in front of him all the time. It felt like the most natural thing in the world, like it was meant to be.

He wondered if it was a one-off, but discovered it wasn't when he rode in the back of an ambulance with a young woman killed in a car accident. But he couldn't hang around waiting for a body to turn up when he happened to be on shift, so he started identifying and grooming his own victims. It was perfect. No one ever suspects a paramedic, but he couldn't push his luck. Sooner or later, the police would start to join the dots so he told his colleagues he'd tired of the hurly-burly of the inner city and was transferring to a rural ambulance service on the other side of the country. Eventually a paramedic's job came up and he applied. That's when he moved to North Devon. He'd changed his name by then. He told his old boss, who was writing his reference, that he changed it because he needed a fresh start after what had happened to Danielle. He didn't question it. He'd had a good run here, too, but he was beginning to think it was time to leave Bidecombe. He had dealt with the CSI, but there would be others. Yes, he should move on. After this one.

He pulls up at the end of the deserted estate behind the Strudwicks' house, TruffleDelite has just ten minutes left until the afternoon lessons begin. Not ideal. Something like this takes time. He fumbles for his special phone and it clatters into the footwell.

'Damn it.'

He retrieves it from underneath his seat and punches in his passcode. Messages pop up on the screen, one after the other.

TruffleDelite: WHERE ARE YOU??????

No fun, is it? Being kept waiting. Now, you know what it feels like to have someone stringing you along, not returning your messages.

TruffleDelite: I'm serious!!! ANSWER ME!! Or I'll go MAD!!!

He'd love to sit there and watch her messages get more and more desperate, but time is short and he needs to think very carefully about how he is going to do this.

Ruggerboy666: Lol! I'm here.

TruffleDelite: Thank God. I thought you'd let me down.

Ruggerboy666: Nah. Would never do that. Just took a bit of organizing, that's all.

TruffleDelite: Soz. Just wanna see my Luke, that's all.

Ruggerboy666: And you shall! Spoke to him just now. He wants to meet.

TruffleDelite: Great, where?

Ruggerboy666: At Breakneck Point. Do you know it?

TruffleDelite: Yeah, it's a bit out of Bidecombe, but I can walk it.

That was easier than he thought. She must be desperate to see this boy. Goodness knows why.

Ruggerboy666: You need to take the lower path down the cliff side. Do you know it?

TruffleDelite: Think so.

Ruggerboy666: There's a bench. Luke'll meet you there.

TruffleDelite: What time?

Ruggerboy666: You need to be there for 1 p.m. Tomorrow.

TruffleDelite: Am at school. 😣 😣 😣

This is the difficult bit. He wants to leap in and persuade her to bunk off school, but if he does that she might panic and change her mind at the last minute. No, this has to come from her. Just how much does she want to see this guy?

The cursor on the screen blinks for an age. Suddenly, it switches to *TruffleDelite is typing . . .*

TruffleDelite: OK. I'll just tell school I've got a hospital appointment. I can forge Dad's signature, easy.

Ruggerboy666: You sure?

TruffleDelite: Yeah. School's shit, anyway.

He raises her three sad face emojis with four laughing emojis of his own.

Ruggerboy666: I'll tell Luke yes, then?

TruffleDelite: Defo. Did he say anything else about me?

Ruggerboy666: Like what?

TruffleDelite: You know?

Ruggerboy666: He might have said he's crazy about you. Lolz.

TruffleDelite: Really? Anything else?

Ruggerboy666: Just that you're a great girl. He can't wait to see you. He said something about wanting to save you from your 'rents.

TruffleDelite: Yeah, they're a nightmare. Did he say he loved me?

Ruggerboy666: 'Course.

He switches the phone off and sits back in his seat. It's on.

52

After the windowless interior of the police custody suite, the early morning light stings my eyes. My shoulders are stiff, and my back is so sore they may as well not have bothered with the wafer-thin plastic mattress they gave me to put on the concrete block they called a bed in my cell.

I've been charged with GBH and bailed to appear in front of the magistrates in three weeks' time. One of the conditions of bail is that I'm not allowed within a mile of Pascoe's home and I'm not to approach him or Jackie. It's hardly my finest hour. As I leave the station, a dozen eyes drill into the back of my head. Turns out that CSI Ally Dymond is no better than the murder detective she called out for corruption in an open court.

I get clear of the building and rummage around in my bag for my phone. A needle of pain threads my temples together, blurring my vision, but there's only one thing on my mind: Megan. I haven't seen her in nearly twenty-four hours. Holt promised me I'd be the first to know if anything happened to her while I was in custody. I believe him. For all his incompetency, he's human like the rest of us.

When I switch my phone on, I am bombarded with messages: a text from Liam, several from Bernadette and a dozen missed calls and voicemail messages from Penny. I ignore them all. All I want to do is see how my girl is. Please, God, let nothing have happened to her while I've been holed up in the police station.

I dial the hospital and Wendy, one of the nurses, answers.

She tells me that Megan has had a very restful night, and all is good. I don't believe in God, but I thank him anyway.

Forty-five minutes later, Wendy clocks me through the glass in the entrance door to the ward and buzzes me in.

'Your mum was here a moment ago. I think she just popped out for a coffee.'

Good, Megan is alone.

'Thank you.'

I take my seat next to Megan's bed. Her mouth is still slack around the breathing tube, but her bruises are yellowing and I'm sure there's a pinkness to her complexion that wasn't there before, like life is slowly restoring itself. She's coming back to me. It feels fitting to begin with an apology.

'Meggy, I'm so sorry I haven't been around as much as I should have been. I've been somewhere else, trying to make things right.' This sounds vague, but what else can I say? I've tracked down your attacker, but he's beaten up his wife with a spanner he stole from the cabin and framed me and now I'm facing a custodial sentence? 'The nurses tell me that you're doing really well, though. It's only a matter of time now until you'll be fully awake. Liam has asked if he can come and see you when you're a bit better. I'm sure your other friends will want to see you too. I miss you so much, Megan. The cabin isn't the same without you. I'm not the same without you . . .' I pause. 'But there's still a few things I need to sort out.'

Movement catches my eye. Through the glass window onto Megan's room, Bernadette has returned with her coffee and is talking to Wendy. It's time for me to go. I kiss Megan's smooth forehead.

'Everything will be all right, Meggy. I promise. I love you.'

By the time I'm in the corridor, Wendy has told Bernadette of my arrival and she's ready for me, armed to the teeth with judgement.

'What, for the love of God, do you think you're doing here?' Invoking the Lord's name – that's strong even for Bernadette.

'I've come to be with Megan, of course.'

'I think it's a bit late for that, don't you?'

Wendy shifts awkwardly, but stays where she is, sensing she may have to call upon her intermediary skills.

'What are you talking about?' I reply in a way that suggests Bernadette's statement is as laughable as it sounds.

'We know you spent the night in a police cell. The detective phoned Penny just before I got here. What on earth possessed you to attack a poor defenceless woman?'

Wendy doesn't even attempt to hide her alarm at this news, but I'm disappointed Bernadette has accepted Holt's version without question.

'I didn't attack anybody, not that I have to justify myself to you.'

Bernadette presses her lips together. She clearly thinks she's exactly the person I need to justify myself to.

'The detective told us you're likely to go to prison for what you did.'

The horror and shame of it forces her words into a whisper, but I've nothing to hide.

'I'm not guilty. The courts will see that.'

'And if they don't? The detective seemed to think it was a foregone conclusion.'

'It's not, but he's right. If I'm convicted, there is a chance that I could go to jail for this, even though I didn't do it, and I need to think about what that means for Megan. Who will take care of her?'

'Well, Penny will have her, obviously.'

'No. She won't. Penny has told me that we have to leave Seven Hills. She's made her position clear. Penny won't have Megan.'

'Oh.'

I lay my hand on Bernadette's upper arm and she's right to stare at it suspiciously. 'Mum, if the worst comes to the worst, would you take Megan?'

'What?

'As her grandmother, you're her nearest living relative. Will you have her?'

She steps away from me and my hand drops to my side.

'No, I can't do that. Megan is your responsibility.'

'I know that, but if I'm in jail I can't look after her, can I? That's why I'm asking you. It wouldn't be for long.'

'No. No. Absolutely not. You're not going to push your problems onto me.'

'Megan isn't a problem. She's your granddaughter.'

'No, Aloysia, I can't have Megan. You'll have to find someone else.'

'There is no one else.'

Bernadette says nothing for a while. Finally, she puts her coffee down on the reception desk and takes my hands in hers.

'Aloysia, I'm seventy-eight years old,' she says quietly. 'I love Megan dearly, you know that, and please believe me when I say I would help you if I could, but I'm not capable of looking after her. I can't give her what you give her.'

The amount of pride Bernadette has had to swallow to admit this doesn't escape me. Too bad. I reclaim my hands.

'You're refusing to help me then? Just like you refused to help me when I got pregnant and when I told you Sean had beaten the living daylights out of me.'

Aware the stakes have just been upped, Wendy takes a sharp breath. Bernadette's face hardens. She wasn't expecting her honesty to be rebuffed, but she's quick to return to her default defensive position.

'Oh, Aloysia, you always have to be so dramatic about everything.'

'There's nothing dramatic about being hit by your so-called husband.'

She rolls her eyes.

'Come on now, Ally. It wasn't that bad.'

'You've no idea, have you? You sit in your big house on the big hill casting judgement on everyone else, but you don't have a clue. Well, I'm sick of you sniping from the sidelines, telling me where I'm going wrong and then, when I ask for help, running a mile.' I pause. 'You've never stopped punishing me for having Megan at nineteen, have you?'

'Because you had everything and you threw it away,' she roars back at me, the coffee cup trembling in her hand.

Wendy decides it's time to intervene.

'OK, I think we all need to calm down.'

But Bernadette is in full flight mode. 'I would have given my eye teeth to have had the opportunities you had. You could have done anything with your life, but you threw it all away by sleeping with the first person who asked you. So, yes, as far as I'm concerned, you made your bed so you can lie in it.'

Her volume increases enough for another nurse to poke her head out of another room. Wendy shakes her head at her as a warning not to get involved. I allow a few seconds to pass to diffuse the situation. I don't want Wendy calling security.

'Look, be angry with me, that's OK, I understand, but don't take it out on Megan. She'll need you more than ever if I have to go away.'

Bernadette shakes her head.

'Maybe you should have thought about that before.'

We've reached attrition. I give up.

'OK. Well, if you won't take Megan, there's only one thing I can do.'

Taking my phone from my pocket, I dial a number I never thought I'd ever have to call again in my life. He answers immediately.

'Sean, it's Ally.' Bernadette frowns. 'It's about the letter you sent me asking for custody of Megan. We need to talk. Meet me at 11 a.m. tomorrow. Don't come to the cabin. I'll meet you at . . . Brandy Cove.'

I ring off and stay silent, giving Bernadette the chance to roll back on her refusal to help. She doesn't.

'Maybe that's the best thing for her,' she says coolly.

'Really? You honestly believe Sean is the best person to look after Megan?'

She gives a little shrug. We have nothing more to say to each other. I can't be here any more.

'Wendy, I need to leave. Can you call me if there's any change in Megan and I'll come straight back?'

'Yes, yes, of course. I'll stay with her.'

'You're leaving.'

But Bernadette's voice is flat and featureless. She knows she's gone too far, that maybe, this time, our relationship is unrecoverable, that it is her that I'm leaving. For good.

'I have to, and you should spend as much time as possible with Megan because once she goes to live with Sean you won't see her. He won't let you. I can guarantee you that.'

'Wait. What do you—?'

But I'm already walking away.

53

Bernadette always liked Sean, once she got past the fact that he fixed roofs for a living. He charmed her like he charmed me, and they seemed to find common ground in their delight in undermining me which they dressed up as harmless teasing. It was for Bernadette, but for Sean, nothing is harmless.

'Bernadette, you need to teach Ally how you make this delicious stew. Ally's looks and tastes like something you'd empty from one of those industrial carpet cleaners.'

Bernadette would laugh and grow ten feet tall at the compliment.

'I did try when she was growing up, Sean, but as you know you can't tell Ally anything. If she doesn't want to do something, she doesn't do it. Stubborn as a mule.'

Of course, Bernadette had no idea she was furnishing Sean with more proof of my ineptness and – when it was just the two of us – he would often say, 'Even your mother agrees with me.' If the two people I loved most in the world, after Megan, thought I was useless they must be right.

Although she has never said it outright, I have always suspected that she never believed Sean hit me and if he did (and that's a very big if) I had in some way provoked it. So, it should have come as no surprise when Bernadette didn't baulk at the idea of Sean taking care of Megan. Megan.

The cabin is too still without her. Those noiseless moments when she was out or asleep that I once craved and cherished have been replaced by an all-pervading and unsought silence that I loathe. I put a reggae song on my Spotify just to lift the mood, but it sounds tinny and its cheeriness jars, so I turn it off again and let the quiet engulf me.

Sinking into the sofa, my eye traces the mural that covers one wall of the living room. Massive palm trees are bent over white sands that slope gently towards a surfless sea where a stick version of Megan and I are standing waist deep, our grins scrawled beyond the inky boundaries of our round faces. I can't help but smile and, after days of watching my daughter lie motionless in a hospital bed, kept alive artificially, her face a passive reflection of her unconscious state, I find myself yearning for a different, more animated version of her so I take out my phone and scroll through her Instagram.

Head tilted to one side like her smile is too heavy to hold upright, her pale red hair lopsided, Megan beams out from her photos. This is my Megan.

There's one of the two of us, taken the weekend before she was attacked. We're sitting at a table at Liam's coffee bar on Morte Sands, our wetsuits peeled back to our bikini tops, our hair clumped and matted by the salty water, our bodyboards propped against the table next to us. After a few failed attempts to take a selfie, Liam took the phone from me. In the picture, Megan is still laughing at my ineptness, my laughter is derived entirely from hers. What wouldn't I give to return to that moment?

I carry on trawling her timeline. Something starts to niggle me. Something I hadn't noticed before. I flick the screen back and forth. Holt's right. Apart from the odd photo, Megan barely used it, especially recently. Then it hits me. I scroll up and down several times, checking and rechecking. There are lots of comments, emojis and likes until around six months ago and then they dwindle to next to nothing, like the user has tired of it – only what teenager elects to come off social media unprompted? Then I get it. The lying little shit. Silent fury that I have been duped so easily seeps through me.

It doesn't take long to find him. He's sitting in a bus shelter near the rec, but he's not waiting for a bus.

I bring the car to an abrupt halt alongside him and leap out, startling him so much he almost falls off the bench.

'Jay Cox. You little piece of shit. Megan had a second phone, didn't she? You gave it to her so you could continue your cosy little chit-chats.'

'No, I didn't.'

I grab a handful of his T-shirt, practically lifting him from his seat. Christ, there's nothing to him. His arms flail and he drops his baccy tin. Its contents splay across the pavement.

'Yes, you did, you lying little fuck. Now tell me where it is.'

'I don't—'

His eyes are wide, pupils dilated. He's high. For fuck's sake. Well, he's just going to have to come down and fast.

'I'm fucking warning you. I'm already on one assault charge, one more won't make any difference.'

'OK, OK. Let go of me, all right, and I'll tell you.'

'No, you'll scarper. Tell me first and then I'll let you go.'

362

'OK, OK, yes, I gave her a phone, but only because I liked talking to her. We were friends, but you wouldn't let her speak to me.'

'Don't you dare put this on me. Where's the phone?'

'Under her bed, that's what she told me anyway.'

I let him go.

'It'd better be there, Jay, or I'm coming for you.'

'It's there,' he says sulkily.

Armed with the information I need, my rage subsides.

'I get that you wouldn't tell the police, but why the hell didn't you tell me?'

He pulls a face as if I've said something so ludicrous it's hardly worth his effort answering, but he does.

'You're one of them.'

I roll my eyes.

'I'm Megan's mother too.'

He shrugs.

'Sorry, all right, I didn't think it was important.'

'She used the phone you gave her to create another Instagram account. The guy who attacked her used that Instagram account to groom her.'

'I didn't know that, did I? Not for sure. I just thought she was using it to text me, like we arranged.'

I stomp back to the car, slamming the door shut. He's not worth any more of my time.

54

Billy and Ken Strudwick are staring down at a card. There's a picture of a quad bike with huge inflated grey tyres and, on it, a smiling girl in pigtails leans forward, grabbing the handlebars. Next to her is an empty wheelchair. Across the top, a caption in loopy red writing reads: *Dunes for the Disabled – Book your trip today for a sand-sational experience!*

The two of them trade looks of wonder, like kids at Christmas.

'I don't know what to say,' says Ken, slightly breathless, his eyes glistening.

'Yes would be good,' he laughs.

'Of course it's a yes. Simon, this is fantastic. Thank you so much.'

'It's my pleasure. I've been meaning to do it for ages. I know you don't get out much. The guy that runs it owes me a favour and I just thought you might enjoy it.'

'It's just about the nicest thing anyone has ever done for me. I can't believe you'd think of us at a time like this.'

He doesn't know what he's talking about and he must be wearing his confusion, as Ken explains.

'We heard about your wife, Jackie. It sounds terrible. Terrifying that someone should break into your home and do that to her.'

'Yes, it is. She's in quite a bad way.'

'I'm so sorry to hear that.'

He seems genuinely upset which is strange as he's never met Jackie.

'Thank you. Working takes my mind off things.' But he hasn't come here to talk about Jackie. 'I've booked the quad bike for 12.15 tomorrow. It's the only slot they had. It's very busy this time of year. I thought Billy could take himself off to Breakneck Point for a walk or something while you're whizzing up and down the beach on your moon buggy.'

They swap laughs at the image.

'That sounds great,' says Billy.

'But it's really popular. If you don't turn up bang on time, you'll lose your spot.'

'OK, no problem. What time do we need to be there?'

'Twelve for the safety talk and then it starts at 12.15. You'll be back at 2 p.m.'

'I can't wait. It sounds perfect, doesn't it, Billy?'

His excitement rubs off on Billy who gives him his widest grin. It'll be one of his last. In a few days, Billy will be facing a murder charge and his dad will be on his own. They shouldn't be so gullible.

'Yeah, it does, Dad.'

'But there is just one more thing.'

His seriousness dampens their cheerfulness.

'Oh?'

'Don't worry, it's nothing bad. I'm not really meant to give gifts to patients. It's against the rules so I'd really appreciate it if you didn't tell anyone about this. I could lose my job over it.'

Ken rolls his eyes like this is just one more thing to add to the list of things proving the craziness of this world.

'What have we become if we can't show each other a bit of kindness?'

'I know, but those are the rules. What's the saying? I don't make them, I just break them.'

Ken laughs.

'Well, thank the Lord for that. Don't worry, your secret is safe with me. Wild horses won't be able to drag it out of me.'

'Hopefully, it won't come to that.' More laughter. 'Great, well, I've got to get going. Have a good time tomorrow. Remember, don't be late. No need to see me out, Billy.'

Passing through the hall, he grabs a tie hanging on the coat rack on the wall and shoves it into his pocket. Sometimes, this is just too easy.

The phone has powered up by the time I reach our bench at Breakneck Point. It didn't take long to find it, taped to the underside of Megan's wooden bed frame. The battery was dead and, still agitated by my encounter with Jay, I couldn't bear pacing the cabin waiting for it to flicker back to life so I connected it to a charging pack and headed out to the coast.

There's no password. There doesn't need to be. As far as Megan's concerned, I don't even know this phone exists. I tap the Instagram icon on the home screen; her username is TwilightSparkle, apparently, which was the name of her favourite My Little Pony character when she was a little girl.

As her timeline flicks into view, a sick feeling masses in the pit of my stomach. What else don't I know about Megan's life?

Her inbox is filled with messages from Jay. They begin smugly discussing how much easier it is to talk now she has a secret phone. I curse the boy under my breath, but my mood softens as their conversations unfurl.

Jay talks of how he misses his mother who died of a heroin overdose when he was twelve. His dad is due out of prison, but Jay wants nothing to do with him as he got his mum hooked on heroin and it is his fault she's dead. He hates the bastard, but he hates himself more for being like him and he's considered ending his sorry life more than once.

Megan shows a compassion I didn't know she had, telling him he doesn't have to be defined by his parents' behaviour. He can take a different route. Her words encourage, cajole and even threaten him to stay alive, to get himself clean and to make his mum proud of him. Megan is Jay's lifeline. That's why he gave her the phone. She kept him alive. I'm bursting with pride for my incredible daughter, and shame for writing Jay off as drug-dealing scum.

I carry on searching her messages and am beginning to give up hope when a name pops up: Ruggerboy666. Rugger is a slang term for rugby. It's quite old-fashioned. Do teenage boys use words like rugger any more? I don't think so. It's Pascoe. I know it is and I can almost sense his breath on my neck as I read his words.

Ruggerboy666: Hi. How's it going?

Its feigned lightness turns my stomach. I can hardly bear to read on, but I must.

TwilightSparkle: Do I know you?

367

Ruggerboy666: Yeah. We're at school together but can't tell you my name. It's complicated.

TwilightSparkle: Yeah, right. Go away or I'll report you.

Ruggerboy666: OK. I was pretty cut up when you hurt yourself at school. Realized then how much I liked you.

TwilightSparkle: Who is this?

Ruggerboy666: Can't say. Soz.

TwilightSparkle: Why not?

Ruggerboy666: Because I'm seeing someone else at the moment. Trying to break it off with her, but she's going through some stuff. Don't wanna make it worse. Can we just hang out here?

TwilightSparkle: OK. Guess there's no harm in it.

Oh Megan. It's so obvious he's playing you. How can you not see it?

Ruggerboy666: Thanks, but don't tell your mates. In case it gets back to her.

The conversation ends but picks up again a few days later.

Ruggerboy666: Hi. How's it going? Just had the biggest row with my mum. Moaning at me for not doing my homework. Who d'you have for maths? I've got Mr Blakewell. He's a total psycho.

Clever. Dropping a teacher's name into the conversation. It wouldn't have taken much to find out who works at the school – a quick check of the school website would do it – but it's enough to persuade Megan he is who he says he is.

TwilightSparkle: Ha! Ha! Yeah, I know. I had him last year. How's your girlfriend?

Ruggerboy666: Pretty mixed up. Am trying to help her. Wish I was with you, though, but she needs me right now.

TwilightSparkle: She's not your responsibility.

Ruggerboy666: I know, but she's got no one else.

TwilightSparkle: Sounds like she's lucky to have you.

Ruggerboy666: Not really. She'd be really upset if she knew I was talking to you.

TwilightSparkle: We're only talking.

Ruggerboy666: Yeah, but it means a lot. Just having someone to talk to who understands.

TwilightSparkle: Yeah, I know what you mean.

The next few conversations bat backwards and forwards, harmless banter that borders on the inane at times, but each time another layer is added to Pascoe's façade as a caring friend.

Someone to be trusted. God, Megan, if only you'd told me. I'd have seen through this shit.

Ruggerboy666: Guess what?

TwilightSparkle: What?

Ruggerboy666: I finally got up the nerve to finish it with her.

TwilightSparkle: Wow, how did she take it?

Ruggerboy666: She was really cut up, but I couldn't go on faking it.

TwilightSparkle: What now?

Ruggerboy666: Can we meet? But not in Bidecombe.

TwilightSparkle: Not sure.

Ruggerboy666: 'Course. Don't worry. I wouldn't want to meet me either!

TwilightSparkle: Lol.

And then there's nothing, not until the night I sent her to her room for truanting from school while I went to Penny's to cool off.

TwilightSparkle: You there?

Ruggerboy666: Yeah. You OK?

TwilightSparkle: No. Bunked off school. Don't want to say why. My mum went mad. Grounded me. The bitch.

Ruggerboy666: That's OK. I'm here if you wanna talk. Your mum was probs just worried about you.

TwilightSparkle: She doesn't give a shit about me. She's never around anyway. Always at work.

Always at work.

Ruggerboy666: 😊 I'm sure that's not true.

TwilightSparkle: You don't know her. She totally lost her rag with me.

Ruggerboy666: Sounds like you need saving from her.

TwilightSparkle: Ha! Ha! Too right I do. Sometimes I can't stand her and I wish I was a million miles away.

Ruggerboy666: Maybe you could be. Wanna meet?

TwilightSparkle: Maybe. Gotta go now. The witch is back.

The conversation resumes a few days later. The night after Cheryl Black's death.

TwilightSparkle: Fancy meeting up?

Ruggerboy666: Yeah, sure. What changed your mind?

TwilightSparkle: No reason. Off school at the mo and a bit bored.

That's it? She met him because she was bored being at home on her own?

Ruggerboy666: OK then. I know a great place.

TwilightSparkle: Where?

Ruggerboy666: Three Brethren Woods.

Three Brethren Woods.

The words swell my insides, expand up into my throat and explode from my mouth in a spew of vomit that splatters the path in front of me.

Three Brethren Woods.

55

It's early when I pull out of the exit of Seven Hills Lodges, take a left turn and head down the hill towards the town centre. There I opt to take the lower road along the seafront, like I always do.

The road climbs out of Bidecombe, passing the turning to the Tarka Estate where Cheryl lived and died, and out onto the main road towards the neighbouring county of Somerset.

Five or so miles out of Bidecombe, I swing into a narrow single-track lane, a grass mohican growing down the centre through disuse; it's a place known only to locals. The high-hedged track twists and turns until suddenly dropping down into a modest car park, enclosed by a low bank.

On the other side of the bank is the pebbly shoreline, no more than thirty metres wide, scooped out of the cliffs a millennia ago. Jagged rocks rise up either side of the inlet, speckled with gulls' nests balanced precariously on a dozen summits. A crumbling stone jetty hints at the cove's illegal past when smugglers, chased by the Royal Navy, would suddenly lurch towards the shore and seemingly disappear like a ghost ship only to drop anchor at Brandy Cove to unload their bounty. They wouldn't stand a chance today. CCTV covers the car park, installed a year or two ago following a spate of car thefts, making it the perfect place to meet Sean.

When I suggested we meet at Brandy Cove, he readily agreed. We used to come here in the early days before the violence started. They were happy times. Or so I thought. Sean would take Megan rock pooling while I laid a picnic on the beach. He didn't have kids of his own and I admired his confidence with her and his firmness when she pleaded too keenly for an ice cream. I even remember thinking, See, Megan, you won't be able to twist him round your little finger. How I hate myself for that now. On one trip, she slipped into a rock pool and the water came over her boots. He told her off, shouting at her for her clumsiness. He went on and on at her and I began to feel a slight unease at his disproportionate anger, but I was still in love with him then and love excuses terrible things.

A white van swings into the car park, and parks on the opposite side to my car. Sean gets out and swaggers towards me, wearing his builders' hobnail boots, khaki trousers splashed with paint and a victorious smirk. I want to get back into my car and drive away, but I can't. I have to do this. It's the only way.

We meet mid-point in the car park. Out in the open. He stands too close to me, invading my space, deliberately using his size to intimidate me and I instinctively want to take a step back, but I don't budge, and this amuses him. This is an Ally he doesn't recognize. He glances down at my hand, holding a white piece of paper.

'You got my letter then.'

'Yes, I did.'

His smirk progresses to a grin.

'I heard you got done for assault too.'

Of course he has. This is North Devon. Everyone knows everyone's business.

'Yes.'

I have no intention of protesting my innocence to Sean. He's not worth the effort.

He shakes his head sadly.

'A disabled lady too. That's well out of order.'

I say nothing. I just want this to be over.

Sean eyes me up and down.

'You're not quite as perfect as you think you are.'

'I guess not.'

He licks his lips and a shudder ripples through me at the memory of the same hands that stroked me and then slapped me all in the name of love.

'I always had my suspicions you were a bit of a wild one. I'd have liked to have seen that side of you when we were together. Maybe things would have been different between us.'

'Maybe.'

He smiles at some memory of what could have been. I swallow my revulsion.

'Anyway, I take it that you're here because you've finally seen sense?'

Finally seen sense. The phrase echoes around me, bouncing off the cliffs, picked up and translated into the cry of the gulls. *Finally seen sense.*

I smile at him. He frowns.

'It's taken a while, but yes, I think I finally have.'

Over Sean's shoulder, the tide is rising, but the sea is calm, enjoying the respite offered by this quiet cove before it rejoins the hurly-burly of the Channel currents.

Right on time, Billy Strudwick appears on the ridge above Breakneck Point. He sinks deeper behind the gorse bush although he's sure Billy won't see him.

He wasn't certain the boy would make it this far. Teenagers aren't known for their love of rambling, but Billy's a good kid. He would feel bad about what's going to happen to him, only looking after his dad is already a prison sentence of its own. Somewhere behind him on the beach, the cripple is being carted up and down the sand dunes in a buggy, pretending to be normal.

Billy pauses to look out to sea, but boredom soon sets in and he turns and heads back towards the beach. Maybe he'll pass TruffleDelite on the way. That would be helpful, but not essential. The timing and his proximity to the scene will be enough, along with his tie, of course. Detectives are always so excited when they find the murder weapon, they never question it.

His watch tells him his shift starts in an hour. He'll make the anonymous call about ten minutes before he starts, saying he saw two people arguing on the cliff, perilously close to the edge.

The police will respond first and more than likely find TruffleDelite. By the time the ambulance station gets the call, he and Trisha will be ready to go. This time, he's not taking any chances with Trisha. He'll be riding up back. He's already texted her that he has a migraine and can she do the driving today.

He emerges from the bush and makes his way down the cliff towards the bench that sits at the lowest point in the path. He's almost there when he sees her and his heart flips. She's sitting on

376

the bench, her back to him, her hood up, hugging her knees against the chilly wind. She's keen. He likes that.

He's about to call out to her when he stops himself and drops behind a gorse bush. The last one was too quick. It was over in a flash. Then Trisha spoiled it all by insisting on riding up back. That's not going to happen again. He wants to savour this one so he stays hidden and watches her a while longer.

She looks around before finally getting her phone out. He thought her parents had taken it off her. Maybe she's got a special phone like him.

His phone vibrates in his pocket. Yes. It's her.

TruffleDelite: I'm here. No sign of Luke. He's coming, right?

Ruggerboy666: Sure, just seen him. He's on his way.

TruffleDelite: It's freezin'.

Ruggerboy666: Am sure Luke will soon warm you up!

She posts the crying with laughter emoji: 😂

TruffleDelite: Thanks for setting this up. Whoever you are.

Ruggerboy666: Told you I'd save you, didn't I?

TruffleDelite: Owe u.

He puts his phone back in his pocket, his fingers brush Billy's tie, giving him a little frisson of anticipation. It's time.

Emerging from behind the gorse bush onto the narrow path, he dusts himself down. He wants to look his best for her.

She doesn't hear him coming. The stiff breeze blowing around them sees to that, drowning out all sounds apart from the screeching gulls overhead. He is less than two metres away. Still she doesn't look up. But that's OK. He's ready. He's waited so long for this.

'Hi there, everything OK?'

Circling high above the cliffs, like tiny white sails against a pewter sky, the seabirds seem greater in number and stronger in voice here as if word got around that what's about to happen is worth an audience. An unseasonably sharp wind gathers into a gust that buffets me hard, trying to force me to move. *You shouldn't be here. You should leave before it's too late.* But Breakneck Point is exactly where I should be.

I've been sitting on our bench for some time now. I wanted to make sure I was here in plenty of time and my meeting with Sean was shorter than I anticipated, but it served its purpose. It gave me the greatest pleasure to tell him to stick his letter, especially as he'd convinced himself I was going to give in to him. I told him if he took me to court, I would reveal that he had been violent to me and then everyone would know what he was really like. He laughed and said I had no proof so I showed him the photo Penny had taken the day I walked out on him and reminded him this was a family court not a criminal court and I had more than enough to expose him for what he was – a wife beater. He called me a 'fucking bitch' and, for a moment, I thought he was going to hit me, but he followed my gaze, spotted the CCTV camera, and thought better of it. Instead, he stomped off to his van and skidded out of the car park in a cloud of dust. I have the impression that's the last I'll see of Sean Parker.

I don't hear Pascoe approach. It's only when he speaks that I know he's there.

'Hi there, everything OK?'

The familiarity and softness of his voice sends a current of fear through me, but his tone is so unthreatening, it's almost impossible to think it could be attached to a monster. Is this how Janie, Cheryl and my Megan felt in the seconds before he turned on them? It's OK. I can relax. I'm safe now. The paramedic is here. But I know what he has done.

For a moment, I can't move, paralyzed by the thought of the minutes that lie ahead, terrified that any move I make will be the wrong move, but I have to do what I came here to do so I stand up.

My legs are weak like they're barely able to support me and my heart is careering out of control. And so it begins, but first I must do something. I turn towards Pascoe and pull my hood down. I want him to see it's me: Ally Dymond. TruffleDelite.

I've been TruffleDelite since yesterday, just after I left the police station. After I left the custody suite, I picked up a message from him telling me he'd succeeded in hacking the Instagram account I'd asked him to take a look at. It belonged to the young girl Simon rescued from the cliffs nearby. With just a newspaper photo and a name to go on, ex hi-tech crime unit Liam took just forty-eight hours to track down her username and crack her password, a record even by his standards. He really is one of the good ones.

I changed her password and took over her account. Just in time it would seem. She'll be annoyed as hell, but she'll never know how close she came to becoming Pascoe's latest victim. I would have preferred not to meet at Breakneck Point, but then it occurred to me that it is the perfect place to meet.

Shock registers on Pascoe's face. His brain struggles to tally TruffleDelite with the person standing in front of him. The CSI in me wants to know what turned him into a killer. But it's too risky. I have only a few seconds to act before he gets himself together. I only need one.

I rush him, grabbing his waist in a rugby tackle, driving him towards the edge of the path and the sheer drop on the other side, but he holds firm, much stronger than his size suggests. He's invincible. Unkillable. And there is no plan B.

I keep pushing forward, but he grabs my back and tugs hard; he's trying to twist me around, fling me over the edge. The gravelly noise is my trainers sliding against the dry loose dirt on the path. It can't end like this. He can't win. Megan needs me.

Deep from within my belly comes a noise, deep and guttural, a war cry of the final onslaught. Now or never. Do or die. I muster everything I've got and, head still bowed and arms locked around his waist, I heave Pascoe just an inch or so from the ground and step towards the edge. His back foot lands, but there's nothing there.

I see this before he does and immediately release him. His eyes flash with panic as his foot continues downwards and his arms shoot upwards, rotating like propellers, but it isn't enough; his balance is lost. He looks to grab on to something, anything: me. I need to move away, but I'm not quick enough. I'm neither flight, fright or fight, just mesmerized by the sight of this man refusing to die.

He catches my sleeve, wrenching me towards him as he tips backwards over the cliff edge, but I'm not strong enough to anchor him. He's taking me with him and there's nothing I can do about it.

He topples into the void, dragging me with him, but a stone jutting up from the path catches my shoe and sends me crashing to the ground, winding me. When I open my eyes, I'm lying face down in the dirt. My chin stings where I smacked it against the ground and my arms are draped over the edge. There's only me. Pascoe is nowhere to be seen.

But there's a weight attached to me, something pulling me down. I peer over the edge. There's a hand wrapped around my sleeve. It's Pascoe, still clinging to me and to life. But there's nothing securing me to the ground and my body begins to slide towards the abyss.

My shoulders clear the edge and I'm face to face with Pascoe. No smug smiles, no enjoyment at my expense. Just an entitlement to life at the expense of mine.

He uses my arm as a climbing rope, his feet searching for purchase on the cliff face, all the while his weight drags me closer over the edge, but I can't die. Not like this. Not at the hands of Simon Pascoe.

My free hand scrabbles blindly for a rock, but there's nothing but loose shingle. Pascoe's hand grabs my shoulder. One more haul and he's safe and I'm hurtling to the bottom of the cliff.

My fingers close around something. Hard, sharp-edged, perfect as if an invisible hand has selected this rock especially for me and placed it in my path.

I lift it and swing it hard against the side of Pascoe's head. It makes contact with a sickening thud and his eyes spring wide with pain and shock. The sight of blood trickling down his cheek humanizes him. He's killable. He knows it too.

He climbs faster, letting go of my sleeve, grabbing the rock face and trusting his abilities. I ram the rock once more into his temple. The resulting crunch deepens his wound. It's too much. His hand instinctively flies up to protect his head from further blows. His eyes search out mine, pinpricks of terror, imploring me to stop. I hit him again. An unnecessary act. He can't hold on with one hand and his grip loosens and his fingers slip from the rock. For a moment, he appears suspended in mid-air before he's released and tumbles noiselessly onto the rocks below.

I wriggle back to safety before I lose my balance and lie there on my stomach, captivated by the sight of the body of the man who wanted to kill my daughter. I half expect him to get up and come at me again because I, too, have bought into the myth that Simon Pascoe must be invincible. He doesn't move, but it's not until the grey slab beneath his broken bones darkens with his blood that I accept it. Simon Pascoe is dead.

Finally, I drag myself to my feet, still unable to shift my gaze from Pascoe, but my window of escape is narrowing; it will be high tide soon.

Penny is moored in a cove a little way beyond Breakneck Point, waiting to sail me back to Brandy Cove. It was the attack on Jackie Pascoe that finally convinced her I was telling the truth because she knew I wasn't capable of such a thing. The boat was her idea. Breakneck Point is eight miles by road, but less than two by sea. If suspicion were to fall on me, the CCTV would show me arriving at Brandy Cove for a walk before getting back into my car and driving away. Holt isn't imaginative enough to think beyond the road network.

At some point, I will have to make it up to Bernadette for what I said at the hospital yesterday. I had to provoke an argument to attract enough attention so that people would remember me calling Sean to arrange a meeting – eight miles from where Pascoe went over the cliff. A very public telephone call plus CCTV at Brandy Cove: my alibi is watertight.

A swell dislodges Pascoe's body, shifting it a short distance only to return it to its same position on the rock as if it's not sure it wants this vile creature polluting its waters. The water laps at his feet until, finally, another wave, more daring than the rest, lifts and carries him out to sea. His body rises and falls carried by the surge until the blackest swell barges in and swallows him whole, dragging him down into the darkness where he belongs. He's gone.

Drawing the juices into the centre of my mouth, I launch a glob of spit over the cliff edge.

'Fuck you.'

And I know, in that moment, that this is what justice looks like. It's obliterating someone's life as they've obliterated yours. I'm not a vigilante. I would have accepted life imprisonment for Pascoe, no parole, but that wasn't going to happen – giving me no choice. I have no regrets either. I have done this for Megan. I'm her mother and it is my job to keep her safe. My only job.

56

Suicide paramedic is suspected serial killer

A local paramedic who committed suicide by throwing himself off the cliff at Breakneck Point is now thought to have murdered at least two women and committed a frenzied attack on a third, police have revealed.

The body of thirty-eight-year-old paramedic Simon Pascoe washed ashore at Morte Sands a week ago. Mr Pascoe worked for Devon and Cornwall Ambulance Services and was based at Barnston District Hospital.

At the time, his death came as a complete shock to family and friends who say Mr Pascoe was in line for an award for his part in the recent rescue of a teenage girl who fell from the cliffs at Breakneck Point some weeks previously.

His wife – for whom he was the sole carer – was too distressed to comment. Mrs Pascoe is not believed to be complicit in her husband's crimes and is even thought to be a material witness in the murder of Janie Warren. She is fully cooperating with the police and is being cared for by social services.

Today in a specially convened press conference,

police say they now believe Simon Pascoe murdered two local women, nineteen-year-old Janie Warren and forty-five-year-old Cheryl Black. He also tried to kill fifteen-year-old schoolgirl Megan Dymond in a violent attack in Three Brethren Woods, which left her in a coma. Police believe there could be other victims including his first wife, Danielle Flowers.

DCI Steven Lowe said: 'We are now certain that Simon Pascoe killed both Janie and Cheryl and attacked Megan. We also have reason to believe that Simon Pascoe's real name is Michael J. Flowers and that he may have been responsible for the murder of Danielle Flowers, his ex-wife, and others. The investigation is ongoing.'

Christopher Banstead, the partner of Janie Warren, was charged and awaiting trial for her murder on Bidecombe Quay in July. Peter Benson was charged with assaulting Megan Dymond. Both men have been released. Mr Banstead's family are calling for a public inquiry.

DCI Steven Lowe added: 'We deeply regret the hurt and distress that have been caused to Christopher and Peter and their families. The matter has now been referred to the Independent Office for Police Complaints.'

Police turned their attentions to Pascoe after they received an apparent suicide note that was posted close to Breakneck Point just hours before he took his own life. DCI Lowe said its contents led police to conclude 'beyond all doubt' that Pascoe was a ruthless killer.

The senior officer added: 'In the days following Pascoe's suicide the SIO in charge of Janie Warren's murder and the attack on Megan Dymond received a letter posted near to Breakneck Point.

'In it, Pascoe refers to certain details of the killing of Janie and the attempt on Megan's life that have not been released to the general public and which only the perpetrator could know.'

When asked if the letter was genuine. DCI Lowe said: 'There were no fingerprints on the letter itself, but Pascoe's prints were all over the envelope. We, of course, called in a handwriting expert who, after extensive tests, concluded Pascoe had written the letter.'

In a separate, but related incident, DCI Lowe said assault charges against Megan Dymond's mother, Ally Dymond, have been dropped. Ms Dymond, a CSI with Devon County Police, was accused of attacking Simon Pascoe's wife, Jackie Pascoe. Police now believe Pascoe carried out the attack.

Ms Dymond was not available for comment. However, her daughter, Megan Dymond, is reported to have regained consciousness.

Epilogue

On the desk in front of me lies Pascoe's get well soon card for Megan. The paper that the envelope is made from is thick and creamy. It's expensive. This is no grabbed-at-the-last-minute-from-a-petrol-station card. Thought went into its choosing. This is a card the buyer wanted the recipient to admire, be touched by, say things like, 'How thoughtful. They don't even know Megan.'

There's no writing on the front of the envelope. Pascoe either wasn't sure who to address the card to or didn't care. Probably the latter. But I'm grateful. It will be his undoing.

My hands sheathed in latex gloves and using a pair of tweezers, I flip the card over. He's made it easy for me. He hasn't licked the envelope down. Sure, his DNA on the envelope would have helped, but steaming would likely have destroyed it and, anyway, Pascoe could be one of those people who don't produce enough DNA in their saliva to get a profile.

It doesn't matter: I have what I need.

I pause a moment, picturing another set of tweezers agitating the envelope in a tray of Ninhydrin, a colourless liquid chemical that releases a sharp vinegary tang into the air as it seeks out the envelope's secrets. Then, those tweezers transfer the envelope to the drying cabinet where the purple swirls and ridges slowly begin to emerge: Pascoe's fingerprints. Smiles all round.

Using one set of tweezers to hold the envelope steady, I use a second pair to prise open the top flap and ease out its contents. The sight of a glossy triangle of green and purple ramps up my heart rate. My brain is screaming at me to leave well alone. Don't give him the satisfaction of thinking you've read it.

But I have to.

Nipping the top edge of the card with the tweezers, it slides out easily enough, revealing a single purple tulip on its cover. And a verse.

> _A Get Well Blessing_
> _Like a flower_
> _nurtured by sunlight_
> _May you grow and_
> _get stronger_
> _In the light of_
> _God's care_

Hot tears blur my vision. How dare that twisted fuck give this to me? He doesn't know what love is and he never will. Blinking my eyes back into focus, I open the card. There's a message inside. Of course there is.

Dear Ally,

All of us at the ambulance station are so sorry for what has happened to Megan, and we are all praying for her speedy recovery.

Please know we were there for Megan. I held and comforted her myself.

Yours,
Simon Pascoe,
First Responder
Devon and Cornwall Ambulance Service

I picture Pascoe in the doorway of the cabin, card in hand, but this time, I don't stand there dumbly nodding, thanking him for attacking my daughter, for fuck's sake.

I ram the tweezers deep into his chest, pull them out and stab him over and over again. Thin straws of blood squirt from his wounds, spattering my face, but I don't stop. I can't stop. Even when he crumples to the ground, clutching his chest, the thin grey metal blade pokes out through my fist and rains down on Pascoe's back, his green uniform crimson red from a thousand cuts.

My hands are trembling like an old lady's. I can't do this; I need a steady hand. Close your eyes and breathe. He's done you a favour, I tell myself. This card is a gift. If he'd just signed his name, you'd be in trouble, but the bastard has gone and written a fucking great missive about how he single-handedly saved Megan. His narcissism is your gain. You just have to do your bit.

I open my eyes. Clarity and determination have calmed my heart, levelled by breathing and stilled my hands. Lowering the tweezers back down onto the desk, I pick up the biro and begin to write.

The hours pass unnoticed, the effort of my concentration

exhibiting itself in my throbbing temples and my aching hand. It's not until I take a slight pause to check my efforts that I notice the pile of A4 paper next to me, filled with row upon row of single letters, words, entire sentences and Pascoe's signature, repeated over and over until I'm confident it's good enough to clean his bank account out. But it's not his money I'm after.

Sifting through the pages, I compare my hand with Pascoe's. My initial efforts are too round, too loopy, too uncertain. Pascoe's letters are much more angular, more jagged, but, by the final page, my hand is firm and sure, like his. It doesn't have to be perfect; it just has to fool the handwriting expert.

The pen is slippery between my latex thumb and forefinger like my sweat has permeated the thin blue covering and, now that it counts, I wrestle with the grip, suddenly self-conscious I'm not holding it right.

The blank piece of paper stares back at me. This needs to be written in one go, otherwise a microscope will expose it as a forgery. Magnifying lenses will reveal the ink thickening at unnatural places in the sentence where the writer has hesitated – the hallmark of a fake.

The tip of the pen touches down onto the paper and begins to move across the page in one continuous action, like an unseen force has taken control.

Seconds later, it's done. The effort drains me, and I sink back into my chair, rubbing the soreness from my eyes that feel like they haven't blinked in days. Leaning forward once more to pore over the words, I track the rise and fall of each letter against Pascoe's card until the end. It'll do.

Bringing the edges of the letter together with the tweezers,

I press the fold down with the pad of my gloved palm and slide it into the envelope, nudging the top flap back under the bottom.

My pen glides once more across the envelope's surface. Holt's address stares back at me.

It's done. Pascoe's death warrant. To be served in a few short hours. Justice isn't always a jail sentence and I was wrong: one more death can fix this.

But making Pascoe pay is the easy part. I, of all people, know there are a dozen ways to kill someone, but that's not enough. That means his secrets die with him and I can't let that happen. Oh no. For Simon Pascoe, there'll be no fawning obituary in the *Barnston Herald*, no letters from colleagues opining his good works and bewailing his loss to the NHS and all who knew him. There'll only be bafflement that someone so normal could commit such terrible acts along with smug whispers that they always knew there was something odd about him.

Killing him isn't enough, the world must know Simon Pascoe as I know him: a cold-blooded murderer.

Dear DI Holt,

I killed Janie Warren and Cheryl Black. I also tried to kill Megan Dymond. I am telling you this because by the time you read this, I'll be dead.

I got to know Janie Warren when she had a miscarriage and I was sent to attend her. I knew she'd be on the quay with her boyfriend that night. I heard them have sex and then they rowed. Her boyfriend accused her of sleeping with someone else and stormed off. That's when I saw my chance and strangled her with my bare hands.

I have known Cheryl Black for some years. She had complex health problems and repeatedly called an ambulance out. I hid my crime by setting fire to her with a cigarette.

I met Megan Dymond because she hit her head in a gym class at school and blacked out so the school called an ambulance. Posing as Ruggerboy666, we got talking online. She thought I was a boy who liked her, which is why she agreed to meet me in Three Brethren Woods where I attacked her using an iron bar I'd stolen from Peter Benson's garden shed. I persuaded Peter to cycle to the woods so I could frame him for Megan's murder, but she survived and that is why I can't go on. Sooner or later she will remember what happened to her and I can't go to prison so I have decided to end it.

Simon Pascoe

I'm a CSI. I know what the perfect murder looks like.

Acknowledgements

A very different version of *Breakneck Point* began when my good friend and fellow writer, Tim Cooke, told me I should write a crime novel, something that had never occurred to me, even though I've written about policing for over twenty years and used to be a scenes of crime officer. Thank you, Tim, for starting the ball rolling and for your ongoing support and friendship.

I would also like to thank the author and my tutor on the Curtis Brown Creative six-month writing course Lisa O'Donnell for teaching me to search for the 'truth and nothing but the truth' in my writing. That course changed my life in so many ways, not least by introducing me to the September Tribe of amazingly talented writers and all-round lovely people who have been a tremendous support to me. I hope I have been able to return the favour. Thank you, Kath, Robbie, Charlie, Sarah and Lolly.

Thank you also to Lucy Morris at Curtis Brown, the best agent any writer could wish for. Your expert guidance, your belief in me and your enthusiasm for my novel have been incredible. I'm so lucky to have you in my corner. I'm not sure there's anyone else I'd rewrite 45,000 words for!

Thank you also to Cicely Aspinall, my editor at HQ. Your brilliant notes are so full of humour and kindness that you made the editing process as painless as it could be. You have been a joy to work with.

I'd also like to thank my brother-in-law Mick for his patience in explaining the intricacies of modern police procedure to me. I am in awe of your knowledge, and any veering off course is entirely down to me.

Thank you to my awesome children, Frank, Rose, Joseph and Alice for accepting as completely normal a mum who spends hours tapping away on a laptop.

And finally . . . Richard, who has not only cheered me from the sidelines for more years than I care to remember, but frequently runs onto the pitch to pick me back up again. I love you for that and for all sorts of other reasons.

Lastly, I'd like to acknowledge the men and women in the forensic suits that you see on your television screens disappearing into crime scenes. Everyday SOCOs or CSIs quietly and diligently go about the business of finding that vital piece of physical evidence that will bring an offender to justice. Without them, the world would be a more dangerous place.

Karin
Slaughter's
Killer Reads
Exclusive to
ASDA

EXCLUSIVE ADDITIONAL CONTENT

Dear Readers,

If you like your crime novels with engaging characters, atmospheric locations and gripping plots, *Breakneck Point* is the book for you. Introducing Ally Dymond, a CSI on the hunt for a serial killer in a quiet North Devon town.

Ally Dymond has been relegated from Major Investigations after blowing the whistle on her colleagues. But when Janie Warren is murdered on her patch, Ally gets the call. Ally finds evidence that contradicts the detective's theory that the murder is domestic. Then another body turns up. Now she's certain there's a serial killer on the loose. What she doesn't know is that he's watching, from her side of the crime scene tape, waiting for the moment to strike.

It might be set in a sleepy seaside town, but *Breakneck Point* will have you up all night.

Karin

READING GROUP QUESTIONS

(Warning: contains spoilers)

1. How do you think the novel switching between Ally and Simon's viewpoints impacted your reading experience? Why do you think the author chose to divide the chapters in this way?

2. 'Megan's stare challenged me to choose between her and my job'. Ally wrestles to balance her responsibilities as a mother and a CSI throughout the novel. Do you agree with how she handles balancing the two? What would you do differently in her position?

3. Simon grooms his young victims via Instagram. How did you react to this aspect of the plot? Do you think young people are educated enough on the dangers of social media?

4. *Breakneck Point* is set in North Devon. Discuss the role you think the rural location had on the plot. How do you think the novel would have been different if it was set in a city?

5. Both Ally and Penny have abusive ex-husbands. To what extent do you think fear of the past impacts the way each reacts to Megan's attack? Do you think Ally killing Simon helped to provide her closure with Sean?

6. Ally and Megan's relationship is the emotional crux of the novel. How did you react to Megan as a character? Could you relate to her teenage misbehaviour?

7. Both Jay and Simon are judged incorrectly, based on faulty assumptions made by other people. To what extent do you think prejudice blinds the characters in the story? What assumptions did you make based on initial descriptions of the characters?

A Q&A WITH T. ORR MUNROE

(Warning: contains spoilers)

The North Devon setting is so integral to the novel, how did you decide on this area and did you ever consider setting it somewhere else?

No, *Breakneck Point* was always going to be set in North Devon. Despite being a lover of urban crime, I wanted to write a crime novel set in a rural area and North Devon was the natural choice. Not only did I grow up there and live there now, but the landscape lends itself perfectly to the crime genre; there are endless places to conceal a body! I'm also fascinated by the juxtaposition of the classic Devon images of thatched cottages and dramatic coastlines (which we have in spades!) and the faded grandeur and ongoing social challenges of the towns that populate the area. This is something I wanted to explore in *Breakneck Point*.

Why did you choose to write from alternating perspectives of Ally and Simon and how did you approach each character?

It happened by accident. I was playing around with writing from Simon's point of view to have a sense of what was going on inside his head and then I found I didn't want to leave! I think including Simon's perspective added to the chills as, unlike the reader, Ally is completely unaware that he's watching her.

Ally's character was already well-formed in my mind before I started writing her. I knew I wanted to write about a female CSI, but I wanted her to be flawed, at times difficult to like and facing the same issues we all face when trying to balance our work and home life. Her mixed and undefined heritage gives her that added sense of at times being on the outside and is a nod to my own background. I wanted Simon to be in a caring profession because this plays with people's perceptions and presumption of goodness. I came across the idea of him being a paramedic when I was out running and I noticed ambulances would park in quiet, out of the way locations, probably because it isn't worth them returning to their base in between calls.

What was the inspiration behind the novel?

Crime novels traditionally have a Detective as their main protagonist, and I thought it would be unusual to write a novel from the perspective of a CSI. I was a CSI, a long time ago, and I felt that I could draw on my own experiences to give a sense of what the role entails, but also the toll that the job can take emotionally on the individual. Ally's impressions of the scenes she attends are largely a reflection of my own.

This is your debut crime novel, why did you want to write crime? Who are your favourite crime writers?

I've always been fascinated by crime. Enid Blyton was a huge favourite of mine when I was growing up, but I've since discovered that where others loved the Malory Towers and St Clare's series, Secret Seven were the only ones for me. I loved the idea of a team investigating a mystery and, unlike the Famous Five, they seemed to have procedures (of sorts!) which I found very appealing. I'm a police journalist so factual crime is my day job, although it wasn't until a friend asked why I'd never written a crime novel that it occurred to me to write one.

I read huge amounts of crime and there are so many fantastic crime writers out there that it is very difficult to choose. Val McDermid is unsurpassed and is consistently brilliant. I've been hooked ever since I read *Cross and Burn*. I'm a huge fan of Peter James' Roy Grace novels and I'm currently enjoying Neil Lancaster's DS Max Craigie, a comparative newcomer, but one that I suspect will be around for a very long time.

What scenes were the most challenging to write?

Without a doubt, the scene where Ally finds out that it is her daughter, Megan, who has been attacked. I have a daughter who is Megan's age, and I knew the only way I could write this with any sense of authenticity was to pretend it was her. It was very, very difficult to do. My husband read it and cried, and I knew then that I had achieved what I was hoping for: realism.

What's next for you – and for Ally Dymond?

I'm delighted to say Ally Dymond will be back. This time, she's heading inland and will be turning her attentions to a terrible murder that has been committed in a remote farming community on Exmoor.

As a side project, I'm aiming to co-write a play based on a real-life trial to be staged locally at the original court where the case was heard. It's been fascinating to see how justice was metered out in days gone by.

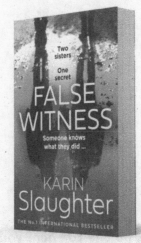

Leigh doesn't like to talk about her sister.

About the night that tore them apart.

About what they did.

But someone else is about to.

How far will Leigh go to protect her family?

THE INTERNATIONAL No.1 BESTSELLER

KARIN
Slaughter

A small town
hides a big secret...

GIRL,
FORGOTTEN

Who killed Emily Vaughn?

A girl with a secret...

Longbill Beach, 1982. Emily Vaughn gets ready for prom night,
the highlight of any high school experience. But Emily has a secret.
And by the end of the evening, she will be dead.

A murder that remains a mystery...

Forty years later, Emily's murder remains unsolved.
Her friends closed ranks, her family retreated inwards,
the community moved on. But all that's about to change.

One final chance to uncover a killer...

Andrea Oliver arrives in town with a simple assignment:
to protect a judge receiving death threats.
But her assignment is a cover. Because, in reality, Andrea is here
to find justice for Emily – and to uncover the truth

before the killer decides to silence her too...

ONE PLACE. MANY STORIES

Bold, innovative and
empowering publishing.

FOLLOW US ON:

@HQStories